RELOAD

KARL HILL

To Robin — The Old Soldier
Hope you enjoy
Karl Hill
2/3/25

BLOODHOUND
— B O O K S —

When you burst into a hut full of enemy soldiers you must remember the drill evolved for such occasions. Shoot the first person who makes a move, hostile or otherwise. His brain has recovered from the shock of seeing you there with a gun. He has started to think and is therefore dangerous. You must then shoot the person nearest to you, because he is in the best position to cause you most embarrassment. Then deal with the rest as you think fit.

Paddy Mayne
Founding Member of the SAS.

ONE

IN THE PRECISE centre of the dome, was a room. Ten feet by ten feet. Floor to ceiling, twelve feet. The walls thick concrete. A cell, rather than a room. One door. No air conditioning. No windows. The heat was unceasing and intense. Illumination was intermittent, supplied by a single blazing strip light. Sometimes, it buzzed and flickered. Sometimes, it remained on for hours on end. Sometimes, it stayed off, and when that happened, the darkness was absolute. Like a tomb, and the only sound was her breath, and the beating of her heart.

The ground also was hard concrete, cool to touch. On it, a pallet, a toilet, a sink. Food and drink were supplied by a metal drawer in a wall. Twice a day, pushed in, pushed out, on metal sliders. In/Out. Food – a bowl of tasteless gloop. Drink – a litre bottle of warm water. She had no idea whether it was breakfast or dinner. Time was meaningless in such a place.

She had been trained to endure. To *tough it out*. And she had been trained by the very best. But training was one thing. Real life was another. The fear didn't go away. Instead, it came in waves. High and low. Like the tides of the sea. *They can't train you not to be afraid,* she thought. But she never screamed. Not once. Another thing she'd learned – *don't let the bastards see you bleed.*

Sometimes, a slat in the door would open. Sometimes, she would see eyes, gazing at her. Sometimes, a voice would speak.

"Soon, you'll be free." The accent was Middle Eastern, educated. Soft. Almost pleasant.

"You think keeping me here changes anything?" she said. She raised her voice, in a display of defiance. But she was exhausted, and dehydrated, and scared shitless. It sounded more like a dry croak. "More will come."

"I'm sure you're right. But I don't care about that."

"You should. Let me go. Turn yourself in. Make it easier on yourself."

"I have never been one to take the easy route in life." A pause, then – "Back home, I have a trophy room. I had it built specially. I'm not an extravagant person." Another pause. She waited, wondering where the hell this was going.

The voice continued. "Nor am I inclined to brag. The trophy room was built as a representation of my power. And as a warning. So that those who would choose to become my enemy would understand the consequences of their actions, should they embark on such a course. To make them think. You understand?"

"Trophies? Isn't that what psychopaths collect?"

She waited, wondering how he would react. But also, she was curious.

"I'm not a psychopath." A patient chuckle. "I'm a businessman. Those who cross me must realise there is a price to pay. I have a glass cabinet on one wall. It's refrigerated, to preserve its contents. The temperature must be exact."

She waited.

"Aren't you going to ask?" came the voice.

She chose not to. She didn't speak. She didn't wish to give him the satisfaction. But the dread escalated. He answered for her.

"There's nothing in it. Just a cold empty space. But soon – very soon – it will hold a prize beyond all others. The best trophy of all."

The voice lowered to a husky whisper. She waited.

"Soon," he said, "it will contain a man's head."

She said nothing. She realised she was holding her breath.

"I will remove it myself, with a sword of finest steel. This man is why you are here. Soon, he will come. And when he does, then you will be permitted to leave."

She blinked, tried to rationalise.

"Who is this man?"

Silence. Then –

"His name is Adam Black."

TWO

Aggression is not anger. Anger might get you killed. Anger is a reckless emotion, displayed by fools.

Aggression is different. Aggression is a controlled state of mind, to be utilised at any required moment. Like a light switch. On/Off. Ninety-nine per cent of the time, the switch is off. But when the switch is on, when that one per cent happens, when the light blazes, then gentlemen, you are unleashed, and you do exactly what you are trained to do, and you bring on your enemies such unrelenting force, you become the embodiment of the devil himself. On/Off. Life/Death. The equation is simple and effective.

Address given by General Graham Lightbody to the soldiers of the 22nd Regiment of the Special Air Service.

ADAM BLACK, in an effort to maintain a semblance of isolation, ventured into town no more than once a week. It was not something he enjoyed. 'Loathed' was a more apt description. But he had to live. He needed food. He needed whisky. And he had made a promise.

Thurso was the nearest hub of civilisation. Not quite a metropolis, but it had a supermarket. From his house, the only reasonable mode of transport was by foot. And it wasn't a house. More of a cabin. Which was doing it justice. Black gave a rueful laugh, as he considered his current place of residence. Cabin was stretching it. But he hardly cared. In terms of personal comfort, his caring days were over. He would have it no other way. He had chosen a path of virtual solitude. All other paths led to darkness. Here, in the shit-end of nowhere, the darkness couldn't trouble him.

Thurso. A town in the north of Scotland. In the winter, grey and dismal. In the summer, much the same. Black went to the supermarket and one other place. A newsagent. The supermarket sold newspapers. Only the newsagent sold the *London Times*. Not that he cared particularly about the quality of the journalism. Nor indeed about events in the outside world. Nor did he have a wistful hankering for reading the written word on good old-fashioned paper, a prehistoric mode of communication in the age of tapping buttons and getting instant access to everything anytime anywhere.

But he had made a promise. More than a promise. A blood oath.

He would buy the damned newspaper every Saturday. Because, if nothing else, Adam Black was a man of his word.

And he was a man of war.

And in that great theatre of death and mayhem, a promise meant something. Thus, the ritual had been observed for over ten years. Every Saturday, regardless of his location, he had purchased the newspaper, scoured each page. And each time, nothing.

And here he was again. Rucksack looped over one shoulder, reaching down and picking up the *London Times*. And wondering at the absurdity of the situation, knowing in the core of his bones, this would continue to the day he died. He opened the paper to a random page. Habit. He would buy it, take it back to his cabin in the hills, and later scrutinise it in more detail. But for now, an idle scan of the first page he opened.

Which, on this occasion, was page twenty-one.

And which, on this occasion, rendered Black in a state of shocked disbelief.

"Jesus…" he muttered. "This can't be real."

But it was real.

And then it all kicked off.

THREE

A RAISED VOICE. Specifically, a man's voice, loud and harsh. Black turned. A young couple were standing outside on the pavement, directly adjacent to the entrance. An argument. But a little more. The action was quick. So fast, one might have questioned it happened at all. Swift and violent. The man, slapping the woman's face, a hard stinging blow. Hard enough for her to stagger back on her feet. Hard enough for her eyes to glaze, and her body to tremble. She didn't respond. She just stood. *Quiet obedience*, thought Black. Someone so used to casual abuse, it had become normalised and accepted. The man loomed over her, tapped his finger on her forehead at a point between her eyes. Black could hear every word.

"You need to learn when to shut that fucking mouth of yours. You understand?"

He was a big man. Maybe six-one. Maybe taller. Late twenties. Possibly older. Well built. The preening type who spent hours in the gym, building large useless muscles to look good in tight T-shirts on a hot beach. Dressed in designer Nike gear. A long-sleeved Lycra top, tracksuit trousers, black running shoes. Dark hair, short on top, tapering stylishly down to a shaved finish either side. Tanned. Brightly coloured tattoo creeping past his top, spreading up his neck, over his pulsing veins, to an inch below his right ear. Looked like a flame-breathing serpent. The guy was all muscle and anger.

She was half his size. Maybe the same age. Maybe younger. Difficult to tell. Tight jeans, a pink pullover, tousled auburn hair. Slim. Athletic. *A couple of gym bunnies*, thought Black. Maybe that's where they met. She pouting over him while he bench pressed one hundred kilograms before a wall-length mirror. The side of her face was reddening, the embryo of a bruise. And her eyes. *Fearful.* Black knew all there was about fear. And he saw it now.

The guy entered the shop. Suddenly the air was thick with aftershave. She waited outside. The shop wasn't large. It sold newspapers and magazines, sweets and cigarettes, some basic groceries. Black remained at the newspaper shelves. The guy gave him a cursory glance. He went straight to the counter. He took out a leather wallet from a zip pocket in his track trousers. It bulged with notes. His hands were big, like shovels. He fished out a fifty, slapped it on the counter.

The man serving was the owner. Black, over the past few months, had grudgingly engaged in some short conversations. Black had established his name was Richard Hornbuckle, that he'd bought the place about five years ago, and he hated the weather, as did his wife, who was a teacher at the local primary school. Beyond that, Black knew nothing, nor did he want to. Hornbuckle had quickly established Black was not the consummate conversationalist, which suited Black fine.

"You sell phone chargers?" barked the guy.

Hornbuckle looked at the fifty-pound note. There was no doubt he would have heard the commotion outside. Hard not to. Hornbuckle gave a weak, conciliatory smile. He gestured to a sign behind him, said, "We do. But I'm sorry. We don't take fifty-pound notes. We've had issues with fake money."

The guy regarded him, forehead wrinkling in puzzlement. Black, still standing at the newspaper section, watched.

"We?" said the guy. "Who's *we?*"

Hornbuckle held his stare. Black was mildly impressed. Hornbuckle was facing unexpected confrontation but was holding his composure. Just. Hornbuckle responded, though his voice sounded small. "I'm very sorry," he said. "We don't accept notes that large. As I said, we've had trouble..."

"Are you deaf?" snapped the man. "I asked you who's *we*. That's twice you've said it. But I only see you." He flashed a wolfish smile, revealing teeth so white they were blinding. He leaned across. "Maybe there's someone hiding under the counter. Maybe you've got some invisible friend. Or maybe you're just talking shit." He lifted the fifty-pound note, stretched it between the fingers of each hand, held it up to one of the spotlights in the ceiling, made a show of examining it, turned his attention back to Hornbuckle. "Looks good to me." He lowered his voice. "The money isn't fake. So you'll take it, and be glad for the business, and you'll give me my phone charger. And if you don't, I'll pin this fifty to your fucking liver. Don't test me. I'm not in the mood. Not today. You understand? Now speed the fuck up." He clicked his fingers. "I'm in a hurry. Chop-chop."

Hornbuckle blinked, swallowed, licked his lips. The situation had turned. The depth of threat in the guy's voice brought the matter to a new dimension. He was treading water way out of his depth. He opened his mouth to speak. Black, stepping forward, spoke for him.

"*We*," he said, "means me and him."

The guy turned his head, appraised Black. The puzzled look returned. "Excuse me?"

Black, newspaper in hand, casually approached the counter, stood next to the guy. Black's estimation was correct. The guy was six-one, an inch smaller than Black. The Lycra top was like a second skin, moulded round large biceps and forearms, a deep chest. Black was leaner, unobtrusively muscular. The guy probably worked out seven days a week, doubtless augmenting his training by a daily dosage of steroids. Black had spent the majority of his life in the army, serving in a most specific regiment, specialising in death and chaos, where killing was as natural as relieving an itch. Black didn't need the muscles. His demeanour exuded lethal competence.

Black smiled, nodded at Hornbuckle. "I'm with him," he said. "And like the man said, we don't take fifties."

The guy cocked his head, stared at Black. Black stared right back.

"And just who the hell are you?"

"Tell you what," said Black ignoring the question, "you give me the fifty, and I'll ask Richard if he'll change his mind."

The guy hesitated.

Black moved an inch closer, spoke softly. "I said, you give me the fifty, and I'll ask Richard if he'll change his mind."

"Is this some sort of fucking joke?"

"No joke. What's the matter? You don't want your phone charger?"

The guy's face flickered with uncertainty. He gave Black the fifty-pound note. Black smiled.

"Thank you."

He turned his attention to Hornbuckle. "Richard, will you accept this fifty?"

Hornbuckle didn't have time to respond. Black answered for him – "No? I understand completely."

Black brought his attention back to the guy.

"He doesn't want to take your money. But I'll take it, if you don't mind." He tucked it into his jeans pocket. "Though I'm treating this as a gift, if that's okay. In fact, call it 'restitution'. Do you know what that means?"

The guy's face creased into a heavy frown.

"It's a fancy word for compensation," continued Black, his tone almost conversational. "I find your behaviour rude, bordering on offensive, and I detest rude behaviour. It smacks of bad breeding. And stupidity. And there's one thing I hate more than rude behaviour, and that's stupidity. So I think it's only fair that you pay me compensation for the inconvenience and hurt

11

feelings you've caused for being rude and stupid. Do you think that's fair?"

The guy reacted with a tremulous smile. He spoke, an edge to his voice. "What the fuck is this?"

Black responded, a shade above a whisper. "*This,*" he said, "is where we are. Me and you. In the moment."

He leaned forward another inch. "Aren't you going to do anything?"

The guy again hesitated. "This is bullshit," he muttered.

Black continued. "Do you know what I would do, if someone had just taken fifty pounds from me, and called me rude and stupid?"

The guy stared.

Black slapped him hard across the face. The guy rocked on his feet, one hand gripping the counter, the other instinctively rising to his cheek.

"That's what I would do," said Black. He moved closer. The guy shrank back. Black slapped him again. The guy lurched away, knocking into a shelf crammed with sweets and crisps. His voice rose to a pitch.

"What the hell's wrong with you!"

"What are you going to do?" said Black, his voice still soft. "Are you going to hit me? Go on. Please. Hit me. Show me what you've got. Use those big muscles."

The guy opened his mouth, perhaps to speak. Black slapped him a third time. The guy yelped.

Black waited, maintaining eye contact. He saw something he had come to recognise, had seen it in all its forms. Fear. Pure and simple. It oozed from the guy as palpable as his aftershave.

The guy took a trembling breath. He made no move to strike back.

Black gave an easy smile. "I understand. You're a man who prefers to hit women. I get it. Easier targets. Less fuss. Less hassle. Slim chance of retaliation. Show them who's boss. I'll tell you what I think." He lost his smile. He spoke, his tone hard and flat. Like a pronouncement of fact.

"I think, if I ever see you hit your girlfriend again, I'll snap your spine. At the top. At the cervical region. Not enough to kill you. But enough to keep your arse in a wheelchair and have you sucking up your porridge through a plastic tube."

Black waited. The guy raised himself up, trying to salvage the remains of his dignity. He opened his mouth, closed it. He looked past Black, at Hornbuckle, who stood a foot back from the counter, transfixed.

"I don't want your shitty fucking phone charger!" the guy shouted. He gave one last indignant look towards Black, shot a venomous glance at Hornbuckle, and left the shop. Black watched him go. He marched past the girl outside, who scurried behind. They both got into a slate-grey BMW X5. The car swept off.

Black returned to the counter, regarded Hornbuckle, gave a wintry grin. He gestured to the newspaper in his hand. "Got change of fifty?"

Black left the newsagent, and went back to the supermarket, and bought something he thought he would never have to buy again. A mobile phone. A basic, pay-as-you-go burner. No frills. He put it in his rucksack, and realised, whether he liked it or not, the action signified something important.

He was re-entering the world.

FOUR

BLACK WALKED the three miles back to his house in the hills. Getting there by car was virtually impossible. A heavy, no-nonsense four-by-four might manage, at a push. And it was a big push. The last mile of the route wound through a landscape of marshland and rock, then into the sheer giddy heights of the Scottish mountains. He shouldered his provisions in an old rucksack, the newspaper wrapped in a plastic bag, and made his way back. The rain had started. Big drops, falling vertically. Looked like it would last forever, and looked like it would get worse. He wore a mountain jacket. He pulled the hood over his head, but he knew, regardless, he would get soaked.

But the rain was not on his mind. Rather the newspaper, and more importantly, what he had seen. It had come as a shock. The shock ran deep, down to the core. He had gone to the shop, expecting nothing. Just another Saturday, enacting the ritual. Suddenly, it was no longer a ritual. Suddenly, it was real.

And seeing it had triggered something else. A spark. A flame in his soul. Something he thought he had lost. A raw revitalisation. A week ago, he would have ignored the guy slapping the girl. A week ago, he wouldn't have cared, and would

14

have let the world around him drift by. But everything had changed. Like he had woken up. Like he was renewed.

The rain got worse. A wind whipped up. It was summer, but here, in the Scottish Highlands, in the mountains, a season was just a name, the weather stubbornly refusing to adhere to expectations. It could snow in June, and it could snow in December. The seasons meant nothing. The consistent theme was unpredictability.

The cabin he lived in was made of heavy timber, with an angled roof of corrugated iron. It was not a pretty structure. The guy who built it had bought up a parcel of land an acre in size, his intention to create three holiday lodges. He hadn't done the maths. The cost to hump the materials across the terrain was prohibitively expensive, the cost to get labour in such a remote place was ludicrous. He got one built, then realised the equation wasn't working, and so abandoned the project before he went bankrupt. Black, by sheer chance, saw it advertised for the same price as a second-hand car. He bought it. It was basic. Utilitarian. No television. Certainly no internet. It was served by a generator, providing a modicum of heat and light. Running water was supplied via the heavens – rainwater collected in a fifty-gallon plastic barrel and pumped into the building through a filtration system. Rudimentary, but effective. One thing Black could rely on. Plenty of rainwater.

He'd been living here for a year and a month. Almost to the day. 'Living' was an exaggeration. *Existing.* With the exception of the occasional hill walker, he rarely met anyone. The Saturday trip to the town was a necessary evil. Necessary, because he needed food. And whisky. Glenfiddich, particularly. Though Black wasn't choosy. Richard Hornbuckle – the newsagent – was the only soul who took an interest. When his endeavours to strike up a conversation with Black were met with somewhat taciturn, bordering on rude, responses, Hornbuckle finally gave up. Which suited Black fine.

He got back to the cabin. It was 11am. The rain had stopped, suddenly. Mountain weather liked to keep you guessing. Shards of sunlight broke through the clouds, spearing the mountainside. Black put the rucksack on the kitchen counter, took out the whisky, immediately poured himself a generous glass into a chipped coffee mug. He went back outside to a wooden porch. On it, a single metal chair, and a small round glass-topped table. He dried them with a towel. He placed the newspaper and coffee mug on the table, sat. He took a breath. He opened the paper, found page twenty-one, ignoring everything else. World affairs held zero interest to him.

He sipped the whisky and focused on the relevant section. The message was simple. The message was exactly as it should be, without deviation. As agreed. Straight to the point. Seven words. Simple and earnest.

Captain Adam Black
I need your help.

FIVE

WILSON SMITH POSSESSED THREE SKILLS.

The first was gardening.

He lived in a modest cottage. He liked living there. It was quiet, and no one ever bothered him. He disliked being bothered. He lived a solitary life. Smith was a very private person.

The cottage came with a quarter of an acre of garden ground. In his own estimation, his garden was exquisite. A work of art. He had never been told this, because no one had ever seen his garden, because he kept it a secret. But he knew. He cared for his plants and flowers and shrubs and bushes with a tenderness and love a parent might lavish on their child. He was sure that if his garden were in a competition that it would win. But that would never happen because Smith was a private man. Private to the point of obsession.

His second skill was patience. He regarded this as a skill, because, to his mind, few possessed it. Patience was not something which came naturally to people. Rather, it was something one had to cultivate over many years, until it was mastered. Thus, in time, it became a skill.

Patience and gardening were intertwined. Gardening required patience, and patience was perfected by gardening.

Smith was a patient man.

Patient men planned. Smith was a planner. Crucial, in his most unique form of occupation. Which was his third skill.

Wilson Smith got paid to kill people. He had a talent for it.

And like his garden, he loved his work.

SIX

BLACK SIPPED THE WHISKY, sat back, considered the vista before him. Rock and heather and grass, the ground veined by a myriad of narrow streams, and close by, the brooding presence of the mountains, snowy topped despite the summer. A man could die in those mountains. Sunshine in the morning, blizzards in the afternoon, death at night-time.

A blood oath.

Be careful what you promise, he thought.

Ten years. Five hundred and twenty weeks. Five hundred and twenty newspapers purchased, one a week, every Saturday. And all that time, silence. Until now. The voice had called.

And Black would call back.

A blood oath.

This was a staged process. The plea had been made. Now the next step. Black remembered. He turned the pages, scrutinising a small section of the *Times* dedicated to the sale of classic cars. It took up an eighth of a page, near the back. Selling cars through a newspaper was an outdated method of advertising, given the monolithic presence of the internet. Still, some diehards used it. There were ten advertisements altogether. Black scanned them,

SEVEN

Black: Colonel?

The Colonel: You're not dead, Adam.

Black: Not yet. At least I don't think so. And if I am, then Hell is much worse than they say.

The Colonel: Where are you?

Black: Scotland.

The Colonel: Sorry to hear that. Can you travel?

Black: Yes.

The Colonel: I'll arrange the tickets. I'll text you the details.

Black: Where am I going?

The Colonel: San Francisco.

EIGHT

BLACK LEFT THE FOLLOWING DAY. He got a noon train from Thurso to Glasgow Queen Street, changing at Inverness and Perth. The journey would take just under eight hours, which Black found amusing – it would take about the same time to travel from the UK to the West Coast of America. He packed light, primarily because he didn't have much to take. All of it contained in a holdall the size of a gym bag. A small gym bag. The sum of his life, packaged in an area no bigger than the size of two footballs. He slept for part of the journey, and for the other part read a paperback he'd picked up at the station for no other reason than the title, given the circumstances, was ironic – *Run and Hide*.

The train arrived at 9.15pm. It was a Sunday night. The place was busy. It was work next day, but people still partied. The noise, compared to the tranquillity of the mountains, was like thunder. Black was to fly to Heathrow at 10am the following morning, and then on to San Francisco. On a whim, perhaps in a sudden bout of nostalgia, he booked a room at the Eagle Arms, in the village of Eaglesham. It was eleven miles from the station. He got a taxi and was there for 9.50pm. The place hadn't changed. He had been away for many years. He had vowed he would never return. Yet here he was.

The room was functional. He dropped his bag on the bed, went downstairs to the bar. It was as he remembered. It brought a thousand memories. He got a Glenfiddich – double – and sat on a leather armchair, which, if he recalled, was part of the furniture all those years ago. The place was quiet. He swirled the liquid in its glass, sipped. The taste never diminished. The dining area was on a slightly raised mezzanine, on the far side of the room, the seating arranged in intimate booths. Where he and his wife had sat, many times, eating, drinking wine, talking, laughing, planning for a future which would never come. Oblivious to the nightmare to follow.

Innocent, he thought. And when his wife was shot, the innocence died with her.

He finished the whisky, left the hotel, made his way to the other pub in the village. The night was warm, the sky clear, the moon unobscured, surrounded by a million stars. He passed the park, set in an incline, running the length of the village. There – the swings where his daughter had played; there – the red bench where he and his wife had sat, watching, drinking hot coffee. The air he breathed held the essence of her perfume, the echo of his daughter's laughter. The place was suffused with memories, each golden and vibrant. It broke his heart. He made his way up the hill, not in any hurry, past rows of narrow terraced houses, past paths and hidden lanes, and always to his left, the sweep of the park, memories unlocked with every step.

He got to the Old Swan. Eaglesham's other pub. Black took a breath. Where the shitstorm had started. He went in. The place was quieter than he expected. A few people sat at high stools at the bar, hunched over pints of beer, the drone of quiet conversation. In a corner, a couple sat sipping red wine.

Despite the warm evening, a real fire crackled in a tiled hearth. He felt its warmth on his skin, making it tingle. He bought a whisky, sat in the shadows. The place hadn't changed. Age-blackened beams tracked across the low ceiling. Walls of weathered stone. Varnished floorboards creaking with every step.

It looked old. It felt old. *He* felt old. He could come back in a hundred years, he thought, and it would probably be the same.

But some things do change. Forever. He wondered where they had been sitting, that night – the three men who had come here with killing on their mind. The three men who had left via the front door, and who, for no particular reason, had attacked him on the road outside, and who Black, in response, and with his bare hands, had killed. In return, in an act of breathtaking vengeance, his family were murdered.

He wondered – had the three men been sitting where he was now? Contemplating the crackle of the flames? What had they been thinking? What had they been talking about? He would never know. They were all dead. Black was good at dealing death. It was his speciality. As a consequence, death followed him, destroying everything he loved.

He wondered – *if I leave now, out that front door, will I see their ghosts? Will they come again, with their knives and fists and hatred?* If so, this time he would run, and never come back, and hope, by doing so, he could start again. *Run and hide.*

But you can't start what's finished. All you can do is keep moving.

Keep moving. And leave the past behind.

Time drifted. Black got three more whiskies. The place began to thin out. Closing time was called. He stirred, left the pub, into the Scottish night. For a minute he stood in the middle of the adjacent road, under the gleam of a streetlamp. The road was narrow and steep, barely wide enough for two cars. There was no traffic. On one side, the glow of the pub. On the other, the deep shadow of the trees. In between, the road he stood on. The killing ground. Where he had been attacked. Where he had attacked right back. All remnants gone. No bloodstains on the ground. All washed away, as if the past had never happened. No ghosts. Only an echo in his mind.

He walked the quarter mile back to his hotel. He passed a group of people. They smiled and nodded politely. Black nodded back. He got to the hotel. He came to a decision. He walked on, another mile, to the outskirts of the village. To a house with red ivy on the walls and windows with white wooden shutters. To a house with a peaked roof of burnt orange slate and an old arched door of heavy oak. To a house where he once lived, with his wife and daughter. To a house where they had been murdered.

He looked at it from the roadside. The ivy was gone. The door had been replaced with white UPVC. The front garden was one large monoblocked driveway. The curtains were drawn shut. All vestige of Black having once lived there, vanished. *As it should be,* he thought. *Keep moving.* Which is what he did, after their deaths. He killed those responsible. Then he killed some more, because he was good at it. But more. He enjoyed it.

He turned away, heart consumed with self-loathing.

They were buried in a cemetery less than a half mile away. He chose not to go there. It would be too much to endure. He bit back his tears. He went back to the hotel, went straight to bed. Eventually, he found sleep and dreamt dark dreams.

———

Black got up early, showered, had a light breakfast, his heart heavy, his mood morose. He called a taxi, and left Eaglesham behind him. He should never have come. He would never go back.

You've got to keep moving, he thought.

Until you stopped.

NINE

THE COLONEL HAD PAID for the tickets. Black collected them at Glasgow Airport. British Airways. Business class. The Colonel didn't stint. Black flew to Heathrow, waited an hour, then got the flight to San Francisco International Airport. Though severely tempted, he stayed off the booze. Better to land in America with a clear head. The flight was punctual. He arrived at 9pm GMT, 1pm San Francisco time. The day was bright, the air clammy. Black hadn't dressed for the cold. He was a virtue of simplicity when it came to fashion. Jeans, dark T-shirt, brown suede bomber jacket, a pair of somewhat battered running shoes. He hadn't worn a suit or tie for years. The thought appalled him. He slung the jacket over his shoulder.

Black passed through customs without difficulty. When asked by the customs officer the nature of his visit, Black had replied *short vacation*. To his own ears, the words rang false. He wondered if they could detect the lie. The Colonel had reached out. Which indicated trouble. This was a million light years from a vacation.

He had no need to wait for baggage collection. The sports bag he carried was small enough to take on board. He left the airport at 1.45. He made his way to the pick-up point, a hundred metres from the main exit. The place was busy. Black weaved his way through a throng of people, until he spied what he was looking for. A man in a dark sombre suit, holding to his chest a placard the size of a dinner tray, and on the placard, written in bold black felt pen, Black's name.

Black went over.

The man gave a small courteous nod. "Mr Black?"

"Yes."

"The Colonel's expecting you."

"Thank you."

Black followed the man to a white Mercedes SUV with brand-new licence plates.

"The Colonel likes to travel in style," remarked Black.

"He's a generous host," replied the man. "My name is Gibson. I'm the Colonel's personal assistant." He gave a small half-smile. "And his driver." He was five inches smaller than Black, but thick in the neck and shoulders, long arms, and rather wide at the hip, suggesting agility and strength. His head was narrow, almost hairless, his features neat. His movements were fluid and easy, consistent with inherent athleticism. His voice was clipped, though Black detected the hint of an accent. Possibly eastern. Maybe Vermont or Maine.

Gibson opened the back passenger door. "I prefer the front," said Black. "And I can get the door."

Again, a polite nod of the head. "Of course, Mr Black." He pressed a button on the car key. The boot popped open. He took Black's holdall, placed it inside.

They got in. Gibson pulled off. The air con in the car was a relief from the afternoon heat.

"Where does the Colonel live?"

"It's a drive, but we'll take the Pacific Coast Highway. It's worth it for the views."

"We're heading south?"

"Yes, Mr Black. To Carmel-by-the-Sea."

TEN

Join the army; travel to exotic, distant lands; meet exciting, unusual people and kill them.

Humorous Aphorism.

THE DISTANCE WAS APPROXIMATELY 120 miles. On his right, the Pacific glittered, sheer as blue glass, the sky a clear blue canvas. The view was like an illusion – difficult to know where the ocean stopped, and where the sky started. *A somewhat different picture from the Scottish mountains*, thought Black. The Mercedes ate the miles, the engine smooth, silent as a whisper, the road long and straight. Gibson spoke with a careful politeness.

"Have you visited California before, Mr Black?"

"I never seemed to get the chance. Or perhaps I never had the inclination."

"It's not for everyone." He gave the slightest shrug. "Most people seem to like it."

"Where are you from, Gibson?"

"Originally from Richford. We moved a around a lot. My

father was in the military. In effect, he went where he was told. A nomadic lifestyle."

"You follow suit?"

Again, a small shrug, as if the matter held little consequence. "Briefly. Served in the navy. Could never tolerate the discipline."

Somehow, Black doubted this. Gibson seemed a man born and bred to discipline.

"You've worked for the Colonel long?"

"He's a good boss. He knows how to get the best from people."

True, thought Black. Though the question wasn't answered.

"What's the weather like in Scotland?" Gibson asked.

"A better question might be – what's the weather *not* like. It's not like this. We Scots have mass celebrations when the sun comes out. Call it mild hysteria. Which might take place one week of the year. If we're lucky. Otherwise, rain. Sometimes, as a change, some snow."

Gibson nodded. "I think you'll like California, Mr Black."

Gibson cruised at a steady speed of sixty mph, never above. Black relaxed back, let the scenery float by. He had visited America several times. Initially, to assess and assist in counterterrorism development, especially in the aftermath of 9/11. Fort Liberty, in North Carolina. Fort Campbell, on the border between Tennessee and Kentucky. Black knew why he'd never had an inclination to return. The place was too damned big. A man could lose himself here, without even knowing it. Lose his identity. Lose his soul. He adjusted his thinking. Perhaps this was the perfect place. Where a man could drift, aimlessly, town to town, forever, without any destination in mind, like a piece of ragged tumbleweed, hostage to the next breeze. Perhaps. Perhaps not. A man could lose himself anywhere, should he choose.

They passed small pockets of civilisation Black had never heard of. The names were from a fairy tale. Half Moon Bay; Miramar Beach; Mercado; Monterey Bay. Soft names. Names echoing an easy and prosperous way of life. Where the sun shone, the soil rich, the vineyards full. For most, a dream.

The journey continued in comfortable silence.

"Would you like to stop for a coffee?" Gibson asked.

"I'm fine."

Two hours later, Gibson pulled off Highway One, heading west, towards the ocean. After ten minutes, they entered Carmel-by-the-Sea. The roads were flat and tree-lined, scrupulously clean. The place possessed a witchy quality. Each building was different, assembled in an almost haphazard, eccentric fashion, as if the owner wished to stamp his own personality on the architecture, untroubled by convention. Again, fairy-tale names – Treetop Café; Sailmaker Inn; The Casanova Vineyard. Boutiques, restaurants, coffee dens. Quaint colourful windows selling art. Bookshops. A shop selling pens. A shop selling fantastical wooden carvings. It possessed a thousand charms and graces. Set back from the road, chocolate box cottages sprinkled with fairy dust. The place belonged in another world, another time. A place for artists and poets and writers to sit in the sun and sip delicate wine, or perhaps the beach, to listen to the swell of the sea.

But for all that to happen, for such a place to exist, there was one crucial ingredient. Money. And lots of it. This, thought Black, for all its romantic olde worlde flair, its slant toward a languid retreat for painters and writers, was a sanctuary for the elite. The rich. People who could afford to live in a fairy tale. Black allowed a soft chuckle. He wondered where you went to get a loaf of bread or a pint of milk. He compared his surroundings to those he had left only twenty-four hours ago – the grey, bleak streets of Thurso, the pelting rain, the skies not blue, rather a blanket of dark cloud. Strangely, Black preferred the latter. It was real. It reflected life, and life was shit.

They drove down Ocean Avenue. As they got nearer the sea, the houses got bigger, more spaced out, set further back. They arrived at the end of the road. Before them, a pavement, then an expanse of perfect white sand, then the water. Gibson pulled sharp right, to a gated entrance. He waited. After five seconds, the gate rolled ponderously open.

They entered.

Gibson turned to Black. "Welcome to the Colonel's house."

The driveway was a one hundred metre cobbled curve. On either side, lush grass, water sprinklers fizzing out cyclical spurts of water. The house was a rambling structure of cream-coloured stone and sun-bleached timber, a high sweeping roof of russet-red slate, a turret-style appendage at one end, sheathed by vibrant green and yellow ivy. Black was reminded of a Spanish colonial villa. Gibson pulled up adjacent to the entrance – a wide, arched wooden door, complete with Gothic-style black hinges.

They got out. Gibson popped open the trunk, gave Black his holdall.

"You travel light, Mr Black," he remarked.

"So it would appear."

"Would you like to freshen up before you meet the Colonel?"

"I'm fine."

"Very good. He'll see you right away. Follow me please."

Gibson opened the front door. Unlocked, so Black noted. They emerged into a vaulted hallway, cool in the late-afternoon heat. The place was bright with sunlight. They passed through, into the rear of the house, to a closed door.

Gibson knocked gently.

A voice, raised, came from inside.

"Come!"

Black recognised it. The timbre. The tone. Perhaps a little weaker. A little frailer. But the Colonel, nevertheless.

Gibson turned, spoke quietly, almost a whisper.

"He may not be as you remember him."

"What?"

"But he's still the Colonel."

Black said nothing, suddenly unsettled. Gibson opened the door, beckoned Black in. Black entered.

Black regarded the man before him. Gibson was right.

The Colonel was not as he remembered, and Black knew, at that moment, that God could not possibly exist. And if he did, his cruelty was beyond measure.

ELEVEN

RICHARD HORNBUCKLE HAD BEEN EMPLOYED by a mid-sized commercial bank for a good portion of his working life. Accounts and investments, based in a business park halfway between Glasgow and Kilmarnock. In the complex hierarchy of pay grades, he was strictly lower rung. He would never head a department. He would never be a manager. He didn't know the right people, nor had he gone to university, which meant, should a promotion arise, the graduate fast-trackers got first bite. Also, he lacked ambition.

Despite being married there were no kids. Remaining childless was not a conscious decision. It was merely a sad fact. In Hornbuckle's opinion, one of the many sad facts of his life. They had lived originally in a suburb of Glasgow called Clarkston. A nice house with a nice garden and a nice car. His wife's name was Elspeth. She was softly spoken and wore her hair long. Working as a teacher with small children had given her a patient and understanding disposition.

And because of those qualities, Elspeth supported her husband when he made, on the face of it, the most adventurous decision of his life.

Hornbuckle, at the age of fifty-eight, was offered early

retirement. The offer had come as no surprise. The bank was downsizing, like everything else. A moderate lump sum, a moderate pension. Certainly not enough to live on. But it seemed the offer had an effect on Hornbuckle. It made him think. It made him reflect, and in what he described to his wife as an *epiphany*, he realised that for the last thirty-five years, he had been sleepwalking through life. That he had woken up. That he had come to a decision.

This was the explanation he gave his wife. Which was a lie.

He saw it, by sheer chance. He and Elspeth were driving the North Coast 500 over a long weekend – a trip along the coast route of Scotland. They had arranged an overnight in Thurso, for no other reason than the hotel was cheap, and the place looked clean. During that afternoon, strolling through the town centre, Hornbuckle spied a sign on a newsagent's window – 'Business for Sale'. Below it a phone number. For reasons he could not fully comprehend, he took a note of the number.

Later, back in Clarkston, he phoned that number. The man who answered was polite and informative. The business was for sale. He leased the premises, and the rental was reasonable, and it still had ten years to run. He explained he had ill health and could no longer run the place.

Hornbuckle listened to the man. He said he would phone back. It was then he made the decision. It was then he knew he had to do something radical.

He spoke to his wife. She smiled, and understood his need to stretch his wings, try a new adventure. Perhaps she shared it. From Clarkston to the north of Scotland. Why the hell not? What was there to lose? And she would get a job. For sure. Teachers were in demand, didn't matter which part of the country.

He phoned the man back the next day. He asked for the accounts. They were emailed to him. He checked them over – it wasn't rocket science to see the business was virtually non-existent. Which was even better. It kept the price down. And it meant a fresh start. A challenge. It would either work, or it wouldn't. And Richard Hornbuckle would make damned sure it worked.

Within six weeks, they had sold their house in Clarkston, and using the sale money, and his pension lump sum, Mr and Mrs Hornbuckle bought a quaint cottage two miles outside Thurso, along with an acre of garden. Neither were gardeners. But, in this new life, in the distant Scottish Highlands, starting afresh, they would make it their new hobby.

Elspeth's prediction came true. Schools needed teachers. She got a job in the local primary. They moved in early August. Richard Hornbuckle took the business over two weeks later. He changed the signs, gave it a lick of fresh paint, reconfigured the interior. New broom. New start. He wasn't expecting much. Throughout his life, he had never expected much. Just enough. Enough to live a life. Enough to allow him the luxury of shutting the doors at 6pm and not have to worry about a goddamned thing, except deadheading the flowers, and lifting the weeds.

But it was all a lie. A lie he told himself; a lie he told his wife.

And then the worry began, five years later. When the quiet man he knew as Adam Black entered his shop.

And when, two days later, they got the letter.

TWELVE

"SHRAPNEL."

One word. Before any introductions, any fond greetings between old friends. Black could think of no adequate response, other than two short words –

"Bad luck."

"You could say that," said the Colonel. "Though that would be an understatement."

Black entered a room of regular dimensions, one wall devoted to shelves of books. At the far end, a tall window, the blinds closed, allowing only a single slender shaft of sunlight. In a corner, an antique writing bureau, opened, documents strewn across its surface. The Colonel was sitting on an armchair, a book resting on his lap. The light was muted, a single tortoiseshell lamp in the corner, providing a soft yellow glow. Enough to read by, barely. Enough for Black to understand the context, when the Colonel said 'Shrapnel'.

The Colonel beckoned Black to a chair opposite. Black sat.

"How have you been, Adam?"

"Surviving. And you, Colonel?"

He gave the slightest shrug. "I can't say I wouldn't welcome death."

Black regarded the man before him. Colonel Daniel Pembroke. The facial features were distorted. The face Black remembered was now no longer. Parts were missing, or horribly skewed – like a child's attempt at a jigsaw, the pieces put in the wrong place. The nose was a gap. A cheekbone was absent, the eye slanting an inch below the other, and the eye itself a socket. The chin also was shorn, a clean cut, as if a laser had inflicted the damage, causing the mouth to droop. A section of his hair was absent, the scalp beneath rippled and raw. Picasso couldn't have done better. The skin was ghastly white, a startling contrast to the black eye socket. Better had the injuries killed him, thought Black.

The voice, however. It remained. Still strong, unaffected by the damage.

The Colonel's lips twisted into something approaching a smile. Black wasn't entirely certain.

"I don't go out often. Don't want to scare the kids. Or anyone, for that matter. Though I might make Halloween an exception. I might blend in. I could have saved you some embarrassment and worn an eye patch, but it itches like a fucker."

Black had seen similar injuries. Unfortunates, caught in the wrong place. IEDs. Improvised Explosive Devices. The Taliban's weapon of choice. They were adept at planting them in places causing maximum impact. Terror weapons. Mindless carnage, on soldiers and civilians alike. One thing about the Taliban, Black knew – when they fought their holy war against the Western infidel, they didn't give a shit who they killed, including their own. Such were the consequences of *jihad*.

The Colonel licked his lips. Black was reminded, rather disturbingly, of a lizard.

"I was due to leave the following day," continued the Colonel. "Ironic. God showing us a little of his black humour. I'd been office-bound in our HQ outside Kabul. Paperwork. Admin. I took a trip into Kabul to say a final farewell to one of our interpreters. He was scared shitless he would get left behind. I wanted to assure him that would never happen. Not on my watch." He gave a dry, humourless chuckle. "My watch didn't end well. The first IED knocked the Land Rover on its side. The driver died instantly. I got out, staggered into another. The majority of the blast caught my face. The doctors said I was lucky. Lucky? I had a different perspective. But no limbs lost. Arms and legs intact. Ten fingers and ten toes. Another irony. I could still run a half marathon. I just couldn't do it in public. I woke a week later, and was left with this." He pointed to his face. "A parting gift from the Taliban."

Black held the Colonel's gaze.

"You're still the Colonel. A man is measured by his actions, not by his looks."

The Colonel responded with a curt nod. "And you, Adam? Surviving? Really? I heard what happened to your family."

Black wondered who, in this room, had the greater wound. It occurred to him, he would take the Colonel's injuries, and a lot more, just to have his wife and daughter back at his side.

"I try not to dwell on it," he lied. "It was long ago. We have to keep moving. That's what we were taught. Words branded into the soul. And our teachers were the harshest on the planet."

"Keep moving," said the Colonel, more to himself. "Sometimes hard to do."

"Sometimes."

"Can I offer you a Glenfiddich, Captain Black?"

Black gave a wide smile. "Never thought you'd ask."

THIRTEEN

DAY 1

RICHARD HORNBUCKLE OPENED the shop at 7am sharp every morning. He abhorred tardiness. Plus, his customers liked reliability. His business depended on it. His wife started at 8.30, but she also liked to leave the house early, to prepare for her class that day. The postman, when he came, usually delivered the mail about lunchtime. Sometimes later. Unlike Richard Hornbuckle, the Royal Mail was not as reliable. Which meant the earliest they got the post was when they got back from work. Not that they got a lot. Communication was mostly done by email. Letters were a dying breed.

Richard had pushed back. He was of an age when he remembered receiving letters through the door. He had a desire to cling to those vestiges of another time. When people actually spoke to each other. When people took the time and effort to pen a letter. When people weren't so damned self-consumed with their mobile phones. At the very least, he had insisted the bank send him paper statements, and the gas and electricity companies send him paper bills. He had won, eventually. The utility companies, the banks, complained. 'Antiquated', a faceless woman at the bank had said. But he didn't care. A small, pathetic victory. But a victory, nevertheless.

Elspeth got home first, usually. Class finished at 3. She stayed on for a little while, got back about 4.15. It was a short drive from the school. About two miles. She tended to walk, but as the summer days were shortening, and the skies were darkening, she drove. It seemed to her, here, in the north of Scotland, autumn was a forgotten month. The days seemed to switch from warmish in the summer, to bitter cold. Straight to winter. One minute sunshine. Next, snow. There was no logic to the Highland weather.

It was Monday. She had stopped off to get two bottles of wine. Red and white. She preferred white. Chilled. Her taste was dictated by her budget. She liked Chablis, but stuck with Chardonnay. She opened the front door, noticed a letter on the doormat. She didn't bother, immediately. She hung her coat on a peg by the door, and went to the kitchen, put the white wine in the fridge, emptied the dishwasher, clicked the kettle on. She sat on the couch in the living room. Long day. Working with kids took its toll. She was fifty-six years old, and the job didn't get any easier. The demands of children, the demands of parents. Especially the parents who, invariably, held the absurd notion that their child was always right, and the world was always wrong. She gave a rueful smile. Perhaps, if she and Richard had children, she would see things through a different lens. Perhaps not. It was pointless to speculate. Some things were simply not meant to happen.

The kettle clicked. She got up, made herself a cup of tea. Richard would make dinner. They took turns. Monday meant chilli con carne. He always made it too fiery, but she didn't complain. She was just glad someone else was doing the work. She opened a cupboard door, took out a tin of cat food, prised open the lid, and with a spoon, scooped out the contents into a small blue plastic food bowl on the kitchen floor. Immediately, from nowhere, almost magically, the cat appeared – *Mr Chuckles*. He smoothed himself against her calf and went straight for the food.

She remembered the letter.

She went back through to the hall, picked it up, glanced at the envelope, paused, studied it more carefully. First thing – whoever had sent it, had handwritten their name and address in block capitals in a childish fashion – how a kid in the classroom might write it. The letters were different sizes, mismatched.

Second – there was no stamp. Someone had delivered it. Which was odd. Perhaps parents, expressing concerns? Or maybe a 'thank you'? For going that bit extra? She got lots of thank you cards. But never one delivered to her home.

She went back through to the kitchen, decided what the hell. It was a Monday, but she didn't care. She would open the wine. She didn't care if it wasn't cold. Something – perhaps a vague feeling of prescience – told her she should have a glass in her hand when she opened the letter. She put it down on the marble worktop, opened the bottle, poured a generous quantity, picked up the letter again, went through to the living room, sat.

She sipped the wine. It tasted sharp. *That's what happens when you buy cheap*, she thought. She held the letter in her hand, felt the texture of the paper with her fingers. For reasons inexplicable, she suddenly didn't want to open it. She felt a tingle of... something. The envelope looked wrong. The words held an ominous quality.

And someone had delivered it.

She took another sip, placed the glass on a side table on a silver coaster.

She opened it.

Richard Hornbuckle got the call from his wife at 5. He knew instantly something was off. Her tone. Her breathing. She was holding back.

"You need to come home," she said. "Please."

"What is it, Elspeth? What's the matter?"

"Please. Just come home."

Richard Hornbuckle closed the shop. The first time he'd closed early since he'd started the business. He didn't have a car. He preferred to cycle. An old-fashioned heavy bike, with ten gears which he'd bought second hand. Like Elspeth, he only had a couple of miles to travel, and the council had created a cycle lane – a flat tarmacadam path, bump free, and running to the edge of town. The journey usually took no longer than ten minutes. He kept his bike padlocked on a pavement railing directly opposite the front door of the shop. The padlock was purely habit. His bike wasn't worth stealing. He unlocked it, set off. His wife sounded worried. Worse. Scared. He pedalled hard.

He got to the house at 5.12pm. Despite the apparent urgency, he opened the garage door, placed his bike inside, up against the wall. Habit. He couldn't change his nature. Routine was ingrained. He closed it up, went into the house.

She was sitting in the living room.

"What's the matter, Elspeth?"

He sat opposite. Her face was pale and tight. She looked straight ahead. On the coffee table between them was an opened envelope, and beside it, a folded sheet of paper.

"What's wrong, Elspeth?" he repeated softly.

She nodded at the letter. She took a breath. *She's composing herself.* With each passing second, his dread escalated.

"There was no stamp," she said. "Someone made the effort to deliver it. Personally."

"No stamp?"

"Read it."

"Is it a bill?"

"Read it," she repeated, her voice low, a hint of irritation.

He stretched over, picked it up. He pulled out his reading glasses from the inside pocket of his jacket.

The letter was written in block capitals, with a black biro. The writing was neat and clear.

43

He studied it, frowned. He looked up.

"What is this?" he said.

She didn't respond.

"And it was delivered?"

No response.

He looked at it again, as if the action might help to clarify the contents. It didn't.

"It doesn't make any sense," he said. "Who would put a thing like this through our door?"

She gave him a fixed stare. "What does it mean, Richard?" Her voice trembled as she spoke. To see his wife scared brought a surge of anger.

"A crank. A nutjob. Or maybe kids, pulling a sick prank. I'll sort this."

"How will you sort this?"

"First thing tomorrow morning, I'll take it to the police."

She gave a hollow laugh. "What can they do?" She took a breath. "I'm worried."

"Don't be," he said. "It's nothing."

"It's not *nothing*!" she snapped. "It's *something*! It was delivered to *our* address. *Delivered! To us!* And it's no kid's prank. It's… serious."

He gave his best reassuring smile, but he knew it looked lame.

"Tomorrow morning, first thing, I'll take it to the police."

She gave a dismissive shake of her head. "We'll need to get an alarm. We should get someone in. Have it professionally installed."

"Of course." He hesitated. "But it might be pricey."

She looked at him. "Seriously?"

"You're right. An alarm would be prudent."

She seemed to slump. Richard went over, sat beside her, put his arm round her shoulders, leaned her in close. He felt the tremble of her body. She began to cry soft tears. "Who would want to do this?"

He said nothing, held her tightly, waited it out, until her tears subsided, the trembling stopped. He kissed the side of her head.

"I'll go to the police," he whispered. "Then get an alarm guy in. I promise, everything will be okay."

"I hope so."

"I'll make us some fresh tea," he said, his voice firm, suggesting the worst was over, that resolution was just over the horizon, that the act of making tea would calm the stormy seas.

She gave a weary sigh, stretched over to the wine glass on the table. "This is better than tea."

He nodded. He couldn't disagree.

"Forgotten what?" she asked suddenly.

"It's nothing. Just crazy talk. I promise. I'll make myself a cup."

He got up.

He went through to the kitchen, still holding the letter. He switched the kettle on, placed the letter on the worktop, stared at it, blinked back the sweat and the fear. He took a deep breath, but the dread squirming in his gut didn't ease any.

The words were clear and unequivocal:

HI RICHARD AND ELSPETH,

JUST DROPPING YOU A NOTE TO SAY 'HELLO', AND ALSO TO SAY WE HADN'T FORGOTTEN.

THIS IS DAY 1. THIS IS THE EASY DAY. THIS CAN BE REGARDED AS INTIMATION. IT WILL GET WORSE, UNTIL THE BIG HURRAH. UNTIL DAY 5. THAT'S A SPECIAL DAY.

THAT'S THE DAY WE GET TO KILL YOU.

SO KEEP COUNTING, AND ENJOY THE LITTLE THINGS.

WITH VERY BEST WISHES, YOUR CONCERNED FRIENDS

Richard ran his finger across the letters, sensing the indentation of the ink on the paper, and with the touch of every letter, the dread squirmed harder, like a living thing.

They've found me, he thought. *After all this time.*

Elspeth was right. The police could do nothing. Not against these people.

And this was Day 1.

FOURTEEN

"WHAT'S it like to die? I never asked you."

Black sipped the whisky. It tasted good. But then, it always tasted good. One of the few things he could count on – the sweet bite of Glenfiddich single malt. A little taste of home.

The Colonel had asked him the question. Black gave a wry smile, remembering. Winter in Afghanistan. When night-time in the great range of the Hindu Kush was so black it was like walking blind, when the temperature dipped to below minus thirty-four degrees Celsius, when the snow fell so hard it crushed the soul. The survival gear the Special Air Service used gave little comfort. Nothing kept the cold out. It seeped into the bones, like a disease.

The mission was simple. Enter suspected Taliban drug territory, cause a little havoc. 'Havoc' was a euphemism. Rather, cause a shitstorm of killing and destruction. No limitations. The intended target was a compound occupied by Bashir Noorzai, a drug lord with a reputation for unparalleled cruelty, which, given the context of the general cruelty inflicted by the Taliban, meant the guy was the real deal. Plus, his opium farms funded a hefty slice of Taliban weaponry, purchased from Pakistan and Iran.

Essentially, Noorzai and his entourage were to be assassinated. 'Havoc' was the coat that covered the ugly cracks.

But everything went wrong within an hour after the drop-off point. As wrong as it could get. They entered a blizzard, from nothing, whipped up in a heartbeat – which was advantageous to the enemy, absorbing the sound of the gunfire. Black and his men didn't know they had walked into an ambush, until two of the five-man unit dropped into the snow, dead before their heads hit the ground. Black and the others reacted, hunkering down, firing into the swirl around them. There was nothing to aim at. Panic shooting, hoping to Jesus Christ a random bullet might hit something. Then the men beside Black stopped firing and fell still. The memories were fragmented. A jumble of images. He'd fired a distress flare up into the sky. The snow got worse. And then, a searing heat above his ear, and Black felt the world shake, and everything turned upside down. Then spikes of mind-numbing pain – shoulder and chest – and then the blizzard turned to darkness.

As wrong as it could get.

The Colonel had flown the helicopter himself, back into the maelstrom, accompanied by a medic and two others. They'd dragged Black and his men into the belly of the Chinook, hovering and swaying a foot above the snow, like a great ungainly bumblebee.

They were all dead. Except Black, who was alive, barely. In the close confines of the helicopter's interior, stretched on a bed held stable by metal joists welded to the sides and floor, Black's heart stopped. Twenty seconds. The medic applied a burst of adrenaline, via an intracardiac injection. It was enough. Life returned. Black came back.

Which was why he gave a wry smile when the Colonel asked the question.

"What's it like to die?" said Black. "Long dark tunnel, white light at the end, lots of angels, and some distant harp music. Or maybe it was violins. It's all a bit vague. And a voice."

"What did the voice say?"

Black grinned. "Told me I was premature."

Now the Colonel smiled. "I dare say you'd heard that before."

"Resurrection," said Black. "You brought me back from the dead. And now I'm here."

"For which I'm grateful." The Colonel paused. "How are you coping?"

Black gave a minuscule shrug. They were skirting on the edge of a conversation he had no desire to enter.

"My family? They were murdered. I murdered right back. With some style, I might add." There was no humour in Black's voice. He was deadly serious. "But retribution doesn't lessen the pain. And after a while, when retribution becomes second nature, it deadens the soul. How am I coping? To use a well-worn cliché – I take one day at a time. Keep moving. That's what you taught us. You wanted us to be killing machines. Bravo. The system worked. But to keep moving takes effort, and sometimes the effort feels too much." He finished the whisky. The Colonel knew him too well. Without prompting, he got the bottle, stretched over, topped Black's glass up.

"Keep moving," echoed the Colonel. "I understand, Adam. It sounds easy. Two paltry words. The army's glib response to the blood and guts, and the aftermath of witnessing such terrible things." He gazed at Black, his single eye bright. In the muted glow, with his face deformed, his skin rippled and stretched and alabaster pale, the Colonel looked like a comic-book villain. "You would give everything to have your daughter again," he said.

Black said nothing, wondering where this was going.

"I have a daughter," continued the Colonel, his voice low and solemn. Another pause. "We aren't... close. But I still love her." He sipped the whisky, seemed to consider his next words.

"I have a problem, Adam. I need your help."

Black waited. He had travelled eight thousand miles for the next part of this conversation.

"My daughter is missing. I need you to find her."

Black said nothing.

"Her name is Elizabeth. Beth. She's thirty-three. She changed when Margaret died. My wife. She died of bone cancer. One of those cancers that eats a person from the inside, whittling them down to nothing. When the morphine stops working, and you just wish to Jesus Christ they'd let go. Beth was sixteen at the time. A hard age at the best of times. A hard age to lose a parent. And Beth had already lost me, because I was never there. I was an absent father. I was more interested in doing my bit in the war against terror, instead of doing my bit looking after my only child. How fucking wrong can a man get?"

Black remained silent, listening. He understood. His own daughter hadn't made it to her sixteenth birthday. Her days on earth lasted all of four short years. He too had been absent. His absence had caused her death, and whether that was true or not was an irrelevance, because Black blamed himself regardless. The question posed by the Colonel was rhetorical – how fucking wrong can a man get? In his mind, Black chose to answer. An absent father – the worst fucking wrong in the world.

"She changed. She fell in with a bad crowd. Drinking. Skirmishes with the law. Then she graduated to other things. Cannabis. Then… harder stuff. I pleaded with her to try rehab. To speak to someone. But I guess that's the thing about addicts. They deny the thing that's killing them. She left the house when she was twenty-one, with some deadbeat. I couldn't stop her, because I wasn't there to do anything about it."

The Colonel gazed at the whisky swirling in his glass. Black waited.

"She kept in touch. Every month she sent me an email. Proof of life, I suppose. Which gave me a little reassurance." He gave a sudden derisive snort – "But *reassurance* wasn't quite on her mind."

"Money," said Black.

"What else? Perhaps I'm stupid. Or naïve. Call me any damned thing you want. But I've been sending her money every month, for the past twelve years. A thousand dollars. I suppose it still gives me a connection. She emails me, to say hi, that she's doing okay. Same day every month. A reminder. 'Don't forget to send the money, Dad'. Which I always do."

The Colonel looked up. "Was that the right thing to do, Adam?"

As if I'm the right person to ask, thought Black. *What would I have done, in such circumstance? The same, probably.* "You were being a father. The choices become narrower."

The Colonel gave a pensive nod. "And then the equation changed," he said. "Or rather, it stopped."

Black waited.

"Three months ago, the emails ceased. Suddenly, radio silence."

The Colonel swallowed, licked his lips, but the motion was awkward. Saliva dripped from the edge of his mouth. He shifted, pulled a handkerchief from his pocket, dabbed his chin, put the handkerchief back in his pocket. His single eye glistened. A tear? Perhaps. "I thought, if I didn't send the money, she would contact me."

"But she didn't."

"I panicked. But I waited. I thought she would respond. The first month rolled into the second month. Still nothing. So, I did the only thing I could think of."

"You contacted the police."

"Who laughed. And who the hell could blame them? A thirty-three-year-old woman doesn't want to speak to her father. Jesus. They must have thought I was crazy."

"And then?"

"I hired a private detective."

A natural reaction, thought Black.

"He was thorough," continued the Colonel. "Maybe too thorough. He tracked her down to a place in the Midwest. He said he was close. I asked him to make contact with her. Let her know I wanted to… what do they say? Reach out. That I still loved her."

The Colonel stopped, stared at Black.

Black cocked his head – "And?"

The Colonel took a breath. "Let me show you."

He got up. He went over to the open bureau in the corner of the room, upon which, a red plastic box, about twelve inches long, six inches wide. He brought it back, placed it on the coffee table.

"This was delivered two days ago." The Colonel gestured – "Please. Indulge me."

Black experienced a frisson of unease. He reached over, prised open the top, looked inside.

Inside, a hand, severed neatly at the wrist, at the junction between the capitate and the scaphoid. The flesh was mottled, bluish black. On the back of the hand, a section of tattoo, which, despite the discolouring of the skin, was distinctive. A vague recollection stirred in Black's mind. Black noted the fingernails had been removed.

Again, the Colonel gestured.

Black lifted it out gently. Secured into the palm by decking screws was a small square of paper with a name on it, with a somewhat grim message –

Jona Lefroy.

He says hi.

Black replaced the item back in its miniature plastic coffin.

"Jona Lefroy was your private detective? You're right. A little too thorough. Your guy stumbled into something he wished he hadn't."

The Colonel's bottom lip quivered. "It's a hell of a message. You noted the fingernails?"

"He was tortured."

"Somewhat medieval, but effective nevertheless."

Black knew the answer before he asked the question. "You have something tangible. What did the police say?"

The Colonel gave a derisive snort. "What do you think they said?"

"Nothing. Because you haven't told them."

"You can see why, Adam."

The mist was dissipating; the picture was gaining clarity, and Black didn't like the signs.

"She's in trouble," said the Colonel. "Bad trouble. For all I know, she may already be..." He finished off the whisky, filled his glass up. His hand trembled.

"If I bring in the police, then..." he nodded at the plastic box, "... I could be signing my daughter's death warrant. You see this, Adam?"

Black spoke plainly. "You said your daughter had fallen in with a bad crowd. Your detective is undoubtedly dead. Perhaps she's not a victim here. Perhaps she's part of the problem."

The Colonel sighed. "The thought had occurred to me. But I need to know. I need to know she's not in danger. And if she is, I need to help her."

Black sat back, appraised the man before him. The man who had braved the snowstorms of the Afghan mountains and the gunfire of the Taliban to save his life. The man who had half his face torn off by a roadside bomb. The man who didn't know if his only child was alive or dead.

The man Black was indebted to. A blood contract, bound by honour and integrity.

"You have skills, Adam," said the Colonel. "Unlike any man I've met. I'm asking you... begging you... to help me."

Black took a sip, swirled the whisky in his mouth, swallowed.

"Jona Lefroy gave you an address?"

The Colonel gave a small sad smile. "Just the town. A place called Fairview. In Kansas."

FIFTEEN

RICHARD HORNBUCKLE HADN'T SLEPT. He got out of bed at 2.45am to make some tea. His mind was in overdrive. He padded downstairs to the kitchen, clicked the kettle on, sat at the kitchen table, took his mobile phone out of his dressing gown pocket and placed it before him. He stared at the blank screen, ran a fretful hand through the remaining strands of his hair. He was prone to overthinking. Agonising. Sometimes over nothing. Sometimes over something. This, he thought, was *something*. This was *real*. A letter had been delivered. *Delivered*! Which meant they were close. And yet…

He searched for reasons to dismantle his theory. How in the name of Sweet Jesus did they find him? He had been careful. The house was in his wife's name, as was the business. Even the car. He was invisible. No assets. No bank accounts. All details in his life precisely manoeuvred to render him practically non-existent. The move to Thurso hadn't been a spontaneous decision. More like a reaction to a bad situation. It had always been his intention to run. Thurso happened to be the right place at the right time.

The kettle clicked. He made some tea, sat back at the table, resumed his focus on the mobile screen. He could phone them. He still had the number. He had never destroyed it. Try and talk his way out of the situation. If it even was a *situation*. But once the call was made, there was no way back. What would he say? Plead? Beg? Ask them to forgive and forget?

Or maybe it was nothing. Maybe it was a crank. Or maybe an aggrieved parent at his wife's school, unable to accept their little fucking Jimmy was a little fucking monster.

His thoughts spun, like a top, battering from one wall to another, always coming back to the same place. Somehow, they'd found him. And now they wanted a little payback. Reasoning with such people was pointless. But yet…

He licked his lips. A simple phone call. Explain the situation. That he was sorry. He laughed out loud. An apology wouldn't quite cut it. Not with these people. And it was way past any monetary solutions. They wanted blood.

But maybe he was overthinking… his mind went round and round. But the phone was on the table before him. A call. A conversation. And maybe a solution. Maybe they could work something out.

Five days. The letter had been specific. There was no give. No room for negotiation. Five days. And then what? Maybe nothing. Maybe something.

He looked up. Elspeth was standing at the doorway. She looked exhausted.

"I couldn't sleep either," she said. She gave a weary smile. She sat opposite. "Remember your promise."

Richard was puzzled. "Promise?"

"That you would go to the police."

He nodded. "I haven't forgotten." Suddenly, another permutation entered his thoughts. *The police.* The last people he wanted to see. Another dimension to the problem.

He tried to sound calm. "Probably it was meant for someone else. Wrong address."

"It had our names," she snapped. "It was meant for us."

"Sure." He hesitated, then said, "Have there been any problems at the school?"

"Problems?"

He paused, weighed his next words carefully. "I mean, annoyed parents. You know how these things can happen. Issues at school. Someone gets a bad report, and all hell breaks loose."

She took a deep breath, forehead wrinkling in thought. "I wish there was. Nothing I can think of. I can ask."

He shook his head. "Better not. Better to keep this a private matter. No need to escalate something which doesn't deserve escalation in the first place." He tried to keep his voice flippant. "It's a piece of childish nonsense."

"But yet, here we both are. Three in the morning. Unable to sleep. Over some 'childish nonsense'."

"That's all it is."

"And you'll get alarms fitted." This was not a question.

"Of course. Alarms. And police. First thing."

This seemed to soothe her. She bit her lip. "Who would want to put such a horrible thing through our door?"

Suddenly, for a brief blazing second, he felt an overpowering urge to tell her. To bare his soul. To come clean, and explain what he had done, and all its consequences. But he didn't. He held it all in, as he had done for five years. He swallowed back his guilt.

"Go back to bed," he said gently. "Sleep. Things will seem better in the morning."

"This is the morning."

"Please."

She gave him a level stare. "Five days, the letter said. And we're now on Day 2. When things will get worse."

SIXTEEN

BLACK STAYED the night at the Colonel's house. They had dinner in the back garden, joined by the man called Gibson. A barbecue set on a pink marble patio, beyond which, a lawn as flat and green as the baize of a pool table. In the precise centre, a fountain whispered. The evening was warm, soothed by the gentlest of breezes, breathing in from the Pacific. *Another world,* thought Black. *Alien, compared to the hail and snow of the north of Scotland.*

The mood was sombre. The Colonel grilled some chilipepper rockfish and thick beefburgers over an old-style half-drum barbeque. He drank more whisky. Gibson abstained, as did Black, grudgingly. An early afternoon flight had been organised, at a small local airfield, and then a three-hour journey to another, equally discreet airfield in a nowhere place in Kansas. Approximately eighteen hundred miles across half of America, to a destination where danger lurked. Black was not brimming with enthusiasm for the trip. A relatively clear head was required.

The soft evening light brought the Colonel's facial disfigurement into sharp relief, the ruined skin of his face shimmering, like the scales of a fish. Black pondered his own past. He had fought numerous battles in numerous countries, and with the exception of the bullets he'd taken in the Hindu Kush, had emerged from the meat grinder relatively unscathed. Unlike many others. Afghanistan – you either lost your mind or lost a limb. Or your life. Black considered himself lucky. He'd only lost his soul.

Black knew a little of the Colonel's background. Rich family, stretching over several generations. Staggeringly rich. A small store somewhere in the south of England grew, over thirty years or so, into several hundred supermarkets worldwide. The Colonel took a different tack, didn't join the business, joined the army instead. Black wondered how the family had reacted. Maybe they were appalled. Maybe they were proud. Black would never know. And now, here the Colonel sat, sitting drinking whisky in the dying sun, face shredded, daughter missing, all the money in the world, and with it, all the sadness.

They sat at a large wooden table, robust and worn, doubtless witness to a thousand barbecues. Cutlery and plates had been laid. Also on the table was a blending machine. Black restricted himself to a cold bottle of beer. Gibson did likewise. Black regarded the man. He exuded a quiet competence, a certain undefinable stillness. Black had encountered men like Gibson before. Capable men in situations of conflict. Men of violence.

"You were in the Navy SEALs?" ventured Black.

Gibson reacted with a quizzical look – "How would you know that?"

"A guess." Gibson was wearing a T-Shirt. Black gestured to a tattoo on Gibson's right forearm.

"The bone frog. Quite a distinct marking. If I recall, a symbol adopted specifically by the SEALs."

Gibson gave a small nod of his head. "That's not common knowledge. Your guess is correct. But I didn't stay for long. As I'd mentioned, I didn't take to the discipline."

Black could have laughed out loud. Gibson appeared the epitome of discipline.

"Gibson's being modest," broke in the Colonel. "Tell Adam what you were in."

Gibson reacted with the merest of shrugs. "SEAL Team 6."

Black raised an eyebrow. SEAL Team 6. Special Missions Unit. Killers' elite.

"We all have something in common."

Gibson tilted his head in puzzlement.

"Afghanistan," said Black. "The graveyard of empires."

"An accurate sobriquet," said the Colonel. "I prefer its old-fashioned nickname."

"The Grim," said Black. "And for good reason. And after Afghanistan?"

"After Afghanistan? I left. Quit the navy. Visiting exotic foreign places had lost its charm."

Black nodded. He understood the sentiment. The military had that effect. It took blood and guts to make a soldier realise the best place in the world was 'home'. It didn't matter where 'home' was. It was still a million times better than a battlefield. But quitting wasn't easy for a Navy SEAL. Black pressed the point further.

"And then?" he said.

"Then?"

"When you left the navy?"

Gibson's lips quirked into a delicate smile. "This and that."

Which meant *security*, thought Black. Or *mercenary*.

The Colonel spoke up. "I needed someone to do my admin. With this…he gestured to his injuries,"… it's difficult for me to deal with things. Lawyers, Accountants. Other bloodsuckers. The business still has to run. Gibson has a mind like a steel trap when it comes to facts and figures. He's an organisational genius. I sit back, and let Gibson take the strain. And you don't seem to mind, do you, Gibson?"

"Admin?" said Black. He looked at Gibson, grinned. "I didn't take you for a pen-pushing type. You both met in Afghanistan?"

Gibson sipped from his beer bottle. "Kandahar. A joint operation. We became close friends."

"Is Gibson your first name or last name?"

Gibson reacted again with a small twitch of his shoulders.

"Does it matter?"

"Probably not," said Black. He switched the conversation. "I'll need a photo of Beth."

The Colonel nodded, slung back his whisky. The lower jaw, part missing, was unable to accommodate the motion. Alcohol dribbled down the remains of his chin, down his neck. He cleaned himself with a paper napkin.

"I don't have any recent ones," he said. "For obvious reasons." He gestured to Gibson. Gibson nodded, entered the house, returned with an A4-sized envelope, which he placed on the table. Black pulled out a colour copy of a photograph – a young woman, maybe early twenties. Not unappealing. Grey-blue eyes under dark lashes, clear and direct. Her face, wide of forehead and cheekbone, slanted across high flat cheeks down to a small chin and curving pink mouth, lips curled in a secretive half-smile.

She was sitting at a table in a restaurant. The table had a red-and-white-chequered tablecloth. On the table was a bottle of wine and a glass and nothing else. Black couldn't read the wine label, not that it was relevant. In the background, other tables, people sitting round them, engaged in their own conversations, unaware the photo was being taken. On a wall behind her, framed photographs, paintings, and a big brass clock, Roman numerals for numbers. The type one might have seen long ago in a railway station. Beside it, a calendar. August 24th 2004. Ten years ago.

Black studied the face. Not instantly the look of a troubled, angry young woman with an addiction problem. Rather, composed, at ease with the world. Seemingly enjoying the moment.

"Who took this?" Black asked.

The Colonel sighed. His shoulders slumped. Gibson spoke for him.

"The Colonel. The last time he saw her. They were at a restaurant together."

"Which one?"

"Is it important?" said the Colonel.

"Probably not. But still. Sometimes the small things matter."

"An Italian place," said the Colonel. "Somewhere in town. The name escapes me." The burgers sizzled. He scooped them up, slid them into six cut seeded buns on a plate, put the plate in the centre of the table. He dropped another burger into the blender.

His alien half-face creased into something approaching a grin.

"Not easy to chew when a chunk of your jaw's been blown off." He switched the blender on. The burger became pulp. The colonel popped open the top, scooped out the contents into his plate with a spoon, and with the same spoon, tilted the food into the side of his mouth. He chewed, swallowed. A slow careful process.

"Sorry you have to see this," he said.

"You don't have to be sorry, Colonel."

The Colonel took another slurp of whisky, said, "Find my daughter, Adam. Wherever the hell she is, get her the hell out of it."

Black said nothing. To such a request, there was nothing to say. He would do his best. Sometimes that was enough. Sometimes, it wasn't. In this particular pursuit, there were no guarantees. Promises were hollow. But his gut told him it would end badly.

His gut told him the girl was dead.

SEVENTEEN

DORNOCH, A SCOTTISH TOWN ON THE
NORTH SHORE OF THE DORNOCH FIRTH.
SIXTY-NINE MILES FROM THURSO.

ROM CALLAGHAN HATED BEING TOLD. He preferred
doing the telling. Giving out orders. The truth was, he took orders
from only one person. His father. And for good reason. But he still
hated it.

His father had spoken. The order issued. It was a special job. It
required a personal touch. Rom, under normal circumstances,
would have delegated the task. The command was specific and
clear. To be fulfilled personally, the idea being to send a message.
That the transgression was of a nature serious enough to justify
the direct involvement of Rom Callaghan, the only son of William
Callaghan, otherwise known as the Gypsy King.

Personal touch. Rom pondered those words. Personal was fine,
provided there was backup. And when he implemented any
command of his father's, Rom always brought backup.

The job was relatively straightforward. The inconvenience was
the distance. Rom lived in a fifty-acre estate three miles from
Dornoch, chosen for its isolation. Separate houses. His father in
one, he and his girlfriend in another. And a third, a large house,
which, at any given time, was occupied by six men. All relatives
or close friends. All on the payroll of William Callaghan. The
notion that Gypsies lived together in a cluster of caravans in some

arse-end muddy field was as wrong as you could get, at least for the Callaghans. Though the same basic structure existed. Only instead of an arse-end muddy field – manicured lawns and neat flowerbeds and dual-toned granite driveways. Instead of caravans – architecturally designed houses. But the family stuck close. Blood was the glue. Blood could be trusted. Which was its strength. The Callaghans' business was organised crime. The backbone of organised crime was loyalty. And the backbone of loyalty was family. Such was William Callaghans' mantra. Rom was less inclined to follow the doctrine, more inclined to do what suited him best.

But his father had spoken.

The inconvenience was the distance. The job was in Edinburgh. A tortuous five-hour journey. He left early. If he got there for midday, and if things went to plan, he could relax in the afternoon, book into a nice hotel, hit the gym.

He took the Range Rover, accompanied by three of his men. Another Range Rover followed, carrying another two. Rom's philosophy – better too much than too little. They set off at 7am. Rom liked to drive. In the front passenger seat sat his childhood friend, Stu Gorman. Loyal as a dog. Lean, pale, and psychotic. Unquestionably an asset in the Callaghan world.

The conversation was minimal. Too early for chat. Rom played music. His choice. Led Zeppelin. AC/DC. Whitesnake. Stuff that got him pumped at the gym. They stopped at nine o'clock at a drive-by McDonald's. Rom got porridge, while the others had burgers. No way was he introducing chemicalised shit into his body. After the job, he would get a proper meal, have proper nutrition. He stuck to mineral water, while the others had coffee.

They sat, all six of them, on high stools, three on either side of a raised galley-style table, hunched over their food. All decked in Hugo Boss and Nike.

"I read something about coffee," said Gorman. "Drink too much of the stuff and it can kill you."

"Drink too much of anything, and it can kill you," said Rom. "Coffee's no exception."

"Heart disease," continued Gorman. "It's all proved. Caffeine and heart disease. I reckon I drink a gallon a day."

"That's eight pints," said one of the men. "No way you drink that much."

"Easy," said Gorman.

Rom grinned. "You could drink a hundred gallons. It'll have no effect on you."

Gorman's pale face wrinkled in bewilderment. "How's that?"

Rom's grin widened. "You don't have a fucking heart." This caused a ripple of quiet laughter.

Gorman reacted with an expression of mock sadness. He clutched his chest – "You're breaking it, boss."

"Sure I am."

They finished up, left the place, continued on their way.

The morning wore on. Food had invigorated them. The conversation lifted, banter firing back and forth, like ping-pong. As they approached their destination, the chat lessened, until only the music played, which Rom eventually switched off, leaving silence.

Ten past midday. They arrived at the north of the city, to the port of Leith. This particular area was zoned for industrial use. They parked their cars hard up on the pavement on Inglis Green Road. On one side, a barren area the size of a football pitch enclosed by chain-link fencing with pounded posts. Someone, once, had the notion of developing something in the space. The notion had gone, leaving a waste of weeds and cement blocks and discarded debris and little else.

On the other side, a steel warehouse and parking bay, filling two acres of land, surrounded by the same style of chain-link fencing. Across one wall, a huge sign – *Fergusons Ltd*. The main gates were open. The place looked busy – lorries parked up at the warehouse entrance, forklifts loading and unloading crates, containers, different shapes and sizes. Clamped to one side, an office-sized building built of grey concrete breeze-blocks, and a flat corrugated roof. Above the front door, the words *Reception Area.*

Rom opened the central console of the car, took out an envelope, tucked it into the inside pocket of his leather jacket. He got out. His men followed. Gorman popped open the boot, pulled out an Adidas sports bag. The six men entered through the main gates, went to the reception area, Rom leading. They filed into a waiting room. Plastic metal-legged chairs lined the walls. In one corner, a coffee machine, offering Americano and latte. Next to it, on a shelf, a stack of plastic coffee cups. The room was devoid of any ornamentation. A typical waiting room in an industrial unit, like a million others up and down the country. On the far side, a wooden counter, behind which, a woman sat. Behind her, another room, the door closed. The woman was on the phone. She gave an automatic smile as the men entered. Rom smiled back. She was maybe late fifties, white blouse, short mousey-brown hair, with a somewhat severe side fringe. He and the others approached the counter. She finished off her phone conversation, appraised them with sharp grey eyes. Her smile was gone. She looked efficient and humourless.

"Can I help you?"

Rom kept his smile up. "We're here to see Jeffrey."

She inspected the men before her, finally fixing her attention back on Rom.

"Do you have an appointment?"

"We don't need one." He leaned closer. "We go way back. Let him know Rom Callaghan is here. I'm sure he'll spare the time."

"Rom Callaghan?" She hesitated. "I'm not sure. Jeffrey only sees people by appointment."

"What's your name?" asked Rom quietly.

"My name? Gladys. I've worked with Jeffrey for ten years. And he insists anyone who wants to speak to him has to have an appointment. It's one of his rules. And he's a man who sticks to the rules."

On the counter was a telephone, a computer and keyboard, a notepad. She had both hands resting on the countertop. Rom placed his own hand gently on one of hers. His smile faded, drooping to a sad frown. He leaned closer still, lowered his voice to a soft whisper.

"Is he in his office?"

She nodded.

"Which is the room behind you?"

Another nod.

"But you need an appointment…" she blustered.

"Hush, Gladys." He raised a finger to his lips, indicating silence. "We're going through to see him now. Three of my colleagues will wait here, to keep you company. Is there a key for the front door?"

"Yes."

"I want you to give it to me."

Again, hesitation.

"If you don't, I'll break your nose and kick your teeth out." He tightened the grip on her hand. Her lip trembled. She blinked, eyes suddenly moist.

"This is real," he said. "And it will happen if you don't do as I say, as God is my witness. Give me the key, Gladys. It's very simple."

With her free hand, she reached under the counter, produced a key attached to a label – *Main Office*.

Rom responded with a polite nod, took the key, tossed it to one of the men, who locked the door. Rom's smile returned. "There you go. Painless. You keep your good looks, and everything's fine." He released her hand, gestured to Gorman and another. He lifted a section of the counter, opened the half-door beneath, went to the interior office door. Gorman and the other man followed. Gladys watched them, face pale and tight.

Rom dispensed with knocking. He went straight in, Gorman directly behind him, carrying the Adidas gym bag.

The office was spacious, with few frills. The walls comprised glossy wooden slats, the ceiling low and artexed, the floor heavy duty carpet tiles the colour of rust. A couple of gunmetal-grey filing cabinets. On one wall, a large aluminium-framed whiteboard, upon which, lists of names, times, places written with a black dry marker pen. Three chairs, the same as the chairs in the waiting room. Not designed for comfort. There was one window, with a net curtain, allowing in a fraction of sunlight. Instead, harsh light was supplied by two long strip lights bolted to the ceiling. In the middle of the room, a desk. On it, piles of papers scattered in no apparent order, a telephone, a framed photograph of two smiling girls. Behind the desk sat a man. His head jerked up in surprise when Rom entered – a long, somewhat equine face, lank dark hair, heavy-lidded blue eyes, skin the colour of paste. Jeffrey Ferguson. Proprietor of Fergusons Ltd.

He was about to speak. His mouth clamped shut.

Rom sat on one of the chairs, stretched his legs out, stretched his arms above his head, swivelled his neck, arched his back.

"We've driven all the way from sunny Dornoch to see you, Jeffrey. Long drive. Feeling a bit stiff. Need to loosen up a little."

Ferguson licked his lips, cleared his throat. "I had no idea…"

Rom raised a halting hand. "No need. Gladys has already explained you won't see anyone unless they have an appointment. She said you were a man who liked to stick to the rules. But I thought, given I am who I am, an appointment would be… unnecessary?"

Ferguson swallowed, gave a flickering nervous smile. "Of course…"

Again, Rom interrupted. "Though you could do something about your décor. Drab is the first impression. And cheap. Drab and cheap. Not a good look. Perhaps a picture on the wall. Some art? Maybe a picture of the two girls in the photo on your desk. That would be nice. Your daughters?"

Ferguson's long face wrinkled in a combination of fear and bewilderment.

"I'm not sure I understand…"

"But maybe I can do better," said Rom. He reached into the inside pocket of his leather jacket, produced the envelope. He opened it, stretched across and placed two photographs on top of the papers on Ferguson's desk. One was a girl of about twelve, in a school uniform, walking towards a parked bus. The other was a girl of maybe fifteen, skating on an ice rink. The same girls in the framed photograph.

Rom was smiling as he spoke. "Your daughters. Taken just a few days ago. The older one looks good on the rink. Think she might go places. Very *lithe*." He paused, said softly – "Do you know why I'm showing you these, Jeffrey?"

Ferguson didn't answer. He gave Rom a limpid stare. The bewildered look had gone. Now, just fear.

"To give you context," said Rom. "To give our conversation a little depth, and to make you appreciate the weight of my words. Yes?"

Ferguson could only nod.

"Here's the situation. In a nutshell, you didn't pay our invoice. In fact, you haven't paid our invoices for the last three months. We don't understand this. The procedure is simple. We send you a bill every month. For services rendered, the services being protection against all the uncertainties of life, and there are many, Jeffrey. Life is one big uncertainty. Not to pay once is… forgettable. Not to pay twice is… bad mannered. But not to pay three times. That is… unforgivable. As you know, Jeffrey, we are not in the forgiving business."

Ferguson's chin wobbled. "Money's been tight. I can sort this…"

"Enough, Jeffrey. It's a little late." Rom took out his wallet, teased out a bank card, placed it beside the photographs.

"Those are the bank details," he said. "Do the transfer now. Plus, add another fifteen. Call it penalty interest."

Ferguson's voice rose to a wheedling plea. "That's a lot to find. I can get it together tomorrow. Just a little time…"

Rom shook his head. "You haven't been listening, Jeffrey. If

the funds aren't transferred in the next two minutes, then Katie…
and he reached over and tapped his finger on the photo of the
girl walking to the bus,"… will have acid sprayed in her eyes,
and Julia… and he next tapped on the girl skating,"… will get
gang-banged by seven men who'll fuck and fuck like rutting
beasts."

Jeffrey stared. Rom made a show of looking at his watch.

"One minute fifty seconds."

Jeffrey gasped, started tapping his keypad. In the glare of the
strip lights, his forehead shone, tapestried with beads of sweat.
"Shit," he muttered. He'd got the password wrong. Rom waited,
yawned. Jeffrey typed in a word, a sequence of numbers.

Rom took out his mobile phone, pressed some digits.

"It's done," breathed Ferguson. "The money's transferred."

Rom's phone emitted a soft chime. He inspected the screen.
"There you are," he said. He tapped his forehead with his index
finger. "The power of the mind."

He stood up. Ferguson looked like he'd aged ten years. "Don't
ever be late again," said Rom. "Not by one minute. You
understand?"

Ferguson nodded vigorously. "It won't happen. Tell your dad,
every month, payment on the nose. I promise."

"That's nice. I'll be sure to pass the message on. Pass my
regards on to the family." He glanced at Gorman, gave a miniscule
tilt of his head, from which Gorman seemed to derive exact
information. Gorman placed the Adidas bag on one of the chairs,
opened the zip, pulled out various implements, and with care,
placed them on the table before Ferguson. Ferguson's face
contorted in sudden panic. He gave a rattling breath.

"What is this? You got the money."

Rom gazed at him. "Really? You think it was as easy as that?
You think the payment and a little interest would cure this? You
need to take your medicine, Jeffrey. You know how it is. It's the
game we're in."

He turned his attention back to Gorman. "Your turn."

Gorman, in a practical manner, began his business, the screams of Ferguson rising to a crescendo.

The men had left. Gladys had heard the dreadful noise from her boss's office. Hard not to. Terrified, she knocked on his door. Silence. She opened it. She gasped, lurched back into the counter, knocked over the computer. Her knees sagged, her legs caved, the office floor rose up to meet her face. The image remained with her – Jeffrey Ferguson, head drooped, unconscious, crucified to the wall behind his desk.

EIGHTEEN

GIBSON WAS to drive Black to San Reno Airfield, a distance of fifty miles. It was small, covering a hundred and eighty acres, with one runway, a single hanger, no tower. An airfield designed for discreet departures and arrivals. An airfield where no answers were given because no questions were asked.

The Colonel had walked Black to the car. The same car Black had arrived in. He wore a wide-brimmed cowboy hat dipped low, and a scarf covering his neck and the remains of his jaw. Even half-covered, his face was monstrous. He handed Black an A4-sized envelope.

"Fifteen thousand dollars cash, in fifty-dollar bills. Plus a bank card you can use at any ATM, should you require more. The pin is 1111. Easy to remember. There's something else."

He gestured to Gibson, who had been standing quietly to the side, holding a wooden container the size of a chocolate box.

He handed it to Black. Black flicked a tiny silver latch, opened it. Inside, in a moulded compartment, a fixed-blade eight-inch KA-BAR Marine hunting knife. Also, a Glock 17.

"Your weapon of choice," said the Colonel. "It has a 'plus 2'. Nineteen rounds. A little bit of insurance."

Black closed the box, put it in his holdall. "Let's hope I don't ever need it."

"I pray that you don't," he said, his voice muffled and lisping. He gripped Black's arm. "Find my daughter, Adam. I beg you. I need to know she's safe. She's all I have. You understand."

Black reacted with the best reassuring smile he could muster, but he knew it played false.

"I'll do what I can."

"I know you will. Good luck, Captain Black."

Black gave no response.

During the journey, little was said. Black was in no mood to talk. He was entering the unknown, at the behest of an old friend. The private investigator the Colonel had hired had been tortured and killed. His hand had been severed. The message was stark – *back off.* Black gave a somewhat rueful chuckle. He was doing the opposite. He was entering the beast's lair, on the basis of an old debt, with nothing more than the name of a town. And two weapons. A typical scenario, he thought, in the life of Adam Black.

Gibson flicked him a side glance – "You find something funny?"

Black shrugged. "Life. No matter what you do, the road runs to the same place."

Gibson regarded him quizzically. "Which is?"

"In my case? A shitshow."

"If you want it to be," replied Gibson. "You want my advice?"

Black said nothing.

"Get to Fairview, do a quick reconnoitre, get the hell out. We both know she's probably dead. The Colonel won't expect anything more. He just needs you to confirm what he already knows. End of."

"Maybe," said Black. *But maybe not.* Black owed the Colonel. But now a little more.

The Colonel had chartered a compact Cessna Citation M2. A four-seater. Other than the pilot, Black was the only passenger. It was waiting on the runway. Gibson nodded a curt farewell, left the airfield. Black had brought his holdall. He carried it on board, and settled in. The passenger section was small but elegant. The seats – all four of them – were comfortable, the side panelling antique mahogany. *No expense spared.* At one end, a large television screen. To his side, a cupboard. He slid the door open. Inside, an array of drinks and a small refrigerator containing more drinks. Also crisps and snacks. Black spied a bottle of Glenfiddich. Perhaps a coincidence. Or perhaps there at the request of the Colonel. Either way, Black abstained, with difficulty, and helped himself to some cold sparkling mineral water. The journey would take roughly three hours. Black delved into his holdall and dug out the book he had bought at the train station in Thurso – *Run and Hide.*

But Black was no longer running. Nor hiding. Black had a job. He had a girl to find.

And a mystery to solve.

The Colonel had lied. And Black wanted to find out why.

NINETEEN

THE JOURNEY WAS SMOOTH, turbulence zero. Black slept a little. He had the capacity to sleep whenever and wherever. A habit instilled in him from his patrol days. Grab it while you can.

The plane landed at a remote airfield which, so far as Black could ascertain, had no name. An area enclosed by a high wire fence, and beyond, endless grassy flatlands, tinted bluish grey, like a massive bruise on the skin of the earth. He disembarked. Within a millisecond of leaving the air con, the heat assaulted the senses. In Carmel, it was warm. Here, under the Kansas sun, it was baking hot. He reckoned he could fry an egg on the asphalt. Already, he felt his T-shirt and jeans cling. There was a solitary hanger, and a long outbuilding of bleached timber. The Cessna taxied towards it, presumably to refuel, and continue on its next scheduled flight.

A young man and woman approached. Both wore matching blue shirts, bearing the yellow and black 'Hertz' logo.

The woman gave Black an award-winning smile – "Mr Adam Black?"

"Yes."

"Hope you had a pleasant trip, sir. Your car is ready. If you'd like to follow us?"

"Of course."

He followed them round the outbuilding, to a section of potholed tarmacadam which, at a stretch, could be described as a car park, holding about a half-dozen vehicles, including a dust-coated Police Dodge Charger. From the car park ran a single-track road, leading to an open gate a mile off.

They took Black to a brand-new metallic-grey Honda Accord Sedan. Black signed for it, was handed the keys. To be returned to the same location in two weeks. All paid for upfront.

It was 5pm local time. He placed his holdall on the passenger seat, took out the box, opened it, took out the Glock. The Colonel was right. Always his weapon of choice. Accurate, powerful, reliable. A one-shot kill. And if you missed the head and hit the torso, then able to punch a hole through jacket, shirt, skin, blood, bone, organ, and back out the other side. Black stored it in the glove compartment. He put the knife in the centre console. He pressed the ignition, grateful for the sudden blast of cool air. He switched on the satnav, keyed in *Fairview*. One hundred and sixty miles. He drove off, the car lurching and bouncing on the single track. He switched the radio on, and was instantly subjected to the grating blare of adverts. Someone selling washing machines, new or reconditioned – buy now, get free delivery, free installation, free removal of the old model and – hey! – we'll throw in fifty dollars' worth of free washing powder.

The land of the free, thought Black. He switched the noise off, preferring the silence.

Two men watched the Cessna land from seating in the outbuilding, at the back, in the shadows, where the sunlight didn't reach. They sat quietly, observing the big man leave the plane, meeting the hire-car reps, and following them round the building, until they disappeared from view. One of them spoke softly into his mobile. His voice lacked any discernible accent.

"He's here."

A voice answered. "You know what to do."

He disconnected. He knew exactly what to do.

TWENTY

DAY 2

RICHARD HORNBUCKLE HAD PROMISED his wife he would go to the police. Also, get an alarm installed. He had almost convinced himself the letter was a prank, some kid's sick stupid joke.

Almost. But not totally. Doubt crouched in the back of his brain, which he couldn't shake. Which made the alarm installation the easy bit. Going to the police was a little more awkward. He had, however, promised his wife. But the way he saw it, he could let matters rest a little time. Perhaps nothing would come of it. That the letter was a hoax. That going to the police would have wasted everyone's time. If essential, he would go. But, in his mind, *essential* hadn't been reached. Not by a long stretch.

It was Tuesday morning. Tuesday was no different to any other day. He followed the usual routine. He opened the shop at the same time – 7am. Which meant getting up at 6.15, showering, shaving. He liked to maintain a degree of discipline. He had dispensed with the suit and collar and tie long ago. There was no need for such regimentation, working in a newsagent. But he liked being smart. Never jeans, always chinos. Never running shoes, always polished-up, laced brogues. Always a shirt, one button undone at the neck, never two, and never ever a T-shirt, which was blasphemous. And he shaved every day and splashed himself with nice aftershave. To skip shaving, he thought, was the harbinger of decline. And what would happen then? An extra fifteen minutes in bed on a cold winter's morning, then a half hour, then an hour, until he stopped going in altogether. And Richard Hornbuckle hadn't upped sticks and moved three hundred miles to drift into a comatose state of retiral. He had come here – to Thurso – to work. To start afresh.

So he told himself. But the reality was different. *To start afresh.* In a way, it was the truth. But not all the truth. It painted a glossy coat over a dark underlay. He gazed at his reflection in the bathroom mirror, and wondered, as he often did, who the hell was the man who gazed back?

To start afresh. Not quite. More like *run away.*

His wife slept on. She also lived by routine. She would get up round about 7. Get ready. Leave for work about 8.

It looked like it would be a fine morning, the sun bright, the sky perfect, save a thin feathery trail of cloud. He hadn't slept well. A single thought bounced about in his head – *Day 2.* He dismissed the unease. Ignore it, and it would go away. Like a minor itch.

He got changed, keeping as quiet as he could. He went out, opened the garage door, got his bicycle. He began his cycle to the shop. He filled his lungs, felt the breeze on his skin. Suddenly, things didn't seem so bad. The letter was a joke – a sick joke, but little more.

He got to the shop, padlocked the bicycle to the lamp-post outside. He unlocked the roller shutters for the front entrance and front window, heaved them up. He checked his watch. 6.55. Mr Punctuality. The way he liked it. He went in. Nothing had changed. Life went on. The letter retreated further into the recesses of his mind.

People came and went. Regulars mostly. At 11am, he called an alarm engineer. He wasn't cheap, but the sad fact was that he was the only engineer within thirty miles who did that sort of work.

The guy wasn't in. Hornbuckle left a message on an answering machine, and half hoped he wouldn't phone back. *Overkill*, he thought. All for a stupid kid's prank.

1pm. There was a small fridge in the back shop. He fixed himself a pork pie, a carton of coleslaw, and some salad. He got a bottle of fresh orange. He wondered what his wife was doing. Probably having lunch as well. Probably in the teachers' common room. Sometimes, to surprise him, she drove from the school, and brought sandwiches into the shop, and they ate together, sipping tea in his little back room.

But not today.

At 2.30pm, his mobile buzzed. He was serving a customer at the time. He glanced at the screen. His wife. Probably reminding him to get the alarm fitted. He let it ring out, finished seeing the customer, phoned her back.

The phone picked up.

'Elspeth?'

Silence.

Suddenly, a flutter of unease.

'Elspeth?'

She spoke, her voice frail.

'Please come home.'

He took a breath.

'What is it, Elspeth?'

Another pause, then –

'I came home early. I'm scared, Richard.'

He kept his voice calm.

'What is it, Elspeth?'

'Come home,' she said. 'Now.'

He was back within twenty minutes. She was standing on the pavement, outside the front gate. He didn't need to ask what the problem was.

Around the perimeter of their front garden was a three-foot-high lap-style wooden fence. He had erected it himself, planted the posts, varnished it. A deep rustic brown. He gave it a fresh lick every summer.

Words in dripping white paint had been scrawled across one half of the front section of the fence. Big capital letters, from top to bottom –

HI GUYS. DAY 2. WE'RE COMING. DON'T FORGET.

He stared at the message. His thoughts tumbled over and over.

"What is this?" whispered Elspeth.

He couldn't instantly articulate a response. Any notion that this was some kid's prank was dispelled. The doubt which he had pushed to the back of his mind, suddenly took centre stage. Only it was no longer doubt. It was fear, raw and stark.

She stood beside him, his wife, her face pale and set. She turned. When she spoke, her voice sounded small. "What did the police say?"

He looked at her, frowned. He couldn't focus. *Tumbling over and over.* "What?"

"The police. When you reported the letter. What did they say?"

He swallowed, collected his thoughts, shook his head a fraction. "They're looking into it," he lied.

"Take a picture," she said. "Show them this. Show them it's real."

"Yes."

He took his phone out, went to camera, took a photo.

"I want them to see. Can you get a hold of someone? Who did you speak to?"

He hesitated, just an instant – it looked like he was trying to remember a name, rather than concoct another lie.

"I can't remember," he muttered. "But I'll speak to them. I promise."

She seemed to accept this. She made her way into the house. He watched her go, and thought –

They've found me.

And now he had no choice. He had to speak to the very people he had no desire to contact. The police.

And by going to the police, he was breaking The Golden Rule.

TWENTY-ONE

When faced with overwhelming odds, run like fuck. And if you can't do that, and the party's over, then smile, and make the bastards earn it.

Whimsical note from Staff Sergeant to soldiers of the 22nd Regiment of the SAS.

THE ROAD COMPRISED TWO LANES, but narrow. Barely wide enough for two cars. Should a lorry or truck come trundling along, he would have to slow and pull over onto the verge. On either side, neglected low stone walls and broken, tangled wire fences. Beyond, the same unending vista – blue-grey flatlands sheathed in shimmers of heat, under the fierce Kansas sun. An occasional house, set miles back from the road. But no people. No human activity. *A dead zone,* thought Black. America was still vast enough to accommodate large areas where no civilisation appeared to exist.

He reached a long straight section. Ahead, maybe a mile, a big camper-van, stationary, at an angle across the width of the road.

Adjacent to it, a dust-covered jeep. He made out five people, hovering round the tail section of the van. Maybe a blow-out, causing the vehicle to swerve, and rest in its current position. Maybe. To avoid it, Black would have to drive onto the verge, and round. Problem was, for most of this part of the road, there was no verge. The road went hard up to a low wall, either side. The camper-van and the jeep, effectively, were a barrier.

Black approached, slowed down. Details emerged. Three men, two women. Two of the men, and both women all possibly in their mid-twenties. Maybe younger. Hard to say. Black found it more and more difficult to distinguish age groups as the years sped by. A consequence of getting older. The third man was easier to place. In his fifties. Pale complexion, grey balding hair, sporting a paunch. Sweat-stained office shirt. Dark trousers bagging at the hips, suggesting the pockets were full. Keys, cigarettes, and such.

The younger group were altogether different. Lean, wiry arms and legs, all taut hard muscle. Athletic. Built like middle-distance runners. Built for endurance. Black recognised the physiology immediately. The men had long hair, swept roguishly back into ponytails, trailing down to mid-spine. Wearing matching red baseball caps. One woman had pixie-short auburn hair. Mirror-effect sunglasses. The other was blonde, bob-cut, wearing a pink straw hat, tilted to one side. The men wore cut-down jeans, T-shirts, one emblazoned with a fist, one *fuck you* finger raised. The woman with the straw hat wore a plain white cotton dress down to an inch above her knees. The other, black Lycra gym gear. All sporting a cute tan. All clean limbed and perfect. They could have come straight from the Californian surf. All looking confused. Four young people stuck in the heat with a broken vehicle, and not knowing what to do.

In the shade of the van, was a pram.

Black stopped thirty yards away. They all gazed at him. The younger ones flashed sunshine smiles. One of them raised a hand, then raised his shoulders, gesturing helplessness, pointed to the rear tyre, conveying a plea for assistance, or at least patience. The older man merely nodded, wiped his brow, turned his attention back to the vehicle.

The problem was obvious. The rear tyre had burst. Plus, the wheel had buckled, slanting at an ugly angle, causing the vehicle to tilt. It would need a tow, thought Black. The older guy, like himself, had probably come across the camper-van, got out to see if he could help, and now was wondering what the hell he could do. Such was the scenario displayed before him. *Displayed.* It was either staged, or it wasn't. And if it was, then it was sophisticated. Black, cynical to the point of obsession, reached over, retrieved the Glock from the glove compartment, placed it on the seat, between his legs. He opened the mid-section, lifted out the KA-BAR, manoeuvred himself, tucked the knife behind the belt of his jeans, at the base of his back.

One of the younger men – the one who had gestured – ambled towards him, to the driver's side. Black waited. He could have reversed. He chose not to.

He let it play.

The man reached the window. Still smiling, though the smile was fixed. Black pressed a button. The window slid open. The man leaned down. His face, close up, was angular, hard lines, flat cheeks. A man fit and trained.

He didn't speak. He looked at Black, intensely, as if seeking verification. He straightened, turned to the others, nodded. Calmly, he put his hand behind his back, brought it round. He was holding a pistol. 9mm. Lightweight. Still enough to lodge a bullet six inches inside Black's skull. Easily concealed. Like Black's KA-BAR knife, presumably tucked behind the waist of his shorts. Looked like a Smith and Wesson M&P Shield. He held it before him, a classic two-handed grip, solid stance, leaning slightly forward to offset recoil. He was a yard from Black's face. The man wouldn't miss, and he knew it, and Black knew it.

"Get out the car, please," he said. He spoke softly. Had he not been pointing a gun at Black's head, he could almost have been polite. But his smile was gone. From now on, it was all business.

Black responded, almost conversationally. "Is this a carjacking thing? I've heard of this."

"You wish. I'm afraid it's not so simple for you, Mr Black."

They know my name. And he hasn't fired. Which means…?

He had the Glock on the seat. Tempting, but the odds weren't favourable. Two seconds to lift the weapon, point, and fire, compared to the millisecond it would take for the guy to squeeze the trigger.

Black gave the slightest shrug. He still had his knife.

He let it play.

He opened the door, got out, stood beside the car, watched as the others at the camper-van – including the older man – began pulling out weapons from the pram. The women had pistols, the men, rifles. They turned, pointed the weapons at Black.

"You understand," said Black, "if your Comancheros start firing, chances are they'll hit you as well."

"I'm sure I'll be fine."

"I'm sure you will. I was merely making an observation."

"Noted, Mr Black. Please. If you make your way to the jeep."

Black did as requested. The camper-van was the decoy, and would presumably be abandoned in the road. Ownership doubtless traceable to a struck-off company with bogus directors. Or perhaps it was stolen. Still, thought Black. It was probably worth over one hundred thousand dollars. An expensive item to be discarded.

He made his way towards the others, the man following, still aiming with his two-handed grip. The older man popped open the boot of the jeep, waited.

Black approached. The older man awarded Black a polite nod, flicked a glance to the side. One of the women stepped forward – the one wearing the white cotton dress – handed the older man her pistol, and using both hands, began to expertly pad Black's T-shirt, his trousers. She found his mobile, and the KA-BAR. She unclipped its leather scabbard, pulled it out, held it up. The blade glinted. *Too bad*, thought Black.

"That's a nice knife," said the older man. "We don't want you cutting yourself."

"That's very considerate."

He beckoned Black towards the open boot. "If you wouldn't mind."

Black stopped a yard away. The older man waited, regarding Black with milk-blue eyes. Close up, he had pockmarked skin, shiny pale and rippled in the Kansas sun. Like melted white rubber. A legacy of old acne. He was heavily built, mostly fat, stomach drooping over the belt of his slacks. He was holding a rifle loosely in one hand, aimed generally in the direction of Black's midriff, without any great care. Which meant, if trouble arose, he was counting on others. In the other hand, he still held the weapon the woman had given him, which he was pointing to the ground. Which meant she was now unarmed, except for Black's knife. But a knife was different from a gun. The odds, slightly, had improved. Not by much. But it was something.

The man who had followed Black had stopped three paces behind, still focusing his weapon. The woman who had searched him remained standing only a yard from Black. The other woman – mirrored sunglasses – held her pistol, like her friend, in a straight, two-handed grip, focused. The third man – *fuck you* T-shirt – watched from ten yards back, positioned in a fighting stance. Butt of the rifle tucked into the shoulder, body at a slight angle, left foot forward, slight bend of the torso. Military-taught.

Black glanced at the car boot, but didn't move. The older man smiled. Unlike his colleagues, his teeth didn't shine. Rather, a faint yellowy stain. "Please," he said. "Get in the car. Let's not make a fuss."

Black cocked his head, as if pondering. "I'd rather not."

The older man frowned, then resumed his smile.

"I can shoot you now, Mr Black. I don't really care whether you're alive or dead. But from a practical point of view, carting about a dead body is awkward, and a real pain in the ass. I'm asking nicely, get in the fucking boot. Otherwise, I'll shoot you where you stand and splatter your brains all over the side of the camper. What do you say?"

Black returned the smile. "No."

The people round him shifted. Indecision hung heavy.

"The way it seems to me," Black continued, "you haven't been told to kill me. In fact, I reckon you've been given strict instructions *not* to kill me. If you had, you'd have shot me already, probably as soon as I got out of the car. But you didn't. Which tells me as much as I need to know. And I'm not getting into that boot. It seems we are at an impasse, gentlemen." He glanced round at the two women. "And ladies. So, if you want me in the boot, you're going to have to make me. And that won't be easy. Because..." and he awarded them all with a sweeping gaze, "...if you touch me, I'll kill you."

Silence. Then the older man nodded. "A real smart-ass. Think you've all the angles covered." He took a step closer. Now, they were in a huddle. Easy for someone to shoot the wrong person. Exactly what Black needed. Confusion and indecision. Two perfect ingredients to defeat the opposition. He braced himself to lunge, to strike.

"I swear, if you don't get into that car..."

He never got to finish his sentence.

His head exploded. Literally. One second – eyes, nose, mouth. Next, an eruption of blood, bone, skin. Face gone. Reduced to particles, spattering out, strafing those around, like flecks of red paint.

Black gasped, crouched low. The man remained standing for two seconds, as if the body was confused, not quite reconciling the loss of its brain. Then it crumpled.

The woman holding the knife released a strangled scream, ending abruptly, as her arm blew off at the shoulder joint, spinning her round. Her back burst open, mid-spine, lifting her from the ground, propelling her into the side of the camper-van.

Black rolled, took cover behind the jeep, and watched as his kidnappers were eviscerated. The woman in Lycra was sprinting to one side, presumably to escape across the Kansas countryside. She got ten yards. Her throat yawned open. She was dead before she fell. The *fuck you* T-Shirt guy turned, tried to duck back into the camper-van, and almost made it. He took it in the base of his back, the force almost tearing legs from torso, spinning him off his feet, flipping him round in a mad ballet. His body smacked the ground. The third man – he who had initially apprehended Black – took it square in the chest – lungs, heart, ribcage showering out behind him in a great sparkle of colour.

Black waited. A silence fell. A unique silence. Black was accustomed to it – the silence that fell in the wake of death. As if the world was in shock and needed space to readjust and set its clock back to regular.

The older man's body had collapsed close to him. His head was gone, now motes of brain and memory. The pistol was two yards away. Black darted his hand out, grabbed it. Nothing happened. No zing of a ballistic-tipped bullet. Perhaps the shooter hadn't seen him. Black couldn't take the chance. If he tried to get into the jeep, he'd be shot in two seconds. Crucially, he didn't have the keys. His own car was too far off to try. He held the pistol close. There was blood on the grip. Black didn't care. It wasn't his, and that was all that mattered. Its solid weight provided instant reassurance.

He could only wait it out. The shooter might wait it out as well. But at some point, cars would come. And even if they didn't, even if the road was seldom used, night would fall, and Black would be better placed to make his escape. Unless they had night vision, which would make matters awkward.

It took less than five minutes.

Lights flashed in the distance. The distinctive wail of a siren. Black took a long breath. He wasn't sure if this was good or bad.

Looked like the cavalry had arrived.

Remarkable timing, he thought.

He gripped the pistol until his knuckles turned white, waited behind the jeep, and braced himself.

TWENTY-TWO

ROM DID EXACTLY as he intended. He booked a room at The Caledonian Hotel, in Edinburgh city centre. A hotel on Princes Street, in the shadow of the castle. A place both exquisite and expensive. After his 'meeting' with Jeffrey Ferguson, his men made their way back north. Rom drove into the city centre, parked the Range Rover in the hotel car park, walked the short distance to Princes Street, got lunch at one of the small trendy restaurants, headed back to the hotel. It was 2pm. He checked in. He went up to the room. He had three calls to make. They would wait. First, the gym. He changed, took his gym bag, got the lift down to the basement area. Here, an entire section of the hotel was devoted to free weights and machines. He spent two hours concentrating on arms and shoulders, then a warm-down on the treadmill. Next, the changing rooms. He had come supplied. The place was empty. He took out equipment from his bag, injected a 100ml shot of Trenbolone in his glutes. Almost immediately, he experienced the familiar pound of his heart, as blood and muscle reacted to the steroids. He sat, allowed his body to calm. He went for a shower, spent twenty minutes under the piping hot water. He padded back to the changing room, and naked, posed before a wall-length mirror, first one way, then the other, flexing and rolling.

He looked good. Better than good. Magnificent. Ripped, muscles sharp, like blades. Bronzed skin. Like a god. A Greek god, he thought. Or a gladiator, of ancient times. Battle ready for the Colosseum. He dried himself off, changed into jeans, T-shirt, went to the hotel lobby, ordered a cinnamon latte.

First call. His father. The conversation was terse. If he was looking for any form of encouragement, or praise, then his father was the last person to speak to. He was merely reporting in –

Rom – 'I spoke to Ferguson. The situation's been straightened out. Money has been transferred. Think he'll be a good boy from now on.'

'When are you coming back?'

Rom – 'Tomorrow?'

'Make it early. We need to talk.'

Rom experienced a prickle of unease.

'What?'

But his father had hung up.

He took a breath, sipped the latte, let his mind relax, which was never easy with steroids flowing through his system.

Next call. To an old friend.

Rom – 'You got the money?'

'Absolutely. Much appreciated.'

Rom – 'You know what to do.'

A soft chuckle. The voice responded –

'Or rather what not to do.'

Rom chuckled with him. He loved this.

'Keep me in the loop,' he said. 'Every detail. It's crucial we know their movements.' He hung up.

The third and final call. The one he was looking forward to. The unease he had experienced in the call to his father was replaced by a swell of excitement.

Rom – 'Hey.'

A female voice.

'Hey.'

Rom – 'And?'

'No problems. It went like clockwork. It felt just fucking awesome.'

Rom – 'You did the whole thing?'

'It was so fucking sweet. I did it. I felt so… good.'

Rom – 'And no one saw?'

'No one.'

Rom – 'I'm proud of you babe.'

'You want to show it?'

Rom – 'I'm at the usual hotel.'

'I'll drive down. I'll be there for dinner.'

Rom – 'And then?'

'You show me how proud you are. All fucking night.'

Rom – 'I'll be waiting.'

TWENTY-THREE

RICHARD HORNBUCKLE HAD NO CHOICE. He had to go to the police. He had already lied to his wife. But then, he had lied to his wife from the beginning. Another would make little difference. But the lying had to stop.

The police station was close to the centre of town. Once, years ago, it was a community hall, and then converted, initially on a temporary basis. Two cells had been installed in the basement. A makeshift reception area and counter built, a couple of offices fitted out. But temporary turned into permanent. Every so often, talk was raised about new premises being built. The talk materialised into nothing, and the converted community hall remained.

Hornbuckle left his bike in the garage, drove the car. The journey took all of ten minutes. He parked in a small area at the rear of the building, designed for six cars at a push. He waited, took a breath, tried to dampen the nerves jangling in the pit of his stomach, but the nerves jangled, regardless. He got out, made his way slowly to the entrance, made an effort to compose himself.

He went in, pushed through the heavy swing doors. He entered the reception. A room devoid of ornamentation, egg-yellow walls, plastic hard-backed chairs lined up on each side. A low table with a scattering of magazines. No windows. Illumination was served by two bright strip lights on the ceiling. Before him, a counter, behind which sat a uniformed policeman, studying a computer screen, clicking a keyboard. He looked up when Hornbuckle came in, held Hornbuckle's stare. He was about thirty-five. Maybe older. Hornbuckle couldn't tell. He sported a full dark beard. Hornbuckle thought fleetingly police weren't supposed to have beards. Other than himself and the policeman, the place was empty.

The policeman smiled, nodded, waited.

Hornbuckle licked his lips, gave a half-hearted smile in response.

"I would like to report a crime," he said.

The policeman tilted his head, half in good humour, half in earnest.

"You've come to the right place."

Hornbuckle approached the counter, kept his voice low, though there was no reason to do so. No one else was listening, because no one else was there.

"Someone has vandalised our fence," he said.

"Vandalised?"

"Painted words on it. White paint."

The policeman nodded again, like a wise owl.

"Vandals," he said.

"Yes," agreed Hornbuckle. "It can only be."

"Let me get your details." The policeman's brow furrowed. He raised a finger –

"I know you," he said. "You own the newsagent at the corner."

Hornbuckle gave a half smile. "Yes." He attempted as little humour. "For my sins."

"I knew I recognised your face. Your fence?"

"Yes. They painted some... words on it." He hesitated. Suddenly he felt stupid. The words themselves weren't offensive. The meaning behind them was.

The policeman sighed.

"Typical. Probably smashed out their brains. Young people these days…"

The policeman went through the required procedure – name, address, date of birth. He clicked all the information on the keyboard. Hornbuckle was mildly impressed at the speed of his typing.

"Have you got a picture?"

Hornbuckle hesitated. "A picture?"

The policeman raised an eyebrow – "The fence?"

"Of course." Hornbuckle patted his jacket – a light rain jacket – then remembered his mobile phone was in his trouser pocket. He took it out, swiped the screen, began the process of scrolling.

"I have a photo somewhere." He gave a self-effacing laugh, as if the process of handling modern technology was a mind-boggling obstacle. Which, if he were honest, it was. He found it, used his index finger and thumb to magnify its size, handed it to the police officer, who inspected it with a puzzled frown. For emphasis, he swivelled the phone round, to make the screen longer. *As if that would help*, thought Hornbuckle. The words remained the same. Scrawled in white paint.

"Odd," said the police officer. He repeated the words slowly. *"Hi Guys. Day 2. We're coming. Don't forget."* He looked up, curious. "It looks like a message."

Hornbuckle cleared his throat. "There's a little more, you understand." The police officer said nothing. He stared at Hornbuckle. His face lacked expression. Like a chunk of wood.

"You see, this is like a continuation of a thing, if you catch my meaning."

The police officer remained impassive. Waiting. Hornbuckle took a deep breath. He was doing something he vowed he would never do. He was breaking the rule. The Golden Rule. Then he thought of his wife, anguished and fearful, and knew he had no choice.

"We – that is, my wife and I – got a letter."

"A letter?"

"Yes."

Silence. "A letter?" repeated the police officer.

"Yes. It wasn't sent through the post. There was no stamp. Someone delivered it. We think the letter and the writing on the fence are connected."

"When did you get this letter?"

"Yesterday."

The police officer waited.

Hornbuckle gave his self-effacing smile again, like the floundering professor who'd forgotten where he'd put his spectacles.

"Yes. I have it somewhere." He knew exactly where it was. He was delaying the moment.

He reached into the zipped inside pocket of his waterproof and pulled out the letter. It was still in its envelope. He handed it over. The police officer carefully opened it and read the contents.

The furrow in his brow deepened.

"You have no idea who sent this?"

"I'm sure it's nothing," said Hornbuckle, lifting his shoulders in a gesture of minor irritation. "A kid's prank, I tell my wife. But she insisted."

The police officer put the letter back in its envelope, handed it back.

"I think it's more than a prank." His voice was solemn. "A letter like this, the message on your fence. This constitutes a threat. You know anyone who has some sort of grudge?"

Christ! thought Hornbuckle. *If only you knew.*

"No one," he lied.

"You sure?"

He nodded.

The police officer took a deep breath. "I'm going to type in a crime report. As it stands there's very little I can do. You have a burglar alarm?"

"I'm looking into this."

The police officer reached down to a shelf behind the counter and handed Hornbuckle a card.

"That's my name and number. If anything happens, you phone me right away. Night or day. I can drop in tomorrow if you want, just to check things are okay."

"That's very kind. But hey – I'm sure it's nothing. Parents, I said."

"Parents?"

"Sure," said Hornbuckle. "My wife works in the local primary. I reckon some kid's parents are upset over nothing."

The police officer made no comment. His face was set. The smiles had gone. "Phone me, Mr Hornbuckle. If you're worried about anything, you phone me."

Hornbuckle read the card.

"Sergeant Harry Starling?"

Starling met Hornbuckle's gaze.

"According to the letter, this is a five day thing. I don't know what it means, but it's logged into the system. Day 5 is what? Friday? I'll come over to your house then, just to check up everything's okay. You good with that, Mr Hornbuckle."

"Richard, please." Again, a shrug and a smile, as if the matter were a bothersome waste of time. "Really. I'm sure there's no need."

"Maybe not," replied Starling. "Maybe it's a kid's sick joke. Maybe a misguided parent. Maybe anything. But I'll come round anyway."

TWENTY-FOUR

THE POLICE CAR approached at a crawl, stopped about twenty yards from Black. Black lay flat on his stomach, was able to watch it through the underside of the jeep. He sat up, back against the driver's door, remained hunkered in. The car sat at right angles to the side of the road. The siren stopped. He heard the growl of the engine. Then silence. Two doors opening, closing, almost simultaneously.

Another silence. Black imagined them scrutinising the carnage.

A voice shouted, "Adam Black! Show yourself. We're here to help."

They knew who he was. The scenario was surreal. Black was mystified. He waited five seconds. He took a gamble.

"I'm standing up," he shouted back.

Instantly – the millisecond it takes for a finger to pull a trigger – the car lurched and bounced to the impact of bullets discharged at close range. Like a spray. The windows exploded, the tyres burst and sagged, the chassis collapsed, reverberating to the dull punch of close high-velocity force. Powerful enough to propel a bullet clean through the driver's door, the passenger's door, and then through Black's skin, blood, bone, punching through his back, exiting out and then beyond, into the camper-van behind him. And probably through that.

Black rolled. He got to the side of the bonnet, took a breath, rolled again. Now nothing but space between himself and those who sought to kill him. The last thing they expected. He spun himself up on one knee – exactly as he had been trained when using a firearm in motion – and for a heartbeat registered the manner of his enemy. Two assailants, either side of the police car. One short, compact, thick in the neck, jaw set and square. The other tall and lean, eyes peering through slits, sporting several days' growth. Each pointing rifles, the butt buried into their shoulders, heads angled, one hand on the grip, the other on the forestock, focused entirely on a specific point. Advantageous to Black. To hit a sudden new target meant swivelling shoulders, adjusting balance, reapplying focus. Which bought time. Two seconds. Two seconds was all Black needed. He fired once, a clean shot to the smaller man's throat, just under the chin. It bulged, then imploded, as the bullet chewed through larynx, trachea, oesophagus. The man gave a gurgling croak, dropped.

Black continued, his movement fluid, adjusting a fraction, re-aiming, hit the second man in the upper chest. The impact whirled him round. Black fired again, the bullet puncturing the area beneath his ribcage, maybe catching the liver. He fell. Black waited. Twenty seconds. No others. He approached the cop car, wary. The smaller guy was dead. His neck had emptied onto the road. His eyes were wide open, as if shocked at his devastating new circumstances. Black made his way round the Dodge Charger, the words *State Trooper* emblazoned on each side. The same car he had seen at the airfield.

The second guy was alive. Just.

He was on his back. His breath was wet and wheezy, in short bursts – in, out. His shirt was saturated. A puddle was forming fast. With all the bodies, the road had taken a vibrant new colour.

Black regarded him. The man's life was now defined by seconds. Black had witnessed the final throes many times.

Youthful men, at an age they considered themselves immortal, realising in these last moments they were not, and death whispered close. Black saw the pain. But worse, the terror.

"You know my name," he said. "You tried to kill me. Why?"

The man stared back at Black. His eyes were distant. His mouth twitched. His voice was low, forced, each syllable a painful grunt.

"Get an ambulance. Need an ambulance."

"Who sent you?"

Another wheezy breath. "Help me."

Black crouched down. "Who sent you?"

The man spasmed. His spine arched, his head rotated up and round, the veins in his neck throbbed. He coughed up a splatter of blood, exhaled, and lay still.

Black stood. He had been in Kansas for less than two hours, and here he was, in the midst of a battle zone. Two dead cops. Five others – three men, two women, strewn in bits across the road. His mind whirled. First thing, he had to leave fast. He removed his T-shirt, wiped the pistol down, tossed it away. Useful to keep, but a link he didn't need. He slipped the T-shirt back on, went to the jeep. The tyres were shredded, the bodywork patterned with measle-like puncture marks. But the damned thing still blocked a section of the road. Black made a guess, searched the pockets of the older guy. His guess was right. He found a car key. The camper-van was merely a ploy, to be abandoned. He was to be bundled in the boot of the jeep, and then they would all take off, sharing the same car.

He started the engine. It offered shuddering resistance, then rumbled into life. Black gave a silent prayer, reversed ten yards. The wheels scraped against the tarmac. He felt the car bundle and bump over the bodies on the road, but Black reckoned the dead didn't care. He got out, retrieved his KA-BAR knife and mobile phone, sprinted to his own car, drove through the space now created between the camper-van and the edge of the road.

He left the carnage behind him. At first glance – and hopefully last glance – a fight between cops and some bad guys. Such was the logical conclusion. No CCTV to put Black in the scene. And no witnesses.

He dismissed it from his mind, which, for Black, was not difficult. Death had been a close companion for a sizeable chunk of his adult life. He knew all its forms, its varieties, and so had become inured to it. Plus, the harsh precepts of his training allowed him to compartmentalise. Tuck the shit away to a dark corner of his brain. *Keep moving.* His mind had already moved on, as he attempted to make some sense of the situation. First, a group of armed assailants had tried to kidnap him. For them, killing him was not an option. They had been instructed to take him alive, that much was clear. Within a minute, they were dead, killed by two rogue cops. Saving Black was not on their agenda. Rather, his destruction. They knew his name. They had been watching. Black was the target.

Common sense dictated he should get the hell out. Back to the UK. The book he had bought on his journey to Glasgow popped into his mind – *Run and Hide.* Wise words. But Black wasn't the type.

Someone knew he was coming. The logical assumption was that the information had come from either Gibson, or the Colonel. Or maybe both. But why?

He had been set a task. To find the Colonel's daughter. He would continue the quest and see it to its end. The whole thing might be bullshit. But he had made a promise. Black would admit, if anything, he was a monomaniac. Given a task, he would continue, regardless. And if they came at him again, then fine. He was prepared. He would come right back.

With fury.

TWENTY-FIVE

The bravest are surely those who have the clearest vision before them, glory and danger alike, and yet notwithstanding, go out and meet it.
Thucydides.

Don't be afraid to admit your fears. But be brave enough to face them.
Instruction by Staff Sergeant to soldiers of the 22nd Regiment of the SAS.

THE REMAINING part of the journey was trouble-free. No more roadblocks; no gunfire; no dead bodies. He watched his rear-view mirror, half expecting a blaze of cop cars. But the road was deserted. Nothing behind him, nothing approaching. The shapes of the camper-van and the cars eventually vanished in the shimmer of the heat. The road became narrower, and potholed and rutted. He had to slow down to a crawl in places or burst the suspension. Rarely used, or so it seemed. But the vista on either side remained constant – vast flat plains of very little. And the other constant – the unremitting Kansas sun.

He drove another twelve miles, got to a junction. The female satnav voice told him to turn left. He pulled onto a two-lane carriageway. Here, the traffic was heavier, both directions. Black felt the tension lift. No one – he hoped – would place him at the scene. Now, he could get lost in the commute. Just another car, going from A to B. Mr Joe Ordinary, blending in like everybody else.

He drove for another four miles, then pulled up at a roadside café, quaintly called The Magic Coffee Bean. He parked, got a fresh T-shirt from his sports bag, changed, dumped the old one in a bin. Ordering coffee with blood-drenched clothing might draw some curious looks. He went in. The place was long and narrow, with a low arched roof, all wood panelling. Like a galley of a medieval ship. Windows on one side, and booths, with yellow cushioned seats and Formica-topped tables and low-hanging lights shaped like tortoise shells. Black sat, and ordered an Americano, large, with a miniature cup of hot milk on the side. He took a long breath, gazed at the scenery – a busy road, beyond which, minor slopes and contours of low, undulating hills. Like the sweep of an ocean caught in a gentle wind.

The coffee came. He took a sip. He couldn't keep the tremble from his hand. Tough day, so far. Fear, for Black, was an emotion he could detach, analyse, dismiss. Sure, he got scared. But he did not allow it to take control. He possessed an ability to consider it, almost as a dispassionate observer watching something from a distance, and then, having understood it, and having rationalised it, he could brush it to one side, and act accordingly. Often substituting fear with a more useful emotion. Such as anger.

And he was angry now.

He took a breath, sipped his coffee, allowed the tremble to pass. *Keep moving.* The antidote to fear. If you could keep moving, then it meant you were still alive. And if you were still alive, then you'd won. Such was the ethos of the Special Air Service. *Life finds a way.*

One group wanted him alive, one wanted him dead. A bizarre scenario. Had the picture not been so grim, he would have felt flattered.

Another sip. It tasted good. Strong and filtered. He didn't generally enjoy filtered coffee, because it was never hot. This was.

What then was he to do? High-tail it back to the cold Scottish mountains was the obvious answer. But Black had never been the obvious type. The Colonel had provided him with the address of his daughter, discovered by the private investigator hired for the job –Jona Lefroy. An address in the town of Fairview, where he was heading. Of course, the whole story could be a concoction, a parcel of lies. But if that were so, what was the point? What had the Colonel to gain from this? Or, for that matter, Gibson? Unless others knew of Black's mission. But even so, the one fundamental question which tossed and rolled in Black's mind was *why?* Black didn't like riddles. He liked answers. To find the answer, he would continue his mission undeterred. Possibly the last thing his enemies would expect. Also, it might draw them out. Expose them, and thus render them vulnerable.

Of course, for the rational man, such a plan was sheer madness. But rational had never worked for Black. Irrational was better. Do what the enemy least expects. Confuse, disorientate. Black allowed a wintry grin. The other consequence was that he got killed in the process. A highly likely scenario. Which made Black such a dangerous adversary. Death held no fear for him. If it came, he would smile and embrace it tightly. Like the old friend it was.

He would drive to Fairview and find out what the hell was going on.

He finished the coffee, broke a fifty to pay for it, left a five-dollar tip. He wasn't being followed. No new cars in the car park. He drove off, rejoined the traffic flow. After an hour, he passed a sign showing a list of towns, and their distances. One was

Fairview – one hundred miles. He put the radio on, expecting the news to be full of gunfights and dead cops. Nothing. Which meant the police hadn't released the incident to the media, or else the police still weren't aware. If the latter, then the bodies lay where Black had left them, and the vultures were feeding. Either way, it was good news for Black. It meant more distance between him and them.

Two hours later. The sun was setting, casting a dreamy bronze sheen to the world. Shadows formed. In the distance, the low hills seemed to glow, red and pale yellow, like dying embers, giving the land a witchy feel. Black came to another sign. First left to Fairview, then another twenty miles. He took the turn, and a half hour later, arrived at Fairview. Population 4,050.

Back home, this place would be categorised as a village. This is where Lefroy said he had found the Colonel's daughter. And lost his hand over it. And then probably his life. Black wondered how the hell she ended up in a place like this. He drove slowly down a main road. Two lanes, shops on either side, cramped up to each other. Most closed for the evening. Fairview Groceries; Greaves Hardware; The Rifle Stop; A barbers with a neon flashing barbers' pole. A chemist shop, still open. A pet store called Furballs. A diner – Jack's Grill. A couple of bars.

The shops ran for about two hundred yards, then stopped, then narrow side roads and houses either side, built roughly of the same design – small single-storey bungalows with wood-clad walls and quaint verandas and low-pitched red slate roofs He drove another half mile. The buildings got a little rougher round the edges. Unkempt gardens, broken slates, worn paint. He passed a sprawling factory building, comprising a main structure, and lots of smaller flat-roofed annexes attached in apparently random fashion, almost as an afterthought. It sat a distance back from the road, enclosed by high wrought-iron fencing, sharp at the top, crowned by nests of barbed wire. Fairview Bottle and Plastics Distributors. The place was deserted and shuttered up for the evening. Outside lights glimmered.

Several trucks and vans were parked in the forecourt. Black speculated – perhaps this was the industry keeping the town alive, providing jobs and money and three square meals on the table.

Black drove another quarter of a mile. The land had resorted back to rolling wilderness. Ahead, he saw what he was expecting. A garish neon sign – *Motel. Vacancies*. There was always one within close proximity to hubs of civilisation.

He pulled in. It comprised a simple ground-level structure of white concrete, with identical doors and windows at spaced intervals. Black counted twelve rooms. In front of each, parking bays delineated in white paint. At one end, the reception area, marked *open* in flashing blue letters. Judging by the parked cars, Black reckoned it was three-quarters full. CCTV cameras on each front corner of the building.

Black got out, made his way to the entrance. The evening was hot and alive with the buzz of crickets. At the side of the door, a couple of vending machines selling soft drinks and sweets. Black entered. The door beeped loudly. He emerged into a brightly lit room. The place was suffused with the unmistakable stink of nicotine. Facing him, a counter of black padded leather, upon which, a computer screen, a telephone, and a display stand with an array of brochures, and at each end, placed upright in miniature glass bottles, a small plastic American flag. One wall, Black noted, was filled top to bottom, side to side, with business cards. A man appeared from a back room, approached his side of the counter. Tall, bone- thin, middle-aged, with a keen birdlike cast of countenance, and a weave of silver hair, swept back in an oily wave. He appraised Black with dark clever eyes.

"Can I help you, sir?"

Black essayed a weary smile – the look of a man who'd spent a long day driving. Which was partially true. Driving and killing and seeing others killed. Black suddenly realised he really was weary. To the core of his bones.

"You have vacancies?"

The man smiled back, his teeth stained brown with nicotine. Black noted the tips of his fingers were a matching colour.

"Sure do. You're in luck. I have two rooms left. Long drive?"

"You could say."

"How long will you be staying with us, Mr…"

Black saw no reason for deception.

"Black. Adam Black."

The man began relaying information into the computer.

"Very good. And…"

"Three nights."

The man paused, looked at Black. "Three nights? You here to enjoy the sights?"

"You could say."

"I guess you've got the tallgrass prairies. But out here, there isn't much else. No, sir. Though I've heard it said the sunsets can calm the soul."

Nice, if I had one.

The man enquired further – "You got family here? Friends?"

"Nobody special."

The man nodded, as if the words gave him all the information he needed.

"I can give you room number twelve. It's the last one down the line. For three nights, that's one hundred and fifty dollars." He remained smiling as he said, "It's payment up front, Mr Black."

"Of course. Cash?"

"Cash is king."

Black handed over fifty-dollar bills.

The man reached to a shelf to his side, lifted out a form, placed it on the counter.

"If you could please complete your details, Mr Black. My name is Miles Danskin. I own this establishment, and I'm here twenty-four seven. If you need anything, anything at all, then just knock my door. If you need the towels changed, then leave them outside, and I'll get fresh ones for you that morning. Every room has a phone, and if you require my assistance, press eleven. Dial zero to get an outside line. Premium rates if you're phoning a friend. Every room has a flat-screen TV, and Netflix comes as part of the package. Yes, sir. We also have wi-fi, and we don't charge for that neither. The password is Miles 1. And we don't allow pets or excessive noise. But we do allow smoking. No one tells us what we can or cannot do in the state of Kansas. So if you want to light up, you go right ahead, Mr Black. Just feel free."

He reached under the counter, produced a key which he handed to Black. "If you're looking for some nice food and maybe a cold beer, I'd recommend Jack's Grill. He fires up the meanest steak, I swear. You like steak, Mr Black?"

"Sounds nice. Maybe I'll try it."

Black completed the answers on the pre-printed form. Name, registration number. The usual formalities. He made the address up. No point in being too honest.

"Is that an Irish accent? My mom was half-Irish."

"Scottish," replied Black. "It's a common mistake."

Danskin gave a pointy-chinned grin. "I've never been. Part of England, yes?"

"Almost."

Danskin maintained his grin. "You guys hunt the haggis? And you love your whisky. Have I got that right?"

"Never caught a haggis. They're nocturnal, and only fly in the dark. And yes. You got it right. We tend to like our whisky." He fished out the photograph of the Colonel's daughter from the front pocket of his jeans. "I wonder if maybe you've seen this person?"

Danskin peered down at the picture. "Damn it. My eyesight isn't what it was. Age gets us all, I guess." He went to the back room from where he had entered, returned wearing dark-rimmed spectacles. He scrutinised the photo. Scrutinised it longer than he needed. He seemed taut. He looked up at Black, shook his head, spoke, voice firm and sure. Way too decisive.

"Don't recognise her."

Black shrugged as if he didn't care. "Fair enough."

Danskin took his glasses off, gave Black an inquisitive stare. "You looking for her?"

"An old friend."

"And you think she's here, in Fairview?"

Black turned his attention to the sprawl of business cards along one wall.

"You must have spent years collecting these," he said.

"Since 1991. Placed in chronological order. The ones at the door are our first customers, way back when. You're standing beside the most recent ones. You got one you'd like to pin on, Mr Black?"

Black studied the most recent cards. "Never bothered with them," he replied.

"And the woman," continued Danskin. "You looking for her? That why you're here?"

He's a curious one, thought Black.

"Jack's Grill? Is that the place?"

Danskin hesitated. "Yes, sir. And the..."

Black cut him off. "Thanks again, Miles. One last thing. Do you have elastic bands?"

Danskin frowned. "You mean, like rubber bands?"

"Yup."

Danskin stared at him for five full seconds, as if trying to divine the reason behind Black's request. Black, however, did not expand.

"You want them now?" said Danskin.

"Two would be nice, if you have them."

Danskin scratched his left ear. "Sure." He again disappeared into the back room, returned with a box, which he emptied on the counter. A loose straggle of elastic bands spilled out. Black smiled, took two.

"Thank you, Miles. You've been more than helpful."

He left the reception. The door beeped as he closed it. He went to his car, got his gym bag, took the KA-BAR from the central console, the Glock from the glove compartment. He reached the last room on the line, unlocked the door, went in. The place smelled of stale smoke, which did not concern him. Bed, wardrobe, chair, table. On one wall, the flat-screen TV. He went to the en suite – shower, sink, toilet. No frills. Utilitarian. You got what you paid for. Black expected no more and had experienced far worse. He tossed his bag on the bed, used the elastic bands to secure the knife to his inner calf, tucked the Glock in his belt at the base of his back, keeping his jacket on. He left the room, locked the door behind him, and drove back into Fairview. He was famished, and cold beer sounded good. Plus, if they wanted him, then he was here, and he was ready.

TWENTY-SIX

ROM HAD to get back home. Early. His father had commanded, and as such, the call was to be answered. Without question. His father was not the type of man to disobey.

Rom pondered the word – *disobey.* It rankled him. Worse, it enraged him. He was a thirty-six-year-old man who shouldn't need to *obey* or *disobey*, or do any damned thing for anyone. In Rom's universe, obedience should be shown by others. To him.

But it wasn't Rom's universe. It was his father's. And his father was not to be crossed.

They woke at 6am, he and Arlene – his girlfriend. As promised, she had arrived at the hotel the previous evening. They'd got dinner in the hotel restaurant, had a couple of drinks, and then proceeded to fuck all night.

He did fifty press-ups while she showered, then he showered. They got changed and went down for breakfast. He ate light. Muesli and some fruit. She had a full breakfast. He marvelled at how she kept her shape. But then, she trained hard like him.

They left the hotel at 7am. He reckoned he'd be back at the farmhouse for 12.

The conversation was sparse. He was irritable. He was always irritable when summoned by his father, and sometimes, when he was irritable, his temper would boil over, and he'd use his fists. It was happening more and more. The consequence of steroids maybe. It didn't matter. For Rom, the end justified the means. And each time he looked in the mirror, he knew damned well the end was worth it. Big deal if he slapped her around a little. She didn't complain. Deep down, she probably liked it. Plus, experience was a good teacher. She knew when to back off, give him space, leave him be.

He played some Rolling Stones. He loosened up a little as the journey progressed. They stopped at Aviemore and had a coffee at one of the many streetside coffee shops.

"I get tense when I see the old bastard," he said. "You know what it's like."

"Sure I do. I get it."

"Do this. Do that. He snaps his fingers, and he expects me to come running. One day, I swear."

"One day, the whole thing will be yours, Rom," she said quietly. "Then you're in control."

"That's right. One day."

"You can bide your time."

"That's right. Bide my time. Until the right moment. I swear, he's got it coming."

"Sure he has." She smiled. "I love you, Rom."

He smiled back. She had a knack for making him feel better, with her soft words. The same applied when he used her as a punch bag. That made him feel better too.

"He wants to talk to me about something."

She made a small questioning twitch of her shoulders. "What about?"

"He wanted me straight back this morning, so I guess it's important. You can never tell what goes through the old cunt's mind."

She nodded solemnly, sipped her latte.

"You've got important things to do as well," he said.

She brightened. "Looking forward to it."

"You've decided?"

"I have. And I'm not going to tell you. I want it to be a surprise. I know you love surprises."

"You know me so well, Arlene. Sometimes I think you know me better than I know myself."

She regarded him archly. "Maybe I do."

"You'll take a picture?"

"Of course."

"Don't forget. I want my picture."

"Like a trophy," she said.

"Sure. A trophy. I like that. Sounds good."

They arrived back at the estate at 12.45. They kissed. Arlene made her way to the house she shared with Rom, a hundred yards further along the driveway. Rom watched her. She moved with the elegant ease of an athlete. He felt his cock stiffen. She got to her own car – an Audi TT convertible. She gave him a swift side glance, raised her hand in a small fluttering wave, drove off and away, tyres scrunching up the tiny white stones.

Rom went into the main farmhouse. The house occupied by his father. William Callaghan. The Gypsy King.

The original building was over a hundred years old. Initially, a solid, square stone-built structure. Callaghan had bought it thirty years back, and trebled the size. He'd stuck on a sprawling half-circle conservatory at the rear. He'd put dormers in the roof, converted the roof space into rooms, added a further side extension in which he'd installed a full-sized snooker table, complete with bar. Now it was a rambling eight-bedroom mansion, appendages added in an almost careless fashion. William Callaghan gave little concern for architectural aesthetics. Nor did he bother with planning or building control. The way he saw it, the house was in the shit-end of nowhere. The authorities would never know what the hell he got up to. Nor would anyone else. William Callaghan coveted his privacy.

Rom knew where he would find his father. He went straight to the snooker room. He heard the smack of snooker balls colliding, and laughter. Laughter meant nothing. Laughter or tears, the level of his father's viciousness remained constant. His instinct was right. He father was there, with Stu Gorman. In a corner was a bar, behind which, a full gantry, glistening with inverted bottles. Whisky, gin, vodka. Every conceivable spirit. Propped with his back against the bar counter, his father. In one hand, a whisky glass. On the bar counter, a bottle of Glenmorangie, half the contents gone. Gripped in his other hand, a snooker cue. Gorman was hunched over the snooker table, aiming his shot.

"The fucking prodigal son returns," shouted Callaghan. "Look, Stu. The big fucking bodybuilder is paying his old dad a visit. We should feel fucking honoured."

Rom said nothing, went over to the bar. His father was drunk. Which made him unpredictable. And terrifying.

"You asked me to come. I'm here. I'm always here."

"And so you are. And so you fucking should be. Pour yourself a drink."

Rom glanced at the bottle on the bar counter. He shook his head. "I'm not in the mood."

Callaghan turned slowly to face his son. Rom faced him back. They were the same height. Rom was big with muscle built from endless gym sessions. Callaghan was just big. Naturally big. Powerful shoulders, meaty arms, thick neck, hands like slabs. Raw vitality. Hair shorn to the scalp three inches above his ears, then a tuft of thick brown hair, cropped short. Not a fleck of grey. Face weathered like ancient wood, all lines and knots. In his left ear dangled a small white-gold ring. It caught the light, glinted like a tiny star. The eyes. They were dead. Rom wondered at the countless times his father's victims had looked into those eyes for a soupçon of compassion, a flicker of mercy, and realised with horror there was nothing.

Dead eyes, thought Rom.

Callaghan leaned closer and spoke softly.

"When I tell you to have a fucking drink, you have a fucking drink. You follow?"

Rom looked away, as he always did. He went behind the bar, found a glass, poured from the bottle, drank it in one, slapped the glass back on the table, filled it up again. He hated whisky. He hated his father.

"Happy?" he said.

"There you go," said Callaghan. "A loving son sharing a drink with his father. See that, Stu?" Callaghan gave a rumbling chuckle. "Happy fucking families."

Rom waited.

"Stu was telling me about yesterday. Some fucking display. Crucified the cunt to his office wall. That'll send a message, for sure. That was clever, Rom. I wouldn't have thought of that. Maybe, after all, you've got a talent for this game."

"I've always had a fucking talent. You just haven't seen it."

Another deep chuckle. "You're right, Rom. Maybe I haven't. Maybe I've misjudged you. Is that how you feel? Misjudged?"

"I don't feel anything," said Rom.

"Sure you don't. But I can see it." Callaghan directed his attention across the room to Gorman. "Can you see it, Stu?"

Stu, standing on the other side of the snooker table, gave a blank expression.

Callaghan laughed. "Sometimes I don't think Stu sees anything." He turned back to Rom. He lowered his voice again. When he spoke, the smile never left his face. "But I see it. I see the fucking hatred all boiled up inside. Boiling and bubbling. All the resentment. Like you're going to burst. And I understand that. That's good, Rom. Hatred keeps you alive. Gives you fuel. Gives you motivation. Keeps the cock iron hard."

"I don't hate you," muttered Rom.

"I couldn't care, one way or the other. We're family. Love, hate. It's a mixed bag. Families are complicated." The smile left. "Just as long as you know your fucking place. And right now, I still give the fucking orders, like it or not. You understand that?"

Rom said nothing. His father was right. His heart burned with hatred.

"That's okay," said Callaghan. "I'll take your silence as a yes. Do you know what you have to do?"

Rom still didn't answer. This was a one-way conversation. A monologue from the acid tongue of the Gypsy King.

"You have to unwind. Relax. Shooting your veins up with all that steroid shit turns your brain to mush. Makes you… unbalanced. Can I trust you to make decisions when you're pumped up full of drugs? That's the question I have to ask myself."

Jesus, thought Rom. *Unbalanced. He's one to talk.*

"My judgement is fine. You don't have to worry about me."

"But I don't worry about you," said Callaghan. "I worry about *me!* Can't have a loose cannon running around fucking everything up."

"What exactly have I fucked up?"

Callaghan took a long slow breath, leant back on the bar again.

He finished the whisky in his glass, and with deliberation, poured himself another, swallowed it down.

"For one thing, your girlfriend."

Rom snapped his head round.

"Arlene?"

"Arlene. Do you trust her?"

"What?"

Again, Callaghan's voice lowered, almost gentle, which made it all the more sinister.

"I asked you if you trust her."

"Of course I fucking trust her. What's that supposed to mean?"

"She knows an awful lot about our business. About the things we do. What I mean is – if things ever got difficult, is she the type to squeal like a fucking whore?"

Rom gripped the side of the counter. The rage rose up. He swallowed it back.

"She's not…"

"Because if she is…" said Callaghan, "I'll slit her throat and bury her six feet deep. Simple as that. So it's down to you, Rom. You follow?"

Rom took a moment, and with effort, kept his voice neutral.

"She can be trusted."

Callaghan leaned forward, rested a hand on Rom's shoulder.

"That's good to hear, son. It really is. You know I love you."

"You asked me to come."

"Straight to business. The way I like it. No chit-chat. We have a new shipment due Friday night. One hundred kilos. Bought and paid for. I want you to liaise with the supplier, check in with him, make sure it goes to plan. Speak to him every fucking minute of every fucking hour if you have to. When it comes, deal with distribution. Get the houses ready. One hundred kilos is a lot of fucking product. If we do this right, keep our heads, we could net fifty million easy. Maybe more. Easy. This is your show, Rom. Don't fuck it up."

Rom took a moment to collect his thoughts. This was the biggest collection they'd had. He was unaware, and it shocked him.

"You never told me about it."

"I'm fucking telling you now!" roared Callaghan. Like that, his mood switched. "You only need to know what you need to know!" He filled another glass, drank it down, topped it up. Rom waited, trying to process this sudden new information.

"It's being flown in on a freight plane," continued Callaghan. "To Prestwick Airport. Friday night. You'll go, you'll check it, you'll get it moved on." The anger vanished. "And you'll not breathe a fucking word to your girlfriend."

"She has a name," said Rom. "Friday night? This Friday night?"

"Is that a problem to you? You got better places to be?"

Rom hesitated. It *was* a problem. And he *did* have better places to be. Suddenly, his timetable would need adjusting.

"Who's the supplier?" he said.

"A new contact." More information he was unaware of. His

father attempted a loud American drawl. "All the way from the US of A."

"America?"

"You catch on fucking quick. Here's his number." He was wearing loose joggers with Velcro-style pockets, which he pulled open. He took out a folded piece of notepaper. He handed it to Rom.

"Now get another drink and play some snooker."

Rom opened the note. Scribbled on it, a mobile number.

"What's this 'contact's' name?"

Gallagher smiled. He'd had all his teeth done. The implants cost over thirty thousand, and they shone like a band of sparkling pearls. Like Rom's. One thing Rom knew about his line of business. When the money rolled in, they all got perfect teeth.

"His name? A fucking stupid one. It can't be real."

Rom waited. The whisky made him light-headed.

"The guy's from the West Coast, so he says."

"And his name?" asked Rom.

"Calls himself Gibson. What a stupid fucking name. Now set the balls up and get another drink."

TWENTY-SEVEN

DAY 3

ROUTINE AND WORK – *two of the antidotes to anxiety,* thought Hornbuckle.

It was Wednesday. Life continued. His wife had to get to school. He had the shop to open. His newspapers were dropped off in big bundles wrapped tight in plastic cord, as early as 7.15am. He hadn't slept well, but that was okay. He might catch a nap at lunchtime. He got up at 6am, showered, changed. His wife looked like she was still sleeping. But he knew better. He made her a cup of tea, placed it on the bedside table, stroked her face gently with the tip of his finger, her cheek, her brow. She didn't stir. Maybe she was sleeping, after all. There were no outward signs of her illness. No evidence it had ever existed. *Maybe all just a bad dream.* The doctors had described the cancer as in remission. That was a good word to hear. They both knew it could come back. But for now, at this moment, it was the best they could have hoped for, and each day was a blessing.

Which made it all worth it. He stood, gazing down at her, and knew, if he had to do the whole thing again, then he would, without hesitation. His mind prickled with unease. Perhaps the recent events might trigger it back. Perhaps anxiety and worry might empower those microscopic black cancerous cells, and make them grow and multiply again.

He went downstairs, scooped out a half tin of cat food into a bowl, mushed it up, put it on the kitchen floor. He couldn't remember if Mr Chuckles had been let in the previous evening. He opened the front door, called his name – as if that would be successful. Mr Chuckles, like every other cat, did exactly as he pleased. No sign. Hornbuckle gave him no more thought. He would turn up as and when he pleased.

Routine. Work.

He did what he did every morning. He left the house, ensuring the front door was locked, went to the garage, got his bicycle, and cycled to work. He made a mental note to phone again about the burglar alarm. The guy hadn't called him back. He would try and get someone out today, and close the shop if he had to.

The morning was cold, the air tinged with the smir of soft but constant rain. He got to work. He brought in the newspapers, arranged them, got the shop ready for the day. He phoned Elspeth at 7.30. She answered drowsily. She had slept a little better, and was getting ready for work. She reminded him she was staying late at the school. Parents' evening. Something she couldn't avoid. Nothing was mentioned of the letter, or the writing on the fence, or that this was Day 3.

At 10am he got a call from Sergeant Starling.

"I was wondering how you were doing?" he asked. Hornbuckle was surprised, but also somewhat reassured at Starling's interest.

"We're fine, thank you. Maybe the whole thing is a storm in a teacup. I might have overreacted."

"Are you at the shop?"

"Yes."

"And your wife. She's at the school?"

"Yes."

"And you're not aware of any disturbances? Anything unusual?"

"All good. As I said, some angry parents. They've had their fun. Now maybe the whole thing will calm down a little."

"I might drive round later, Mr Hornbuckle. Check things out. See how the land lies."

"Please. It's Richard. Mr Hornbuckle is far too formal. And only if you have to. But I don't want to cause a fuss. I'm sure you have much more pressing things to do than deal with this."

"It's fine, Richard. You're not causing a fuss. You have a good day. And if you're worried about anything, if anything happens, you pick up the phone. You have my number?"

"Yes."

"Enjoy your day, Richard."

The conversation ended.

Hornbuckle looked up the number of the alarm fitter, phoned him. A man called Billy Watson. The phone was answered. It was Billy Watson himself. He could be out that day, fit motion sensor alarms at the front and back doors, and also the ground-floor rooms, height adjusted for the cat. 4pm. The job would take about two hours. The package came with a five-year guarantee, plus the first annual service was free.

The day wore on. Business was slow. Wednesdays, inexplicably, were always slow. Events weighed heavily in his mind as the minutes ticked by. *Day 3*. Maybe there would be no Day 3. Maybe the whole thing was bullshit.

Maybe not. It was the *maybe not* which was the root of his anxiety.

He avoided napping at lunchtime. If he did, he knew he wouldn't sleep that night. He sat behind the counter of his little shop and watched the clock. The rain got heavier, then at around 2pm, it suddenly stopped, weak sunlight filtering through the clouds. It still felt cold. Or perhaps it was because he was tired.

He shut the shop at 3.15. He wanted to be ready for the alarm guy, in case he came early. He cycled the two miles back. The sun had disappeared, swallowed up by rolling clouds. A wind whipped up from the east, sharp and strong. Looked like a storm was coming.

He approached the house. He had repainted his fence the previous evening. His heart was heavy with dread. He half expected fresh letters scrawled in white garish paint. He took a deep calming breath. The fence was untouched. The world seemed wonderfully normal. He went to the garage, parked his bike in the usual place, made his way to the front door.

And stopped.

The dread morphed into fresh, gut-wrenching horror.

Using steel cord wrapped excruciatingly tight round its neck, someone had strung his cat to the front door. It hung, lifeless, a sack of dead flesh, suspended from the handle. Beneath it, nailed into the wood, was an envelope.

Hornbuckle took a moment. Tried to arrange his thoughts. Tried to contain the terror. Tried to ignore the thump of his heart and the pulse in his head, pounding strong as a jackhammer. He felt nauseous. He bent to one side, retched. Nothing came up. He remained bent over, hands on his knees, staring at the ground. He felt dizzy. He took another deep breath, couldn't keep the shudder from it.

And so Day 3 had arrived. With a fucking vengeance.

"Jesus fucking Christ," he whispered. He suddenly thought, maybe they're still here, close by, waiting. He experienced a new surge of terror.

He straightened, looked out beyond the front fence, to the road, the trees beyond. There was no one there. At least no one he could see. What seemed normal before was now fraught with danger. Perhaps he was being watched. Perhaps they wished to witness his reaction and hovered in the shadows. But there were no shadows. Their house was two miles from town, with no one nearby. Remote. Other than a thin group of birch opposite, the landscape was sparse – rolling plains of heather and low gorse and the occasional outcrop of rock. If they were watching, he'd surely see them.

Several long slow breaths, as he made the effort to compose himself. He reached down, tore the envelope off the door, opened it, and read its contents.

HI RICHARD AND ELSPETH.
CAT GOT YOUR TONGUE?
WELCOME TO DAY 3. AIN'T IT A PEACH? POOR
PUSSY. HOW THE LITTLE FUCKER SCREAMED. AND
IT DIED SLOW. I MEAN SOOOO SLOW.
TICK-TOCK. DAY 5 SOON. YUMMY. CAN'T WAIT.
REGARDS.
YOUR SPECIAL FRIENDS.

Hornbuckle read it twice, tried to keep his lip from quivering. He'd been this scared once before. When his wife was diagnosed with the cancer. But that was a different type of fear. A slow fear. A fear of loss. This was entirely different. This was raw and sharp and vicious.

He kept his mind focused. The alarm guy was coming. His wife was working late. He would make sure she would never know. He went back to the garage, got a thick rubble bag. He carefully unwound the wire cable from the door-handle. He gently placed the cat in the bag, tied it tight. He went back to the garage, got a shovel. Carrying the bag and the shovel, he scurried across to the patch of trees. The earth was damp and loose. With great energy, he dug a hole about three feet deep, placed the bag in the hole, filled it up, patted the ground flat. He stood, staring at the small grave, unable to focus, thoughts rolling and tumbling. He blinked, wiped sweat from his eyes, took a long breath, then another, tried to find calm in the havoc. But the calm was gone. In its place, nerve-shredding terror.

. . .

He went back to the house, replaced the shovel in the garage. He read the letter for a last time, ripped it up into tiny pieces, put it in the main plastic recycle bin kept at the front of the house, which would be emptied the next day.

Welcome to Day 3.

He checked the front door. No sign of a forced entry. He unlocked it, went inside, waited, listening. Silence, save the pounding of his heart. He made his way straight to the kitchen, fixed himself a large whisky, drank it straight and in one swallow. Then another. He hated the taste. But at this moment, in this particular situation, it was called for. Something strong to beat back the fear. He put the bottle back. If his wife discovered the whisky was out, she would know.

His choices were narrowing. In fact, there had never really been a choice since the saga had started. In his heart, he knew, deep down, his course of action was inevitable.

He would make the call.

His thoughts were interrupted by the sound of a vehicle pulling up outside. His heart rose to his throat. He peered through the living-room window – the alarm guy. On the side was emblazoned the words *Call Billy Watson, Alarm Specialist. No job too small.* Below it was a mobile phone number. The driver got out. Presumably Billy Watson. Dressed smartly in navy-blue overalls, and a blue skip cap. Hornbuckle watched as he opened the front gate, approached the door. The bell rang. Hornbuckle took a second, composed himself, answered.

"Mr Hornbuckle?"

"Yes."

"I'm Billy Watson. You phoned about installing an alarm?"

"Yes. Thanks for coming at such short notice."

Billy Watson liked to talk, and Hornbuckle was content for him to do it. Turned out Watson recognised him from the shop, had seen him about town. Hornbuckle listened, nodded, agreed, let him blabber. His mind was elsewhere. Three hundred miles elsewhere.

"I can install motion sensors in a corner of each room. Very discreet. You'll hardly know they are there. You said you had pets..."

Hornbuckle interrupted him. "A cat."

Watson nodded, as if the information was of profound importance. "You don't need to worry. I can set the sensors just..."

Hornbuckle interrupted again. "You don't need to worry."

Watson gave him a quizzical look. "Worry?"

"About the cat," said Hornbuckle drearily. "It's no longer an issue."

Watson said nothing, obviously waiting on Hornbuckle to expand. Hornbuckle was in no mood to explain. Watson reacted with the slightest shrug, continued smoothly – "In which case, my job becomes a whole lot easier. I'll fix a keypad by the front door. Simple to operate."

"Thank you," replied Hornbuckle. He was suddenly exhausted. He was still in shock. Plus, the man's endless conversation was draining. He wanted to curl up on the couch and die. "I'll let you get on. I'll be in the kitchen."

Watson had brought in a large canvas bag, which he plonked on the floor. He opened it, and began the process of lifting out gadgets and equipment. Hornbuckle took zero interest and did what he said he would do. He went to the kitchen, where the whisky beckoned. Another wouldn't do any harm. He would need its courage to make the call.

He poured himself another glass, sat at the table, trying to formulate a strategy as to how he would deal with the situation. He could plead. Or negotiate. He gave a frosty laugh. There would be no negotiation with these people. He had nothing to negotiate with. He had little money. No real savings. The shop was leased. The house was in his wife's name. Zero collateral. Back to pleading. And pleading would get him nowhere, because these people didn't care.

Regardless of strategy, one thing was certain. He had to make the call. He had to ask them to stop, knowing they wouldn't.

The doorbell rang. He jumped round. He hadn't touched his whisky. He glanced at the clock. Twenty minutes had passed, and he had barely noticed. He got up, went to the door. Billy Watson was in the hall, installing the keypad, whistling some tuneless sound.

Hornbuckle took a breath. He had no idea who it was. The presence of the alarm guy provided a modicum of reassurance. He answered the door. Before him stood Sergeant Harry Starling.

With effort, he kept his voice level. "Hi."

Starling gave a brief nod. "Hope I'm not troubling you, Mr Hornbuckle. Thought I'd check up. Make sure you were okay."

Hornbuckle swallowed, and for a millisecond, had a desire to unburden the whole sorry mess. But he didn't. He couldn't. Not yet.

The Golden Rule.

"No problems," he said. "Really."

Starling was about to speak. Hornbuckle raised a halting hand. "And I promise, if anything... untoward should happen, you'll be the first person I'll call. But we're fine."

Starling acknowledged the comment with another slight nod of the head. "Okay then. You have my number."

Billy Watson, who was standing four feet from the door, interrupted.

"The keypad's installed. I've set it up and used the factory code, 1234, then press 'enter' to activate, then same again, only 'exit' to deactivate. Easy-peasy, lemon squeezy. Though you might want to change it. Four numbers. Something personal, that you won't forget."

Hornbuckle hesitated. He couldn't concentrate. His head was splitting. He had too much to think about.

"Year of birth," suggested Watson. "Easy to remember. That's what I use."

"Yes," said Hornbuckle, absently. "That's what I'll use. Year of birth."

Starling left. Billy Watson took another thirty minutes to install the sensors. Hornbuckle paid him cash, which he accepted gladly. Then he too left.

Hornbuckle was alone. He returned to the kitchen, downed the whisky he'd left on the table. He went upstairs to their bedroom, to the wardrobe. He had a collection of jackets on coat hangers. Some he had forgotten he had. He slid them individually to one side, until he found the one he was looking for. He hadn't worn it – hadn't looked at it – for over five years. An old winter ski-jacket. All zips and buttons. He rummaged through the inside pockets, until he found it – a coffee receipt from the Windmill Café. He had chosen never to destroy it. Perhaps, on a subconscious level, he knew this day might come.

He had a call to make.

To those who might wish to kill him.

And he was terrified.

TWENTY-EIGHT

Law cannot rule where enforcement cannot follow.
Anonymous.

Of course we abide by the rule of law. Our Special Forces are trained to kill, but as a last resort. They're not trained to murder.
Response by General John 'Polly' Stewart to a question raised by a BBC reporter regarding alleged war crimes in Afghanistan.

You're killing machines. Pure and simple. That's why you're here. It's in your training, it's in your nature, it's in your blood. To think otherwise is naïve and foolish, and will get you dead.
Address by Staff Sergeant to soldiers of the 22nd Regiment of the SAS.

BLACK DROVE INTO TOWN. He was famished. He went to Jack's Grill and ordered himself a hamburger, salt-and-chilli fries, a carton of potato salad, a token smattering of veg. The food was stodge, plenty of it, and cheap. The restaurant held little memorable features. Small, and a quarter full. Little rectangular wooden tables with chequered tablecloths and matching plastic table mats, and round each table, four high-backed plain wooden chairs. On the walls, framed, somewhat faded cinema posters of movies all the way back to the seventies – *The Sting*, *Dirty Harry*, *Jaws*. A couple of Bond movies. The place was basic. Zero frills. Somewhere like this, in the shit-end of nowhere special, where money was tight, a business couldn't afford to be expensive. Such a place would not survive a single day. Black didn't care. He'd eaten in worse places. He downed the food with a cold bottle of Budweiser. He sat at the window. Outside, the main road was quiet. Dusk had fallen, illumination provided by the yellow glimmer of streetlights. The only other place which looked open was a bar called The Old Winery, lit up in red neon.

He waited. He was in the open. In plain sight. An easy target. It was brutally simple, and dangerous to the point of madness. But it was the most effective plan he could think of. Like pus from a boil, he had to bring it out, expose it, then react. For the thousandth time, he wondered why he didn't get the hell out. But he knew he wouldn't. He'd see it to the end. Maybe the Colonel's daughter was missing. Maybe she wasn't. But he had to get to the truth, because that was simply the way he was built. And if he died in the process, well then, he would thank the fuckers for it, and maybe take a few with him.

But he had a knack for not dying.

The waitress cleared away his dishes, asked if he wanted some dessert. He politely declined, but opted for a coffee. She was thin, skin brown as parchment, hair tied severely back. She looked like she smoked maybe forty a day.

He showed her the photograph.

"Have you seen this person?" he asked.

She made a show of studying it. She darted a glance at Black, then back to the photograph, frowned.

"She your girlfriend?" she asked.

"Just a friend."

She nodded slowly, scratched the back of her ear. "I've seen her," she said. "Sure it's her. She was here, sitting in the corner table. Maybe ten days back."

"You're certain it was her?"

"Pretty certain. We don't get many strangers stopping here." She pointed over to a vacant table, as if the action endorsed her certainty. "She was sitting right over there. With a guy. I remember him because he wore an expensive-looking suit. Looked like a fancy city boy. They only came in the once." She looked at him meaningfully. "They left a measly tip, if I recall."

Black acknowledged the remark, leafed out fifty dollars, left it on the table.

"How do you like it?" she asked.

"This place?"

"The coffee."

"Black. And strong. Please. Did you happen to catch where she was staying, or what she was doing?"

"Nothing I can remember. They looked serious. Like they had real business. Maybe on their way to the Walled City. I haven't seen them since."

"The what?"

"But most people don't stop. Not here. The buses drive by, as if we don't exist, and drop them off up yonder. They come and go. Maybe two every week. Taking people in, taking people out. That's probably where your girlfriend was going. That's where everyone goes."

"She's not my girlfriend." He held back his exasperation. She was talking in riddles. "What's the Walled City? Who goes there?"

People at a far table attracted her attention. She gave Black a courteous nod. "Black and strong."

He watched her take fresh orders. He had loose verification that the Colonel's daughter had been here, to Fairview. Which was something. Or maybe she was mistaken. But she sounded sure.

The door opened. A man entered in full police uniform. Strapped to his belt a black leather holster, holding a .357 Magnum. He stood for a moment, gave a friendly salute to a woman standing behind a glass cake display counter, made a show of searching about, spied Black, came ambling towards him. Black watched, nerves heightened, senses sharpened to an increased competence. But he was intrigued. Such interest, he thought. *News travels fast.* Presumably the motel owner had relayed the information.

The police officer stopped at his table. He was a big man. Wide and barrel-chested, a gut sagging over his belt, a fat round face perched on a fat round neck, bald as a stone, shiny in the restaurant lights.

His face crumpled into a smile.

"Did you try the rib-eye? The best in town."

Black raised an eyebrow. "Maybe next time."

The police officer gestured to the chair opposite Black. "May I?"

Black nodded his assent. The policeman sat. The chair creaked under his weight. He rested two large hands on the table. His smile never wavered.

The waitress came over. She placed Black's coffee on the table. "Can I get you anything, Sheriff?"

The sheriff picked up a paper napkin, dabbed his brow. "How's about a cold beer. Make it real cold. Like freezing."

He turned his attention back to Black. "It gets hotter every year, I swear."

"Global warming," said Black.

"Could be. Takes a lot of getting used to. Some folks never get used to it. They don't tend to last long."

"If you can't stand the heat…"

"… then get the hell out the kitchen," finished the sheriff. "That's what they do, they get the hell out."

Black sipped his coffee. It wasn't hot. He hated tepid coffee. He thought it prudent not to complain.

"I was just passing," continued the sheriff. "I noticed a new face. Thought I would introduce myself. To be polite, you understand. It pays to be polite." He paused, as if expecting Black to respond. Black said nothing. The sheriff continued: "I can tell from that accent you're not from these parts."

"I'm from out of town."

The waitress appeared, put a frosted bottle of Budweiser before the sheriff. He nodded in appreciation, pressed it to the side of his face, rolled it side to side. Still smiling.

"You visiting someone?"

Black sipped the coffee. He smiled back.

"Not visiting."

The sheriff seemed to divine some hidden information from this. He pursed his lips, nodded thoughtfully, then took a glug from the bottle. There was no discernible movement in his throat as he swallowed. Like liquid flowing down a hollow tube. Under different circumstances, Black might have found the situation amusing.

The sheriff gave Black a level stare.

"Not visiting? Then just passing through."

"Not quite. I'm looking for someone. An old acquaintance. Perhaps you can help." He reached into his pocket, took out the photograph, placed it on the table. The sheriff picked it up, scrutinised it.

"Nice-looking young woman. She your girlfriend?"

"Old acquaintance."

"Can't say I've seen her. Have you tried the motel? Miles Danskin knows all the faces who come through."

Black held the sheriff's gaze.

The sheriff's smile flickered. He handed the photo back. He rubbed the back of his head. The smile returned, broader than before.

"You know, now that I think about it, maybe I did see her. Yeah. Jesus." He shook his head in exasperation. "You know what's worse than the goddam heat? Old age. I'm not getting any younger. No, sir." He emitted a wheezy chuckle. "The memory goes, yes? We're only human."

"Sure," replied Black in a measured tone. "The memory goes."

"Yup. Definitely." His forehead wrinkled, the expression of a man trying hard to recall an elusive fact. "She asked me for directions. That's it. Think she must have got lost. Maybe a couple of days ago." He leaned forward in the chair, bulk stretched over the table. Black noted the guy wasn't entirely bald. Above each ear, a fuzz of near-invisible blond hair. "I think I know where she's staying."

"That's handy," said Black. "Do tell."

The sheriff sat back. "But where's my manners." He stretched out one meaty hand. "My name's Sheriff Len Kinnermont."

Black shook it. It was like shaking hands with a bear. "Adam Black."

"I hope our little town of Fairview is treating you well, Mr Black."

"I don't intend staying long."

"You've more important business elsewhere. I understand. For most folks, Fairview is a 'passing through' place. An 'interlude' you could say." He flashed a glance at the framed posters on the wall. "Like in the old days, the bit between the movies, for popcorn and hotdogs and Coke – back in the day when cinemas played two movies in the one slot. I'm old enough to remember that. When you got what you paid for, and you got a bang for your buck. Fairview's kinda like the popcorn and hotdog bit. You're there for the movies, but it's part of the package, so you make the most of it. You like the movies, Mr Black?"

"I haven't been for many years."

"Me neither. I used to like the action stuff. Thrillers. But then I came to realise that the more these Hollywood guys tried to make it real, the less real it became." Black watched, as one of his great bear paws slapped the holster carrying his Magnum. "The damage this baby can do can't be replicated on the silver screen.

No, sir. It isn't real life. Not by a long way. You ever seen a man shot, Mr Black? It's not pretty. No, sir."

Black took another careful sip of his coffee. "You mentioned that you might know where she's staying."

"I think I might. But it's not an easy place to get to."

Black said nothing.

"If I recall, she'd rented a place a couple of miles out of town. A quiet spot, hard to find."

Black waited.

The sheriff cocked his head, as if coming to sudden realisation – "She might still be there. If you want, I could take you out?"

"Now?"

"Yup."

Black made a show of pondering. "I have my car outside," he said. "I could follow you."

The sheriff seemed to consider. "That sounds like a plan. Yes. That would work. You want to go now? There's no hurry."

Black gave a wolfish grin. He hated tepid coffee. He would leave it.

"Let me pay my bill," he said.

"Of course. Take your time. I'm not going anywhere."

I'm sure you're not, thought Black.

He would follow the sheriff, and take his chance, and see how the cards fell.

TWENTY-NINE

THE KILLER CALLED Wilson Smith hadn't always lived in a cottage in the village of Haworth, and would admit such a place would not normally have been his first choice. Nor would he deny the move to the Yorkshire countryside held a dark irony. Often, he would reflect on the matter, and consign the circumstances to fate.

Six years ago, he had been contracted to murder a retired CEO of a mid-range oil brokerage company. The reason why was never given, and Smith didn't care.

As ever, Smith's identity was securely protected. Secrecy in his chosen profession was sacrosanct. Contact was via texts on burners and encrypted emails. And as per the norm, he carried out detailed and painstaking diligence on his target, including the proposed location of the strike. He decided the individual's house was ideal. Relatively isolated, private, and simple to fabricate a scenario for the police.

The kill had been easy. A burglary gone wrong. Smith got paid for his work. The world moved on. But the house – the killing ground – held appeal. Perfect for a man like Wilson Smith. And the garden…

He waited. Smith was a patient man. He could wait an

eternity, should he choose. The target was divorced. No kids. No close relatives. The house went on the market seven months after his death. Using the money he had been paid for the kill, Smith bought it. Bought it cheap. No one wanted it. Blood and violence. The place was tainted.

Irony indeed. Smith found the situation comical. And, in a further ironic twist, he resolved to enhance the garden, as an amusing tribute to the man he had killed.

He laid a patio, about the size of a tennis court. He had carried out the work himself, with his own two hands, his own labour, his own sweat. He had used aged Yorkstone paving. Designed to appear distressed and weathered. Once down, it looked like it had been there a hundred years. In the precise centre he had erected a green marble fountain. The task had taken him four weeks. He was meticulous. It was a perfect square, flat as glass. At night, he would sit on his patio, and listen to the whisper of the water, and watch the night sky, and perhaps sip a cup of green tea.

Smith did not drink alcohol. He did not smoke. He did not partake in the use of drugs. He kept rigorous control of his diet. He was, in his own estimation, a master of discipline. Essential if he were to survive.

One of the slabs, with a certain twist and a pull, could be lifted. Under it, a metal lid, secured by a combination lock. When opened, it revealed a box sunk into the earth, six feet square. In the box were items Mr Smith required for his particular trade. Knives. Pistols. Rifles. Ammunition. Other items, all lethal.

Smith had been given a new job. Just as he had carefully planned his garden, and his patio, and indeed every facet of his life, so he had planned the killing of his next target.

He was ready. All he needed was a text, and an instruction.

And then Wilson Smith would fulfil his contract.

THIRTY

ELSPETH HORNBUCKLE GOT BACK FROM PARENTS' evening at 7.30. Hornbuckle still hadn't made the call.

He tried to remain bright and breezy, as if everything was fine with the world.

She was in the hallway, in the process of taking her coat off.

"What do you think?" he said.

She looked exhausted. For a moment, he felt a yawning terror – her face, so pale, so drawn, was not dissimilar to the look the cancer had given her. The look it gave everyone.

"What do I think about what?"

He turned, pointed to the keypad on the wall.

"Ta-da!"

She reacted with a weary smile. "What's the code?"

"The year I was born. Plus, there's sensors in the hall, and all the ground-floor rooms. And one above the back door. Like Fort Knox. So you can rest easy."

"Rest easy? What about Mr Chuckles?"

Hornbuckle's hesitation was barely noticeable. Enough time to frame an answer.

"No problem. The alarm activates at a certain height. It's not an issue." Another second of hesitation. He hated lying to her. But then, the last five years had been one long hidden lie. "He'll be fine."

"That's good."

He moved on quickly.

"How was it?"

They made their way to the kitchen. He went to the fridge. He had chilled a bottle of white, which he opened, and poured her a glass, and placed on the kitchen table. She sat, kicked off her boots, ran her hands through her hair, massaged her temples.

"I feel I could sleep for a week," she said.

He got himself a glass of red, sat at the table opposite.

"Rough time?" he ventured. He attempted flippancy. "Parents wondering why their chicks aren't child prodigies?"

"Not so bad." She fixed her gaze on him, spoke barely above a whisper. "Did anything happen?"

He assumed a look of puzzlement, again in an effort to scale the situation down. "Anything happen?"

She reacted with a small incredulous blink of her eyes. Her voice rose.

"What do you think I mean – this is Day 3. The letter said. Did anything happen?"

Christ, he hated this. The spectre of the inevitable phone call rose up in his mind, for the millionth time, black as death. He shook his head. He needed those two seconds to keep his voice neutral.

"Not a thing. Nothing happened. Nothing's going to happen. We've got an alarm. I've been to the police. The whole thing is a sick joke." He added, somewhat lamely – "Put it from your mind. Please."

She sighed, drank some wine. "The day's not over yet," she said.

At least, in respect of this statement, he could respond without lying. "Nothing's going to happen," he said with assurance. He repeated his initial question. "How did it go?"

The corners of her lips rose into a small wintry smile.

"A couple of indignant mums not understanding why, when their kids swear at their teachers, the kids should get detention. As if swearing and shouting is a perfectly normal response when the little bastards are asked why they haven't done their homework."

Another drink. Then – "I reported the thing to the school. The letter. The graffiti on the fence. Just in case."

He nodded, and wished, deep down, she hadn't. "Good idea. They can make enquiries."

"Sure."

"No cooking tonight. I'll order a takeaway."

She gave a listless response. "I'm not hungry."

"You have to eat. Keep your strength up. I'll order, and drive in to collect."

She acquiesced with a small movement of her head. She got up, went through to the living room. He remained in the kitchen. He heard the sudden noise of the television, and decided he would make the call on his way into town.

———

He made the order, left at 8pm. He shouted goodbye, but doubted she'd heard him. He drove a half mile down the road, pulled into the grass verge. He took the coffee receipt from his trouser pocket. On one side, a printed date, time, destination, price. The details were irrelevant. The other side of the ticket was infinitely more important. A handwritten mobile phone number. His handwriting. The phone number of someone he had spent the last five years hiding from. Hiding with painstaking effort.

All for nothing, he thought.

He felt the texture of the paper in his hand, felt the imprint of the number. Blue biro. He remembered the moment well. Over five years ago. He had used a cheap plastic pen he'd taken from the office. He remembered using the receipt, because at the time he had nothing else to write on.

The contact number. The person to speak to. To confirm arrangements for repayment.

And that was the problem. He'd never used the number, because he'd never made the repayments.

He took a breath, composed himself as best he could. But his heart thrummed fast and hard, his mouth was dry, his hands trembled. He concentrated, looking out at nothing, sight focused inwards, trying to catch the thoughts whirling in his mind, slow them down, bring order to the chaos.

He got his mobile phone, switched it on, stared at the screen, and wondered, not for the first time, how the hell they had found him. But they had. There was little doubt in his mind. It was pointless to agonise over the 'how' of the past. He had no choice but to deal with the 'how' of the present – how the hell he was going to get out of the mess he'd started.

He swiped the screen, brought up the keypad, and pressed the number.

The number rang. Good start. At least it was still active. Which meant he could talk. Plead.

He waited. His pounding heart kept time with the ring of the phone. It picked up. A voice answered. A woman's voice. Not young, he thought.

"Hello?"

"Hi," he said.

Silence. His mind raced. He said – "I'm looking for Tommy Windle."

A pause. He heard her breathing.

"Who is this?"

"Someone…" he began, then stopped, as he tried to regulate his thinking. "Someone who needs to talk to him. It's important."

The voice became harsh. "What's your name?"

"My name is Richard Hornbuckle. He'll be expecting my call."

The statement brought a brittle, wheezy laugh.

"Somehow, I don't think so. How did you get this number?"

"He gave it to me."

"Really? That must have been a while ago."

"It was. Five years back."

"And you're phoning him now?"

"Like I said, he'll be expecting my call."

Another pause.

"What do you want? Are you the police?"

"No."

"What the fuck do you want?"

Hornbuckle's voice cracked with the pressure. "I want him to stop. Tell him, I'll make it up. I'll do anything. Just tell him to stop."

She erupted into a wild cackle.

"Tell him yourself. Why should I care?"

"Who is this?"

The line went dead. Hornbuckle stared at the blank screen. He felt numb. And shocked. He had no idea what had just happened. His finger hovered over the keypad, to press the number again. He held back, and instead slumped in his seat, and took a long slow breath.

Tell him yourself.

The woman might have been his girlfriend. Or perhaps his wife. Or mother. Her answers made no sense. There was no escaping the situation. He tapped in the number again.

It went straight to voicemail.

"Please," he said. "I need to talk to Tommy. Tell him to phone this number."

He disconnected. He was swimming in a deep sea, and the current was dragging him down, and he was drowning.

Day 3. It kept repeating compulsively, like inch-worms traversing the inner surface of his skull. He thought of Mr Chuckles, gutted and hung, displayed on their front door, a stark message. He hunched over, began to cry into his hands, soft shuddering tears. He was lost and helpless and shit scared. He needed help, but no one on the planet could provide it, because the mess he'd created was his mess, and no one else's, and he deserved all he got.

He straightened, grasped the steering wheel, composed himself. Tommy Windle might phone back, but somehow he didn't think so, given the cryptic conversation. He came to a decision, and remembered an old quotation from somewhere in the bible – *And the truth shall set you free.*

He would tell his wife. Tell her everything. And perhaps together they would come to a solution.

His phone sparkled into life, buzzing and vibrating on the passenger seat. His breath caught. For a moment, he froze. Panic bubbled up, from the pit of his stomach to the back of his throat. He snatched the phone up, looked at the screen.

The number calling was his wife's.

He took a second to regain a degree of normalcy.

He answered. Elspeth spoke in a gasping, choked voice, the words stumbling over each other, rendered incoherent.

"Slow down. Tell me what's wrong."

"It's… it's on the…"

"Easy," he said. It took effort to keep calm. But he had no choice. "Catch your breath. Slowly. What's wrong."

He heard her inhale, exhale. "Please… come home."

He waited.

"It's on the front path."

"What?"

"It's still there."

"Tell me."

"The fucking cat. It's slit wide open. You hear me. Someone's killed our cat. And…"

He sat, motionless, staring at the phone, trying to comprehend what she was saying.

"And…?" he whispered.

"They left a note."

A note! He was unable to speak. She spoke for him.

"Nice try."

"What?"

Suddenly her voice went flat, as if there was no more emotion to give.

"That's what the note said. *Nice try.*"

THIRTY-ONE

SHE HEARD a noise she thought she would never hear. The rattle of keys, the turning of a lock, the creak of old hinges. Her prison door was opening. She experienced a raft of emotion. Elation, that perhaps this was her release; dread, that this was her doom.

The light was on, glaringly bright, bringing details into sharp relief. A man stood in the doorway, two others behind. They each were casually dressed. Jeans, T-shirts. Each probably in their mid-twenties. Tanned. Athletic. Each with long hair, trailing past their ears. And each with a rifle looped over their shoulder and a short sword sheathed to their belts. The one in the doorway wore a roguish red silk scarf. He nodded politely at her. He spoke in a soft Californian lilt –

"He would like the pleasure of your company. If you will?"

Her voice was dry. She realised she hadn't spoken for days. She swallowed, licked her lips, composed her words.

"Where are you taking me?" The words came out strange, like someone else had spoken. A voice she didn't recognise.

The man gave a sardonic laugh. "Somewhere a little more comfortable. Please. He's waiting. And one thing he hates, is to be kept waiting." He gestured to the hall outside. "Shall we?"

There was little for her to say. He stood to one side. He followed her as she made her way out, flanked by the two other men. She emerged into a winding cylindrical stone tunnel, devoid of any ornamentation. Like a wormhole in the rock. Underfoot was cold and smooth on her bare feet. Illumination was served by the same strip lighting as in her cell. They escorted her to a plain wooden door. One of the men unlocked it. They entered a broader passage. Same winding route. A carpeted floor. Also, small porthole windows at head height. She had no sense of time. They stopped at a door. Beside it, a chair, draped over which, jogging trousers, a grey sweat top, pants. Under the chair, a pair of trainers.

The man pointed to the door.

"A shower cubicle. There's towels and soap and other stuff. All you need. Take the fresh clothes in with you. Put the old clothes in the bin. Twenty minutes. One second longer, we come in and get you. Yes?"

She did as requested. She was grateful for this small luxury. She hadn't washed properly in days, had slept and sweated in the same clothes. The shower room was spacious, comprising cubicle, toilet and a cupboard filled with fresh towels. A metal unit in which she placed her old clothes. On a shelf, a range of gels and soap and shampoos. Unlike the grey stone walls in the hall, the walls in the shower room were adorned with frosted white marble tiles. No windows. The opportunity of escape was zero.

She showered, washed her hair, dried off, changed into the new clothes. They were a size too big, but she didn't care. The trainers fitted perfectly, which was the main thing. She could run if she had to.

She re-entered the hall, feeling about two hundred times better. The procession moved off, she and her three escorts, along the winding stone corridor.

Another door, then steps – thirty in all. She counted them. Then into a further passage. Here, the walls were brightly painted, with windows on either side at regular intervals. They were at a height of maybe fifty feet above the expanse of the grounds. It was night-time, but the surrounding land was illuminated by light globes set in posts in random fashion. People beneath her milled about, undertaking tasks, conversing, oblivious to her presence. The site stretched easily a half mile in every direction; a landscape of cultivated fields, animal pens, wooden barns, white-blocked structures where people slept and ate. And close by, dominating everything around it, a church of white panelled wood, complete with spire, and a high crow-stepped gable. The focal point of the commune. Where people massed every morning and every evening to listen to the wisdom of the savant known simply as Zain. But the church was quiet. The sermon was over.

They reached another door at the end of the corridor. On either side, sitting on soft chairs, a sentry. Young men. Tanned and supremely fit. Dressed like those around her – faded jeans and T-shirt. This, she realised, in its strange way, was a uniform. Casual. Informal. Blending in perfectly with the ethos and attitude of this place. On the surface, carefree and relaxed. Lurking just beneath, darkness and extreme violence.

The man behind her stepped forward, knocked gently, opened the door, beckoned her inside. Without a word, she entered.

The room was exquisitely decorated. The floor was polished herringbone hardwood, the walls smooth and curved. Suspended from a low ceiling, a light fashioned from rock crystal, casting a soft yellow hue, creating an almost dream-like quality. In the centre a low glass table set on ivory legs, upon which, a platter of fruit. Mangos, peaches, plums, strawberries. Her mouth watered. She felt she hadn't tasted fruit for a thousand years. Beside the platter, wine bottles and champagne resting in a silver ice bucket, and tall fluted glasses.

Also on the table, a box wrapped in glittering silver paper, tied and bowed with red silk ribbon.

Scattered about, a selection of wide leather chairs. On one, stretched back in a pose of languid ease, was a man clad in a hooded velvet robe of deepest grey, his features neat and compact, blond hair in a boyish crew cut, cheeks flat and wide. Startling blue eyes. The robe could not disguise the taut physique beneath. In one lolling hand, a glass of red wine. This was the preacher known as Zain. The man thousands flocked from all over North America to hear. The man she had come to investigate.

In the shadows, watchful, a bodyguard.

Zain waved a hand to a chair opposite. "Please. Come and join me." His voice was soft, lilting. Almost musical. Lacking any discernible accent.

"Do I have a choice?" The question was rhetorical. She sat. She waited.

"I call this my inner sanctum. Away from all the hustle and chaos. Where I can find a little... peace."

She gave a sardonic grunt but said nothing. She was too tired to be afraid any longer. The fear had spent itself. Maybe hours ago, maybe days ago. She was uncertain. Time had been a meaningless concept in her little stone cell. But the fear had gone. Instead, a tingle of disgust. And disappointment that she might never get the chance to bring some justice to the monster before her.

Zain continued. "We've never been introduced. Perhaps introductions are redundant. You already know who I am. And I know who you are."

He tilted his head, as if expecting her to respond. She reacted with a stubborn set of her jaw.

Zain remained unfazed. "You are Elizabeth Pembroke. The daughter of Colonel Daniel Pembroke, I believe. And rather beautiful." He tipped his wine glass in salute. "And who is both talented and ambitious, and who happens to work for the Federal Bureau of Investigation." He sipped his wine, lips curling at the edges into a fox-like smile.

She said nothing.

"What field?" he asked. "I believe the Bureau has many different departments."

Elizabeth fixed him with a level stare, replied in a flat voice,

"The department that takes down scumbag drug-dealing bastards."

Zain laughed in easy glee. "Fearless and bold. You can't tame a wild cat, for sure."

She responded, voice rising in anger. "You understand you're finished. Other agents are coming. You can't escape this. They'll blow this whole cult shithole open." Her anger descended to desperation. "Better to hand yourself over to the authorities."

Zain gave a look of exaggerated surprise. "Others are coming? Really? They seem to be taking their time." Again, a tilt of the head, prompting a reply. "Maybe they've lost their paperwork? Or perhaps they've forgotten all about you?" His smile changed to a sad frown, his voice lowered to a conspiratorial whisper. "Or maybe they don't know you're here."

She concentrated, tried to rationalise what he was saying. A doubt which had nibbled the edges of her mind, and which she had stubbornly refused to acknowledge, began to bite hard.

"They know I'm here," she said, containing the tremor in her voice. "Bet on it. My partner…"

Zain raised a hand, cut her off. "Your partner, Jona Lefroy? Is that who you mean?"

The doubt blossomed into something different. Dread. She said nothing.

"I think you need to grasp a new reality," he said, his tone almost affable. "You came here with Jona, your fellow FBI colleague. We know this. You infiltrated our little commune, which was very rude. But you got discovered. Got unmasked. Or, as they might say in an old gangster movie – *got ratted out.*"

She reacted with a tight-lipped smile. "Jona wasn't in here when you took me. I phoned him on his mobile. Warned him. He was out of the compound, in Fairview, liaising with other…"

"Federal agents?" said Zain. "Whipping up a strike force to come and save the day? Is that what you think?"

She sat silent. Her world was imploding.

Zain shifted to one side, took out a mobile phone from his

pocket. He held it up. "This is Jona's." He placed it gently on the glass table. "Sorry to disappoint."

She realised she had been holding her breath. She exhaled slowly, inhaled, tried to keep calm.

"Where is Jona?"

"I'm glad you asked. Aren't you a little intrigued?"

"I don't understand."

"Aren't you curious?"

"What the hell are you trying to say."

"About the box on the table," said Zain. "Don't you want to open it? It's a gift. For you."

She shook her head. "Go fuck yourself."

"That's no way for a guest to behave. Nor is it very ladylike."

"I'm no lady."

"Let's approach this from a different perspective." He glanced round, snapped his fingers. The man waiting in the corner of the room approached.

"Fetch me the gun."

The man wordlessly went to a double-doored cabinet, the doors fashioned from darkened glass, opened them, took out a silver handgun, returned. He handed it to Zain, who balanced it in his hand, as if judging its weight. He pointed it at Elizabeth.

"From this range," he said, "and from this pistol, the bullet would shear your head from your shoulders. Or, if I were to fire at your chest, it would burst your heart and eviscerate most of your vital organs. Now please, open the box. I got it specially for you, and it would seem a cheap way to die, over such a paltry request."

She took a deep breath. The situation was past flippant rejoinders and defiant retorts. The situation was real. He would squeeze the trigger on a whim. She knew this man, had studied his past. He was the worst kind of killer – one who enjoyed doing it.

"Please," he prompted. "Ten seconds."

She studied the box on the table. It scared her almost as much as the man holding the pistol. It was a cube. About the same dimensions as a container for an air fryer. Or maybe a twelve-pack of beer cans. Or perhaps something else.

She stretched over, picked it up, placed it on her lap. It was solid. Not cardboard. Made possibly of wood. It wasn't heavy. Nor was it light. It held something. She was too terrified to consider what.

Zain gestured with the pistol. "Please."

She pulled the red ribbon, tore the paper off, let it fall to the floor. Her guess was right. A plain wooden box. She thought of her partner, Jona Lefroy. The fear intensified. She glared at Zain. "What the hell is in this?"

"Surprise."

The box had a lid. Two small grooves had been created for fingertips. She opened it.

Inside, white polystyrene filling chips.

"It's precious," said Zain. "Be careful."

She put her hand inside, breath held, as she waited for the touch…

Her fingers brushed an object. She gasped, jerked her hand back, then teased her fingers forward. She felt something solid. Something hard. She pulled out another box – long, slim, leather-bound, held closed by a tiny latch. She frowned, twisted the latch, opened it. Inside, set in a grooved velvet compartment, a short-handled hand-axe.

"What is this?"

"The shaft is made of fibreglass. It's known as a 'woodchopper'. It's my gift to you."

The dread diminished. She thought the box contained something very different. Still, the fear remained. She had been given the axe for a reason.

"Why would I want an axe?"

Zain reclined back in his seat. He still held the gun, vaguely pointing in her direction.

"It's not just any axe. It's special. It's something to be treasured."

"I don't understand."

"Allow me," said Zain. Another wordless glance at his bodyguard, who nodded an acknowledgment. He padded back to the double-doored cupboard, opened it, carefully removed a white plastic bag. It appeared to contain something resembling the shape of a football. He came back, stood beside Elizabeth.

"Now you might understand," said Zain

She looked up at the man standing beside her. He turned the bag upside down. The head of Jona Lefroy tumbled out and onto her lap. She lurched to her feet, uttered a short shrill scream. The head rolled onto the floor.

Zain straightened his aim, pointed the weapon at her. "Please, Elizabeth. No dramatics. Sit down."

It took five seconds to find her voice. It cracked with emotion. "What the fuck have you done!"

"Given you a present. Sit down, please."

She sat. She stared. There, on the wooden flooring, Jona Lefroy's head, face gazing at the ceiling, eyes open and strangely alive, mouth and chin contorted, neck, where it had been cleaved, revealing white bone and pale tissue.

"The axe in your hand was the implement used," said Zain, tone conversational. "Which is why you should treasure it."

She turned her head, mind numb, registering what she was holding. She dropped it to the floor, as if it were white hot.

The bodyguard stooped, grasped Jona Lefroy's head by the hair, placed it back in the bag, returned it to the cupboard.

Her mind whirled. She found her voice. It sounded small. "Treasure?"

Zain gave his head a shake, as if in mild exasperation. "You both tried to infiltrate my organisation. Your task was to destroy me, bring down everything I have worked for, send me to prison. Possibly to kill me. You must have considered death as a possible consequence of your actions, should you be discovered. One of the downsides of working for the Federal Bureau of Investigation. Yes?"

Her voice was a mumble. "I don't understand."

Zain gave an idle wave of his hand. "Why would you? You're an innocent, Agent Pembroke. Your innocence makes you vulnerable. Jona Lefroy betrayed you."

"What…"

"He struck a deal. He and an old friend came up with a plan. And it revolved all around you. Which is why you are still alive."

"Old friend?"

"Someone Jona met in Afghanistan. The war against terror. This 'friend' discovered you were assigned with Lefroy to take my organisation down. This information was potentially very valuable. Lefroy approached me two weeks ago, and revealed your plan. And in particular, he revealed your identity. They were right. This was the most valuable thing in the world. He thought – they both thought – that by doing this, they would be rewarded. But in Lefroy's case, how can a Judas be trusted. He suffered the consequences. But he gave us what we wanted. He gave us you."

She waited.

"You're the connection," he said.

"Connection?"

He smiled. She sensed the finale was coming.

"Soon."

She tried to swallow, but her mouth was too dry. The sound in her ears was the thump of her heart.

"What are you talking about?"

"I'll let someone else tell you."

"Someone else?"

"It's not for me to explain. There is another. A person who has taken great interest in this situation. The same person who cut Jona's head off."

She struggled with this. Nothing made sense. She paused, grappling with a disturbing new thought. "The man who spoke to me when I was imprisoned," she said. "Who is he!"

"Soon."

She carried on, words tumbling. "He mentioned a name."

"Of course he did."

He glanced at the guard, who approached. He gave him back the handgun. The guard returned it back to the cabinet. Zain sipped his wine, resting his startling blue gaze on Elizabeth.

"Have some champagne, Elizabeth. Relax. Enjoy the moment."

She didn't respond.

"Do you not understand what you are in this game?"

She waited.

"A bargaining chip."

"Bargain for what?"

He sighed, as if bored with her questions.

"The man called Adam Black."

"Adam Black. Who the fuck is Adam Black?"

"He'll be here very soon. I'll introduce you. Then you'll understand."

THIRTY-TWO

When, where and how. These are the relevant questions for a soldier to ask. Never ask why. There's simply no point. You'll never get an honest answer.
Anonymous.

BLACK FOLLOWED the sheriff from the restaurant. On the way out, he caught the waitress's eye. She gave an easy smile.

"The sheriff arrested you?"

"Not yet," replied Black, smiling back.

"How was the coffee?"

"Cold."

They emerged into the main street. The evening was balmy and dark. A moonless black velvet night. The street-lamps emitted a soft shadowless luminescence. Up in the sky a million stars glittered. Traffic was non-existent. The place was quiet. Black experienced an undefinable emotion. His senses tingled. Danger was close. Things were stirring. Events would flow, and he would flow with them, to a destination, the substance of which was uncertain. His senses heightened to needle sharpness.

His car was parked adjacent to the restaurant. The sheriff spoke casually. "I'm just round the corner. I'll come past, then you follow. Okay, Mr Black?"

"Okay, Sheriff."

Black got into the car, watched the sheriff walk away. There was a suggestion of dominance in his stride. A swagger. This was his kingdom. He ruled, and he knew it. A man used to getting his own way. A man no one dared cross.

For someone who had parked his car *just round the corner*, he took longer than Black imagined. Probably making the call, he thought. Arranging matters. Giving orders, marshalling the troops. Black expected no less. His distrust of his fellow human being was born not from paranoia, but self-preservation. He had a knack for recognising bad men, developed and honed over most of his adult life.

Black waited. The pistol the Colonel had given him was tucked in his belt under his jacket. The knife was bound to his calf. A patrol car eased up beside him, like a shark. A window slid down. The sheriff nodded. Black nodded back. The sheriff drove off. Black followed.

They kept at a steady thirty miles per hour, heading back out of town, passed the bottling plant, the motel, and beyond into the greater darkness, the landscape caught in shifting shadows. The sheriff had said two miles. They were approaching four, when the sheriff turned off the main road. The car bounced and lurched. More of a track than a road. This continued for a further two miles. Suddenly, to one side, a structure rose up from the dark, framed fleetingly in the glare of the headlights. A house.

The sheriff stopped. Black pulled up behind him. The sheriff got out, beckoned Black out. Black waited a second, scrutinised his surroundings. The car headlights were not pointing directly at the house, rather at right angles, creating a perspective shrouded in half shadow. Details were obscured. The place looked neglected. The front garden was a jungle of waist-high grass, the surrounding fence bleached and tilting. It was a one-storey wooden-clad structure. The wood looked like it was peeling. The windows were blank, lacking curtains or blinds. Grass and other vegetation was growing in tufts on the roof. It looked abandoned.

Black got out.

He assumed a puzzled face. "It doesn't seem anyone's living here, Sheriff. Are you sure this is the house?"

The sheriff put on a show of tilting his hat back and scratching his scalp, as if he too were perplexed.

"This was old Mrs Willow's place." He turned to Black. "But you see, Mrs Willow died a few years back, and I guess you could say the place got a bit... run-down." He brought his hand down, swept his Magnum from its holster, held it in a two-handed grip, pointed it at Black's chest. He was less than eight feet away, in the full beam of the headlights. He couldn't miss, even if he wanted to.

"I'm sorry, Mr Black. And you seemed a nice polite gent. I do what I have to do. But that doesn't mean we still can't have some fun." His teeth gleamed when he smiled.

Black said nothing. He let it play.

The sheriff, retaining the weapon in one hand, reached into the top pocket of his shirt, pulled out a whistle. He blew into it, twice. It cut the air, sharp and shrill.

"Okay boys," he shouted. "All clear."

Black sensed movement. He turned to the house. Shadows emerged from round the back, merging into human form as they approached the lights. Three men. Black recognised one of them. Miles Danskin, the motel owner. Their cars parked behind the house, he assumed, invisible in the darkness.

They sauntered up to the sheriff, without any apparent urgency. Black wondered with some trepidation what the sheriff meant when he said *fun*. Danskin was grinning. He wore a white T-shirt and grey jogging trousers. In the full beam, he looked scarecrow thin. Arms and neck like frosted twigs. Another was large, similar build to the sheriff. Bulky, with fat and old muscle and good living. Middle-aged. Blue eyes set in a round moist face.

The third was smaller and younger. Maybe late twenties, with a flush of blond hair brushed high over his forehead. Compact build, thick shoulders, long muscular arms. Of the four men facing Black, this one possessed most potential for inflicting harm. He was the one who spoke first –

"Jesus, Len. You gone and captured a big one. Like a fucking king-size whopper."

Danskin laughed. "Guess you came to the wrong town, Mr Black."

The large one turned to the sheriff. He had something in his hand. An inhaler. He placed it to his lips, gave it two quick inhalations, then spoke, his voice wheezy and laboured. "You sure this is okay?"

The sheriff – Len – kept his attention on Black. "Sure it is. The man said we bring him in alive. That doesn't mean we can't have a little sampling. Hear that, Mr Black?"

The agitation on the other man's face didn't leave. "But we buried the others, Len. This one might get to tell his story. We gotta keep this thing secret. Don't you think, Len?"

"Enjoy what we got," piped up the man with the blond hair. "You fucking worry too much. We got here some prime fucking beef. We're not passing this one up. No way."

Miles Danskin could hardly contain his glee. "Hear that, Mr Black! You're a piece of prime fucking beef. Yummy!"

"Take it easy, Clive," said the sheriff, referring to the large man with the inhaler. "This one isn't telling any goddamned story. The way I hear it, when he's up there in the Walled City, he's gonna wish he was back here with us boys, being buck-ridden like a fucking wild mustang."

"If you say so," said the man called Clive. He studied Black, lips twitching. "He's a mustang, all right. As God is my witness, I'll ride him hard."

Danskin clapped his hands. He was clearly enjoying the moment. "What do you say now, Mr Black? All the way from

England with your fucking accent and your fucking attitude. Asking dumb questions."

During the entire exchange amongst the four men, Black had said nothing. Now he spoke.

"I think you have that wrong."

Danskin looked puzzled. "I ain't got nothing wrong."

"I'm all the way from Scotland, not England."

"Same fucking place."

"Not quite."

The sheriff cut in – "Enough." He had both his hands back on the pistol, which he twitched to the direction of the house. "In there. That's where we take them. We like our privacy, Mr Black. You understand, I'm sure. We don't want these intimate moments being interrupted with any unnecessary distractions and such."

"I'm sure you don't," said Black

"Christ, he's a cool one," said the blond man.

"Shut up, Johnny," said the sheriff. "In the fucking house, Black. Try anything stupid, and I swear to Jesus fucking Christ, I will shoot you in the back of the head and bury you deep in Mrs Willow's back garden."

"Like all the others?" said Black.

"You catch on fast. Now move."

Black considered his position with an almost analytical detachment. He viewed himself, his enemies, his surroundings, as a neutral observer, part of his mind alive to the prospect of danger, another part formulating a response. And yet another, bristling with the thrill of expunging evil men.

Black considered his options. The building was better. Containment. Less chance of them escaping into the night.

Black walked towards the house.

"Hands up to the sky!" barked the sheriff.

Black complied, pushed the front gate open with his knee, hinges grinding out a rusty complaint. There was a front path of sorts – broken slabs, weeds. Either side, the tall grass wavered, stirred from a sudden warm breeze. He got to the door, the four men behind him.

"It's not locked," the man called Johnny said, laughing.

Black turned the handle, pushed. The door stuttered open. Darkness, deep and solid. The unmistakable smell of rot.

"Stay there," said the sheriff.

Torchlights flashed on. Images sprang into vision. A short hall. A worn carpet, a broken pendant light hanging from a low ceiling. There, on a wall, a picture of a nameless landscape, hanging askew. At the far end, another room. Without any instruction, Clive, Johnny and Danskin brushed past Black, went through the hall into the far room, torchlights bobbing. Ten seconds later, soft yellow light flickered. *Well-practiced,* thought Black. *No newbies in this game.* He could hear Clive coughing.

"On you go now," said the sheriff.

Black turned his head, looked at the sheriff over his shoulder. "I don't think Clive likes the damp."

The sheriff gave a deep rumbling laugh. "You're a cool fish right enough, Scottish. That's the last thing you need to worry about right now. Please. Follow the boys into the back room. Keep your hands where I can see them. Nice and easy."

Black did as requested. Through the hall. He emerged into what once was a living room. The remnants were still there. A tiled fire surround, a couple of torn leather seats, a faded green cloth sofa. A couple of side tables. The room flickered and danced in the warm hue of a dozen candles, placed in random fashion throughout. In one corner, an ancient television, small and deep, with an arial made of two wire loops on top. The screen was smashed. In the centre of the room was a thick blue rug, discoloured with an array of stains. Even in the candlelight, Black recognised the colour. Blood. Old and new. He'd seen such stains a thousand times before.

The sheriff beckoned with his pistol – "Stand in the centre. Keep your hands up. I swear, twitch a finger, and I will shoot you in the head." He flicked a glance at Johnny. "Search our new friend."

Johnny stepped forward and positioned himself behind Black. He leant in close, whispered in Black's ear – "Don't move, big boy." He began the process of searching – patting, pressing, probing, and immediately uncovered Black's handgun. He pulled it from under Black's belt, dangled it between his thumb and index finger, as if it were red hot.

"Lookee here!" he shouted triumphantly.

"Nice," said the sheriff. "Toss it on to the couch. He said you would be armed, and he wasn't wrong. But then he said you were a lot of things, Mr Black. He said you were a dangerous man. Well, seeing you standing there, you don't look so dangerous. Does he, boys?"

"Looks like he's ready for it," breathed Danskin, licking his lips. Black noted he was rubbing the front of his trousers. "Looks like he wants it."

Johnny had stepped away, to stand beside the others. It seemed the search was over. *Amateurs*, thought Black.

"Now a little bit of fun time," said the sheriff.

Black regarded the four men standing in a line, watching him.

"This is a regular thing for you guys? Instead of pool and some beers, it's a bit of rape and murder?"

The sheriff gave his deep rumbling chuckle that seemed to emanate from the depths of his chest. "We have our sport. Boys and girls. No one misses them. What with the crowds that go on up to the Walled City. Runaways, mostly. Looking for salvation."

"But they find you four pilgrims instead," said Black.

"We like our fun. Where you're going, it won't matter if you've been through a little rough and tumble."

"Watch him, Len," said Clive. "He's a tricky one." In the close confines of the room, in the glow of the candles, his round face shimmered, like a circle of sweat.

"I'm watching all right," said the sheriff. "Enough of this idle chit-chat." He straightened his arms, pointed the handgun in the direction of Black's head. "Take your clothes off, every piece, and lean up against the chair. Like a good boy."

Black frowned. "I don't get it. I really don't. Is it stupidity? Is it a genetic fault? Too much inbreeding?" Then he smiled, his expression one of sudden enlightenment. "That must be it – too much inbreeding."

The sheriff blinked. Then he spoke with a snarl. "Quit the smart mouth. Take your fucking clothes off."

"Watch him, Len," said Clive.

Johnny bristled forward. "He said take your fucking clothes off."

Black seemed the epitome of calm reason. "But that's what you're not getting." He looked directly at the sheriff. "I'm not like the others. You can't kill me and dump me in a hole in the ground. Your boss wants me alive. You daren't shoot, sheriff. Otherwise, if I'm dead, then I guess you're dead too."

Danskin spoke up. "Shoot him in the leg. That'll make him easy."

"He's not my boss," retorted the sheriff. His eyes were pinholes set deep in the fleshy folds of his face. "I can do what I fucking want. And right now, I want to do you, you understand. To fucking *do* you. Hear my voice, Black. I'm not asking again. Take your fucking clothes off, or I swear by God almighty, I will blow your fucking head off."

The smile never left Black's face. The four men were about six feet from him, standing in a loose cluster. Johnny – the blond-haired guy – and Danskin were standing either side of the sheriff. Behind the three hovered Clive, like a great white moth.

"You're sure this is what you want?" said Black quietly. "Once you start the dance, you never quite know how it ends."

Johnny guffawed. "You're the one gonna be dancing. All fucking night, I swear. Dancing and howling, for sure."

"Fair enough," said Black. "Shoes first?" Without waiting for an answer, he crouched down, as if to untie the laces of his right shoe. The manoeuvre was executed for an entirely different reason. Black pulled up the bottom of his jeans by six inches, grasped the hilt of the knife attached to his calf, snapped the elastic bands, and in a single swift movement, threw it underhand fashion, lunging forward simultaneously, in a bowling style pose. As he had been trained. The knife was blade heavy, allowing for accuracy and greater penetration. Plus, given the short distance, there was no spin. The blade entered the sheriff's upper thigh with force, lodging hilt deep.

The sheriff lurched back, bellowing like a bull, arm jerking down in reflex, finger twitching the trigger, firing into the floor. Black continued forward in one fluid motion, his stride uninterrupted. He kicked the sheriff in the groin. The sheriff sank to his knees, dropped the handgun. Instantly, Black swivelled, struck Johnny a fearful blow in the neck using the heel of his hand, crushing his larynx. He swivelled again, struck Danskin across the temple with his fist and felt the crush of bone. Turning at a crouch he hurled forward, knocked Clive off his feet. They rolled across the floor, Clive screaming and shouting. Black caught him in a clamp, thrust him onto his stomach, jammed his knees between Clive's shoulders, reached down, cupped both hands under the chin, jerked up and back and snapped his neck.

Panting, Black rose to his feet. In less than fifteen seconds, he had killed three men. He turned his attention to the sheriff, who tried to stand, shifting on one leg. Black slapped him hard across the face. The sheriff toppled on his side, dazed. Black picked up the handgun, placed it in his jacket pocket. He retrieved his own pistol from the seat where it had been left. With one hand, he grabbed the sheriff by the back of the collar, dragged him to the couch, sat him up.

He waited. Awareness returned to the sheriff's face. His eyes adjusted, focused on Black. He swallowed. He looked down at his leg.

"You stabbed me," he muttered.

"You started this," said Black. "Allow me." He leant down, and in a quick movement, yanked the knife out. The sheriff grimaced, gave a short grunt of pain, put his hands over the wound.

Black pointed the gun at the sheriff's face.

"Your friends are dead. Not quite what they were expecting, I imagine. Indulge me, sheriff. How many people have you killed over the years?"

The sheriff's jaw muscles bulged and twitched. His skin shone, tight and pale. His breathing came in short wheezy gasps. He had both hands over the wound on his leg. The blood wasn't spurting. He was lucky. No major arteries clipped. But the blood kept coming. And as the seconds passed, the shock would diminish, and the pain would escalate.

"I need to get to a hospital."

"Sure you do. How many? Focus... Len? May I call you Len? Good. How many have you and your little club buried, Len?"

The sheriff swallowed. "You've killed them. Clive. My brother."

Black shook his head, tapped the muzzle of the handgun on the sheriff's forehead. He leaned closer. "You don't need to worry about him. But you do need to focus, Len. How many. If you don't tell me, I'll slice both your ears off."

"Since the Walled City became a thing. It wasn't my idea, I swear. It was all Johnny. We did it once, as a dare. Then it became... a habit. It was easy. It just seemed... to happen. Like God intended it."

"A habit," echoed Black. "How many?"

"Ten. Maybe more. I guess I've lost count."

"I understand. Looks like God was on my side this evening."

The sheriff's breathing got more ragged. "We can work this out, Black. I have money. Cash. It's yours. I can take you to it right now. A trade, yes? If you let me go."

Black sat cross-legged on the floor opposite the sheriff, handgun in one hand, dagger in the other, and said, "Maybe later. Now tell me about the Walled City."

THIRTY-THREE

HORNBUCKLE HAD RUSHED BACK when he got the
call. The remains of the cat were strewn across the front path. The
conclusions were terrifying. Someone had been watching the
whole time. Perhaps they still were. The thought escalated his
fear. Standing in the front garden, he scanned the landscape. Now,
suddenly, he saw a hundred places to hide – woodland; rocks and
boulders; the contours of the low hills. The shadows. He cursed
his complacency.

He took long slow calming breaths, went to the garage, got
necessary implements, carried out the grisly business of disposing
of Mr Chuckles' remains. *Déjà vu*. He shovelled up the body, the
entrails, tipped it all into another heavy-duty bag, tied it tight,
placed it in the bin. He would deal with the stain later. It looked
like it would rain. Maybe the rain would wash it away.

His wife was in the living room, sitting on the settee, staring at
the opposite wall. Her expression was one of vague
bewilderment. *Shock*. He sat next to her and took her hand. It was
limp and lifeless and cold. And the skin so white. Like she had
been bleached of life. Now was the time. Now, he had to explain.
To his surprise, she turned and spoke first.

"I've called the police," she said. Her voice was flat. "I spoke to a nice young man. Sergeant Starling. He'll be here any minute, I imagine." He looked into her eyes. They glistened with tears. He held her. She put her arms round his neck, began to sob softly into his shoulder. He said nothing, absorbing her despair.

"Who would do such a thing?" she whispered. He felt her tears on his skin. *Let me tell you.* He took a breath, summoned up his courage.

The doorbell rang.

She drew back. "The policeman," she said, her voice a monotone.

He clenched his jaw in frustration. The last thing he needed. He kept his composure. He carried a burden he now had a desperate need to unload. For his sanity. And his wife's. The policeman was an intrusion.

"I'll get it," he said. He went to the front door. Starling stood on the doorstep, in full uniform.

"I got a call from your wife," he said. He tilted his head, as if prompting Hornbuckle to respond.

"Yes, of course. She called you. Please. Come in."

He opened the door wider. Starling entered, stood in the hallway, waited.

"Please," said Hornbuckle. "Come through."

He led Starling into the living room. His wife hadn't moved. She rotated round when they entered, gave a wan smile, said nothing. Hornbuckle beckoned him to sit on an armchair opposite. He didn't offer tea or coffee or any damned thing. He wanted him out.

Starling met Elspeth's eyes, gave a warm smile. "How are you, Mrs Hornbuckle?"

She replied, a little more energy in her voice. "Please. Elspeth. No need to be formal. I'm scared. I don't know why this is happening. It doesn't make sense. Does it, Richard?"

Hornbuckle lied easily. The more he did it, the easier it became. "No sense. It's crazy."

"Sure," said Starling. With his right hand, he reached up to the top-left pocket of his jacket, pulled back the Velcro, fished out a notebook, with a small pen attached.

"I have to get some details." He focused on Elspeth, still wearing the reassuring smile. *Like he knows all the answers,* thought Hornbuckle. "You said the cat…"

Elspeth broke in. "Our cat was dead on the front path." Her voice had lowered back to a monotone. "I had gone out to empty the bin." She bit her lip, struggling. "I saw something on the slabs, at the far end, at the garden gate. I thought maybe a black bag had somehow blown in. Maybe from the garage. Or the road. A burst bag with some rubbish smeared on the ground. But it wasn't that at all."

Silence fell. Neither Hornbuckle nor Starling spoke. She needed the moment. She nodded, as if finding the resolve to continue. "I made my way up the path, and realised it was our cat. We called him Mr Chuckles. We gave him the name in a burst of sarcasm. He was the grumpiest cat in the world." Another staggered breath. Five seconds passed. Then – "He was stretched out, on his back. His tummy…" Her voice faltered. She spoke through sudden hot tears. "Who would do such a thing!"

Starling waited a second. "If you could let me know what you saw." His words were gentle. "Please. I know it's difficult."

She continued. "His tummy had been slit, all the way, top to bottom. His… insides had been pulled out and lay in a tangle." She shook her head, as if still in disbelief, went on. "There was a note. Inserted inside him, sticking out."

Inserted inside him! thought Hornbuckle. *The cat had been dug up, slit open, returned, laid out like an exhibition. The perpetrator had taken the trouble to leave a note. Like icing on a cake. Inserted.* The word sickened him. He swallowed back a sudden surge of fear, raw and sharp.

Starling was writing in his pad. He looked up, regarded Elspeth, spoke in his soft, measured voice.

"Do you have the note?"

"Yes."

She got up, went to the mantelpiece. She picked up an envelope tucked behind a Napoleon-style clock, came back, placed it on the coffee table.

"May I?" said Starling.

She nodded.

He opened it carefully. *"Nice try.* Handwritten. Does this mean anything to you?"

"No," she said. Hornbuckle merely shook his head. He had no desire to vocalise the lie.

Starling replaced the letter in the envelope. "Do you mind if I keep this?"

"No problem," said Hornbuckle, perhaps too quickly.

"Fingerprints?" said Elspeth.

Starling gave a small shrug. "I don't think so. But it's handwritten. The last letter was different. Written in block capitals. Maybe I can check with our experts. Who knows? It's worth looking into. You didn't see the cat when you came back from work?"

"No," said Elspeth.

"You work at the school? When did you get back? I'm trying to get a time frame for this."

"I got back at about 7pm."

He nodded, smiled. "Parents' night."

"Yes."

"And you saw nothing."

"No."

"You went out to empty the bin. Do you know the time?"

"About 8.15."

Starling focused his attention on Hornbuckle. "And when did you get back from work, Mr Hornbuckle?"

Hornbuckle cleared his throat. He hadn't anticipated this. His mind whirled. "I got back about 4. I left early." He tried to make light of the situation. "To meet the alarm guy."

"Sure." Starling never stopped writing. "I came round earlier today. And you saw nothing then, I assume."

He nodded.

Starling looked up, fixed his gaze on Hornbuckle. "When Elspeth called, she said you had gone to get a takeaway. Yes?"

Another nod.

"You left the house when?"

He blinked, licked his lips. "I can't remember exactly."

Elspeth swivelled round to face him. "Sure you do. You left at 8."

Starling wrinkled his forehead, in an age-old expression of puzzlement "You left at 8. And you saw nothing."

"No."

Silence. Then, "Whoever carried out the attack did this in a space of fifteen minutes. Give or take."

Neither Hornbuckle nor his wife spoke.

"They committed the act." He repeated his statement. "All in fifteen minutes."

Hornbuckle found his voice. "Someone close by. An impulsive act."

Starling twitched his head in the negative. "Not when they've left a note. That's not an impulsive act. That's planning and forethought. And it means they were close by." He focused back on Hornbuckle. "To have arranged things in such a short space of time…"

Hornbuckle shifted in his seat. "Yes. Of course. Makes sense."

He closed the notebook, tucked it and the pen back in his top pocket. He folded the envelope with care, placed it in a side pocket. He stood up. Hornbuckle stood with him. Elspeth remained seated.

"Someone clearly has a grudge. Please, think back. Anyone you may have crossed or upset? You don't have any neighbours, so this isn't a neighbour dispute. Anyone at work?Or maybe someone you may have met at work. Have you had any traffic altercations? Anything at all?"

"An angry parent," said Elspeth, her voice low. "Blaming me for something."

Starling looked sceptical. "It's possible. But unlikely. This..." he patted the pocket containing the envelope, "...runs deeper. This is vengeance." He pursed his lips, thoughtful, regarded Hornbuckle. "Any irate customers?"

Again, a shake of the head. It didn't feel like lying when he didn't speak.

"You have my direct number. I'll make enquiries. Be vigilant. Anything at all, you phone."

Elspeth looked up at him. "This is Day 3."

Starling offered no response. *What the hell can he say?* thought Hornbuckle.

He saw the young policeman out.

"Thank you for coming."

"I wish I could do more. And the alarm's working?"

"It's fine."

"Keep the code simple."

Hornbuckle gave a knowing smile. "Year I was born."

They shook hands. Hornbuckle watched as Starling made his way along the garden, watched him pause at the stain on the slabs, watched him get into his car and drive off.

He returned to the living room, sat where Starling had sat, faced his wife.

"Why are you lying?" she said. Her voice was flat calm, which made it worse.

"I have a story to tell," he said.

"Tell me."

He sighed. Now was the time. Perhaps he knew it had to come. As inevitable as death.

"It began in a village," he said.

She kept her eyes fixed on him. He took a deep breath, continued –

"The village is Eaglesham, and it was there I heard about a man called Peter Grant."

"Who is Peter Grant?"

"He's the man doing all of this."

THIRTY-FOUR

ROM DID NOT FIND the prospect of travelling to Prestwick appealing. Another five-hour drive. Yet he had mixed emotions. His father had given him the responsibility to arrange and oversee their biggest drug import. A portion of his brain felt flattery. Pride, almost. Another portion felt entirely different. It still rankled him, that he had been ordered. *Told.* Like a child. He was *humiliated.* Still, the fear he felt for his father outweighed any notion of displaying outward insubordination. He wondered, fleetingly, if his father would have him killed if he should choose to disobey. Possibly.

Rom left the house after three further hours of drinking whisky. He drank rarely. He was intoxicated. Which he hated. But his father had insisted. And when that happened, there was no choice. Another reason to hate him. His father and Stu Gorman had remained, playing snooker, and would doubtless be there all day. Which was something else that rankled. Gorman was supposed to be his man. Not his father's.

His own house was one hundred yards along the driveway. A property built on the land they owned. Not as large as his father's. It was nevertheless an impressive structure – a long low bungalow, surrounded by dark varnished composite decking, like a moat, sheltered under a white awning. Clean white stucco walls, the roof glittering with solar panels, and at one end, somewhat incongruously, a two-storey conservatory, appended like a tower, constructed entirely of glass, the upper floor reached by a spiral staircase. It was on the upper level he kept his gym. When he trained, he liked to have a view. And the view was clear and unobstructed. On all sides, a landscape of low rugged hills, merging to distant woodland, beyond which, the mountains. The only blot was his father's house, which, on a sudden notion, he decided he would flatten when his father died.

He got in, showered, changed into a loose tracksuit, flopped on the couch of his living room. On one wall, a television the size of his father's snooker table. He got the remote, found a sports channel, kept the volume low, glanced at his mobile – no messages. Perhaps too early. He drifted off to sleep.

He woke with a start, eight hours later. Light outside was failing. Here, in the Scottish wilderness, when it got dark, it was an absolute darkness, thick as blindness. His mobile had dropped on the floor. He reached down, picked it up. Two messages. One from Arlene. Received a half hour ago. 8.15.

> On my way home. Can't wait to tell you. You'll love it. Fucking awesome.

As promised, she had attached photographs.

This made him smile. *Fucking awesome.* It had gone well. She was right. He *would* love it. She couldn't wait to tell him. He couldn't wait to be told.

Second message. No name, other than X. They had agreed, for this particular task, names were not to be used:

170

> Went ok. Did as requested. Checked the
> aftermath. All going to plan nicely.

Aftermath. He loved the use of that word. This second message also pleased him. He felt suddenly invigorated. He typed in his passcode, brought up his bank details, arranged an instant transfer of £20,000 to the nominated account. As agreed. A further £20,000 when it was over.

He got up, padded across to a switch, turned the outside lights on, then dimmed them. The decking was bathed in a soft amber hue. He pressed a button – bi-folding doors, which made up the entire front wall of his living room, concertinaed open in one smooth motion. He got a cold bottle of mineral water from the fridge in the kitchen, went outside, breathed in the Scottish air. The world was silent. He was still light-headed, adding a surreal dimension to his surroundings. The creeping darkness, the soft lighting, the quiet, all blended to create a dreamy quality to the evening. He spied headlights. He sat at a table, watched its slow approach – along the curving section of driveway from the main road to his father's house, then past it, towards him.

Arlene's car. His excitement rose, her words playing in his mind – *fucking awesome.*

THIRTY-FIVE

After the Iranian Embassy siege, when suddenly the world's media was interested in, and somewhat in awe of, the special forces unit known as the Special Air Service, a BBC reporter allegedly asked an army general what the main difference was between soldiers of the SAS, and regular soldiers, to which the general replied (allegedly) – "They're all mad bastards."
Anonymous

BLACK HAD TUGGED Johnny's T-shirt off, and, using his knife, had torn it into three sections, each roughly the same size. He wound one section round the top of the sheriff's thigh, applying it as a tourniquet. He used another to bind the sheriff's wrists. The sheriff offered no resistance. Black sat back. The sheriff was dazed, had lost blood, was in pain, but he was a long way from dying.

"Who do you work for?" asked Black.

Sweat dribbled into the sheriff's eyes, causing him to blink and twitch. He croaked out a response – "What do you intend to do?" He licked the sweat off his lips. "I'm an officer of the law..."

Black laughed. "Nice answer. Let's try again. Who do you work for? It's a simple question. If I don't get the right answer, I'll cut off your right ear. Try again."

The sheriff's voice was a mumble. "Like I said, I have cash. You can have it all. I'll take…"

Black leant across, gripped the sheriff in a tight headlock, and in quick savage movements, sliced off his ear. The sheriff howled, tried to squirm away, but the effort was feeble. Black sat back, gave the sheriff the third section of Johnny's T-shirt. The sheriff, gasping, placed it awkwardly on the side of his head to staunch the blood.

"You're a fucking animal."

"I'm in good company," said Black. "I'm going to ask you again. If you fail to answer to my satisfaction, I will cut off your other ear. I will continue cutting off your appendages – nose, fingers, balls, etc. – until I get a sensible response. By the end of the night, if you continue resisting, you'll end up an unrecognisable lump of flesh, no longer a man. You understand the programme of events?"

The sheriff nodded.

"Who do you work for?"

"He calls himself Zain."

Black pondered. The name meant nothing.

"Who is Zain?"

The sheriff took a long slow breath. Black could almost read his thoughts – what was more dangerous? The consequences he faced should he spill information on 'Zain', or the consequences of Black's wrath? The decision was easy.

"Zain runs the Walled City. He's the leader of some crazy cult. He's been called *The New Messiah*. Kids from all over come to listen to him. It's a sort of commune. Two thousand acres. Has its own living accommodation, fields for crops and livestock. Even a fucking school. And a big fucking church in the middle. Any one time, there's easy eight, maybe nine thousand people living there.

Self-sufficient. There's movement all the time. People arriving, people leaving."

"What do you do for Zain?"

"I make sure his... operation... runs smoothly. Keep people in line, so to speak."

Now they were reaching the nub of the matter, thought Black.

"Operation? I'm intrigued. Explain."

The sheriff took another long breath. Black waited.

"The whole thing's fucking bullshit. It's a front. There's an airfield on the site. It brings in heroin. Vast quantities. As I said, there's always a flow of people coming in and out. Some of them are couriers, delivering drugs to all over the country. Also, he utilises the bottling plant in town. Uses the lorries to transport the gear. He pays me to make sure no one gets uppity about what's going on. To make sure there's no unwanted interest in the operation." He gave a sardonic snort. "And no one ever fucking complains, because it doesn't go well for troublemakers."

"And Zain pays you?"

The sheriff nodded. The T-shirt he held to the side of his head was saturated in blood. Altogether, the sheriff looked a sorry mess. Black couldn't have cared less.

"Sixty thousand dollars a month. To keep things smooth. To look the other way."

"That's top dollar," said Black. "Corruption pays. What did Zain ask you to do with me?"

"To bring you in. To the City."

"He was expecting me then."

The sheriff shifted where he sat. "I can't feel my fucking leg."

"Your leg's fine. He was expecting me?"

"I guess. I was given the command. Keep an eye open for an English guy called Adam Black."

"Scottish," said Black.

"What?"

"It doesn't matter. The motel owner tipped you off?"

The sheriff became almost accusatory. "The guy you killed."

Black ignored the remark. "You rounded up your little posse to bring me here, to this shithole, before delivering me to Zain."

The sheriff didn't respond.

"Why does Zain want me?"

"I honestly have no idea. Like I said, I get given a job, and I don't question the man."

Black believed him. The sheriff was a lower rung in the organisation. A thug with a badge, possessing a peccadillo for rape and murder. He reviewed the situation. He had been asked by the Colonel to search for his daughter. Upon his arrival in Kansas, a group of men and women had tried to bundle him in the back of a car. Killing was not on their mind. Within minutes, they were shot by two men, possibly cops, probably not, with killing definitely on their mind. They'd tried to shoot Black, but failed. Black had arrived at Fairview. Someone – Zain, he assumed – knew of his coming. Zain didn't want him dead. He had instructed the sheriff to bring him in alive.

The underlying question was – who the hell was Zain? And what was their connection? Black had no answers. Plus, he seemed no closer in establishing the whereabouts of the Colonel's daughter. The woman at the diner had said she remembered her eating with a guy at one of the tables. The motel owner – *the ex-motel owner* – clearly remembered her when Black showed him her photo.

The affair was mired in mystery. The individual called Zain – *The New Messiah* – seemed to hold the key.

Black resumed his attention back to the sheriff.

"What about the girl....?"

"She went to the Walled City with another guy," blurted the sheriff. "That's all I know. She's probably still there. I didn't know anything about her, except that you might be asking around for her whereabouts. That's it, I promise." The sheriff began to sob. "I'm sorry. I truly am. Things just got a little out of hand. We wouldn't have done you any real harm. It was just a bit of crazy fun."

Black considered the man before him.

"What have you told Zain?"

"About what?"

"About me."

"I told him I was bringing you in."

Black shook his head. "You know, for a guy who earns sixty thousand dollars a month you're a stupid fucker. All you had to do was tell me the girl I was looking for was at this 'Walled City', take me there, and you would have accomplished your mission, and right now you'd be sitting at home on your fat arse in front of your cinema-screen television watching a movie and filling your fat stupid mouth with beer and pizza. But you wanted your bit of fun. You and the boys. You just couldn't resist it. And look where it's got you. Stabbed and missing an ear. And staring at the barrel of a Magnum. Poor decision, yes?"

The sheriff's sobbing subsided, his voice reduced to a low mournful sound. "Please… I'm sorry. I can sort this…"

"Of course you're sorry," said Black. "But sometimes sorry isn't quite enough." He reached over, searched through the sheriff's jacket, pulled out a mobile phone.

"You can contact him using this?"

The sheriff nodded. He kept his head down, T-shirt still clamped to his ear, staring rigidly at the floor.

"I once had a dog like you," said Black, his tone conversational. "He thought, if he couldn't see me, then I couldn't see him. From his perspective, I suppose, a logical assumption. But of course, I did see him." He tapped the sheriff on the shoulder. "Look at me."

The sheriff raised his head, regarded Black with eyes burrowed deep with pain. And fear. Black had seen it a million times and saw it now. He was a connoisseur in all its forms.

"Phone Zain. Please." He handed the mobile over. The sheriff, awkwardly, clutched it in his bound hands, manoeuvred it round in his fingers, the T-shirt pressed on his ear now dropping to the floor, revealing a moist red patch of blood. He switched it on, swiped the screen, tapped contacts, tapped a name. It rang.

Black took the phone from him. A voice answered. Smooth and deep and lacking any discernible accent.

"Sheriff? You're on your way?"

"Not quite," said Black. "Am I talking to Zain?"

A short pause.

"Adam Black. Such a pleasure. What have you done to our poor sheriff?"

"You don't have to worry about him. We got a little sidetracked, but I think he sees the error of his ways. He tells me you want to meet up. Any specific reason?"

"I hear you're an interesting man. I enjoy meeting interesting people."

"So it seems. Though you have a peculiar way of showing it. I think you'll have to do a little better."

"I have the one perfect reason."

"Do tell."

"Elizabeth Pembroke."

Black said nothing.

"You remember her. She's the reason you're here. She's with me now. Sitting opposite. I believe she's not in the best of moods. Her mind is focused on other things."

"That's not a good enough reason," said Black.

A harsh chuckle echoed from the phone. "But I think it is, Adam. Here's the situation. You get here in one hour. One second longer, and I'll gouge her eyes out with a spoon. No debate."

Black responded instantly. "I have the sheriff."

"Good for you. You do what you have to do. If you call for backup, the girl dies. Tick-tock."

The phone disconnected. Black regarded the sheriff.

"Tell me how to get to the Walled City."

In stops and starts, between sobs and tears, the sheriff stuttered out directions – *follow the main road a further ten miles. Take the turn-off marked Yellowbird Holdings. It's a single lane, easily missed, leading once to a coal mine, closed down sixty years back. Keep to the road about five miles. The outer perimeter is stock wire fencing. The gate's always open. Drive another mile or so, then you'll come to a low concrete wall. The entrance is always open too. You'll see lights and buildings and people. That's where they live. The commune. Those who worship The New Messiah. You'll pass a church. Keep driving. Don't get off the road. Another couple of hundred yards, you'll come to a massive structure, like a fucking fortress, with a dome in the centre, surrounded by high walls. You don't get into that. That's invitation only. You wait until the doors open. That's where he lives.*

Black thanked the sheriff for his cooperation. The sheriff looked up at him, eyes suddenly alight with... what? Hope? Salvation? Black would never know.

"What now? I've told you where he is. I've got money..."

Black thrust forward, hard, stabbed the sheriff through the throat. He left the blade inside, leaned back, watched him convulse and gurgle.

Black considered his options. There was really only one. Zain may or may not have Elizabeth. The whole thing might be bullshit. Black couldn't take that chance. Zain wanted to meet.

Black would oblige.

THIRTY-SIX

ZAIN PLACED the mobile phone on the arm of the couch, gazed at Elizabeth. His eyes glittered, like blue marble in the sun. She kept his gaze, kept her voice steady, despite her fear. She refused to allow him the satisfaction. *Keep talking,* she thought. *Engage.* Something might go her way. As she had been trained. But the conversation he'd had with the man called Adam Black was terrifying.

"Spoon?" she said. "That's original."

He spoke, his voice soft and silky. "I've always had a good imagination." He gave the merest shrug, allowed a sad smile. "I was maybe a little poetic. But I can think of other things equally as horrific. A bullet to the head, for example. Let's hope Mr Black is punctual."

"Let's. I don't know who Adam Black is. Why is he so important to you?"

"Your father would know," responded Zain. "Please, have some champagne. Enjoy the moment."

She ignored the comment. "What has my father got to do with this? I'm here. And I'm asking the question."

"You have a fire, for sure," said Zain. "Perhaps it needs to be dampened a little. Patience. Soon, all will become clear."

"You're talking in riddles." She asked suddenly – "Who was the man who spoke to me through the cell door? It wasn't you."

Zain reacted with a languid stretch of his back. "So many questions. Have some champagne. It's very good. It's very expensive."

Her anger, once again, rose to the surface. "I don't want your fucking champagne!"

She sensed the bodyguard tense. Zain waved him to relax with a careless gesture. He brushed invisible crumbs from his lap.

"The man you spoke to is waiting. Unlike you, he is a patient man. He has been waiting for many years."

"Waiting?"

"Of course. Can't you guess? He's been waiting for Adam Black. And you hold the key."

"The key to what!" Her defiance rose again. She felt her cheeks flush in sudden hot anger. "How do you know he'll come! He would be mad to enter this place, on account of someone he's never met. I don't know who Adam Black is! He doesn't know me. What the fuck is going on!"

Zain regarded her with his 'bluest of blue' eyes. At that moment, she sensed the presence of the man. His smooth pale face, the clear penetrating stare, his easy fluid movements. People came to this place to listen to him preach. He looked the part. A man who was so confident in his own skin, he looked like he might know all the answers.

"You know why people come here?"

She said nothing, waited.

"It's because when I speak to them, they hear what they want to hear. And you know why that is? Because I can read the crowd. I suppose it's a gift. But I'm good at it. I would go so far as to say I have an exceptional talent at it. I can read people. I get into their minds and hearts. And once I've done that, then the rest is easy."

He crossed his legs, the corners of his lips rising into a smile.

"I haven't met Adam Black either. But I've heard a lot about him. Enough, shall we say, to understand the working of his soul."

"Fucking bullshit."

Zain carried on unperturbed. "He has a code. How would you describe it? A moral code? A warrior's code. He believes in honour. Good over evil, that sort of thing. He's the very man to come here, and rescue the damsel in distress, because to behave in such a manner is in his DNA. He's a killer. Ruthless, even. But his every action is dictated by his sense of honour. Which is his flaw, and which, in the end, will destroy him."

"What are you going to do to this man? This Adam Black."

A soft laugh. "Me? Nothing. I have no quarrel with him. It is for another to take his vengeance."

"Who?"

"He's waiting. He has been waiting for a long time. When Adam Black arrives, then he will show himself."

A silence fell.

Zain said, "Relax, Elizabeth. Let the situation unfold. There's nothing you can do to change its outcome. Let it flow, and you'll be the stronger for it."

She reached over, grabbed up the glass of champagne, downed it in one, flung the glass on the floor.

"It tastes like shit. They call you The New Messiah."

Zain made a gesture with his hands, as if to say – *well, if that's what people want to call me.*

"You'd better be fucking careful, Zain."

"Why is that, Elizabeth?"

"Because the last one got crucified."

Time passed. Maybe fifteen minutes. Maybe a half hour. Maybe a year. Nothing made sense in this crazy world, except the simple fact that her life was in peril, and there wasn't a goddamned thing she could do about it. More guards had entered, and now stood, silent as stone, one in each corner of the room. A fifth stood six feet to her side, watchful for sudden movements. All armed, rifles hanging from their shoulders, each looking like they knew how to use them. Zain sipped his red wine, picked from the tray of fruit on the table, offered her some, to which she gave a flat refusal. She was in no mood for eating. Nor talking. They sat in silence, the only sound the heavy drum beat of her heart.

Zain's phone buzzed. He answered. He nodded. He looked at Elizabeth.

"Exactly as anticipated. Adam Black is here."

THIRTY-SEVEN

PETER GRANT, thought Hornbuckle. A name he had hoped never to say aloud again. But yet he was, at this very moment, and to the last person he wanted to tell. His wife sat, silent, pale as death, listened as he told his story...

... just over five years earlier.

They had gone to the consultant together and held hands as he relayed the results in that quiet sincere manner people adopt when conveying bad news. Breast cancer. And it was aggressive, and had spread to the lymph nodes under her arms and near the breastbone. Maybe treatable. Just. Difficult to say. The problem was time. And waiting lists. And availability. *And bureaucratic NHS bullshit*, thought Hornbuckle.

There's the option to go private, the doctor had suggested, which only compounded Hornbuckle's self-loathing. They didn't have medical insurance, because it was a luxury they couldn't afford. Hornbuckle had failed the woman he loved. He was bitter and enraged.

It was winter, and it was cold. An evening with some friends – work colleagues. Liam Findlay and Robin Thomas. A small, quiet pub called the Old Swan, in the village of Eaglesham. Hornbuckle had never been to the place. Liam lived locally and had recommended it. Hornbuckle had agreed, grudgingly. He would drive, exit early. He hated leaving his wife alone. She was on medication. Her every waking hour was straddled with exhaustion. It was her idea. *You need a life,* she had said. Spoken as if she had already given up on hers.

Perhaps it was fate. Or merely a random culmination of events. Two men entered the pub. Hornbuckle watched them, thought little of it. Both well dressed. *Immaculately* dressed. Robin leaned close, like a conspirator.

"The guy in the camel coat. You know who that is?"

Hornbuckle, sipping fresh orange and lemonade, shook his head. "No idea."

"He comes in here usually once a month. That's Peter Grant."

"Who?"

"You need to get out more," said Liam.

"Peter Grant," repeated Robin, words tainted with the slightest slur. He was on his fifth pint. "He owns fucking everything."

"He's a property developer?" said Hornbuckle.

Liam gave a mischievous grin. "He's a little more than that, by all accounts."

"Peter Grant," said Robin, as if, by continuing to repeat, Hornbuckle might suddenly know who the guy was. "Property developer, businessman, benevolent altruist. 'Poor boy done good' story. One side of the coin. Flip it over, and you get extortionist, drug dealer, loan shark. Fucking kingpin gangster. And you've never heard of this guy? Seriously?"

"Seriously," said Hornbuckle.

"There you are," said Robin. "A night out with me, and your eyes are opened to the world."

"So it seems," said Hornbuckle. He studied the man standing at the bar. The man called Peter Grant. Tanned, compact build, clean shaven, chisel-faced, mouse-brown hair cropped short. Five-ten, at a push. *Boxer,* thought Hornbuckle. A confident, capable man. He oozed money. Three-piece suit, white silk tie, white button-down shirt. His watch glittered. Probably a Rolex. Hornbuckle wouldn't know the difference. He looked relaxed. He was laughing with his friend, and his teeth were Hollywood white.

"And they say crime doesn't pay," he said, more to himself than his friends.

"You got to be born with it," remarked Liam. "You can't learn the street."

The following morning, he got a call at work. A sympathetic voice, breaking bad news. Another refusal. The tenth. He had applied initially for a loan from his own bank. But for the amount he needed – the cost of a private hospital and the follow-up care – the arithmetic didn't add up. He was mortgaged to the hilt, his credit cards were maxed out, he had a personal loan on the car. Their income wasn't enough. He had applied to other banks. Then loan companies. Lenders of 'last resort'. But the risk was too high. Default was likely. It was thanks, but no thanks, and a swift rejection.

They had no family to borrow money from. No friends with that type of money. Nobody. They were on their own. His wife was dying, and he was powerless to help.

His thoughts turned to the quaint little pub in Eaglesham. To the man called Peter Grant. His expensive suit and camel coat and dazzling white smile, and he wondered, perhaps, if such a man might be an answer. The mere thought terrified him. But then, terror had different levels. To Hornbuckle's mind, nothing could compare to the unparalleled agony facing his wife.

He googled the name *Peter Grant*. It was too generic. He narrowed it down. *Peter Grant, Scottish businessman*. Lists of information appeared. He scrolled down, scanning each section. His friend had described him as an altruist, and he was right. The guy was wealthy. He headed youth schemes, opened drug rehabilitation centres, big on poverty in deprived areas. A real local hero. He typed in *Peter Grant, Scottish gangster.* More lists, of an altogether different sort, but nothing verified. Gangland gossip. Inferences to organised crime. Members of his family serving lengthy sentences. But nothing specifically connecting Grant to any crime.

Hornbuckle brought up pictures of the man. The same easy smile, as if life were simple and money didn't matter. Pictures of him with celebrities, politicians, with people on the street. There – a photo of his house. A mansion in the trendy west end of Glasgow, set back from the road, enclosed by a wall and high gates.

He had an address.

He got home that evening. His wife had received a letter from the hospital. The likely timescale for an operation was three months. At the earliest. He saw the defeat in her eyes, the hope crushed, and knew then, at that precise moment, he had no choice.

The following weekend, he went to Peter Grant's house. The wrought-iron gate was set between two stone pillars, upon which, CCTV cameras. Set in one pillar, a metal speaker panel. Underneath, a buzzer. He pressed it, waited. After five seconds, a voice answered.

"Who is this?"

"My name is Richard Hornbuckle. I would like to speak to Peter Grant."

"What is it regarding?"

"A business arrangement."

"Do you have an appointment?"

"No."

"You'll have to make one."

"How do I do this?"

"Phone the office. Blue Yonder Enterprises."

It clicked to silence.

Hornbuckle got an appointment the following Tuesday. It was scheduled for midday. Blue Yonder Enterprises had an office comprising the third floor of a rather grand Victorian building in the centre of Glasgow. A concierge met him at the front entrance, beckoned him into the reception area. The walls gleamed from top to bottom with ice-blue marble tiles, flecked with silver veins. He approached a counter, constructed of the same material. A young woman sat behind it. On one wall, a large sign listed the various businesses occupying the building, and the corresponding floor they were situated. Insurance brokers, solicitors, surveyors. Floor 3 – Blue Yonder Enterprises. Impossible to determine from its name the type of business it conducted.

He introduced himself, informed her of his appointment. She gestured to the lift. He thanked her, went in, pressed number 3. The walls of the lift were mirrored. The reflection staring back was of a somewhat haggard man, hollow cheeks, pasty white complexion, shapeless suit hanging from his body. He felt how he looked. Exhausted and desperate.

The lift stopped at level 3. He got out. He emerged into a corridor, at the end of which, a single door with glazed windows. At the side, a metal plate the size of a dinner tray, in which were engraved the words *Blue Yonder Enterprises*.

He went in.

Another reception area. Small, nowhere near as ostentatious as the one on the ground floor. Simple and functional. A plain wooden desk, and behind it, a middle-aged man in a neat suit, studying the open screen of a laptop. Opposite, a couple of chairs.

The man looked up.

"I have an appointment with Mr Grant. My name is Richard Hornbuckle."

"Sure you do," replied the man. "Have a seat."

Hornbuckle sat on one of the chairs. There were no magazines to read. He stared at the far wall, hoping the man at the desk didn't hear the thrum of his heart.

He did not need to wait long. Within five minutes, a door at the end of the room opened. A man appeared. Slim, casually dressed in jeans, open-necked shirt, a navy-blue sports jacket. Sharp inquisitive eyes, which were now fully focused on Hornbuckle.

"You're here to see Peter Grant?" said the man.

Hornbuckle stood.

The man beckoned him to follow.

Hornbuckle was led into an office, as basic as the outside waiting area. The man seated himself behind a desk. Functional, basic. On it, a few sheets of paper, a pen, and not much else. The walls lacked any ornamentation – no pictures, no photos, not even a clock. Plain white. One window, offering a view of a brick wall – the side of the neighbouring building. Hornbuckle sat on a chair on the opposite side of the desk.

The man did not shake hands. He kept his gaze fixed on Hornbuckle.

"My name is Nathan Grant. What can we do for you, Mr Hornbuckle?"

Hornbuckle answered quietly. "I would like to see Peter Grant."

The man called Nathan Grant gave a curt response. "Peter Grant is my uncle. He doesn't do appointments. I handle most of his business affairs. You mentioned on the phone you had a business proposal to discuss?"

Hornbuckle felt ridiculous. His plan was ill-conceived and ill-judged. An impulsive act born from desperation. But he was here. He would see it through.

"It's complicated."

Nathan offered no comment.

Hornbuckle continued: "I was hoping your uncle might lend me some money."

"Do you know my uncle?"

"No."

"Have you tried a bank?"

Hornbuckle nodded.

"I'm afraid we can't be of assistance, Mr Hornbuckle. Lending is not our business." He stood. "I wish you luck."

Hornbuckle mumbled a vague *thank you*, left the office. The man sitting outside ignored him. Hornbuckle left the offices of Blue Yonder Enterprises.

───────

He got a call on his mobile that evening, from a man called Tommy Windle. The conversation was short and to the point – Windle was aware Hornbuckle required a loan. Perhaps Windle could help. A meeting was arranged next morning in the tea room at the windfarm on Eaglesham moor. 10am. Hornbuckle got time off work, feigning illness. He arrived fifteen minutes early. The tea room was empty. No wonder – the morning was heavy with wind and rain. One side was constructed entirely of glass, offering a panoramic view of the moor, and the great white turbines, blades revolving in ponderous cycles. He got coffee, sat. At 10am precisely, a man entered. He was tall, wearing a raincoat, under which a hoodie, the hood drawn over his head, rendering his features indistinct. He surveyed the room, caught sight of Hornbuckle. He approached.

"Mr Hornbuckle?" The voice was low and polite.

"Yes."

The man drew back a chair, seated himself. He removed his hood to reveal a heavy boned face, jutting brow, hair shaved into a bullet-shaped skull.

"My name is Tommy Windle. I might be able to help you."

"Nathan Grant told you about me?"

"I understand you need a loan?"

"Yes," replied Hornbuckle.

"Maybe I can assist."

A girl no older than sixteen appeared at the table – "Can I get you anything?"

Windle tilted his head to a questioning angle – "Double-shot latte?"

"Of course." She looked at Hornbuckle, who was still drinking his first coffee.

"I'm fine," he said. She smiled, went off.

Windle clasped his hands, placed them on the table. Large, thick fingered. A ring on the index finger, and on each of the others, tattooed above the knuckle, a symbol too small for Hornbuckle to recognise.

"How much do you need?" asked Windle.

Hornbuckle had given this question considerable thought. The cost of the operation, approximately forty thousand. There was post-op treatment. At a guess, another fifteen. Then add a little more, just in case.

"Seventy," he replied, trying to keep the quiver from his voice. "Seventy thousand."

Windle's face remained expressionless. Whether he was surprised at the amount was impossible to say. It was like trying to read a chunk of rock.

"You must understand," said Windle, "if we agree to providing you this amount, there are strict terms you must follow. These terms will not be put in writing, and are very simple. First, however, you need to write down my mobile number."

"Yes. Of course." He had a pen in his inside pocket. He had no paper. He used the back of the coffee receipt, left discarded on the table. Windle gave him the number, repeated it. Hornbuckle wrote it down.

"That number," said Windle, "will be your only port of call. You will only speak to me. No one else. You understand?"

"Yes."

"I want you to text me your date of birth, your full address, your place of employment."

"That's all? You don't need anything else. You don't need to know why I need the money?"

Windle stood, looked down at him.

"Three items of information. Date of birth, address, employment. Once we have these, we will make a decision. Then, and only then, will we provide you with the terms of the loan." His demeanour suddenly changed – a broad smile split the big bones of his face. "Don't fancy the weather much. Ruins the hair." He pulled out a five-pound note, left it on the table. He flipped the hood over his head and left the tea room. A second later, the waitress returned with his coffee.

"He had to leave," said Hornbuckle. The waitress shrugged, disinterested, returned to the kitchen area.

Hornbuckle sat, staring at the number he had written down, and wondered if he'd dreamt the encounter. But he hadn't. It was real. And he faced a decision. A crossroads. Continue, or retreat. He had no choice. He texted the information requested, and wondered what the hell would happen next.

He received a text two days later. A meeting at an address in Govanhill, the southside of Glasgow, at 4.30pm, Thursday afternoon. 200 Westmoreland Street. Flat one, up left. He used satnav to find the address, parked opposite an old sandstone tenement block, comprising ten flats. The main common door was locked. He checked the panel on the wall – names and flat positions, each with a buzzer. The only one without a name was one up left. He pushed the button, waited five seconds. The main door clicked open. He entered. The walls were painted pale cream, the stairs wide and solid grey stone, a smooth wooden hand railing on metal balusters running up one side. He climbed to the first landing, got to the door on the left. No name. He rang the bell, waited. The door opened. Tommy Windle stood before him. Dressed, so it seemed, in the same gear he wore at the tea room.

"Hello, Richard."

"Hi."

He followed Windle through to a hallway with nothing in it – bare floorboards, bare walls – and into a living room equally devoid of any ornamentation or furniture, save two chairs opposite each other, and between them, on a low table, a black leather briefcase.

"Sit, please." Hornbuckle did as requested. Windle sat on the other chair.

"You'll be pleased to hear," said Windle, "we're happy to loan you the money. Seventy thousand."

Hornbuckle's heart raced. Here was salvation. And dread. He was poised to enter a new world, radically different from anything he had known. He said nothing.

"The money is in the briefcase," continued Windle. "In fifty-pound notes."

He hesitated. "It's cash?"

Windle reacted with a sudden sardonic laugh. "We don't do bank transfers. Do you wish to count it? Take as long as you want."

Hornbuckle blinked. His mouth felt dry. He nodded. He reached over, clicked open the briefcase. The money was there, in neat little bricks, bound by white elastic bands. He had never seen so much. He glanced at Windle, who was sitting back, arms folded, a secret half smile playing on his lips. Hornbuckle picked out a batch, peeled off the elastic band, counted out one careful note at a time, placing each on the table. He was methodical. After twenty minutes, he confirmed to Windle the money was correct. He put the money back in the briefcase, closed it, turned his attention back to Windle, waited.

"Here are the terms," said Windle. "The funds require to be repaid within six months from now. Plus fifty per cent. I will phone you on the day prior to the repayment, and arrange a meeting place. Repayment must be paid in full. If you fail to repay it, we will impose a penalty of twenty per cent a day."

"That's... rather severe."

Windle carried on as if he hadn't heard. "If, after seven days, you have not paid the debt plus penalties in full, then the situation moves on to a different level."

"What does that mean?"

Windle gave an easy smile. "It means we will not tolerate lack of payment. But you needn't worry, Richard. I'm sure you won't let things reach that stage."

"I'm sure I won't," stammered Hornbuckle.

Windle stood. He stretched his hand out. "Do you agree to these terms, Richard?"

Here was the moment, thought Hornbuckle. He could say no. He could walk out the door. And then what? His wife would die.

He shook hands.

"The contract is sealed," said Windle. "The money is yours. One last thing. It's The Golden Rule."

Hornbuckle waited.

"You never, ever, go to the police."

Hornbuckle mumbled his agreement. He had the money. He felt no elation. No cause for celebration. He had entered a nightmare. He picked up the briefcase and left the flat...

"... but Windle never phoned," said Hornbuckle. His wife had not spoken during his story. Which made it worse. "I used the money to pay for your operation. Used it all. There was no chance I could pay it back. I waited for the day to come. For Windle to contact me, like he said he would. But he never did. The call didn't come."

Her tone was flat when she spoke. "You lied."

"Yes. I lied. But it was for you..."

"Don't!" she snapped. "Don't foist this on me. I had cancer.

Lots of people get cancer. I could have waited. I might have been fine. But you gambled our lives with gangsters. You didn't give me a choice." Her voice cracked with emotion. "You didn't give me a fucking choice!" She took a long shuddering breath, then said, "Was it all bullshit?"

Hornbuckle nodded. His self-disgust had reached a new level.

"I lied about my pension. About my lump sum. It was nowhere near what I told you. The money for the operation came from Windle."

Her voice was back to flat and toneless. "You told me you wanted to sell the house because you wanted a change. A change for both of us. *Something different,* you said. *Something new,* you said. But it wasn't that at all."

"No."

"You wanted to sell the house because you knew you couldn't repay the debt. You wanted to go to the north of Scotland because you thought you would be safe. That no one would find you. You weren't searching for something new. You were running. You wanted to run and hide."

"Run and hide," he repeated in a hollow voice. "Yes. Because I could never repay them, and I knew they would do terrible things." He looked into her eyes, seeking that iota of understanding, and finding nothing. "But he never contacted me. I thought, maybe I had a chance. I thought, I can use the time for us to get away. And they never came looking…"

"Until now."

"Yes."

"They've caught up with us. And now they're going to kill us."

"I don't think so. They're trying to scare us. They want their money. I can maybe reason with them."

"Reason with them? How does that work? We have nothing to reason them with. Sell our home? Because that's all we have."

He tried to straighten his thoughts, but everything was jumbled. "I don't know. It's been five years of nothing. Where have they been? Have they just suddenly realised we're living here? It doesn't add up. I need to talk to Windle. I need to understand why now."

"We need to go to the police," she said. "Tell them everything. Tell them about Tommy Windle. Tell them about his connection to Peter Grant. They'll protect us."

"Nothing can protect us," he said quietly.

"I'm going to phone that young policeman."

"Please!" His voice broke with sudden sharp anguish. "If we go to the police, then there's no going back. Give me one more day."

Her forehead wrinkled into a frown.

"What will you do?"

"I know where Peter Grant lives. I'm going to drive there early tomorrow morning. I'm going to speak to the man. And I'm going to fucking beg him to stop."

She bit her lip. Her mouth quivered. She reached over, embraced him, held him tight.

"I love you," she whispered. "And I'm coming with you."

THIRTY-EIGHT

BLACK HAD DRAGGED the bodies out through the back door of the house, dumped them somewhat unceremoniously against the rear wall. The moonlight cast an oily dark sheen on their blood. Parked close by was an old pickup truck, presumably the mode of transport for the sheriff's buddies. He had returned to the front of the house, had driven the sheriff's car round beside the truck. Hidden to a casual observer. Questions would be asked in time, searches organised, and eventually the discovery made. A bunch of dead bodies. More, if the authorities chose to use initiative, and dig about in the back garden. And then what? Black had allowed himself a frosty grin – suddenly the sleepy shitty little town of Fairview becomes the sensation of the century.

Black got into his car, drove to the Walled City, following the sheriff's directions, which proved to be accurate. Yellowbird Holdings, turning off, following the track road to the stock wire fencing, and then on to the low perimeter wall, and then on through.

He pulled off the track a quarter-mile back, parked, got out. His was the only vehicle. The landscape before him was illuminated by scores of soft glow lamps; dotted in apparently random fashion, low buildings, half hidden by shadow. He made his way past the church, towards the structure the sheriff had described as a fortress. People milled about. Mostly young. Dressed in casual summer wear – jeans, T-shirts, sandals. The air was warm and held the faintest scent of cinnamon. Not unpleasant, he thought. A young woman smiled at him, tanned, flashing white teeth –

"Welcome."

Black nodded.

"You hear to find salvation?"

"I'm here to find Zain," responded Black.

"Cool." She laughed, a soft lilting sound, and sauntered away.

The main doors to the building were thick cast iron, high and broad. Five men approached. Similar in physique to the men who had initially attempted to abduct him. Broad-shouldered, lean hips, moving with unconscious poise, suggesting training and agility.

One spoke, smiling like he was greeting a long-lost friend. "Adam Black? Is that you?"

"Yes."

"Welcome."

"I think there's an echo."

The man disregarded the comment. He and the others had formed a loose circle round him.

"If you'd like to come with us. Zain is expecting you."

"That's very comforting."

They moved as one unit, towards the entrance, Black in the middle, a solitary fish guided by a school of sharks.

One of the men – the one who had spoken – thumped the doors with the palm of his hand. A three-second wait. They rumbled open, pulled from inside.

They entered. The doors were pushed closed. Black stood in a courtyard. The style was almost rustic. The ground was cobbled. In the centre, a circular pond, around which glistened small citrus trees heavy with lemons and oranges. Light was supplied by flaming candles set on silver brackets on the walls, flickering soft yellow. In the pond, a fountain whispered.

Three more men were waiting, each clutching rifles, each pointed at Black. The spokesman approached, searched him, patting arms, torso, legs. Black, on reflex, had come armed, knowing it would prove of little use. The man, within five seconds, discovered his small arsenal of weaponry – the Glock in his inside pocket, the Magnum tucked under his belt, his KA-BAR knife.

"That's not very hospitable," remarked the man, still smiling his glowing smile.

"I'm not the hospitable type," Black remarked back. "I hope you don't take offence."

"I'm sure I won't." He produced a set of handcuffs, clicked them closed round Black's wrists. Black offered no objection. Given the circumstances, objection carried little weight.

Black, now escorted by eight men, was led out of the courtyard, and up a set of stone steps, to a door of the main building. They filed through, three in front, then Black, then five behind, emerging into a large, cathedral-ceilinged reception hall, plush with heavy rugs and paintings and bright tapestries on the walls. In the centre, suspended, a black candelabra, glittering in a confusion of twinkling lights.

"Zain likes his home comforts," said Black.

On either side was a staircase, sweeping up to a top landing. They went up, a careful procession, and reached the upper level. More doors. Not only was it huge, thought Black. It was a labyrinth. Intentional, no doubt.

They got to a corridor, leading to a wide arched wooden door, Gothic style, complete with cast-iron strap hinges and studded iron nails. Each side, sitting, was a guard, rifle on lap.

The man leading the group knocked respectfully, opened the door, and gestured for Black to enter.

"Thank you."

The room was large and well furnished. An armed guard

standing in each corner. On a couch sat a man, blond-haired, pale-skinned. Opposite, on a soft padded seat, a woman. She looked round as Black entered. Shoulder-length hair, red as flame, high aquiline cheekbones, eyes bluish grey, cold as crystal. *Athletic,* thought Black. A sprinter's build.

Unmistakably the girl in the photo. The Colonel's daughter.

The door closed behind him. The lock clicked. Of his entourage, only one remained. The guy who had spoken. He stood a step behind Black, watchful, armed with a pistol.

The man on the couch pointed to a seat adjacent to where the woman sat.

"Please, Adam. May I call you Adam? Take a load off. I'm sure you've had a busy evening."

"Thank you," replied Black. "It's been a tad stressful."

He sat. The woman said nothing, stared at him.

The man clapped his hands. "Introductions. My name is Zain. This young lady is Elizabeth Pembroke…" he switched his focus to Elizabeth, "and this," he said, gesturing to Black, "is the man of the moment. This is Adam Black."

She looked at Black. "Who sent you?"

"Your father."

She shook her head a fraction. "I don't understand this."

Black regarded Zain. "For 'The New Messiah', you look decidedly ordinary. Bordering on pathetic. God needs to up his game, I think."

Zain responded with an easy brush of his hand, as if the comment lacked relevance.

"I've heard so much about you, Adam. A military hero. Do you know Adam's history, Elizabeth? It's a tale… what would you say… of trials and tribulations. Would you care for some champagne?"

"Maybe later," said Black.

"But I don't want to tell your story," continued Zain "It is, I think, for someone else to tell. Someone who has waited many years for this moment."

Black surveyed the man before him. "Then it's not you."

Zain's eyelids took on a languid droop. "Not me?"

"It's not you who has such a keen interest to meet me. And they've tried twice. First, a group of gun-toting hippies tried to bundle me in the back of their car. Then, an overweight sheriff and his friendly pilgrims. But it wasn't you." Black had sudden insight. "You're a front."

He turned to Elizabeth, mind in overdrive. "You were undercover? You tried to infiltrate?"

She glanced at Zain. She spoke as if he weren't there. "FBI. We suspected the little bastard's been using this fucked-up commune to distribute drugs."

Black turned back to Zain. "But you didn't kill her. And I'm not dead. We're here for a reason."

"As I said. Someone has waited a long time to meet you."

"Like a school reunion. I'm getting all nostalgic."

"Not quite," said Zain. "The consequences will be a little more... impactful." He sipped his glass of red wine, placed the glass carefully on the table, sat back, crossed his legs, and said – "He's coming now. He's dying to meet you."

As if on cue, a far door opened.

A man walked into the room.

It took Black five seconds to understand who he was looking at.

And the mystery only deepened.

THIRTY-NINE

THE RENDEZVOUS WAS SET for just after midnight the following night. Prestwick Airport. A cargo plane was due to arrive one hour earlier. A Boeing Dreamlifter. Modified to extend its volume to sixty-five thousand cubic feet, it could carry up to three times more freight. Flying from San Francisco to Dublin, then to Prestwick, then on to Hamburg, and finally Stockholm. Carrying general cargo, ranging from furniture to refrigerators, from pet food to timber. Sixty-five thousand cubic feet. All packaged and crated.

Rom had arranged for a truck to pick up a quantity of goods – crates of South American kidney beans. The truck was supplied courtesy of Jeffrey Ferguson, who still owed interest on the late payments, and who would do anything to avoid a rerun of the crucifixion on his office wall. The plane was to be taxied adjacent to a specific hanger. The freight handler would oversee the crates escorted from the belly of the plane to the consignee. He had been given a hundred thousand in hard cash to be discreet. The crates would be forklifted into the back of the lorry, the lorry would depart, driving to Jeffrey Ferguson's industrial unit in Edinburgh. Then, within the warehouse confines, the crates would be opened, the drugs then transferred to other destinations, to be distributed.

Such was the plan.

Rom ate a leisurely breakfast in his house, which he fixed himself – muesli, a protein shake drink, and some poached eggs on toast. Arlene sat with him, sipping coffee. Also, he had asked Stu Gorman to join him. Gorman had been drinking most of the day before, yet outwardly exhibited no obvious signs of a hangover.

"How was my father?" asked Rom.

"He drank a gallon of whisky," replied Gorman. "But he was still standing when I left him. I don't know how he packs it in."

"A lifetime of practice," said Rom in a dry voice. "He'll live forever."

"He might just do."

"More's the pity." Rom fixed him with a steady gaze. "You're ready for tomorrow night?"

"Of course. Big night. The drugs are flying in."

"This is true," said Rom. "And tonight's an important night as well."

Arlene giggled.

"Is something funny?" said Gorman.

"She's excited," said Rom. He lost his smile. He regarded Arlene. "But you're not going with Stu. It's a one-man job."

The giggling stopped. She frowned into her coffee. "I get to miss the best bits."

He ignored her. He focused his attention on Gorman. "I need this done right."

Gorman looked puzzled. "What is it you want me to do? Your father said we were to relax today…"

Rom slammed his fist on the table. Arlene jumped, spilling her coffee.

"I don't give a fuck what the old bastard said! You understand me?"

Gorman nodded solemnly. "Sure I do, Rom. Sure I do."

"Because you and he are getting awful fucking cozy, playing snooker and drinking fucking shit whisky all afternoon."

"He asked me…"

"I don't give a shit if Jesus fucking Christ asked you. You work for me. You do as I say, because it's me that pays you, and that's the way it is. You understand this concept, Stu?"

"Sure I do, Rom. That's the way it is. That's the way I like it. Me and you." He swallowed, looked at Arlene as if for support. She stared straight ahead, all humour gone.

"Look what you've made me do. Arlene's spilled her coffee. I've spilled some milk." He fixed Gorman a measured stare. "But we don't cry over spilled milk."

"No," said Gorman.

Rom resumed a conversational tone. "Now that we have reminded ourselves how things work, then I would like to repeat, this is a one-man job, which you will not tell anyone about, and which is important to me. And I want it done tonight."

"Okay. Tell me what I have to do."

Rom's smile returned. His temper worked like that. On/off. Like a light switch.

"Listen carefully…"

FORTY

THE MAN who entered the room hadn't changed significantly from the photographs Black and his team had been given ten years ago, in the command compound in Helmand Province. Still, it took time to register. But Black remembered. He was good at recalling faces. It was his speciality. Especially the faces of those he had been ordered to kill. And back then, in those dark days, Bashir Noorzai was top of the list.

The man stood next to the chair where Zain sat, spoke to Black in a voice of hushed pleasure.

"You remember me, Mr Black. I can tell."

"You're hard to forget, despite my best efforts."

"Such a treat to see you here. You can't imagine my sheer joy at meeting you."

"I'm flattered," replied Black. "But please don't feel such joy is reciprocated. It was you who ordered my abduction. The camper-van, the broken wheel, four hippies and a fat guy. An over-elaborate display. It didn't end well. Two cops spoiled your fun."

The man reacted with the faintest of shrugs. "Not everything goes to plan. A mystery. Someone didn't want you to get here. But a minor irritation only. The fact is, you have arrived, and I have the pleasure of your company."

Black allowed a cold smile. "It's funny. When we were given your photograph, we all thought you were ugly. Truly. It was unanimous. Like movie-monster ugly. Seeing you in the flesh, you're much worse. My condolences. Your mother must have been profoundly disappointed."

The man seemed unperturbed by Black's remarks. He made his way to an adjacent couch, sat. Black examined the man before him, seeing a man of middle weight, a squat head – the face wider than high – the nose like a beak and dark of nostril, the mouth wide, thick-lipped. His hair was a glossy black pelt, his skin darkly tanned, and his eyes. Soft dead olive-drab.

"God must be smiling," said the man. He ignored Elizabeth. His concentration was focused entirely on Black. "I have prayed for this moment. And behold!" He clapped his hands lightly. "My wish has been granted."

"Be careful what you wish for," said Black.

"I am always careful. It is a prerequisite of my... occupation. Do you believe in serendipity, Mr Black?"

Black said nothing.

"The gift of finding good things unlooked for. Events, seemingly random, coming together to merge into surprising conclusions. Like Elizabeth coming here. Like her partner betraying her. Like her father using you as leverage. Like you, with your naïve, misguided sense of chivalry, coming here, to this place, to rescue her like the shining knight. The pieces combined make a bigger picture. You understand?"

Elizabeth turned to Black – "What the fuck is he talking about? And who the fuck is he?"

Black sat back. He still couldn't grasp the connection. He answered her –

"Let me tell you who he is. The man sitting opposite is Bashir Noorzai, the man responsible for the biggest and most elaborate heroin trafficking industry in Afghanistan. Known commonly as a drug lord. Distributing heroin globally. A dealer in death and misery. A close ally to the Taliban, who depended on a portion of his income to fund terrorism and slaughter. Otherwise, a glorified drug-dealing fuckbag."

She looked at Noorzai, blinked in puzzlement. "But I thought it was Zain..."

"I suspect he was merely a cover," said Black. "If you came here thinking Zain was the head of the operation, you were looking in the wrong direction."

"Very perceptive," said Noorzai. "Please, tell Elizabeth the rest of the story."

"Why not?" replied Black. "When I was on tour in Afghanistan, I headed a small unit of soldiers whose primary function was to hunt and kill this man. As you can see, we failed. Regrettably." A whisper of a smile played on his lips. "Though there's still time."

Noorzai nodded slowly. "I think, perhaps, time is running short. But please. Allow me my turn. Elizabeth must be curious about... well... about everything."

Black said nothing.

Noorzai turned his head to regard Elizabeth.

"Adam Black. Captain Adam Black. I have made it my business to know as much as I can about him, for reasons which will become clear. He was quite a force, back in the day. A captain in the Special Air Service. The famous *SAS*. As he said, team leader of a small internal unit, specialising in terror and carnage. Set loose by his superiors, to kill. Like a mad dog. We Afghans remember him well, he and his band of assassins. Then they awarded him a medal. The Victoria Cross. And then what? Tragedy. His wife and child murdered. Poor Captain Black." Noorzai's mouth drooped at the corners in exaggerated sadness. "Perhaps it was fate. Perhaps this was the hand of Allah, redressing the balance. And then Captain Black disappears. Goes off-grid. Until now. Until this moment, when he was delivered into my hands."

"My only regret," said Black, "is that we didn't kill you." Soon, he hoped, this thing would make sense.

"March 7th, 2004," said Noorzai. "Does that date mean anything to you?"

"No."

"Elizabeth's father, Colonel Pembroke, arranged a mission. You and your men were dropped deep into the Hindu Kush. The mission was to kill me. Do you remember?"

Black said nothing.

"Of course you do. You were ambushed. Arranged by me. Your men were killed. You survived. You were badly wounded. I understand you died, briefly. But you came back. Like Jesus Christ. The Colonel flew back himself to get you out. A wild night, by all accounts."

Black waited.

"Some of my men were killed that night. In particular, one man."

Close now, thought Black.

"One man," repeated Noorzai. He paused. Black said nothing.

"My brother," whispered Noorzai. "You killed him."

A silence fell.

Black gave a small shrug. "Is that the big reveal? Too bad. For the record, I'm glad he died. One less scumbag fanatic drug dealer to worry about. But there's more, isn't there?"

Noorzai reacted with a thin-lipped smile. "You're a cool one, Mr Black. Yes. There's more. You were betrayed. You and your men."

Black waited. Dread blossomed in his chest. A premonition of something bad.

"The Colonel," said Noorzai, "was working for me."

He turned his gaze to Elizabeth. "Your father. From the very beginning." He paused, perhaps for dramatic effect. He resumed his attention back to Black. "He had been accepting substantial payments for telling me all the army's little secrets. He told me about your men, the mission. He told me about you. Which was how we planned the ambush. When he came back that night with the rescue team, he played the part well, the caring brave commanding officer. All a lie. He thought you would all have been killed. But you lived. And my brother died. And I swore revenge."

Elizabeth stared at Noorzai, at Black. She spoke, her voice brittle. "My father..."

"... is a traitor," finished Black, in a hard flat tone.

"Indeed," said Noorzai. "Isn't it wonderful? And when I discovered his own daughter was here, masquerading as a follower of our 'New Messiah'..."

"You're a fucking liar," spat Elizabeth.

But Black saw the truth in his words. It made sense. But the riddle was still incomplete. Elizabeth, in sudden heated passion, articulated the question in his mind.

"How could you know?" she said, her voice shrill. "How could you know who I was?"

Noorzai sighed. "Greed. It always comes down to greed. Your colleague Jona Lefroy knew who you were. Your Judas. He knew how important that information was. He knew about Mr Black, and that he had killed my brother. And voila! It seemed only logical he should sell you. But his price was too high and look what he got."

"What happened to him?" said Black.

Elizabeth turned, gave him a leaden stare. "They cut his head off."

"Careless," said Black. "Sounds like he had it coming. Though I don't know how he could know about me. Someone must have told him..." He paused, grappling with a disturbing new thought. He experienced a flash of insight. "Unless..."

Noorzai reacted with an easy wave of his hand. "Enough. It hardly matters. What does matter, is that you are here. Both of you. In the 'Walled City'. This time tomorrow, Mr Black, you will be somewhere very different. A homecoming. Back in Afghanistan. Where I will perform on you terrors you cannot begin to understand. And you, Elizabeth..." Again, the sad droop of his mouth. "You understand, I can't allow you to leave."

Elizabeth motioned with her foot, tapping it gently on the floor. Black caught the action from the side of his eye – there, under her seat, almost invisible, the edge of a blade. An axe, Black realised. He twitched his head, an almost imperceptible nod, hoping she would understand.

Distraction.

He stood up, suddenly. The men in the room bristled at the movement. Five men. One close. Four others at each corner, who now advanced towards him. All armed with rifles. The one closest spoke, his tone harsh. "Sit the fuck down." He raised his rifle to emphasise the point, the muzzle two feet from Black's head. Black had one distinct advantage. Noorzai didn't want him dead. And when it came down to the shit and sweat of intimate close combat, rifles were no damned good.

Zain, silent up to this point, laughed suddenly. "Where are you going!" There's nowhere to run."

"I'm not running," said Black. He grinned, flicked a glance at Elizabeth –

"I'm doing what I do best."

FORTY-ONE

DAY 4

AS ROM WAS DOWNING his breakfast protein shake, Hornbuckle and Elspeth were beginning the journey south. It was 7am, Thursday morning. They spoke little. The radio was on, but Hornbuckle hardly heard it. They took turns driving. They stopped halfway, and got some coffee and a bite to eat. They arrived in Glasgow at 1pm. He knew where to go. The details were ingrained into his memory cells. *Like a cancer*, he thought.

The office building where he had met Nathan Grant – nephew of Peter Grant – had not changed. It still possessed its architectural elegance and grandeur. The main entrance was as before. He and his wife went in. The concierge met them – the same individual. He gestured politely to the reception area. Again, nothing had changed. Same marble walls, same reception desk. Different receptionist, however. Hornbuckle was good at remembering faces, and he didn't remember hers. She looked up, smiled. Hornbuckle was in no mood for smiling back.

"I would like to see Nathan Grant," he said. "I don't have an appointment. But I need to see him. It's urgent."

The receptionist's brow furrowed in puzzlement. "Nathan Grant?"

"Yes."

"Do you know which office he works with?"

Now it was Hornbuckle's turn to display puzzlement. He pointed up to a sign on the wall. "Sure…" He stopped short. His eyes roved the list of names, and their corresponding floors. Floor 3. Blue Yonder was absent. Replaced by a new company. JK Radcliff. Commercial Surveyors.

"Where is Blue Yonder?" he asked.

The receptionist looked from Hornbuckle, to his wife, back to Hornbuckle.

"I can't say I've heard of them," she replied, hesitating. "Maybe they were here before I started?"

The concierge, standing at the entrance to the reception hall, stepped forward. He was possibly in his late sixties, a round owlish face, wispy grey hair, eyes enlarged by silver-framed Coke bottle glasses.

"Apologies for interrupting," he said, his tone quietly respectful. "I couldn't help overhearing you. You're looking for Blue Yonder?"

Hornbuckle appraised the man. "Yes. I was here, about five years ago."

The concierge nodded. "That would be right, sir. But they upped and left. Very sudden it was. Literally one day they were here, next they weren't. The furniture and office equipment were taken away, and the place was left vacant. Their name was removed. About a month later, the surveyors took occupancy. I never saw Mr Grant again, nor any of his staff."

Hornbuckle was perplexed. "They just disappeared?"

"That's about right, sir."

"And you don't know what happened to them?"

The concierge leaned closer, like a conspirator. "There're facts, and there're rumours, you understand. Who's to know?"

"Who's to know what?"

"It was in the papers. Front page stuff. Peter Grant – the multimillionaire – who owned the company."

"He was in the papers?"

"Why yes, sir. It happened up north, in his mansion in the mountains. No one knows what really went on. But I reckon it was hushed up."

Hornbuckle's perplexity was fast becoming frustration.

"What happened up north? What was hushed up?"

"Don't you know, sir?"

"No, I don't."

"Peter Grant was killed."

———————

They left the building, and sat at a bench on George Square. It was late afternoon, the sun hidden behind a straggling trail of grey cloud. The concierge was unable to provide further information, except hints and gossip about Peter Grant being connected to a Glasgow crime family, which was of little use to Hornbuckle. He searched Peter Grant on his mobile phone, and there it all was, in typically lurid detail. Death in the Scottish Highlands. A boating accident on a remote loch. Questions raised, but none answered, only opinion and hypothesis. But the implication was clear – it was no accident.

"What does this mean?" said Elspeth. Her face was pale and tired in the grey light.

"I know where he lived," said Hornbuckle. "We'll go there. Maybe I can find someone. Talk to someone. Maybe Nathan lives there. He seemed a reasonable man. Maybe I can plead with him."

"Plead," she echoed. "You've been to this man's house? This *Peter Grant?*"

He gave a sour laugh. "Not quite. I didn't get past the front gate."

She said nothing. He took her hand. It was small and cold. "I promise this will stop."

Her lip quivered. He thought his heart would burst. "These people are animals," she said quietly. "Maybe it won't stop, until..."

He squeezed her fingers gently. "It *will* stop. And if I can't reason with them, then I promise, I'll go to the police. I'll phone Sergeant Starling and tell him everything."

She said nothing. The square wasn't busy. People, leaving somewhere, going somewhere, thinking normal thoughts, doing normal things. What normal people do. Unlike himself. Indebted to a dead gangster, planning to visit his domain, to beg his family for the nightmare to end. He was an aberration, and deserved all he got.

"Nathan will see sense," he said, more to himself. "Once he knows why I did it."

She gave him a side glance, her expression unreadable, but said nothing.

He remembered where Peter Grant lived. The events surrounding the affair, from the minute Peter Grant walked into the warm little pub in Eaglesham, to the second Hornbuckle struck the deal with the man called Tommy Windle in a shithole flat in the south of Glasgow – all these events were scorched into his brain, embedding details never to be forgotten.

An hour later they reached his mansion. He parked the car outside the high gates. They were half open. They both stared at the building, set back a hundred yards from the pavement. Unlike the offices in the city centre, this place had changed. Ravaged, thought Hornbuckle. The windows were boarded up. A section of guttering hung broken, slanting to the ground like a frown, the walls splattered with graffiti. Weeds grew in the driveway, like the scribblings of a child; the front grass was knee-high.

"I don't think anyone's in," remarked Hornbuckle in sour amusement. "Let's see."

They entered via the open gates, approached the house. The closer they got, the worse it looked. A man appeared from the side, presumably from the back area. Wearing a suit, a tie, looking flustered. His face was flushed, his collar was loose, his tie askew.

He waved to them. "Everything's fine," he shouted. He half jogged towards them. "Someone reported kids in the back garden. But it's all fine." He looked at them, as if expecting an answer. "You here to take pictures?"

Hornbuckle and his wife glanced at each other.

The man sensed their uncertainty. "You're from the auction house?"

"No," said Hornbuckle. "We're... friends of the owner."

The man gave them a blank look. "Oh."

"We heard he died."

The man pulled out a paper tissue from his pocket, dabbed his forehead. "Sorry," he said. "I've been rummaging through the grounds all afternoon. I thought you were here to take the pictures. She's going up for auction next month. No one wants to buy her. Been on the market for years." He turned, gazed at the building. "Lucky if we get a million. Though the land might fetch something." He turned back to them. "Where's my manners. I'm Frank Joss. I work with the lawyers winding up Mr Grant's estate." He grinned. "I'm the man they call to make inventories and checklists and do admin. All the exciting stuff. Glorified stocktaker."

"The house is being sold?" said Hornbuckle, in an effort to keep the dialogue going.

Joss shrugged. "It has to go. Death duties don't disappear. That's been five years. HMRC would backdate Jesus Christ himself, if they had an angle. You were friends of Peter Grant?"

Hornbuckle had to think on his feet. "We've been out of the country. Thought we would look in. Maybe speak to a member of the family. To catch up. To pay respects. Maybe speak to Nathan?"

"You won't find anyone here," said Joss. He assumed an air of concentration. "I don't know anyone called Nathan. Peter Grant has a sister, if I recall. Have you spoken to her?"

Hornbuckle hesitated. "I can't remember her name. It's been a while. Would you know how I can reach her?"

He smiled. "Give me your mobile number. I'll contact the office and text you the details. What did you say your names were?"

"John Smith," said Hornbuckle. "And this is my wife, Wilma."

They got back into the car. For the first time in as long as he could remember, Hornbuckle detected the ghost of a smile on his wife's face.

"Wilma? Really?"

"I like it. You look like a 'Wilma'."

"You look like a 'Fred'."

He chuckled. "You're showing your age."

They made their way back to the city centre, somewhat aimlessly, hoping for the text. Within thirty minutes, the text came. Name, address. Susan Grant. 64 Cherrytree Road.

Hornbuckle logged it into the satnav. Only four miles from where they were. He switched direction, headed for the house of Susan Grant.

Cherrytree Road was in the east end of Glasgow, a quarter of a mile from Parkhead football grounds. A long straight street, comprising rows on either side of white, flat-roofed, roughcast cubes, each cube containing four flats. Two on the ground, two upper. They got to 64. Lower flat. A trimmed hedge. The path to the front door was clean, well maintained, as was the tiny front garden. They got out of the car, made their way in. He rang the doorbell. Inside, he heard movement. The pad of footsteps. An image appeared through the bevelled glass. The door opened. A woman stood before them – sharp-faced, sunken cheeks, dark inquisitive eyes, hair a mass of black roiling curls, a startling contrast to her parchment-pale skin. Wedged between her fingers was a lit cigarette. She wore a long black skirt, a pale-blue blouse, the colours accentuating her thin physique. Witch-like, thought Hornbuckle.

She said nothing. She stared at them with disconcerting intensity.

Hornbuckle gave a tremulous smile. "We're looking for Susan Grant?"

She responded. Her voice was low, like a growl.

"Who's looking? You the police?" Her eyes narrowed. "You don't look like cops."

"No. We're looking for Nathan Grant." He recognised the voice. The same woman who had answered when he'd phoned Tommy Windle's number.

She raised an eyebrow. "Why you looking for him?"

"You know him?"

"I asked you a question."

"I... we need to talk."

"What about?"

Not for the first time, he felt his frustration build.

"Please. Can we come in?"

She took a deep drag, exhaled two streams of smoke through her nose, flicked ash onto the steps.

"Okay."

She turned, went inside. They closed the door behind them and followed her through into a small living room. Basic. The air was heavy with the smell of cigarettes. A couch, two chairs, a coffee table, upon which, an ashtray formed from a lump of pink glass. Beside it, an open book, face down, and a packet of cigarettes. Marlboro Reds. In a corner, a television, which she turned off. She sat on one of the chairs. Hornbuckle and his wife sat on the couch opposite.

She was blunt in her questioning. Pleasantries were ignored.

"What is it you want to speak to Nathan about?"

"It was you," said Hornbuckle. "When I phoned. You answered."

"What of it?"

"Are you connected to the man I was trying to speak to?"

"The man you wanted to speak to was Tommy Windle." She leaned over, stubbed the cigarette out in the ashtray. "Tommy Windle was my husband."

Hornbuckle waited, said nothing. There was more to come.

"Tommy Windle is dead."

Hornbuckle and his wife exchanged glances.

"I'm sorry," said Elspeth.

Susan reacted with a wheezy cackle. "Don't be. I hated him. When I heard he died, I went out and got drunk. Not to commiserate. To fucking celebrate. He was a bastard, through and through. So don't be sorry. I'm not."

"Can you arrange for us to talk to Nathan?" said Hornbuckle.

"Why do you want to talk to him?"

"It's… a business arrangement I'm trying to sort out."

Her lips curved upwards; her teeth were nicotine coated.

"Business arrangement," she repeated. She stretched across, picked up the packet of cigarettes, teased one out. She reached into a pocket in her skirt, pulled out a cheap plastic lighter, lit up. She took a deep inhalation. Smoke coiled around her. She sat back, inspected them through heavy-lidded eyes.

"You really want to talk to him?"

"Yes."

"Then you'll need to be Jesus fucking Christ, and raise him from the dead."

Hornbuckle was shocked. "They're all dead?"

The same cackle. "Sure they are. But I guess they had it coming. My brother was Peter Grant. Millionaire businessman. But everyone knew what he was. A fucking gangster. A pyscho. I never wanted any part of it. Don't care what you say. But my husband did. Tommy craved the high life. Look where it got them.

But in their line of work, there's no retirement. Just death. As I said, I guess they had it coming."

"And Nathan?" ventured Hornbuckle.

She took another deep drag.

"You really don't know?" she replied.

"Know what?"

She nodded slowly, as if weighing up her next sentence.

"Five years ago. When hell came calling. Peter owned a big house in the mountains up north. He and Nathan and a whole lot of others were there. A guy had crossed my brother – and no one ever crossed Peter Grant." In the nicotine haze, her eyes glittered. "Everybody was summoned. Don't ask me what they were doing. But it was bad stuff. They'd captured the guy, and taken him there. Not to enjoy the Scottish scenery, I think." Another wheezy laugh. "Far from it."

Another drag. She suddenly erupted into a coughing fit. From the same pocket, she took out a paper tissue, used it to cover her mouth. Ten seconds later, the coughing subsided, but the rattling in her lungs continued. She tucked the tissue back in her pocket.

"Emphysema," she explained. "They said I should give up those cancer sticks. But I say, fuck 'em. They're all I've got."

Hornbuckle remained silent.

She continued: "As I said, hell came calling. The night they brought the guy to the big house, they all died. Killed. Peter, Tommy, Nathan. All the men. The house was burned to the ground. They were killed by one man. Seemed like they'd bitten off more than they could chew. And my brother could chew a big fucking mouthful."

Elspeth spoke up. "They were killed by one man?"

"The cops kept quiet. The Peter Grant crime family was destroyed in one sweep. Case closed. The guy had done them a massive favour." She shrugged. "Done everyone a favour."

"They're all dead," said Hornbuckle to himself. The implications only deepened the mystery. "Who was this man?"

She flicked ash into the pink-glass ashtray.

"The devil himself," she replied. There was no humour in her voice. "Tommy told me all about the guy. Said he was an ex-soldier. SAS. Said he was a handful, but they had him, and he was gonna pay big style. Seemed like Tommy paid instead. Said the guy was a fucking stone-cold killer."

Hornbuckle waited.

"He told me his name," she said.

"Yes?"

"He said his name was Adam Black."

She saw them out, during which time, she had lit up another Marlboro Red.

"You said you had a business arrangement. Looks like any arrangement you had with the Grant family is dead in the grave. Looks like you might be a lucky man."

He looked up into the sky. He felt spots of rain. Clouds had thickened. He regarded Susan Grant, whose brother and husband were dead, and who held no sorrow. "Adam Black. Do you know what happened to him?"

"Could be dead, for all I know. But I don't think so."

"How do you know?"

That cackling laugh – "The devil never dies."

They got into the car, drove off. Something to eat first, then the long haul back to Thurso.

"It makes sense," he said. "Why I was never chased for the money. Five years ago. About the time I met Tommy Windle. All that must have been going on in the background. Before they got round to collecting it, they were all killed."

"By the man called Adam Black."

He drove in silence for a further ten miles, then said – "I think I know who he is."

She looked at him askance.

"A man comes into the shop every weekend. He buys a specific newspaper. The *London Times*. He seems... different."

She shook her head disparagingly. "You're kidding. There's a million 'Adam Blacks'."

"Maybe," he said. "But like I said. He's different."

"How different?"

He thought about it. About the incident in the shop only a few days ago. How Adam Black had handled himself. He groped for the right words.

"I don't how to put it. He has a presence." He found the right word. "He's formidable."

Another silence fell. Then Elspeth said – "You think this Adam Black might be mixed up in all this?"

"I don't know. The whole thing's crazy. It might not even be the same guy."

"What are we going to do? If it isn't Peter Grant or Tommy Windle that's doing this, then who?"

But Hornbuckle had no answers. Maybe the stranger who came into his shop had the answers. Maybe not. He didn't know. He was floundering in the dark.

Time passed. They stopped for a break. A coffee and a cake. Hornbuckle said he would keep driving. Darkness fell. It was 10.30pm, and they were a hundred miles from Thurso, when his mobile buzzed, and they got the call.

And their world caved in.

FORTY-TWO

SHE UNDERSTOOD. It was all down to timing. And distraction. Black got up from his chair. His wrists were handcuffed, but at the front, not behind his back, thus providing a degree of mobility. He flicked another knowing look at her.

Then struck.

She watched, in those first five seconds. Black moved with agility and purpose. He spun, leapt over the back of the chair, to the nearest gunman, grabbing his rifle, jerking it up to the ceiling, simultaneously rendering a ferocious headbutt, forehead slamming the bridge of the nose. The man staggered back, grappling with Black, still clutching the rifle. Black was relentless, head pounding the other's face. The guards rushed forward, reluctant to shoot, poised rather to use their weapons as clubs.

Distraction. She took her chance. Noorzai was nearest, sitting opposite. She swept up the axe from the floor, and in two strides was on the table and across, scattering bottles and glasses. Noorzai, surprised, made to rise from the couch. She was on him in less than two seconds, raising her knee, buffeting his chest, forcing him back down, she remaining on top. He tried to wrestle her away. She brought the axe to his throat, the blade was needle sharp.

"Don't fucking move..." she hissed, "... or I'll slice your fucking head off."

She felt his body go limp. She adjusted her position, now sitting next to Noorzai, close up, facing Black and his assailants, one arm gripped around Noorzai's neck in a semi-headlock, the other hand pressing the axe at his throat.

Movement stopped. She was the focal point of the room. She made a curt gesture with her head – *back off*. The men surrounding Black stepped away. Black disengaged his hold on the rifle. The man he had attacked lurched back, disoriented, to collapse on his knees, nose and cheeks rendered to pulp.

"Glad I have everyone's attention," said Elizabeth. She kept her eyes on the men before her. Black's plan, whether intentional or not, had concentrated the guards together into a manageable space, thus giving her greater control.

"Drop your weapons. Please."

They were uncertain. Zain, sitting on an adjacent chair, was rigid, face ashen. She had chosen the right man. Noorzai was the leader, Zain just another guy on the payroll. And she could tell Zain was scared, because if his boss died, who would pay the bills?

"I won't ask again."

Noorzai, despite his situation, appeared to remain composed. "You'll not kill me," he said. She could sense the axe blade roll minutely back and forth with every syllable. "What then, Elizabeth? You'll have no leverage, and my men will kill you and Adam, and what will that achieve?"

"Who said anything about kill?" In one quick motion, she tilted the axe, sliced off a wedge of his chin, down to the bone, adjusted the axe back to his throat. Noorzai gasped. She held him tight, keeping the blade hard to his skin. "Next time, I'll cut four inches off your throat. Then we'll see what that achieves." She focused back on the men, raised her voice. "Now drop the fucking weapons!"

"Do it!" Noorzai's voice was shrill, composure vanished.

Blood pulsed from the gouge in his face, wetting the blade, wetting her fingers. She tightened her grip.

The men, showing some hesitation, placed their rifles on the floor. Black immediately approached the nearest to him, raised his wrists. "If you don't mind."

The man looked at Noorzai for instruction, who responded immediately. "Free him."

The man pulled a small key from his jeans pocket, unlocked the handcuffs. Black picked up two of the rifles, went to Elizabeth, handed her one. She tossed the axe to one side, stood, pointed the rifle at Noorzai.

"Good thinking," she said to Black.

"And you," replied Black. "Dab hand with an axe." He turned his attention to the group of men, standing in a loose group. His rifle, waist high, was pointed in their general direction. "Everyone on their knees, hands behind your heads." More hesitation. More looks of guidance towards Noorzai.

"You don't need to worry about him," said Elizabeth. She had positioned the barrel of the rifle hard up against the side of his neck. "Concentrate on not getting shot. That's the best advice I can give."

"Do as he says!" snapped Noorzai. His face glistened. The languid pose had evaporated. She saw before her just another terrified drug dealer, desperate to survive. The men complied, grudgingly.

Black approached. He picked up the remaining rifles, dropped them in a corner. One of the guards had a knife sheathed to his trouser belt. Black relieved him of it, buckled it to his own belt. He focused on Zain. He gestured to a far door, from which Noorzai had entered. "I'm assuming that's another way out?"

Zain nodded eagerly. "It leads down to a small courtyard. There's a back door. It's locked. There's no guards." He pointed to one of the kneeling men. "Rosco. He has the keys."

Black tilted his head politely. "Thank you."

Rosco was closest to Black. Heavily muscled, deep torso, twin buttresses of ropy sinew expanded up to support his jaw, his head seeming narrower than the neck. Unlike his colleagues, his scalp was shaved to the bone, revealing a patchwork of scars and rippled skin. His expression was one more of minor inconvenience than fear.

Elizabeth sensed an edge, a motion. The man shifted suddenly, hand reaching down behind him, to the waistband of his jeans. He drew it round, a pistol in his left hand. She shouted, to warn. There was no need. Black shot him in the head, and then, in rapid succession, shot the others. Now, five dead men lay on the floor.

"Jesus," she muttered. "You go the whole nine yards."

Black said nothing. He rifled through the pockets of the man called Rosco, found a set of keys. The gunshots had alerted the guards outside. There was a hard knocking at the door.

"We don't have much time," said Black. Next to her, Noorzai was still as stone. Zain was more animated. The shocking violence appeared to have provided him with renewed focus.

"I never wanted this to happen!" His voice had sharpened to a wheedling whine. "I just front things, you understand? I never wanted you killed, I swear. I do what I'm told."

"I didn't think Messiahs took orders," said Black. He looked at Elizabeth. "We need to go. We need him." He cocked his head at Zain. Then he nodded at Noorzai. "Him, however, we don't need."

She took a breath. The knocking at the door grew more urgent. Men were shouting.

"He's why I'm here. I need to bring him. Make him accountable for his crimes."

Black gave her a smouldering gaze.

"Listen, Elizabeth. He's a liability. If we take him, they will not stop while he's alive. If we kill him now, his goons get upset, posture a bit, a bit of road rage, but the motivation's gone. The biggest problem they'll have is wondering where they get their next pay cheque from. And then they'll be fighting each other over who takes charge of the business."

As Black spoke, Noorzai's pinpoint eyes darted from Black to Elizabeth to Black, like he was watching a tennis match. He spoke suddenly, voice a hoarse croak –

"Five million dollars each. I can do the transfer right now. Two minutes. I'll tell my men to back off. You go your way. We all get to live. You become rich in the process." He licked his lips. The guy was bargaining for his life with the only thing he had. Money.

Elizabeth regarded him, hesitated, said, "You killed my partner. You cut off his damned head. You need to pay for what you did." She turned to Black. "He needs to go to prison."

The shouting outside escalated.

"What will happen then?" responded Black, an edge to his voice. "You think a scumbag like this forgets? Your life won't be your own. From prison, he will seek to destroy you, and everything about you. Psychopaths do not forget. We keep him alive, this whole thing stays alive. We kill him now, then it ends. You know this, Elizabeth! We need to leave! He'll only slow us down."

"Ten million," rasped Noorzai. "Don't listen to..."

"Fair point, Black," she said. She adjusted the rifle, shot Noorzai through the head. Black followed up, shooting him twice in the chest. "Making sure."

They left the room by the other exit, Black grabbing Zain by the scruff of the neck.

"Don't kill me! I want to help."

"Shut up," said Black and Elizabeth in unison.

Black used one of the keys to lock the door. They emerged onto a concrete landing. At the end, a stairway. From the room they had just left, the unmistakable sounds of gunfire, indicating the other door had just been blown open.

They raced down the stairs, half-dragging Zain with them. At the bottom, another short passage and a metal door. Black tried one key, then another. It was taking too long. He pressed the nozzle of the rifle against the handle, fired. The hall echoed with a tinny clang. The door bounced open. They were in a courtyard.

Featureless. A flat asphalt square, high walls on either side. At one end, an arched space, leading out into the open area, and the general commune. No guards.

"That's the way," gasped Zain. "Please. I've shown you. Don't kill me."

They made their way across the flat ground in a half trot, half crouch. Life continued undisturbed. People milled about, groups chatted, despite the lateness. Campfires dotted the landscape. In the distance, buildings wreathed in shadow.

"What now?"

Behind them, a muffled boom. The second door being blown open. She reckoned they had maybe twenty seconds.

"Time to hear The New Messiah," replied Black, and despite their situation, he grinned a wolfish grin, and for the hundredth time, she wondered about this man, Adam Black.

FORTY-THREE

THURSDAY EVENING.

THEY DROVE the last hundred miles in virtual silence. The caller had been the young policeman, Sergeant Starling. He had relayed his message; they had responded in disbelief. It seemed to Hornbuckle that time was suspended. That he felt a disconnect. That the news he had been given could not possibly relate to him. That this sort of thing happened to other people.

His wife had cried. Soft tears. Tears of someone who knew it didn't matter whether she cried or not, because it wouldn't make one iota of difference. Tears of quiet desperation, he thought.

His mind churned. The overwhelming question – who the hell was doing this? The Grant family, and all connected to them, were dead. There was no one left to seek redress over the unpaid debt. Again, his thoughts veered towards the man called Adam Black. There was a connection. Perhaps a coincidence. The guy who came into his shop once a week might not even be the same person. Just a guy who bought the *London Times*. But what if…?

None of it made sense.

"What are we going to do?"

"I don't know," he heard himself reply. Ashamed. He understood the implication behind the question. She knew the police couldn't help. And she knew there was no answer. And he felt pathetic. And the old feeling of self-loathing bubbled up inside him.

They didn't speak again for the rest of the journey.

They got to Thurso. They didn't go home. He wanted to drop her off at the house. She had insisted. She wanted to see it.

He drove straight to the shop. It was late, but despite the hour, a crowd had gathered. He couldn't park within fifty yards. The police had cordoned off a section of the road. He found a place. They got out and made their way slowly. Suddenly, she clutched his hand, held it tight.

Two police cars, and a fire engine. The fire had been extinguished. Smoke coiled lazily up into the night sky. The air was suffused with the smell of incinerated wood and brick and plastic. Strangely, it was not unpleasant. A portion of the roof had collapsed, parts of its framework exposed, like a corpse burnt to the bones. The front window had shattered to non-existence, the interior blackened, the stock melted to ash.

The shop was destroyed.

Starling was there, along with two other policemen. He spotted them, and immediately went over.

"I'm so sorry," he said.

Hornbuckle spoke in a dreary monotone. "What happened?"

"I got a call about two hours ago. Someone passing saw a blaze from inside. By the time we got here, it had spread…he gestured helplessly at the ruin,"… to that. There was nothing we could do."

"Did anyone see…?" asked Elspeth.

Starling shook his head, spoke before she finished – "Nothing. It's too early to say. It could have been anything. An electrical fault, maybe. Or…"

"Or not," said Hornbuckle.

The policeman spoke solemnly. "If this is arson, and if this is connected to the recent threats you've been receiving, then the problem's escalated. Until the fire department investigate this, we won't know for sure."

"We fucking know!" said Elspeth. Her voice shook, her anguish vibrant and raw. It cut his heart, deep as any blade. *This is killing her,* he thought. *And it's killing me.* "You don't have to be a fucking rocket scientist to figure this one out!" She kept her eyes locked on Starling, daring him to disagree. He answered softly, in conciliatory tones.

"I've spoken to my superiors. We're taking this very seriously. We'll have a policeman outside your house 24/7, until we have a grip on what's going on."

"We can't live like this," she said. "Living in fear. And you can't give us protection forever."

Starling didn't respond. What could he say? thought Hornbuckle. She spoke the truth.

A sudden noise split the air. A crack of timber, a thunderous rumble of great weight shifting. The remains of the roof had given way, collapsing to the floor, wafting a fresh plume of thick smoke into the sky. The fire crew waved people further back. But there was little need. His shop was hollow and dead. It had given its last.

"Who the fuck is doing this," he muttered.

"There's no point in you being here," said Starling. "You should get back home. I'll follow you, and get you safely in."

"And then what!" snapped Elspeth. "A police escort every time we leave the house! If we go to the shops, do we come back alive! If I go to work, will they kill me in the fucking classroom!" She gasped. Her shoulders trembled. "I'm... sorry." Like the shop, she caved. "It's just... impossible to comprehend."

"Let's go home," said Hornbuckle gently. He held her close. "There's nothing for us here."

They went back to the car, drove to their little house in the country. Starling followed them. Hornbuckle parked in the driveway, Starling parked on the road at the front. They made their way to the door. As they approached, the outside light beamed on automatically, sensitive to movement. His heart leapt to his throat – nailed into the wood was an envelope. Starling came up the path behind them. Carefully, he pulled the envelope free. The envelope wasn't sealed. He teased the contents out, producing a single folded sheet of A4-sized paper. He glanced at them, opened it out, holding it at diagonal corners with the tips of his fingers.

He studied it for ten seconds, looked at Hornbuckle and his wife, then turned it so they could read what it said.

NOTHING LIKE A NICE FIRE TO COZY YOUR TOES.
CATCH UP SOON FOR THE BIG REVEAL.
STAY SAFE.

Hornbuckle looked at Starling, and said, "I don't think you need to wait for the fire department."

FORTY-FOUR

BLACK, jacket draped over his hand, had the rifle pressed against the small of Zain's back. Elizabeth was at Zain's side, arm interlocked. They approached a group of eight young men and women, involved in quiet conversation, sitting on long benches – rough, carved from wooden logs, positioned round a metal firepit. Flames flickered and crackled.

Black leaned close, whispered in Zain's ear. "Tell your flock God's spoken from on high. Play your part, do what you do, and you might get to live. Otherwise, I'll put a bullet in your spine."

Zain understood. His lips stretched into a beaming smile. He raised a welcoming hand. Black was impressed.

"Ring the bell!" he shouted. His voice had changed. Strong and confident. A voice to be listened to. A proclamation. *A true performer*, thought Black.

The group turned, jumped up, faces a combination of joy and confusion.

"Zain," they muttered, almost in unison. "It's Zain."

"I have a message! Ring the bell! Ring the bell! Tell others! Tell everyone! I have a message!" One of the group – a young man still probably in his teens – sprang away, sloping into the night, fast as a deer. Others now approached.

"To the church!" shouted Zain. "Ring the bell! I have a message! Sent to me in the night! Ring the bell!"

Within five seconds, close by, a bell clanged, like the sound of an old-fashioned janitor's school bell, then followed by another, a little further away, and then another, until the clamour of ringing bells filled the night.

More had arrived. They moved quickly, a throng of maybe forty or fifty people now clustered round them, heading towards the church. All the time, Zain repeated the same words – "I have a message, children. A message to give you." And all the time, Black stayed close, rifle angled discreetly into Zain's back. He glanced round. Through the crowd he glimpsed six men, bristling with sinister intent, following at a short distance, weapons hidden.

They approached the church, impressive in the gloom, the spire illuminated by coloured globes and twinkling net lighting. The entrance was a large arched double door at the top of five wooden steps, with architraves of burnished oak and black iron hinges. Gathered there were hundreds of people, and more were flocking towards it, some carrying flaming torches.

The men and women around and behind them began to chant – *Zain, Messiah! Zain, Messiah!*

Black looked back again – the six goons following were lost from view. They reached the steps. People pressed close. Black flicked a glance at Elizabeth. She disengaged from Zain, just as he began to climb the stairs. She and Black melted into the crowd, weaving and dodging.

Black had left his car a short distance away. He hoped it was still there, otherwise it was a long and fraught walk back to town. The crowds still came on, thick and fast, and everywhere, the night reverberated with the sound of clanging bells and repeated chanting.

He saw the car. They drew nearer. He spied two figures, out of place amongst the people heading towards the church. Leaning against the bonnet. One was smoking. Guards, assumed Black.

Perhaps stationed there as soon as Black's initial arrival was public. Their posture and apparent lack of concern suggested they hadn't yet been contacted by the others about Black's escape. Or perhaps they were just lazy. Or perhaps anything. Black and Elizabeth were heading towards them, against the tide of people. As such, they would be easily spotted, which meant they would have to veer in a wide circle around and behind the vehicle, then approach it from behind, and catch them unawares. Black felt a prickle of tension. He glanced behind. They were undoubtedly still being followed by those who sought revenge for the death of their leader. For now, the crowds had formed a screen. Soon, all would change. Time was running short.

He nodded towards his car. "You see them?"

"That's your car?" responded Elizabeth. "Must be special. Looks like you've got a couple of valets."

"Not that special." As he neared, he noticed a rifle resting on the bonnet. "We go round and back."

"If we shoot them, we'll cause a frenzy. And you'll give them our position."

"They know our position already. It's just a matter of time before they get here. And who said anything about shooting? But I could do with your assistance."

FORTY-FIVE

ELIZABETH, bumping and jostling with those swarming to the church, emerged to stand before the car, hands raised. "I'm here," she said simply.

The two men, surprised, became instantly alert. The one smoking flicked his cigarette to the ground, snatched up the rifle, kept it pointed to the ground to avoid attention. The other pulled a pistol from a holster under his jacket, and like his friend, kept it from view. The one with the rifle was stocky, hair bristle-short, black beard. The other was lean, arms all veined muscle, hawkish features, long somewhat greasy hair tucked behind his ears. Under his right eye, a small red crucifix tattoo.

"You're the woman?" he said.

"I sure hope so," said Elizabeth.

"Don't fucking move."

He reached into an inside pocket, took out his mobile, spoke, all the time eyes concentrated on her.

"She's here. Just handed herself in." A pause, as he listened. Then he snapped his focus back on Elizabeth. "Where's the guy?"

"The guy?"

"Adam Black."

She gave a miniscule shrug. "Think he got shot. I don't care about him. Can you take me out of here? I can pay."

He turned his attention back to the phone. "Says he got shot." Another pause, listening. "Here?" he said. Another pause. With deliberation, he put the mobile back in his pocket, cast a meaningful glance to his partner.

"There's others coming," he said. "No way you're leaving, little lady." He nudged his pistol towards a low wooden structure twenty yards off. "Let's go."

"I can pay each of you a million dollars."

"Sure you can. Move it."

"Please."

"Move it. Or I shoot you here."

She made her way to the building, the two men following. The building was timber-framed, flat-roofed, the size of a double garage. No windows. The door was locked by a straight metal bolt. The other guy – the one with the rifle – slid it open. He flicked a switch. A single strip light flickered into life. The place was a storeroom. Bags of rice and grain, crates of tinned food, sacks of potatoes and vegetables, shelves stocked with random stuff. Bottles of water, toilet rolls, cleaning fluids, plastic buckets.

They entered. The man with the rifle hovered at the doorway. "Make it quick," he muttered, closed the door, waited outside. The other – Red Tattoo – held his handgun – a .357 Magnum revolver – in a careless manner, somewhere in the region of her midsection.

"You killed the boss. That's what they're saying. You and the guy called Adam Black. Place has gone to shit. Never expected you to head back to his car. Sure didn't think you'd hand yourself in. Should have run, darlin'. Run the hell away. But they want blood. Said I could do it. Right here. " He emitted a deep rumbling laugh – a smoker's laugh, she thought.

"But I gotta do it real quiet," he said. "Don't want those pilgrims getting all upset and creating all sorts of shit." He was chewing gum. He made a show of spitting it out. "So, I guess we'll just get right to it."

She watched as he reached both hands behind and under his jacket, to produce a leather scabbard. He unclipped the top, drew out an antler-handled bowie knife.

"Jesus," she muttered. "Just make it quick, why don't you."

The guy looked puzzled. "Make it quick?"

"Not you, fuckface. Why the hell do you think I'm here?"

The door cracked open. The other guy staggered in, clutching his throat, fell to the ground, writhing in a spray of blood. Adam Black followed, crouching, knife in hand. Red Tattoo spun round, face clown-like in shock. Elizabeth strode forward, kicked him hard in the groin. He doubled over. She continued, acting instinctively, delivering a hard undercut blow to the neck. He staggered back, gurgling and choking. Black finished things off, deftly slitting his throat.

"You took your time," she said.

"Damned rude of me," he said. "Let's get the hell out of here."

They left, locking the door. Someone was in for a shock when they went to collect their can of beans. They darted back to Black's car. He knelt at the front tyre, reached round the inside, picked up the opening key. He pressed a button, the doors clicked, they got in. The bells were still ringing, though the herding crowd had thinned, now massed around the church some three hundred yards distant. Running at speed toward them, the men who were following, broken free from the throng of people.

Black spun the car in a tight circle, drove back along the single-track road, the church, the people, their enemies diminishing into specks, then swallowed up by the night.

Elizabeth relaxed back in the passenger seat, took a long slow breath. "We're out," she said. "How the hell did we do that?"

"Maybe The New Messiah spoke to his god and asked him to help us."

She responded with a frosty laugh.

"I wonder what his message was."

"We'll never know. The guy's a master of improvisation. Maybe to tell his flock the game's up, and it's time to go home."

"It soon will be. Once I call it in. I wonder what they'll call him in a state penitentiary."

"I know what they'll call him by the time he gets out," said Black.

She looked at him.

"The Old Messiah," he said.

FORTY-SIX

EIGHT HOURS EARLIER. THURSDAY AFTERNOON.

"WE'VE BEEN INVITED FOR DINNER," said Rom. "Tonight. He does this. A sudden fucking decision, and we all have to jump. And it's not a fucking invitation. It's a fucking command."

The cargo was due in the following evening. Rom had been liaising with both the supplier and the intermediaries. His father had given him the name of the American called Gibson. The supplier. The conversation had been succinct and brisk. Gibson acknowledged receipt of the money. The packages were en route. Gibson assured him there were no difficulties at his end. He spoke with the solid confidence often displayed by educated Americans. Rom liked that. No false bonhomie. No smart unnecessary bullshit. Matter of fact. Reliable.

He had contacted those officials in customs, reiterating their importance, reminding them of the payout they had already received, and the payout they would get once the job was accomplished. And reminding them of the consequences of failure.

And he had contacted Jeffrey Ferguson, who was putting up vehicle transport and storage. Ferguson required little encouragement. He was indebted already. He understood intimately the consequences of crossing the family, having been nailed to the wall of his office.

He had contacted his small army of dealers, in Aberdeen, Glasgow, Edinburgh and Manchester. Preparing them, arranging distribution, coordinating the smooth transport to each of the main drug houses. He had felt damned good. Until the call. His high spirits evaporated. He was enraged. And humiliated. Yet again, he was hostage to the whims of his father.

"We?" replied Arlene.

They were sitting on the decking at the front of the house. It was mid-afternoon, the weather pleasantly warm, the sun bright, the air still. The lack of breeze enticed the midges. He had twelve 'midge magnets' spread evenly around the periphery of the house. Small machines sucking up the little bastards in their hundreds of thousands. But they still got through. And they still bit. Each of the machines made a faint humming sound, which was almost therapeutic. He had been making calls most of the day. He sat at a table, drinking chilled sparkling mineral water. Arlene was lying back on a recliner chair, reading, a white wine on the table. She was wearing a wide-brimmed hat and sunglasses. Sometimes she wore sunglasses to hide the bruises. This time, she wore them for their intended purpose.

"You heard," he snapped. "He wants you there."

"He hates me."

"He hates everybody. Don't feel privileged."

"What does he want?"

"How the hell should I know."

She took her sunglasses off, placed them on the table, awarded Rom an even stare.

"Do you think he knows?"

Rom gave a dismissive shake of his head.

"Not a chance. Unless someone talked. And no one talked, because no one knows, except you and me. So he doesn't know. And if he did, I'd be dead by now."

"If you say so."

"That's right. I do say so. So shut the fuck up."

With obedience cultivated from a thousand bruises, she put the sunglasses back on, and resumed reading.

But his mind churned. What if he did know? The thought had never crossed his mind, until this moment. He pushed the thought from his head. He knew exactly why his father wanted them for dinner.

To remind them. To remind *him*. Who the boss was. And to keep Rom in his place.

Idly, he used the tip of his index finger to scroll down the phone numbers collected on his mobile. He stopped at one in particular.

Mr Smith.

If anything should happen – should his father push too far – he would send the message, and by sending the message, the instruction would be given, and the deed would be done.

And he would be free.

Dinner was set for 5pm that evening. William Callaghan didn't cook. Cooking and cleaning and most other household tasks were arranged by a live-in maid called Elsie, who occupied a small outhouse at the back of the main building. When Rom's mother was alive, the notion of an external agency doing the cooking was unthinkable. But his mother was dead. Bone cancer, consuming her insides, hollowing her down to nothing, dead within eight weeks of the initial diagnosis.

The cooking stopped. William Callaghan, Gypsy King, had no time or inclination. Someone was brought in.

They got there punctually. Almost impossible to be late, given their houses were one hundred yards apart. The maid had answered and asked them to go straight to the dining room. They made their way through. The room was of regular dimensions, the walls rendered back to the original stone, the ceiling rail-tracked with glossy oaken rafters. At one end, a log fire, unlit. The walls were adorned with paintings. Landscapes. Rom had never expressed interest in them. In the centre, a solid table of rough wood, around it six high-backed chairs. Three places were set. Callaghan was there, sitting at the head, a place set on either side. He was drinking from a crystal glass. On the table before him, a bottle of Glen Moray single malt whisky, which, so Rom noted, was almost finished.

His father's face was flushed. His eyes were bright. He beckoned them to sit on either side.

He fixed Arlene an unnerving stare, said, "Would you care for some wine?"

Clustered on the table was a group of open bottles. Red and white.

"Thanks," she replied. "Red, if you don't mind."

"Why would I mind? Red it is."

He filled her glass.

He turned his attention to Rom. "And you'll be having a whisky, for sure."

"I'm working tomorrow, if you remember."

"You'll be having a fucking drink, because I say so."

He poured the remnants of the whisky bottle into a glass, placed it before Rom. He raised his own glass to his lips. "Here's to happy families."

Arlene slipped a glance at Rom. Rom said nothing, sipped his drink.

"We should do this more often, don't you think?" continued Callaghan. "A father and son need to bond. Talk. Laugh together. What do you think, Arlene? Do you think your boyfriend should visit his father more often?"

"Yes," she said quietly.

Callaghan gave a hoarse wheezy laugh. "There you are, Rom. Your good lady agrees."

The maid entered with plates, laid them on the table. T-bone steaks, green vegetables, fluffy mash.

The maid left. Callaghan got up, went to a side bureau, swung it open, returned with a fresh bottle of Glen Moray. He ripped open the seal, screwed the top off, filled his glass, took a large swallow.

"Bodybuilders like steak, yes? Protein and all that."

Rom nodded. The steak was overcooked. He preferred it rare. Prudence, however, counselled him to say nothing. His father began to eat, urged Rom and Arlene to do the same.

They ate, Arlene nibbling at her food, casting furtive glances at Rom's father.

"I won't bite you," he grunted, laughing. "I think your girlfriend is frightened of me. Are you frightened of me, Arlene? Speak up."

She reacted with soft nervous laughter. "Of course not. Why should I be?"

"No reason at all. I'm all big and cuddly. Isn't that right, Rom?"

"If you say so."

"Whereas Rom here," continued Callaghan, "I think he's shit scared of me." He jabbed his knife at Rom to emphasise the point. "Tell her, Rom. Tell her you're shit scared of me."

"Why did you ask us over?" said Rom.

"To eat!" said Callaghan, voice raised. "And to have some friendly family discourse. A bit of banter! Is that such a crime?" He drained his glass, filled it up, took another healthy gulp, plonked the glass back on the table. He shovelled more food in his mouth, spoke as he chewed – "You like that word, Rom?"

"What word?"

"Discourse."

"Wonderful," said Rom.

"I like it. It's an educated word." He leaned towards Arlene, his great bulk sliding across the chair. "But I'm not an educated man. No chance. Far from it. Everything I've known..." and he tapped his temple with his forefinger, "I've got from the street. Because that's where I was born. Not in any fucking fancy mansion. And one thing I can say with certainty, you can't learn the street. You follow?"

She nodded, dipped her head, concentrated on the plate of food.

"She understands what I'm saying," he continued. He took several more mouthfuls, belched, finished the glass, filled it up. He pushed the plate away.

He sat back, glass in hand, regarded Rom with a glittering gaze.

"Big day tomorrow," he said.

Rom likewise pushed his plate to one side. He'd hardly touched it. "Is that why you asked me here?"

Callaghan nodded slowly. "This is what you have to understand. Everything you see, everything around you, that big fuck-off palace you live in, that big fucking four-wheel beast you drive, the Rolex wrapped round your wrist, your fucking designer clothes – all of it came from me. From what me and your mother built." He spread his spade-like hands on the table. "I built it. From scratch. From being fucking street smart, a bit of cunning, and having no fear to spill a little blood along the way. Therefore, the answer is fucking yes. That's why I asked you here. To make sure you're ready. To make sure I know you won't fuck this up."

Rom swallowed back his resentment. "Why do you think I'll always fuck up?"

"Because you always fucking do!" roared his father. He thumped a fist on the table. The plates rattled. He swigged down the whisky, topped it up again. He pursed his lips, lowered his voice. "Face it, son, you're full of piss and wind. Swaggering about with those stupid schoolboy muscles. I need to be sure you're ready. I need you to understand this is a serious bit of work. That you can wrench yourself away from the fucking mirror for two minutes and get your head into some real business."

"He takes his responsibilities seriously," said Arlene suddenly. "You should give him a chance."

Callaghan remained motionless for five seconds, then swivelled slowly round to focus his full attention on her, like the manoeuvre of a Great White.

"And what do you know about his responsibilities?"

Her voice shook, but she held his stare. "Enough to know he takes them seriously."

He kept his gaze on her. She blinked, lowered her head again.

"Pillow talk." He turned once more to Rom. "Is that what happens? After you've ridden the fuck out her, it's all sweet secrets and whispers. You tell her about our business?"

"She doesn't know anything," muttered Rom.

His father's lips curled at the edges into a crooked smile. Once more, he gave Arlene his full attention.

"Sure she doesn't. Look at me, Arlene." She raised her head. She was pale, her eyes wide. "Listen to what I'm saying. My son, your boyfriend, is organising the biggest drug deal this family has ever done. We're importing one hundred kilos of heroin, being flown in from North America. The goods are arriving at Prestwick tomorrow evening. Your lover is organising this. He's going to ensure its safe arrival, its transport to a warehouse in Edinburgh, and then its distribution to a number of drug houses we have up and down the country. The street value of this merchandise is over a hundred million. You see now this is a serious business."

She flicked a glance at Rom, nodded, kept silent.

"Do you know why I'm telling you this?"

She shook her head.

"Because now that you know, you can never fucking leave. We have a bond, you and I. You're tied in. And if you do think about leaving, then here's what I'll do...He accentuated each word, a second's pause between each –"... I will rip your heart out. You follow?" He sat back, finished off the whisky, smacked his lips, suddenly becoming jovial. "So you'd better be good, and not say a word, and stick to opening your legs, and keep his cock hard, and pray to Christ above that Rom doesn't get fed up with you." He lowered his voice. "Now you begin to understand what serious means."

"I'll get this done!" said Rom, voice raised. He felt a mixture of emotion. Rage, embarrassment. But above all, fear. The man beside him, his father, terrified him.

"Too right you fucking will," retorted Callaghan. "You spoke to the American?"

"Yes."

"And?"

"All good."

"And?"

"You want everything?"

"What do you fucking think I want!"

"The shipment is leaving the West Coast later this evening. It'll land at Prestwick at midnight tomorrow. It'll be on the street in less than two days' time. I've got it covered."

Callaghan nodded like a wise old owl. "And our man at the airport?"

"He knows what to do. He knows the rewards, and he knows the penalties."

"And our friend Jeffrey Ferguson? He's got the transport all ready? He knows the pick-up times?"

"He won't let us down, for sure."

Callaghan gave a low rumbling laugh, coming from the depths of his lungs. "For sure." He turned to Arlene. "Do you know what Rom did to the fella? He crucified him to his office wall." The laughter stopped. He focused back on Rom. "Which was imaginative." His eyes narrowed to slits. "And which is what I'll do to you if you fuck this up." He pointed to the wall at the opposite side of the room. "There. And I'll hammer the fucking nails in myself. I won't ask someone else to do it. You follow?"

Rom gave him a hard bitter stare. "A hammer won't cut it," he whispered.

"What?"

"The walls are stone. You'll need a drill."

His father, eyes bloodshot with the whisky, turned him an acid look. The type of look perfected over a lifetime of unremitting violence. A look that burned through blood and bone, and with laser efficiency, shrivelled the soul. "Just don't fuck this up."

It was at that moment Rom experienced blazing clarity. And with it, a wondrous sense of freedom.

He knew what had to be done. His father had given him no choice. He had pushed and pushed. Now was the time for Rom to push back.

They left shortly after. They saw themselves out. They passed a night-time sentry. Six men lived in a lodge fifty yards from the main house. At any given time two men patrolled the grounds. Despite his bravado, the Gypsy King still required protection. As did he, thought Rom grimly. From his own father. As they made their way back to his own house, he implemented his plan.

He glanced at Arlene. She seemed to detect his purpose.

"You going to do it?" she said.

"Too fucking right."

"That's good, Rom. It needs to happen."

He found the number on his mobile phone and sent the text.

To Wilson Smith.

FORTY-SEVEN

BLACK GLANCED in the rear-view mirror every few seconds, but no one followed.

"They won't come after us," he predicted. "The impetus has gone. To come hunting will expend too much energy. Much better to work out how to minimize the fall-out from Noorzai's death. With any luck, the organisation will implode, fracturing into squabbling factions, and then everything goes to shit."

"You've got it all figured out," said Elizabeth. Her tone was flat, hollow. *Shock,* thought Black. And no wonder.

"Not really. It's just common sense. We're dealing with guys whose loyalty is measured by the size of the dollar. Criminals are easy to read."

She closed her eyes. "I could sleep for a century."

"I know just the place."

———

Black drove back to his motel, a mile outside Fairview. The reception door was locked, the lights out. The owner was unlikely to return, presumed Black, given he was lying stone dead with his pals somewhere on the Kansas plains.

They parked the car round the back of the building, went to his room. Elizabeth sat on one of the beds and used the telephone at the bedside cabinet, contacting her immediate superior, explaining what had happened. She did a lot of listening. She hung up.

"I've got nothing to pay the phone bill," she said.

"Don't concern yourself," replied Black. "The motel owner's beyond caring."

Elizabeth seemed to accept this without further enquiry. She was either too tired to care or had bigger things on her mind. Black waited.

"They'll strike tomorrow," she said. "I've spoken to my field agent. He went further up the line to an assistant director. I only had to mention Noorzai's name. It'll still need sanctioned. But it will happen, and Zain and his crew will be in a shit-tornado."

"Shit-tornado," said Black. "Nice one. I'll need to remember that."

She responded, her voice flat – "They had no idea."

Black waited.

"I've been held captive in that shithole, and no one – not my field officer, not one fucking agent in my team – knew there was a problem. Because no one told them."

"No one?"

"Special Agent Jona Lefroy. My colleague. We went into this together. Undercover. But then I get caught. And then I discover that the bastard betrayed me. Sold me out. He was the liaison agent. It was in his interests not to tell anyone about my situation. But look what he got for his trouble."

"He had his head removed, if I recall," said Black.

She lay stretched out on the bed, placed her hands behind her head, stared at the ceiling. "I need a shower."

"Why do you think he betrayed you?" asked Black.

"Money. What else?"

Black lay on the adjacent bed, and likewise cupped his hands behind his head, and likewise stared at the ceiling as he spoke.

"A whole lot of money, I think. He had something to sell. Namely you. Because he knew you were important."

"I don't understand any of this."

"Because Noorzai knew that by using you, he could get to me. Through your father."

She remained silent for a minute. Then she spoke, her voice soft.

"He said bad things about him. He said he took money. A lot of money. To provide military secrets. To commit treason."

Black considered the matter, reviewed the facts, lined them up in his head, tried to rationalise with analytical detachment.

"I have a theory, and it's not rocket science. But I have to ask you – did you tell anyone about this operation? I mean, anyone outwith the FBI?"

"No. Of course not. We can't do that. It's against the rules."

Black gave a low chuckle. "Rules. I like that."

She didn't respond.

"Here's what I think. It's speculation, but it makes sense. Noorzai, through the information given by your headless friend, Special Agent Lefroy, became aware you were the Colonel's daughter. The Colonel, during the war in Afghanistan, was selling secrets to Noorzai. Noorzai therefore would know the Colonel was in command of a unit deployed in Afghanistan to… let's say, shake things up a little. Cause a little irritation to the drug lords. Ergo, Noorzai would be aware I was the captain in that unit. On one specific excursion into the badlands, we were caught in an ambush. Presumably your father had tipped Noorzai off. During the exchange, I killed Noorzai's brother, without even realising it. It was night-time, and we were caught in the middle of a snowstorm…" He stopped, the details vivid in his mind. The darkness, the mad swirl of the snow, those around him – his fellow soldiers – dropping silently to the ground, like puppets with their strings cut. He swallowed, spoke in a measured voice. "All my men ended up dead. I was the sole survivor. Your father mounted a rescue operation. Flew the helicopter himself and got me back to safety. Presumably an act. A show, to add another layer of innocence to his actions. Noorzai, naturally, blamed me. I was taken to hospital back in Britain, your father got badly injured by an IED, and got sent home. The unit was finished, neither me nor the Colonel returned. Case closed."

"Until now," said Elizabeth.

"Noorzai wanted revenge, beyond all else. He wanted to kill me. This was his chance. Through you. By having you as a hostage, he could use your father to get to me."

She remained silent for a full two minutes. Black reckoned he could hear the gears of her mind grind and chew this information. Considering, analysing. Exactly as he would do.

"But the picture's not complete," she said.

"I know."

"There's a gap in your logic."

"I know."

"Noorzai would have to know who I was. Special Agent Lefroy would have to know how important I could be. And once Noorzai knew this, he would have to have the means to contact my father, to use me as a bargaining piece. You can't account for these things."

"No." Black pondered. "Can you remember if Lefroy had any tattoos? Any markings?"

Silence. Then – "On his forearm. Stretched midway down past his wrist and onto the back of his hand. The Bureau didn't like it, but he never got it removed."

"What was it?"

"It was weird. It was horrible. Like a frog."

"A bone frog," said Black.

"What does it mean?"

"Tragedy. A symbol of Special Forces. And something else."

"What?"

Black took a long breath, fitting pieces into slots, and arriving at the most tenuous conclusions. But yet… "Barbecues and expensive whisky," he replied. "Loose talk and a whole lot of bitterness."

"I don't understand."

"Me neither."

"You're a strange one, Adam Black."

"I've been called worse. And better, I might add."

"Will we be safe here?"

"Perfectly. Zain and the hired goons have much bigger problems than us. They have ten thousand devoted disciples to deal with, plus the impending horde of the FBI to contemplate, because they'll know you'll have called this in. They have dead bodies to think about, and probably a warehouse full of Class A drugs in the compound. We're the least of their problems. If they had any sense they would cut their losses and run like hell. But they won't, because their greed will blind them. So yes. You'll be safe."

"Then I'm going to have a shower."

Black smiled. "Thank God."

She turned on her side, looked at Black on the adjacent bed. "You're from Scotland."

"For my sins."

She gave a crooked grin. "My dad never mentioned you. Is Scotland like… part of England?"

Black grinned back. "You could say."

"I've never been."

"It has some advantages. Predictability, for one."

"How?"

"It's always wet. And it's always cold."

"Sounds nice."

"It's a place," said Black simply. "You okay?"

"I've just learned my father sold military secrets to a Taliban drug lord. Struggling to get my mind round this. He's all I've got." Another pause. "What have you got, Adam?"

"Nothing."

She didn't respond. Black, not inclined to bouts of melancholic introspection, nevertheless found himself continuing – perhaps it was exhaustion. Perhaps it was self-loathing. Perhaps he was sick to the soul.

"My wife and daughter were murdered. Five years ago. A man entered our house and shot them. My wife was in the kitchen. My daughter was watching television. Two innocents. Killed because of me. Since that day, I decided on two things."

She stared at him, said nothing.

"That I would make it my business to expunge evil men," he said. "And make it my business to die trying. That's the answer to your question, Elizabeth. I've got nothing. Nothing at all, except a capacity to kill people."

"You came for me," she said quietly. "You entered that place, knowing you would probably die. Alone. Outnumbered. For me. Who you'd never met. A stranger. I'm not sure I've met anyone quite like you, Adam Black."

Black gave a weary smile. "Which tells you something else."

"What?"

"I'm insane."

"Or remarkably chivalrous."

"I'm not the chivalrous type, I can assure you."

"You're certainly something. What now?"

"What now? I have answers to seek." The impact of what he was saying was not lost on him.

She sat up, regarded him solemnly. "My father?"

"He needs to explain himself. I'd like to have a chat."

She nodded curtly, as if coming to an instant and irrefutable decision.

"I'm coming with you."

Black frowned. "Aren't you going to wait..."

She raised a halting hand. "I need to hear his answers. I need to hear the truth. The Bureau can wait. This is family. Give me this, please."

There was nothing Black could say, except –"How do you propose to get to Carmel? You don't have a passport."

She got up, went to the en suite, turned. "But we have a car."

Which was true. But it would slow him down. For a fleeting moment, he was tempted to leave her while she was preoccupied in the shower, creep out, take the car to the airport, and hike a flight to San Francisco. He still had the wad of cash the Colonel had given him. He heard the rush of water. He dismissed the notion. He could do with the company, he realised. Plus, he liked her.

Next stop, the Colonel.

He drifted off to sleep, his last waking thought tinged with a familiar dread – people who tended to get close to him usually ended up dead.

FORTY-EIGHT

DAY 5 - FRIDAY

A POLICE CAR remained outside their house the entire night, down to the persistence of Sergeant Harry Starling, for which Hornbuckle was grateful. But the night passed without event. Dawn arrived, the sky the colour of grey gauze, clouds splintering the sun into dreary fragments. *More rain,* thought Hornbuckle. *It never fucking stops in this godforsaken place.* A place of his choosing. It wouldn't have mattered where they had gone. Whichever lunatic was doing this would have found them. For revenge? For something he had done in the past? For the sheer thrill? For the thousandth time he racked his brain. The Grant family were all dead. No one cared anymore about his unpaid debt. What then? Adam Black. The name kept popping into his head. He was linked with the Grant killings. The same guy? A coincidence? And even if that were the case, why would Black carry such a crusade against them? No reason. The guy came into his shop once a week to buy the *London Times*. End of. Probably no connection.

He had no answers.

He hadn't slept. He was pretty sure his wife hadn't either. It was 7am. He was sitting at the kitchen table, staring at an empty coffee cup. His shop was gone. Suddenly, he had no income. Not that he got much. But it helped. He would have to brace himself for the ensuing torture of dealing with his insurance company. Weeks, if not months, of protracted correspondence, argument, long hours of fruitless telephone calls. He pushed it from his mind. Irrelevant to consider such things. Getting out of this thing alive was foremost in his thoughts. The rest was inconsequential.

He heard his wife's footsteps coming down the stairs. He got up, clicked the kettle on. He felt ancient. He was bone tired. His head throbbed. His back was stiff.

She came in. She gave him a wan smile, sat.

"Did you sleep?" she asked.

"Did you?"

She shook her head. They said nothing more. The kettle boiled. He fixed her a cup of tea, and another coffee for himself, and sat opposite her.

"I never said it," she said.

He looked at her quizzically. "Said what?"

"Thank you. For saving my life."

He blinked, tried to grasp what she meant. The penny dropped. He struggled to respond.

"It was all I could do. I had nowhere else to go. I was desperate…"

"You did it for me. You went to dangerous men and risked your life. All for me. You're a brave, kind, foolish, wonderful man, Richard Hornbuckle. And I'm thanking you for saving my life. And I love you."

He felt tears well up. He wasn't able to keep the tremble from his voice. "I love you too," he whispered.

"We can get through this," she said. "We carry on as normal. The police are there. Starling is on our side. If they intend to do something bad, then they have to show themselves to do it. And when they do that, then they expose themselves, and we can catch them."

"You're much braver than I am," he said.

"No, I'm not. I'm terrified. But I've made a decision. I will not allow this thing to beat us. Today, I'm going into school, and I'm going to teach, and I'll do all the things I normally do. I'll be fine. The school's probably the safest place I can think of. Then I'm going to come home, and we're going to have dinner tonight, and watch television. We have the police looking after us. And we have each other."

"If you say so," he said.

"And you've got to get the insurance sorted. That'll be your job today."

He couldn't help smiling at her pluck.

"If you say so."

She took his hand in hers. In the bright kitchen light, she was pale, skin etched with weariness. But her sudden strength was infectious.

"I do say so," she said. "We'll get through this. If we keep our heads." She squeezed his hand. "I love you."

"I love you too."

His wife had showered, changed, went to work. He followed suit – showered, changed. He would cycle to his shop, take proper stock of the extent of the damage. Then, he would contact his landlord – a pension company based down south somewhere. He had had little communication with them. He paid the rent through the bank. They collected it. The matter would be complicated. Insurance companies, loss adjusters, lawyers. But suddenly the task before him strengthened his resolve. He had something to do. A challenge. And a welcome distraction. And his wife was right. They had each other.

But still, despite his new-found vigour, nothing could shake the shadow in his mind.

The note had been most specific. Five days. On the fifth day they would die.

And this was Day 5.

FORTY-NINE

ROM GOT up at 6am and went straight to his gym. He'd received a text at 9.30 the previous evening from the American called Gibson. The plane had left San Francisco airport along with the merchandise. No problems. The customs guy had waved it through, which was Gibson's part of the deal. Then, it was down to Rom. After its various stop-offs, the plane would arrive at Prestwick Airport at 11.45 that night.

Rom hit the gym hard. He'd slept well. He felt good. Events were in motion. The dinner with his father had sealed matters. Any doubts were extinguished. In their place, certainty. A burden had been lifted. His father had only himself to blame for the consequences of his actions.

Big changes.

He worked arms and shoulders. His gym had every conceivable machine, plus free weights. He'd spent over forty thousand on the equipment, and it was the best money could buy. Two hours, pumping iron, keeping recovery time between each set down to thirty seconds, and at the end, muscles burning, veins swollen, blood pumping, he presented himself before a full-length mirror, designed to catch exactly the right type of light, and he thought, truly, he was invincible. Empowered.

Tonight, how things would change, and he laughed loudly, and posed himself, arms raised, like Atlas, holding the world in his mighty grasp.

He showered, standing beneath the waterfall flow of steaming hot water, enjoying the moment. He changed into loose jogging trousers, muscle-tight running top, trainers. He glugged down a pint of high-protein solution, comprising milk, whey powder and six eggs. He left Arlene sleeping. Last night, after his father's behaviour, she had been distraught. When he explained what he had done, the transformation was almost miraculous, her mood turning to excitement. Elation, even. One thing he liked about Arlene. She had a lust for blood.

"That means we've got two things to look forward to," she'd said.

Which was true.

Two things.

Big changes.

FIFTY

IT WAS APPROXIMATELY 1,500 miles from the town of Fairview to Carmel. Provided the traffic was light, provided they didn't crash, provided they didn't get stopped by the bad guys (or the good guys, reflected Black), and a hundred things Black couldn't think of, then they could do it in under twenty hours without breaking too many speed limits. They could take turns driving, maybe four-hour shifts each. It was feasible.

They left the motel at 6am. They'd slept for five hours. They were both tired, but they'd catch up on sleep when they took turns driving. California was two hours behind, which meant, if luck was with them, they would reach Carmel by about midnight, local time.

Black stuck the address in the car's satnav. The route appeared wonderfully simple. The Interstate 70, passing through Colorado, then catching the I-15 at Utah, slicing through the southern tip of Nevada, and then into California, until Barstow. Thereafter, following Highway 58, a jagged stretch north, until reaching the Pacific Ocean, and Carmel-by-the-Sea. *Easy,* thought Black ruefully. He added another possible reason for delay – they might get lost.

Elizabeth drove first, claiming she didn't need to sleep. They drove fifty miles out of Fairview. She stopped to fill up at a twenty-four-hour petrol station combining as a discount store, and using some of Black's cash, bought some new cheap clothes, which she changed into at the ladies toilets – couple of T-shirts, pants, a pair of unbranded jeans, some deodorant. The whole lot came to under twenty-five dollars.

"My type of place," remarked Black.

They kept the radio on. Elizabeth wanted country and western. Black wanted sixties rock. Black tossed a coin. He lost. In desperation, he suggested time restrictions. No more than two hours, then they swap channels. Elizabeth, grudgingly, accepted.

At midday, it hit the news. The details were sketchy. A massive raid at the religious encampment ten miles from the town of Fairview, conducted by the FBI. Zain, the leader and self-proclaimed Messiah arrested in possible drug-related offences and involvement with organised crime. The place was cordoned off, the information restricted. People – *disciples* – were interviewed. All of them protested ignorance. The reporter interviewed one young woman, who described Zain as a prophet from God, and who flatly refused to believe that he might be connected to criminal activities.

"It's all lies," she said bluntly in a Midwestern drawl. "They did the same to Jesus and look where that got them."

"They arrested Jesus on drugs charges?" replied the reporter mischievously.

"It's all lies, I say. You can't put God in prison."

Black smiled. Elizabeth reacted with a sour laugh. "Watch us," she said.

"If they've seized the drugs," said Black, "then there's going to be a lot of dissatisfied customers out there."

"Good," said Elizabeth. "We've destroyed the head of the snake. The empire will wither and die."

"Until there's a new one."

They sat silent for a spell. The news had changed back to music. It seemed to Black the landscape on either side was constant, as if he were trapped in a weird time loop, going over the same road, through the same territory, under the same sunshine, endlessly, starting nowhere, ending nowhere. Until this moment, he had never really appreciated the vastness of the country. *Tempting,* he thought, *to give up and lose yourself in such a place.*

His mind, not for the first time, retraced back to an event for which he could not explain. An anomaly in his thesis. An event which didn't stack up.

"Something happened when I got to Kansas," he said.

"That's the understatement of the century," replied Elizabeth. "I think a lot of things happened when you got to Kansas."

"Something in particular. Something which breaks the pattern."

"I'm listening."

"I picked up a car at the airfield, courtesy of your father. The road from the airfield to the main highway was narrow, almost single track, about thirty miles long, going through nowhere in particular."

"Still listening."

"I encountered a camper-van blocking the way. Broken down, apparently. But not really. It was a ruse. Three men, two women. Their intention was clear. To kidnap me, presumably to truss me up and take me to Noorzai. Killing me was the farthest thing from their minds. Otherwise they would have done it."

"They knew you were coming," she said.

"Tipped off by your father. To ensure I was brought in as a trade for your life. But we know this already. That makes sense. What doesn't make sense is what happened."

"And what did happen?"

"Two guys appeared. Policemen, though I suspect that was a disguise."

She waited.

"They killed the men and women. Shot them from a distance. Clinical and professional."

"To save you?"

"The opposite. To kill me. It was sheer luck I didn't get hit. But they came looking. Drove up to the camper-van. They knew my name. Once they had established I wasn't dead, they made it their business to finish the job. Their efforts, as testified by me sitting here driving this car, failed. But not for the lack of trying."

"You killed them," said Elizabeth.

"I've always been lucky when it comes to killing."

"You're sure they weren't real cops?"

"If they were, we'd be hearing about it. Two dead cops, five civilians, all lying on a desolate road, shot to pieces. That's major news. Even if they were bent cops, it would be on every channel, every station, everywhere. Which leads me to the conclusion they weren't cops at all..."

"... and someone cleaned up the mess after you'd gone."

"Someone didn't want me to get to Noorzai."

"If you hadn't made it to the compound, he would have had me killed. Without compunction."

"And would have taken great enjoyment in the process," said Black.

She pursed her lips. "My father wouldn't have given such an order. His single motive in this entire affair was to serve you up, in the hope I'd be set free."

"Which is the anomaly. Someone knew I would be there, and they wanted me dead. The picture doesn't fit."

"Who would know? My father, obviously."

"And his friend," muttered Black to himself.

"His friend?"

"He called himself Gibson."

She snapped her head round. "Gibson?"

Black glanced at her, focused his attention back to the road. "You know him?"

"More than most. He's my ex-husband."

Black listened. Life never ceased to surprise him. There was no pattern to it. Or perhaps the pattern lay in its endless inconsistencies, as wild and scattered as the stars in the sky.

"He was one of my dad's army buddies. He served in the Navy SEALs. My dad did a lot of liaison work with the Americans when they were in Afghanistan. They were real close. Gibson would come visiting when he was on leave. Dad offered him a job. A management role in the company."

"The company?"

"The family business. Shops up and down the length of the country."

Black said nothing. He kept his thoughts to himself.

"Gibson left the navy," she continued. "He moved into a rented house in Carmel, close to home."

"And your father?"

"He stayed on in the army. He seemed content for Gibson to help with the business. He was efficient. Good at admin and paperwork."

"And that's how you met him."

"He was round regularly. We went out for dinner. We went to the movies. We went on dates. We did all the normal things that couples do when they're seeing each other."

"You were at college?"

"I was in my final year, studying English lit and politics. He was ten years older but what the hell." She gave a frosty laugh. "Young love."

"And your father was okay with this?"

"He didn't seem to mind. He liked Gibson a lot. I guess he thought it was a good match."

Black said nothing.

"I had always dreamed of joining the FBI. But then it was just a dream. An idle fancy. Gibson asked me to marry him. I was twenty-three. I said yes, and suddenly I forgot all about the FBI, and was more intent on keeping my new husband happy."

She looked out of the car window as she spoke, her voice distant.

"He was getting a good salary in the business. I got a job working for a big recruiting firm in Monterey. We stayed in his rental. We were maybe going to buy something. A flat, maybe a small house. Dad said he would give us the deposit. I had everything planned, from the colour of the carpets to the range oven in the kitchen. I was ready to move."

"But you didn't," said Black.

"The marriage lasted one year."

"Brief," remarked Black.

"I never saw it coming," she said.

"What?"

"That he was a narcissist of the worst kind. The psychotic kind. Every situation was a chance to abuse. And when he used my jaw as his personal punch bag, I got out."

"That took courage," said Black.

"Not courage. Fear. That the fucker might kill me. I left, then spent the next six months of my life wading through the courts trying to get a divorce. Which I did, in the end. But the bastard didn't make it easy. Not one bit. In fact, I think he enjoyed the process."

"The behaviour pattern of a true narcissist," remarked Black. "Blame everyone but yourself, and when at last confronted with the truth, make everyone pay."

"You into psychoanalysis, Adam? You don't seem the type."

"I'm not. But I've met psychopaths, and they seem to share certain traits. What did your father do?"

She remained silent for ten seconds. Black waited. Here, perhaps, was the root of the problem.

"He did nothing. He was still serving in the army when all this shit went down. When he came back to Carmel on leave, he allowed Gibson to continue to work for him. He said we should try and patch things up. That Gibson wasn't all that bad. That I should give the guy a chance. That I was *overreacting*."

Black raised an eyebrow. "Interesting. It maybe explains a lot."

"Like what?"

"I'm not sure. Maybe nothing. Maybe everything. Then what happened?"

"I did what I should have done at the beginning. I applied to join the FBI. They accepted me, and before I knew it, I was in Quantico, up to my ass in mud and learning how to kick the shit out of the bad guys."

"Which you do with aplomb," said Black.

"I lack your clinical edge," she replied.

Black smiled. "You'll learn that as you go along. Then what happened?"

"The relationship with my father broke down. We became estranged. To be candid, I hated him. I didn't see him, or speak to him, for years. Then he came home. I was aware he had been badly disfigured. I visited. To my horror, I discovered Gibson had moved into the house, still doing the admin work, but also as my father's carer. The meeting was short. I wished my father well, but told him straight I had no desire to see him again. That's how we left it. That was four years ago."

"And here we are," said Black.

"Here we are what?"

"Going back to see him. A reunion of sorts."

"Not the nice type. He sold army secrets to a terrorist. He betrayed you. He betrayed his country. And ultimately, he betrayed me." She hesitated. "None of it makes sense."

"It never does."

She continued – "Special Agent Lefroy – my friend – must have known how important I was to Noorzai, otherwise he would never have taken the risk. When he sold me out, he must have known I could be used as a bargaining tool to get my father, who in turn, could get to you? How would he have known that?"

Black took a breath, thinking more out loud than responding to her question – "The bone frog. Whisky. And barbecues."

She shook her head dismissively. "I don't know what that means."

"I'm not sure I do either. But maybe we'll find out."

FIFTY-ONE

HORNBUCKLE, despite his brave words, was agitated. The timescale was clear. This was to be the last day. Day 5. Friday.

They had agreed he would drive his wife to the school and pick her up at 4.30. She hadn't objected. A police vehicle had waited outside their house the entire night. He went out, offered the guy some coffee. He squinted up at him, gave a smiling response and said he would love one. Milk, two sugars.

"All quiet?" Hornbuckle asked.

The policeman gave a thumbs up. *Jesus,* thought Hornbuckle, *shouldn't you be at school? Or am I just getting so damned old?*

"I'm driving my wife to work," said Hornbuckle. "Then I'm going to head to the shop. Or what's left of it. Then head back here maybe. Or perhaps go to the library."

The policeman nodded. "Might be better to go to a public place. Just to be safe. We'll have another police car come round this evening."

"Okay."

He dropped his wife off at 8am, watched as she made her way to the main entrance of the school building. The place was already filling up – with staff. It was too early for kids. She met a friend at the doors, and went in. She turned a brief glance back at him, fluttered her fingers, disappeared inside.

A fraction of the burden lifted. There, in the cloistered sanctity of the school, at least for a little while, she was safe. Unless the pupils attacked her. Which wasn't such a bizarre notion in these crazy times.

He drove to his little shop, parked the car. He was vigilant, looking right and left, all about. Nothing seemed untoward. The place was quiet. He inspected the remains. His little shop was no more. A blackened shell, imploded, the roof collapsed, the windows gone, a space where the door once stood, splintered shafts of timber sticking out, like crooked fingers.

"Total loss," he muttered. He experienced a surge of desperation. He thought of his wife, her resolute bravery. The feeling subsided, replaced by sadness. His business was gone. But then, he reflected, the business had always been secondary. A means to an end. The real reason he was here was to escape the fury of Peter Grant and his crew and the repercussions of an unpaid debt.

Run and hide. The story of his life, he thought. But it had all been for nothing. The Grants were dead. Destroyed, so it was claimed, by a man called Adam Black.

Adam Black.

He was struck by a sudden thought. He reached into his memory. His conversations with Black over the months had been minimal, bordering on terse. The man was relatively uncommunicative, possessing a somewhat saturnine self-assured disposition. Economical of motion, detached. He tried to remember... A fragment rose to the surface. Once, Black had divulged how he'd had to walk three miles in the rain from the foot of the mountains. Hornbuckle went back to his car, googled the details. Nearest mountain was Ben Dorrery. He had cycled near it once, a year or so ago. He remembered the lodge there. Remote. Isolated. Perfect, for a man like Adam Black.

Perhaps this man had an answer. Or perhaps he had no answer at all.

He started the car up, drove out of Thurso.

The library could wait.

Hornbuckle thought it through. His hypotheses made sense. Ten minutes later, he bumped his car onto a heathery verge, got out. It was on foot from here. He wriggled his body through an old narrow turnstile in a rough stone wall, made his way along a rocky path through sparse woodland, thinning to rolling hills of rock and gorse. In the distance, maybe a mile, the mountain loomed. In its shadow, a shape too regular to be natural. A small house. He picked his way along the route, concentrating on where to place his feet rather than his surroundings. It was uphill. He cycled to work every day, and thought he was mildly fit. But this was tough. He vowed, should he ever get through this shit in his life, he would join a gym.

He stopped a hundred yards from the building, or what remained of it. There was little point in going closer. His puzzlement only increased. And his despair. He looked about. The place was desolate, devoid of any other signs of human existence.

Who would have done this? And why?

He turned, headed back, suddenly afraid, glanced round, ensuring the image was not something conjured from his imagination. But it was real. Now the landscape held new perspective – the shadows cast by the mountain held lurking danger behind every rock, every contour. He half ran, half stumbled back to the car, thoughts racing.

If Black had indeed lived in that house, and Hornbuckle strongly suspected he did, then he and Black shared a common theme. Perhaps then, there was a connection?

He might never know. He might never see Adam Black again, and his question might never be answered.

For all he knew, Adam Black was dead. And this thought brought new terrors. Black was a link – albeit tenuous. Without him, the link was gone, the thread broken, and Hornbuckle was left floundering in a world he didn't understand. A world of madness, where people he didn't know wanted to kill him for reasons he couldn't explain.

And this was Day 5.

FIFTY-TWO

THE DRIVE DOWN to Prestwick was smooth, trouble free. Some minor roadworks on the A9, causing a fifteen-minute delay, but Rom had factored this in. There were always delays on the A9. Foolish to think otherwise. Stu Gorman accompanied him, sitting shotgun in the passenger seat, two men behind him. Cousins. The job merited the involvement of family rather than outside agencies.

During the journey, he received three calls from his father, which he'd placed on loudspeaker. Each call was asking where he was, if there was any trouble, was everybody ready. Rom knew exactly why he was doing this – so that each of them was aware of the level of importance of the task, and that failure of any kind was not an option. But Rom was confident. He'd checked, double, triple. People were in place, greedy for the rewards, terrified of mistakes. He was more than confident. He was riding on a wave of euphoria. Plans were in place. Plans within plans. Let his father bark orders out, he thought. He didn't care anymore. He'd made the call. The call had been answered.

They made a couple of stops. The weather changed as they drove south, as it always did. It had started cloudy. The air was damp with impending rain. Further south, the clouds broke, sunlight filtered through, the day grew warmer. The rain stayed away.

They got to Prestwick at 11.30pm. Rom had been here once before. A dour little town, forgettable in almost every aspect, with the exception of the airport, which, to Rom's mind, was the only thing useful about the place. Especially tonight. Big enough to handle freight. Small enough to avoid unwanted inspection.

They parked the car in a twenty-four-hour supermarket car park a quarter-mile from the airport, and adjacent to the planned route. Nothing to do now but to wait. Rom got a call from his inside man. In fact, he'd paid two men. One in customs – a senior officer – and a freight handler. The news was good. The news was excellent. The plane was on time. No issues.

Despite his confidence, Rom felt a flutter of nerves. Seconds ticked by. The moment was looming. It was almost midnight. The clouds had gone, the night sky clear, the moon a pale disc encircled by a swirl of stars. His mind reached across space and time, to his father's house two hundred and fifty miles north in the Highlands. What would he be doing? Drinking, probably. Mobile phone at his side. Waiting for news. Waiting for his son to tell him the merchandise had landed, and everything was sweet in the world.

Gorman bought some snacks from the supermarket. Crisps, cans of energy drinks, dry roasted nuts. Rom declined the food. He sipped from a carton of fresh orange.

"How can you eat that shit?" he said.

Gorman gave a dry chuckle. "Tastes good."

"Zero nutritional content," said Rom.

"Fuck nutrition," said Gorman, laughing. The cousins laughed with him. The conversation tailed off. A few cars floated in and out. Late-night shoppers.

At 12, his phone pinged. Rom opened the screen. The plane had landed. They waited. At 12.45 another message. The merchandise was being loaded into the delivery truck. At 1am, a third message. The truck was leaving the airport.

All good.

Two simple words. A multimillion-pound payload.

"Okay," he said. "Keep your eyes peeled." He started the engine up, nerves sharpened. He sensed it with the others. All of them hyper-alert, adrenaline flowing, like jackals, alive to the scent of blood.

Gorman pointed. "There."

Three hundred yards away, approaching on the adjacent road, rumbling at a sedate speed, the HGV they were expecting, carrying a fixed container. Emblazoned on the side – Ferguson's Haulage and Freight.

Rom moved off slowly towards the car-park exit, timing it. The HGV passed. He slipped in behind, followed at a respectable distance of fifty yards. The phone rang again. His father.

"What the fuck is happening?"

Rom held his anger back, with some difficulty. A calm disposition was required, as part of the façade. He responded in a neutral tone.

"The lorry has left the airport. We're following it now."

"That's good. Phone me when you get to the warehouse. I mean it. Fucking phone me."

Rom disconnected. He kept a constant speed behind the vehicle. It made its slow trundling way out of the narrow streets of Prestwick, eventually reaching the M77 heading east. At this speed, and at this time of night when traffic was light, Rom reckoned the journey would take an hour forty-five. The fear was being stopped by traffic cops, but the risk was low. Safe speed, nothing erratic, nothing to arouse suspicion.

The motorway merged onto the M8. As they neared Edinburgh, tensions eased. The atmosphere changed. Conversation started. Even laughter. Rom let the others talk. He was in no mood for chat. He had things on his mind. One thing in particular, which dominated all else. He kept glancing at the clock on the car dashboard, double-checking with the Rolex on his wrist.

Gorman seemed to sense his mood.

"Relax," he said. "The worst is over. The customs guy came through. It went down a fucking treat."

"Sure," he said. "But until I see the shit with my own fucking eyes, and I know it's all there, every last fucking ounce, until that moment, I'll give relaxation a miss."

Gorman raised his hands, a placatory gesture. "I get it. No problem." He grinned. "But the signs are good."

Rom grinned back, keeping the façade going. "The signs are good," he said. "So far."

And then he received the text. *The* text. The phone vibrated, heralding its package. He picked it up from the central console, swiped it open, read its simple, wonderful, life-changing message.

Job done.

And he was King of the World.

FIFTY-THREE

WILSON SMITH WAS a master of detail. He had committed the layout of the house to memory. Every room, every cupboard, every step. He knew the contours of the surrounding land, the incline of the driveway, its width, its length. He knew the height of the walls, the number of windows, the types of locks on the doors. He knew the number of men who guarded its perimeter, the type of men they were, the routine they followed. He knew everything about everything. When it came to understanding his victim, his knowledge was such, he felt he knew more about the individual than the individual knew about himself. Of herself. He wasn't choosy.

And in this particular task, he'd been given an abundance of intimate information, which was advantageous.

And he had been given a key.

He parked his car a mile from the house, in a lay-by shrouded by overhanging trees. The car was hired using false ID, from a small rental company in York, paying cash. He would return it within two days, and no one would care. None of the roads in the immediate area had cameras. No one knew he was here. No one would ever know.

It was a quarter to midnight. He wore a plain black long-sleeved Lycra top, black Lycra leggings, black training shoes devoid of any luminous markings, black gloves, black balaclava. Wrapped round his eyes, Gen 3 night-vision goggles, favoured by the US military. Strapped to his outer thigh, a tactical leg holster, carrying a SIG Sauer M17 pistol, complete with silencer. Crisscrossed over his shoulders and chest, holsters either side, each carrying a Glock 17, each Glock holding seventeen rounds, each bullet hollow-tipped. Velcroed to a waist utility belt and around each calf, black nylon sheaths holding Gerber fighting knives. In a zip pocket, as a last resort, a knuckle-duster.

In Wilson Smith's profession, half-measures could prove fatal.

He knew the way. He would cut across the terrain – all wild and barren, with mild sloping hills and intermittent rocky outcrops. Too difficult to be cultivated. Perfect for travelling unseen. He sloped off, invisible.

There was no wind. The night was still, the sky clear, unblemished by cloud.

He reached his destination twelve minutes later. A group of buildings spaced apart, bright with outside lighting. One hundred yards off, he removed his night goggles, crept closer, hunkered down, surveyed the scene. The private road. The big house. Several outhouses. Further away, another house, all illuminated. As he expected. At the front, a couple of cars.

He waited. A man sauntered into view. A patrol guard. He stopped at the front door, rummaged in his pockets, pulled out a packet of cigarettes, lit up. He pulled out his mobile, the glare of the screen reflected on his face. He gave a loud laugh. Perhaps in response to a text. Perhaps he was on Facebook, or Instagram, or anything. It didn't matter. What mattered was that he was complacent, and lazy, and inept. He sauntered off, to do his tour round the grounds. Smith knew there were two guards. If one was at the front, then the other was at the back. Now then was the time to move.

He ran forward, in a half crouch. He knew there was CCTV, but it was an irrelevance. A camera above the front door, two on the roof each side, one at the rear. Should the recordings ever be scrutinised at some later date by the authorities, they would discover an intruder with no discernible features. He got to the front door, used the key, went in, quiet as a whisper.

He had committed the internal configuration to memory. He unclipped the leg holster, eased out the SIG. His weapon of choice, when tasked with close killing. Perfect weight, low recoil, easy to handle. He crept through the hallway, illumination solely from a single brass lamp by the telephone. Doors on either side, which he ignored. Stairs on one side, leading to the first floor, to the bedrooms, which he also ignored. His employer had been most specific. The target, at this time, on this specific night, would not be in bed. His employer spoke with certainty. A room at the back – a snooker room, and a bar.

He got to the door at the end, the entrance to the kitchen. The door was closed, but the light was on, evidenced by a slender gleam beneath the frame. He turned the handle, pushed gently, six inches, looked round. There, a woman bent over an open dishwasher, removing items, placing them on an adjacent counter.

A blip, nothing more. She shouldn't be there. But she was. Her problem. He replaced the pistol back in its holster, unsheathed the Gerber. She was placing plates into a cupboard, head height, her back to him. He entered, strode forward. She may have sensed the movement. Too late. She turned, managed a half-startled gasp. He was behind her, cupping one hand under her chin, thrusting upwards, his other hand working the knife, stabbing the neck. Death was relatively quick, and relatively silent. Five seconds, a short gurgling groan. Her body went limp. He laid her gently on the kitchen floor. He was pleased. No blood on his clothing.

He wiped the blade on a dish towel, inserted it back in the sheath, pulled out the SIG. He made his way to a far door, opened it slowly. The dining room. Closed curtains, lighting provided by the kitchen. He closed the kitchen door. Darkness. He knew the way. He went across the room. Another door, to a passage. A final door, at the end. He heard noises from beyond. Two men talking. Laughing. The unmistakable sound of a snooker game.

He reached the door. He took a breath, collected himself. This moment, seconds before conclusion, brought a wondrous clarity of vision, of purpose, which no other experience could emulate. All planning, strategising, rehearsing, crystalised down to this last act.

He opened the door.

Two men. One bent over the snooker table. One sitting at the bar. The one at the bar, he recognised immediately. William Callaghan. He had a glass in his hand, poised at his lips. He froze, his face registering dull shock. Almost laughable. The man over the table played his shot, straightened, turned to speak. Smith aimed, fired twice, both head shots, the silencer rendering the sound down to a soft thwump – like the sound of a pillow being punched. The man's skull burst in a glorious profusion of blood, bone and hair. He bounced back onto the snooker table, scattering the balls, the baize a bright new colour.

Smith, in a second, adjusted his aim to the target, marched forward. Callaghan tried to speak, failed, words strangled into an incoherent jumble. At a range of three yards, Smith shot him in the stomach, chest, neck. Callaghan collapsed to the floor, barstool skittering away. Smith, in two strides, loomed over him, shot him three times through the forehead, in rapid succession, the sound morphing into one. Like his snooker buddy, Callaghan's skull exploded in wondrous bright colour, his startled features fracturing into a thousand pieces.

Smith left the room, back through the passageway, the dining room, through the kitchen, ignoring the still form of the maid, and to the front door. He waited, then, once establishing the route was clear, left the house and disappeared into the deep darkness of the Scottish Highlands.

He sent a message to his employer:

Job done.

FIFTY-FOUR

THEY REACHED Carmel-by-the-Sea just after 10pm local time. Earlier than anticipated. They debated about parking the car. Whether they should park a discreet distance from the Colonel's house and walk. Or simply drive straight there, and audaciously park at the front entrance.

Black preferred the former. Caution, vigilance, surprise.

Elizabeth countenanced the latter – "It's my father," she said simply. "You think he's going to kill his daughter? He gave you a task. You performed successfully. You are returning the merchandise intact. Namely me."

"It's not your father I'm worried about," Black answered.

She shook her head adamantly. "This is my home," she said. "I'm not returning like a thief in the night."

Black offered no disagreement. There was a naïve logic to her argument. Nevertheless, he was thankful he still carried weapons.

The night was quiet and balmy. Restaurants were still open, and bijou wine bars, and couples strolled. The place held a quiet civility – as if boisterous conduct was alien, something simply not to be tolerated.

They approached the house. Just beyond, the beach, and the sea. The air stirred with the faintest breeze, carrying the sound of breaking waves. Inconceivable that dark crimes could be committed in such a place, thought Black. But then, where people existed, regardless of paradise, dark deeds always followed. The nature of man, he thought. As natural as the elements.

The front gates were open.

"Is that good or bad?" questioned Elizabeth. Black had no answer.

He eased up to the front courtyard, where, only three days before, he had shaken hands with the Colonel, who had wished him Godspeed, but who had neglected to mention the dice were loaded from the start.

There were no lights from the interior. It looked empty. Black's nerves prickled. The drive here had been long and tiring, the previous couple of days had been dramatic. He was weary. He was running on adrenaline, and the tank was almost empty.

Elizabeth stepped forward, turned the handle. The door was unlocked. She glanced at Black, shrugged, her expression unreadable, went inside. Black followed.

The place was in darkness, save for a soft lamp on a corner table, casting shadows.

She went straight to his study, Black keeping a step behind. She turned the light on. There, the Colonel's chair as Black remembered. The bookcase, the antique writing bureau. The room was empty.

"Maybe he's gone to bed," said Elizabeth.

"Maybe," said Black. "Maybe not. Let's try the back."

They went to the rear of the building, passing through empty rooms, all of them unlit. They got to a set of French doors, leading to the large expanse of garden. They went out and approached the decking area. Here, at last, was illumination. Candles were lit, and scattered randomly on the floor, ledges, on the rough wood table. At one end, the half-barrel barbecue. Under a red awning, sitting on a chair, dressed in a neat dark suit, white shirt, dark tie, black Oxford brogues, was the Colonel. In one hand, a full whisky glass. At his feet, on the wooden timbers, a bottle. Beside it, a revolver.

Specifically, a Colt Single Action Army. A 'sixgun', as it was nicknamed in Westerns. In the shadowy flicker of the candlelight, the skin on the Colonel's face had a scaly shine, his injuries rendered all the more horrific. Black felt little sympathy.

The Colonel cocked his head, saw them approach. He half rose from his chair, sank back down. His expression lacked emotion. A lifetime of discipline, thought Black. An inability to display feelings. Another legacy of the harsh regime inflicted by the Special Air Service. Or maybe he was overthinking it. Maybe it was his disfigurement which prevented any real expression.

They stepped onto the decking and sat opposite the Colonel. Black placed his handgun on the table between them, the message simple – *hey! You're not the only person in the room with a gun.*

The Colonel gazed at his daughter. His lips twisted into something approaching a smile.

"I knew you'd come back," he said softly.

She said nothing. The Colonel switched his gaze to Black.

"You did it, Adam. You brought her back. I could always count on Captain Black to see a mission to its end."

Black kept his voice neutral. "Interesting observation. Let's consider the 'mission' for a moment. You asked me to find your daughter. But you already knew where she was. And you knew Noorzai held her captive. You struck a deal. My life for your daughter's. The 'mission' was to wrap me up, package me, and send me to my death. And I would do it gladly, because you knew you could rely on my loyalty and my friendship to blind me from the truth. Where's Gibson, by the way? I would like to renew my acquaintance."

The Colonel took a wheezy breath. He leaned down, picked up the bottle, plonked it on the table beside Black's semi-automatic.

"Would either of you care for a drink?"

Black raised an eyebrow. Glenfiddich. His favourite. No point in refusing. Without speaking, he went to a cluster of glasses on a tray by the barbecue, got two, placed them on the table, filled them up, gave one to Elizabeth. She took a tentative sip. Black was less restrained. He downed it in one, filled the glass up, drank half, rested the glass on his lap.

"I remember," said the Colonel. "Glenfiddich. Your tipple. Many an evening, you and I spent drinking the stuff under the Afghan stars."

Black considered the man before him. The man with half a face. He experienced a plethora of emotion. Sympathy; rage; disbelief.

Betrayal.

Regardless, Black maintained a flat, imperturbable disposition.

"My enthusiasm to share your company may have waned somewhat had I known you were selling military secrets to a drug lord."

The Colonel disregarded the comment. He gazed at his daughter. "It's so good to see you, Elizabeth. When I realised you were Noorzai's prisoner, my world crumbled. But you're back. You're safe. You're here."

She took another sip of the whisky, put the glass on the table carefully, regarded her father.

"Why? Please. For once, the truth."

"Karma," replied the Colonel. "Look at me. Look at my face. This is my penance, for my sins." Suddenly, his voice took on an edge. "Isn't this enough? The truth doesn't matter anymore. I'm paying for what I did, every minute of every day."

"The truth matters to me, Colonel," said Black quietly. "And the men who were killed as a result of your treachery. You still have your life. They were robbed of everything."

"And it matters to me," said Elizabeth. "I need to understand who you really are. I need to make sense of this… fucking nightmare."

"You wouldn't understand," muttered the Colonel.

"Try me," said Black.

The Colonel sighed, stared at the ground. He lifted his head.

"The business was failing. It was haemorrhaging money. My

father was CEO, but the board had made bad decisions. High interest rates, credit fucking crunch, every fucking permutation of disaster. The company was going to fail. He reached out. He asked me to leave the army, help him to steady the ship. Otherwise...he made a vague gesture,"... we would lose all this. Lose our status. Lose respect." He took a deep breath. "Then who would have paid your college fees, Elizabeth? How would you have survived?"

"Don't you dare spin this fucking thing," she retorted, spitting the words. "This isn't about me."

The Colonel finished his drink, filled up the glass. His hands trembled. Black didn't care.

"You lied to me, Colonel. I knew when you showed me the photo of your daughter. You told me she had fallen in with a bad crowd, that you were giving her money, that her life had gone in the wrong direction." He looked at Elizabeth briefly, turned back to the Colonel. "The picture I was given was of a young, confident woman, at ease with the world, and at ease with herself. But that was merely speculation on my part. The photo had a clock on a wall in the background, and the clock had a date. You claimed to have taken the photo. But that wasn't possible, because on that date you and I were several thousand miles away in Afghanistan, trying to duck bullets from the Taliban. So you lied. And that was a bad start."

The Colonel blinked, shook his head. "I trained you well, Adam. And yet..."

"And yet I continued."

"Your nature. To seek the truth."

"Which you have trouble telling," responded Black.

"There's more," said Elizabeth. Her face was taut, her cheekbones harsh in the candle-flame. Her eyes never wavered, accusatory. "Jona Lefroy betrayed me to Noorzai. He must have known how valuable I was. How would he have known that? He gambled everything to give me up. So he was expecting a massive payout. But how the fuck would he know I was your daughter?

And how the fuck could he have made the connections? Between me, you, and Adam? Speak to me!"

The Colonel sighed again, wiped his eyes, swallowed. He reached over, tapped the top of the bottle. "That," he said. "And my big mouth."

"Barbecues and whisky," said Black. "May I?"

The Colonel said nothing. Elizabeth looked at him. "What's this about, Adam?"

"*Esprit de corps.* Friendships sealed in blood. Loose talk. And greed. Please, Colonel. Feel free to correct any flaws."

The Colonel responded with a fractional nod of his head. He remained silent.

"You showed me a severed hand," continued Black. "Remember? You claimed it belonged to a private investigator you had hired to find your wayward daughter. Another lie, I might add. It belonged to Elizabeth's erstwhile colleague, Special Agent Lefroy. His wrist and hand bore a section of tattoo. Quite a distinctive one."

"A bone frog," muttered the Colonel.

Elizabeth frowned in puzzlement.

"Exclusive to Navy SEALs," said Black, his voice low. "A tribute to fallen comrades. Something to bond brothers in arms. That evening, as we sat here, on this deck, drinking beer and whisky, I noticed Gibson had an identical tattoo on his left forearm. Both men Navy SEALs. A coincidence? Maybe. Maybe not."

Black took a drink. It tasted good. It served a need.

"Let me theorise," he said. "Gibson and Lefroy were old navy veterans. Navy SEALs, no less. Buddies, who had seen a whole lot of shit and blood. I imagine they kept in touch. Drank together. Reminisced. One night, one afternoon, one morning – who the hell knows – Lefroy tells Gibson he's going after a religious preacher called Zain. With a female. Special Agent Elizabeth Pembroke.

"Gibson is now confronted with startling possibilities.

Elizabeth, his ex-wife, the Colonel's daughter, is suddenly in the picture. And he knows all about Zain, because – and here, I'm taking a leap, but correct me if I'm mistaken – I reckon he knew that Zain was a front for the drug lord, Bashir Noorzai. He sees a connection he can exploit. Am I right, Colonel? How would he have found out? Was he sitting here one evening, in this seat, sharing a bottle of Glenfiddich? What were you doing? Flipping burgers? Grilling steaks? Or have I got that wrong? Enlighten us, Colonel."

Elizabeth spoke through gritted teeth. "What the hell are you talking about?"

The Colonel took another rattling breath, broke into a coughing fit. Black wondered if it was an act. It sounded too real, and too damned painful. The Colonel was dying. Black no longer cared.

They waited for the coughing fit to lessen. The Colonel wiped his mouth with a tissue, found his breath, spoke –

"You're right. You were a soldier like no other. Captain Adam Black. More than a soldier. A warrior. I spoke about you because I was damned proud to have you in my regiment. Proud to fight at your side."

"But you betrayed me. Tell us what you said."

"We spoke a lot about the war, Gibson and I. The war on terror. The things we did. I told him about you. I told him about that night, deep in the mountains of the Hindu Kush. How you and your men were… ambushed. How you killed the brother of Bashir Noorzai. That I was the only person in the world who knew that. How you survived."

"What else did you tell him?" said Black quietly. Another sip.

The Colonel heaved another long sigh. "Everything. I told him about the promise you made, should I ever need your help. How you felt indebted, because I saved your life. That you would come to my aid, if ever I needed it, because it was in your nature to do so. I told him how Noorzai would pay a king's ransom if he could capture the man who killed his brother. Capture Adam Black." He looked pleadingly at Black – "And I told him nothing would ever compel me to give you up. But…"

"But you did," said Black simply.

"He had my daughter. What the hell else could I do?"

Elizabeth nodded thoughtfully, regarded Black. "So Gibson hatched a plan with Lefroy. Lefroy made the gamble. He told Noorzai who I was, and how he could use me to force my father to contact you, and then deliver you up on a plate." She snapped her head round to the Colonel. "Is that right?"

The Colonel merely nodded. The remains of his mouth quivered, as if he were about to speak. He said nothing.

"But things went badly for Special Agent Lefroy," continued Black. "He was expecting a big payout for this information. As was Gibson. Noorzai, being both psychotic and unpredictable, rewarded him by cutting off his hand – which he sent you, to this address, all neatly packaged – and then his head. So long, Special Agent Lefroy. His Lambs were well and truly Silenced. But I think we're all missing something. The elephant in the room, so to speak. Am I right, Colonel? Like, how did Noorzai know where to deliver the severed hand? How would Gibson connect Zain and Noorzai? Your drunken *tête-à-têtes* with Gibson beside a hot barbecue would indicate your acquaintance with Noorzai was more than a memory from the war. Tell us, Colonel?"

The Colonel swallowed, cleared his throat. His voice was a croak.

"He knows where I live," said the Colonel. "He's always known where I live. Since I returned from Afghanistan."

Black watched Elizabeth's expression. Her eyes widened in shock. Then her brow furrowed, her eyebrows lowered. Puzzlement. Then the slightest shake of her head. Disbelief. Then her face straightened, her jaw tightened. Enlightenment. And anger.

"You and Noorzai," she said. "You're…"

"Partners," finished Black. "Yes, Colonel? Or am I reaching?"

The Colonel cast his rheumy gaze, first to his daughter, then fixing on Black. He licked his lips with the tip of his tongue. *A lizard,* thought Black.

"I came home. The business was dead. I'd tried to prop it up. I'd failed. I needed money. Badly. I was... connected... to Noorzai. We decided – Gibson and I – to maintain the relationship."

"What the fuck did you do?" whispered Elizabeth.

"We became his distributors for the West Coast. And beyond. To Europe. To Britain. Gibson was adept at it. He possessed a skill for making contacts, striking deals, arranging transport. He created a vast network. A web. He was a fucking genius at it. And so we carried on the business."

"A glorified drug dealer," remarked Black.

"But it stopped," continued The Colonel. "When Gibson and Lefroy told Noorzai about how I knew you had killed his brother, that I could make contact with you should I choose, then Noorzai felt this as a personal betrayal. I think he felt affronted. The relationship we had ended. Badly."

"Gibson misjudged his reaction."

The Colonel nodded. "A rare lack of judgement. But monumental. He double-crossed me and sacrificed my daughter. And instead of the king's ransom, he lost everything."

"I love your clichés," said Black. "He lost everything? I don't think so. There is one last thing he still has, and which I hope to help him lose fast."

"Which is?" said Elizabeth.

"His life."

FIFTY-FIVE

THEY REACHED the warehouse a couple of minutes before 2am. Jeffrey Ferguson was there, a hunched figure, hands bandaged, white as death, eyes flitting left and right in nervous agitation. The forecourt held ten vans, each to take a portion of the merchandise and transport it to drug houses dotted up and down the country. The high doors of the warehouse were open, the place illuminated by a gantry of spotlights on the ceiling. The truck pulled in, eased into the main building, Rom following. The main doors slid shut. The truck came to rest, the thunderous sound of its engine stilled. Rom stopped behind it, got out, along with Gorman and the two others. In the background hovered Ferguson. The driver opened the cabin door, jumped down. Rom handed him an envelope containing two thousand pounds in twenty-pound notes. The driver took it, tucked it into a pocket in his jeans, went round to the back of the vehicle, opened it up.

Inside, piled head height, wooden crates, and on the side of each, a stamp of the Brazilian flag, and underneath it, *Ambroco Red Kidney Beans.*

"I didn't know that was where they came from," said Gorman.

"You learn something new," replied Rom. "Look for the unstamped crate." The driver folded out a rear step and began unloading. Rom nodded at Gorman, who in turn flicked a glance at the two cousins, and they all began to unload, Rom overseeing the process.

Ferguson sidled over, to stand beside him. He cleared his throat. "After this," he said, keeping his voice low, "are we good?"

Rom turned to look at him. Ferguson flinched.

"What do you mean 'good'?"

"You know…"

"Spit it out."

"I'm just saying, after tonight, are we even?" He licked his lips with the tip of his tongue, skin so pale, glistening like alabaster under the sheer glare of the floodlights. "I've done what you asked. Arranged all the transport. I haven't let you down."

Rom turned back to the men unloading the truck, said, "You need to understand the situation, Jeffrey. Your new reality."

"What new reality?"

"That we're never even. You're in it for life. So shut the fuck up, and don't make me lose my temper. Are the vans ready?"

"Yes."

"Good boy."

The crates were being placed on the concrete floor adjacent to the truck. They were heavy, the going was slow, producing a clamour of grunts and groans. A forklift might have proved useful. Rom made a mental note. He would arrange one next time.

"We're looking for the crate with no stamp," he reminded them. Slowly, the truck emptied. Rom experienced a tingle of nerves. Had he been mistaken? Had he misheard the American?

Gorman, from the back of the container, gave a triumphant shout.

"Got it!"

The tingle disappeared. Confidence resumed. Gorman manoeuvred the crate down onto the ground. He opened the boot of the Range Rover, took out a crowbar, used it to pry open the top. Inside, packed in rows of ten, were two hundred cans, each the same, each bearing the same label – *Ambroco Red Kidney Beans.* Underneath, the slogan – *A Taste of Brazil.*

"Let's get a little taste, shall we?" quipped Rom. He and Gorman and the cousins congregated round the open crate.

"Are you going to phone your father?" said Gorman.

"In good time. Let's get these tins open." He twisted round, spied Ferguson standing by the side of the truck. He waved him over. Ferguson approached, the skin of his forehead wrinkled in puzzlement.

"You see these cans?" said Rom.

He nodded.

"I need you to open them."

His frown deepened, eyes blinking and shifting round the group of men.

"I'll need to check in the kitchen."

"Check for what?" said Rom.

Ferguson stared at Rom for five seconds. He spoke, hesitation in his voice.

"For a can opener? Won't I need that?"

Rom gave a barking laugh. He felt fucking good. "A can opener? We haven't got time for that."

"We haven't?" Gorman looked from face to face, as if searching for some meaning behind the conversation. Finding nothing, he said – "Do you want me to use a knife? I might have one back in the office, somewhere."

"I don't want you to use a knife," said Rom. He was enjoying this. "Then what…?"

Rom leaned closer – "I want you to use your fucking teeth."

This caused a ripple of laughter. Ferguson swallowed, stepped back, face moist with sweat. "My teeth…"

Now Gorman chimed in. "Sure. Your teeth." He bared his own teeth, placed a finger on each of his incisors. "Use these ones. Pierce the top and start chewing."

"Start chewing…" stammered Ferguson. "You really mean…"

"I really mean I want you to start chewing them open with your fucking teeth."

Rom plucked out a tin from the crate, tossed it to him. He fumbled the catch, dropping it on the concrete floor. He picked it up, held it in both his hands, turning it over and over. He looked up at Rom.

"I can't," he whispered.

"You can't?"

"I wear false teeth."

They laughed. Rom shook his head despairingly, snatched the tin back.

"Jesus, Jeffrey. Learn to take a fucking joke."

He went to his car, got four tin openers from the glove compartment, passed them about.

"Right, gentlemen," he said. "Get opening. Let's see those kitchen skills. Don't cut deep. We can't tear the goodie bags."

They each picked up a tin, began the process, twisting the handle, slicing the top off, tipping the contents onto the concrete. Then another. And another. The ground was awash with red gloop.

But there were no little white pouches. No sealed containers. No secret parcels.

No drugs.

The last tin was opened and emptied. They all stared at the mess at their feet, as if, somehow, the stuff would magically morph into physical substance. Gorman, the two cousins, turned to Rom.

The tingle returned, only it wasn't a tingle. It was a tsunami of strong mingled emotion. Helplessness. Rage.

"He must have made a mistake," Rom muttered. "Fucking American. Must have picked him up wrong."

Gorman regarded him quizzically – "He said the crate without the label?"

"Check every fucking one. I don't care if we're here all fucking night. All fucking week." His voice was shrill. "Check every fucking one!"

Gorman turned to the other two – "You heard the man."

They began the task. Rom pulled out his phone, pressed contacts, tapped the number for the American. It went to voicemail.

"He must have made a mistake," he repeated. He relayed the conversation in his mind. The smooth American accent was clear and unequivocal. *The unmarked crate.* He phoned again. This time he left a snarling message – "There's no fucking gear where you said. We're checking the others. If we've got nothing here, I fucking swear you're a fucking dead man. You hear me, a fucking dead man."

He hung up.

The American had twenty million pounds of their money. Arranged by his father. Endorsed by his father. Unless…

Suddenly, he had a wild, mad notion. A mental leap, from one unthinkable scenario to another. He remembered a snippet of the dinner conversation with his father the previous evening, one which he had considered insignificant. His father's words –

And our friend Jeffrey Ferguson? He's got the transport all ready?

He turned to Jeffrey Ferguson. He and the HGV driver had retreated, towards the far wall, to a side exit door.

He pointed to them. "Where the fuck are you going!"

The driver bolted. In his haste, he stumbled, twisting his ankle. He continued in a half-hobbling crouch, got to the door, pushed. It was locked.

He turned to Rom, eyes wide and terrified, cast a darting glance at Ferguson, who hadn't moved.

Rom beckoned them with his finger. "Over here. Both of you."

They made their way towards him, the driver limping. Ferguson appeared more hunched.

Rom regarded them. Ferguson fidgeted, eyes flitting towards the main entrance doors. The driver kept his gaze focused on the ground.

"What the fuck is happening here?" said Rom.

Ferguson appeared agitated. Distracted. Rom snapped his fingers an inch from his face.

"Look at me. Concentrate. How did my father know you were supplying the transport? You and him having little confabs?"

"I phoned him…" said Ferguson.

"Why?"

"I told him you'd contacted me about getting the stuff moved from the airport." He licked his lips, trying to find his voice. "I told him you wanted to use my warehouse."

"Why!" demanded Rom.

The driver suddenly raised his arms – "This has nothing to do with me!" He took a step away. "He told me to do it. Honest. I don't know what the fuck is going on."

Rom grabbed Ferguson by the front of his pullover, jerked him forward.

"Speak to me, you fucking rat."

Ferguson was shaking. He muttered something, too low to be coherent.

Rom pushed him away.

"Fair enough."

He cast a meaningful look towards Gorman. He and the two cousins had stopped opening the cans, watching the events unfold, faces etched in confusion.

"Give me your gun," said Rom.

Gorman, wearing a leather bomber jacket, unzipped it, pulled it to one side, to reveal a Glock tucked in a shoulder holster. Without a word, he unclipped it, handed it over.

Rom pointed it at the driver's face, and shot him. The driver fell back onto the concrete. Rom stepped forward, stood over him, shot him three more times in the head. It cracked open, like an egg, the contents spilling into the widening pool of Brazilian kidney beans.

Rom focused back to Ferguson, raised his arm, directed the pistol at Ferguson's lower jaw.

"Talk to me. Or not. The choice is yours. If you don't. I will blow your fucking face off."

Ferguson stared at the muzzle of the gun, transfixed. His breath came in short sharp gasps. His throat pulsed with every swallow. His skin was parchment white, every line, every wrinkle brought into sharp relief.

"I don't feel well," he said.

"I don't give a fuck."

Ferguson's eyes swivelled from the tip of the pistol to Rom, back again, like two shiny globes.

"Please. This was your father's idea."

Rom waited.

"I phoned him to say..." another swallow, "... I wasn't happy about doing this. Not after what you'd done. That I wanted out. That I wanted nothing to do with you."

"Uh-huh."

"He said..." his eyes swivelled to the three men watching, then back to Rom, "...he said he had a plan."

"Do tell."

"He said he'd made a deal."

"A deal?"

"With the cops. He said they were coming down on him hard. He said he would give them you, for immunity."

"He would give them me? His son?"

"He said you were... trouble. The arrangement with the American was a hoax. A ruse. He told me he paid the American five hundred thousand dollars to play this game. That it was worth it. There were never any drugs coming from America. He told me to plant two bags of heroin in the driver's cabin. And he would plant some in your car. A 'double whammy'. That's how he described it. Caught with it in your possession, caught trying to buy more."

Rom digested this information with incredulity. But it made sense. His father could have hidden drugs in his car any time. He pondered, turned to Gorman.

"Check under the fenders."

Gorman remonstrated. "You don't believe this fucking bullshit."

"Check it."

The three men went over, crouched, began to check the underside of the wheel wells, feeling with their fingers.

"Jesus," muttered Gorman. He lay flat on his back, shone the torch of his mobile. "There's something here." He placed both hands under, tugged, pulled out a polythene bag stuck to the chassis with black tape.

He raised it up. Ten kilograms easy, thought Rom. Pure white. Equating to maybe three-quarters of a million street value. Equating to fifteen years easy. He had been a fool. But a fool who would get the last laugh.

He resumed his focus back on Ferguson.

"So how is this supposed to work, Jeffrey? I'm curious."

The eyes now were steady. They stared straight back at Rom. He seemed to straighten slightly. He knew his fate, thought Rom, and he was doing the best he could, to see it to the end.

"Once he knew you were in the warehouse, for sure, he would call the cops. Give them the green light. They would come, find you here, with the gear, arrest you."

"That's why he was so keen for you to phone him when you got here," said Gorman.

"They might still come," said Ferguson. He gestured at the fallen HGV driver, his head reduced to an oily mix of clumps and shards. "How will you explain that?" His demeanour changed into sudden vitriol. "You'll go down for life. Do you know how I felt when your own fucking father told me he wanted you out? My fucking heart sang. I fucking rejoiced. You understand?"

Rom gave an easy smile. "And yet… I don't hear the blazing sounds of sirens. I don't see any sign of our boys in blue. Why do you think that is?"

Gorman approached, spoke urgently. "We should get the fuck out of here, Rom."

Rom raised a finger, indicating silence. No one spoke.

"Still nothing," said Rom. "Shall we phone my father, and get to the bottom of this mystery?"

Gorman was agitated. "Fuck's sake, Rom. Let's get the hell out of this shithole."

"Patience," said Rom. He took out his phone, tapped his father's number. He put it on loudspeaker. It rang for thirty seconds, then went to voicemail.

"He's not picking up," said Rom. "That's a shame. I would have enjoyed a chat. Never mind." He put the phone back in his pocket, turned his attention back to Ferguson.

"Let me provide a sense of reality to this fantasy. My father hasn't made the call. The police aren't coming. Seems like we've both been let down. We share a bond, don't you think? What's your thoughts?"

Ferguson blinked away sweat. "He said they'd come," he whispered.

Rom stepped forward. His eyes blazed. "The old cunt is dead," he hissed. He pressed the pistol into Ferguson's stomach, shot three times. Ferguson released a low moan, fell on his backside, both hands cradling the wound. He sat, hunched over, studying the blood oozing through his shirt. He looked up, seemed as if he was about to speak. Rom rammed the barrel of the gun into his mouth.

"I should have killed you the first time." He squeezed the trigger. The back of Ferguson's head erupted in a puff of red particles.

Rom addressed Gorman and the two cousins.

"My father tried to grass us up. You heard it yourself. But he's dead. I'm in charge. We get rid of these fuckers." He glanced at Ferguson and the truck driver. "Then we head home."

Gorman looked uncertain. "How do you know your father's dead?"

"Because I had him killed. Now let's move. Big day tomorrow. Business to conclude."

Business to conclude, he thought. And he could hardly wait.

FIFTY-SIX

SILENCE FELL. The night buzzed with the sound of insects, and not far away, on the periphery of the senses, the sound of the sea. The Colonel drank his whisky. He didn't replenish. He straightened in his chair, looked directly at Elizabeth. "Where do we go now?"

Elizabeth wasn't finished. "What happened when Adam got to Kansas? He told me that two men tried to kill him? Do you know about that?"

Black said nothing, let it play. He thought he knew the answer. He waited.

"When it hit the news," replied the Colonel, "about the FBI raid on the commune, Gibson told me everything. The man was... full of hatred."

"Hatred?"

The Colonel looked at his daughter. "For you." He took a breath. "His pal in the FBI was dead. He wasn't getting any big payout from Noorzai. The drug supply had stopped. All he had was his hatred for you. He clung to that. He arranged for assassins to kill Adam near the Kansas airport, so he would never reach the compound, whereupon your death was assured. He told me all this last night. He enjoyed it. It broke my heart, I swear. I had no idea whether you were alive or dead. Until…" His voice broke. He swallowed, regained composure. "Until now. He told me all this, and I wanted to kill him. I wanted to tear his fucking throat out."

"What happened, Colonel?" asked Black softly.

"He left. There was nothing I could do. For Christ's sakes, look at me!"

"Do you know where he went?"

The Colonel shook his head. He slumped back in his chair. Any fire in him had gone. "He has money. We have a contact in Scotland. A guy called Callaghan. Some sort of Gypsy King bullshit. This time it was different. He wired five hundred thousand dollars. The deal was simple. We were to give him nothing, but act as if the merchandise was being delivered. I have no idea what his game is. But Gibson got the money, and he's taken it with him."

"And you don't know where?" said Elizabeth.

"He's clever. He's vicious. And he has a skill for survival. If he doesn't want to get caught, then he won't."

Again, a silence fell, save the sounds of paradise around them.

Black gazed at the old, disfigured man sitting on his decking. Eventually he spoke.

"We were friends. I looked up to you. We fought together. But you betrayed me, my men, and your country. Put simply, you committed treason. Your actions caused the deaths of many people. You worked with a drug lord, and continued to do so, up until the last few days. Your accomplice – Gibson – married your daughter, whom he abused. Yet you did nothing, because his importance to your drug operations was paramount over all else. You're self-serving and duplicitous. You are the embodiment of evil, Colonel. And one thing I cannot abide, is an evil man. I hope you were going to put that revolver to good use."

The Colonel bowed his head, stared at the ground, said nothing.

Black stood. Elizabeth, face pale and solemn, stood with him.

She regarded her father. Black wondered at the feelings running through her mind. Confliction, for sure. The man before her was a villain. But also, her father.

She spoke, her voice deadpan. "I will never see you again. I will leave this house, and never return. I love you, because you're my dad. But I hate you, as a man. I hate everything about you. Everything you are, everything you've been. You're a monster." Her lip quivered. Her face flickered. Trying hard to keep it back, thought Black. The raw emotion.

Suddenly she knelt, her face level with her father's. They looked at each other. She took his hand, whispered – "As Adam said, I hope you put the revolver to good use."

She got to her feet, glanced at Black, said, "Let's get the fuck out of here."

They left the house. As Black opened the door of the car, a sound echoed from within, clear and distinctive. A single gunshot. He caught the look on Elizabeth's face. A momentary spasm. Like pain. Then it was gone, and in its place, a cold, implacable veneer.

They got into the car. Elizabeth was in the driver's seat. She drove carefully out of the long driveway, through the open metal gates, and into the warm Carmel night.

"What now?" she said.

"I need a lift to the airport."

"I'll take you."

Silence. Then Black spoke.

"What will you do?"

"Go hunting," she said.

"Gibson?"

"Yes."

"He's a dangerous individual."

"Good. Makes the hunt worthwhile."

"And if you find him?"

"I intend to kill him."

"Sounds reasonable."

Silence. Then Elizabeth spoke.

"And you?"

Black considered the question.

"Go home, if home is how it can be described. To say I live frugally would be an understatement. I've been living one day at a time. Pardon the cliché. Though it's true. Wake; eat; drink; walk; sleep; repeat. An occasional sojourn into town. A mindless series of events, culminating in nothing."

"Why?"

"Why what?"

"Why live like that?"

Now there was a question. He pondered, and realised how difficult it was to frame the answer into something she would understand. That *he* would understand.

"I'm bad luck," he replied.

"I don't follow."

"People I'm close to have a habit of dying."

"Join the club."

"And people I'm not close to have a habit of dying."

"Join the club."

"And in the latter case…" he hesitated, "… I enjoy the process. Which isn't right."

She didn't speak for a minute, then said –

"You're ridden with guilt, and you hide yourself away, like a hermit. Penance."

Which was the truth. She'd captured the essence of Adam Black, he thought. Thanks to behavioural science at Quantico, no doubt.

"But in the last few days," he said, "it's like I've woken up."

"Rejuvenation."

No, thought Black. *Resurrection.*

They arrived at San Francisco Airport at 1.15am. Black still had a large tranche of the Colonel's money. He suspected the Colonel no longer had any need for it. He booked business class. Unlimited drink. Unlimited whisky. The Colonel's parting gift.

Elizabeth escorted him into the airport. It occurred to Black they hadn't had a proper sleep for over twenty-four hours. He was exhausted. Skip the whisky on the plane. Sleep instead, he decided. He imagined Elizabeth felt the same, though she exhibited no apparent signs. *The thrill of the chase,* he thought. The flow of adrenaline kept you going. Until it stopped. And then? Crash and burn, big style. He'd been there a million times.

He purchased a ticket; the flight to Heathrow was leaving in just over two hours. Black got a drink. Glenfiddich. Elizabeth, a fresh orange and lemonade. They sat on high stools at a cute little bar called Blue Oyster Bay, tucked in the corner of the airport. It was dark, unobtrusive, quiet.

"I never said it out loud."

"What?" said Black.

She gave a small smile.

"Thank you. For saving my life."

Black sampled the Glenfiddich. Straight. No ice. A taste of home. Its taste never failed to hit the spot. Not once.

"My pleasure."

"Will I see you again?"

Already Black had thoughts crystallising in his head.

"You might need help."

"I might."

"The weather here is definitely…"

"Agreeable?"

"…different."

"And if I were to need your help?"

Black, in a moment of dark humour, almost suggested she place an advert in the *London Times*. Instead, he gave her the number of the mobile phone he'd bought a million years ago in a Thurso supermarket.

"If you need me, phone me."

"Sure. Like the Dark Knight. I shine the lamp up into the sky, and you'll come calling."

"Yes. I will."

She nodded slowly, noting the deep sincerity in his voice.

"Goodbye, Adam Black."

She stood, her fingers touching his for the briefest of moments, and without a further word, left.

She hadn't touched her drink.

FIFTY-SEVEN

ROM HEADED BACK on his own, to his house in the Highlands. Gorman and the others were left to dispose of the bodies. Rom didn't ask, nor did he want to know. The procedure in such situations was consistent and reliable – the cadavers burnt, the charred remains dissected, each part wrapped in plastic sheeting, then loaded with weights, to be dropped somewhere deep. Gorman possessed many talents. He was particularly skilful at tidying things up. Rom liked to think of him as the perfect housekeeper.

Rom drove through the night. He was on a high. The moment was delicious. During the journey, via his mobile phone, he arranged an online transfer to Mr Smith's account. The First Caribbean International Bank in the British Virgin Islands. Four hundred thousand pounds. Worth every penny. Cheap, almost. Rom would have traded his soul to see his father killed. He already had, he thought grimly.

He phoned Arlene, explained what happened.

"The old bastard tried to sell me out. He had it all planned out. But he died before he could call the cops. Goes to show. If I hadn't had him killed, I'd be looking at fifteen years serious jail time. Guess what goes around comes around."

She responded tentatively. "Where is he?"

"Probably still in the house." He chuckled. "I should have asked for a little extra."

"A little extra?"

"Like maybe arranged for his fucking snooker cue to be rammed up his arse."

She tittered – a high fluting sound. "That would be funny. What will you do with him?"

"His body? Bury it somewhere no one will ever find. It's not as if we're short of space."

"But you'll keep something, yes?"

"A memento? Jesus, you're twisted. Sure. Maybe a finger. Or an ear. Or maybe an eyeball, and you can pickle it and store it in a jar."

Again, light laughter. "You're funny, Rom. You make me laugh."

Rom smiled. Life was good. Life had never been better

"And you're going to be laughing plenty tomorrow night. You all set?"

"Yes."

"That's good, baby. I'll see you soon."

Rom arrived at 6am. He went straight to his father's house. The two men guarding it were oblivious to earlier events. From the outside, all was peaceful. Mr Smith was a consummate professional, thought Rom, doing exactly what he said he would do. Unnoticed by the guards. A shadow.

He got to the kitchen. There, on her back in a puddle of congealed blood, face stricken in a combination of shock and disbelief, the dead body of the housekeeper.

"Careless," muttered Rom. His estimation of Mr Smith decreased a notch, though peripheral loss was part of the agreement, within tolerable limits. The housekeeper was an immigrant. No one cared. She was well within the limit. Nevertheless, he'd liked her.

Her body would be dealt with, like the others.

He went to the snooker room. Instinct. His father rarely left the fucking place. He entered. Before him, two bodies. One, a man he knew a little, a friend of the family, but in essence, just another hired gun. The other was his father. Shot numerous times. Unmistakably dead. Top of his head a profusion of spiky bone shard and stringy veins and gelatinous lumps. Like someone had dropped a bowl of spaghetti on him, which Rom found an amusing comparison.

He knelt, stared into his father's eyes.

"You did this," he whispered. "Not me."

FIFTY-EIGHT

THE AFTERNOON for the Hornbuckles had passed without incident. Hornbuckle chose not to deal with any paperwork. He was in no mood to face the impossible bureaucratic idiosyncrasies of faceless organisations. Insurance would wait another day. His landlord could wait another day. Life could wait another day. He went for a long walk – six hours, picking his way through the Scottish hills. The purpose, he told himself, to clear his thoughts, clear his head, rationalise. But his head didn't clear. The question remained, rolling around in his mind like a ball in a lottery machine – who was conducting this campaign of terror? And why? And was this man – Adam Black – connected? He had no answers. And the ball kept rolling.

He got back to the house at about 4.30, unlocked the front door, entered, immediately met by the welcoming beep-beep of the alarm, counting down its thirty-second timer. He tapped in the code. Silence. Nothing untoward. Still, he experienced a tingle of dread. Given the last few days, he never knew quite what to expect.

He got a call from Sergeant Harry Starling, checking up, ensuring no issues had arisen. Hornbuckle felt like telling him that other than their lives being fucked up back, front and sideways, all was good. He chose not to. Hornbuckle thanked him. The guy was doing his best. And Hornbuckle needed all the friends he could get.

Elspeth got back at 5.30. He'd made dinner. She looked tired. She'd asked him how he'd got on. He said he hadn't done anything, that he'd gone for a long walk. She'd given a bleak smile and said she would have done the same. Tomorrow was Saturday. Perhaps they could both go for a walk, and he kissed her on the lips and held her tight.

The evening passed. They went to bed. Nothing happened. The night was quiet.

Perhaps the fire was the end, he thought. Perhaps their enemies dared go no further.

Perhaps.

———

He awoke early to a dreary, insipid morning, the sky a grey-black monochrome.

It was Saturday. Day 5 had passed. They were still alive. He dared to hope.

FIFTY-NINE
SATURDAY

BLACK SOUNDLY SLEPT on the plane. He awoke a half hour before landing at Heathrow, much to his chagrin. He'd missed out on the booze.

"Hope I wasn't snoring," he remarked to a cabin steward.

"In business class," the cabin steward replied, grinning, "no one ever snores."

"Of course they don't."

He got a connecting flight. His perspectives had altered. What had Elizabeth said? Rejuvenation? He reckoned it was true. The Colonel, by a strange quirk, had been the orchestrator of Black's revival, despite his treachery. He remembered the thriller he'd bought. *Run and Hide.* He still had it in his holdall. He fished it out, gazed at the cover. No more running now, he thought. No more hiding. Time to change.

What next, he wondered? Sell the shithole he was living in. He laughed out loud. Who the hell would buy such a thing? They'd have to be mad. Like himself. Perhaps he'd keep it, use it as a base. He had a little money in the bank. Not much, but enough. He could get a job. Anything. Or he could drift. The thought of drifting appealed to him. The thought of drifting back to America held considerably more appeal. Not for the first time, his mind returned to Elizabeth, who was, without doubt, a capable and fascinating woman.

Black arrived back in Glasgow at 1.10pm.

Saturday afternoon.

SIXTY

RICHARD AND ELSPETH HORNBUCKLE went for a walk mid-morning. They'd got prepared. Mountain boots; waterproof trousers; gloves; hats; rucksacks holding essentials – sandwiches, some fruit, a flask of hot tea. Plus a map and compass, in case of disaster. They reckoned they'd try thirteen miles, travelling a circuitous route, avoiding roads, following some cycle paths.

The plan was to walk at a leisurely pace, make a day of it. It looked like it would rain, but that didn't matter. What mattered was that they were venturing out, with each other, into some fresh calm air. Calm is what they needed. Plus perspective. Two components difficult to find in the current situation.

The rain stayed away. They got back at 5pm. Their boots were muddy. They'd eaten the sandwiches. They'd drank the tea. For a brief period, they'd stepped out of themselves, and as a consequence, their spirits lifted. But Hornbuckle felt the leaden weight return to his heart when they reached the house. His wife undoubtedly felt the same, but she wore a brave face, and he loved her for it.

At 6.48 he got another call from Sergeant Starling, once more checking on their welfare, and imparting some bad news.

"I can't spare anyone this evening," he explained. "There was a football match on at Dingwall. Sometimes there's trouble in the evening when a big club comes up. To avoid it, we need a presence. I've spoken to my superiors…his voice faltered,"… and I can't make an exception. Not even in this case."

We're a case, thought Hornbuckle. *Just another statistic. Another hassle to be handled.*

"That's okay," he said. "I understand."

"But I'll be at the station," said Starling. "You have my direct number. You phone me if there's a hint of a problem."

"That's okay," repeated Hornbuckle. "I understand."

He didn't tell his wife.

They had dinner. He made chilli con carne. They shared a bottle of red wine, and watched a little television, and went to bed around 10.30.

The day had passed without incident. Hornbuckle began to believe that maybe, just maybe, it was over.

It was Saturday night.

SIXTY-ONE

IT SEEMED TO BLACK, after the pristine spotlessness of Carmel, that Glasgow felt unclean. Grime-ridden, a deep engrained grime in the buildings, the streets, the people.

But it felt real. A gritty, hard truth. *This is life,* thought Black. *Not fantasy.*

The thought of the train journey dismayed him. Seven hours. A mischievous thought entered his head – that he should hire a taxi. After all, he still had some of the Colonel's money, which he'd changed for pound sterling. He dismissed the notion instantly. Going business class on an aeroplane was the extent of Black's new 'splashing the cash' philosophy. Also, the thought of having a taxi driver as company for several hours was not an enjoyable prospect.

He went to Costa, bought a sandwich and a coffee. The train left at 2.20pm. The journey was uneventful.

The train pulled in at Thurso at 10.30pm, just as the Hornbuckles were going to bed.

It was Saturday night.

SIXTY-TWO

ROM DIDN'T clear up the bodies immediately. He locked his father's house, allowed no one inside. Matters would be attended over the next few days. He had more important things to deal with.

He slept through the morning, got up at 12.45. Arlene fixed him some lunch. The euphoria hadn't left. He felt... magnificent. His father was gone. He was free.

At 3pm, he hit the gym, blasting calves and thighs, performing supersets until his muscles ached and his body trembled.

Stu Gorman got back from Edinburgh at 6pm, accompanied by the two cousins. The disposal had been completed, the bodies of Jeffrey Ferguson and the lorry driver gone forever, their existences vanished. Rom didn't ask for the details. Gorman didn't offer any. In due course, the process would be repeated for his father and the maid.

And the others.

But not yet.

He and Arlene had a light dinner. Nothing much was said. He knew she was excited. They watched a movie on Netflix, but he couldn't concentrate.

At 9.30pm, one hour before Black's train pulled into Thurso, Rom was joined by Gorman, the cousins, and two other men. They sat round his dining-room table, talking quietly, making final arrangements.

SIXTY-THREE

BLACK HAD a three-mile trudge to endure. The thought filled him with gloom. Plus, he didn't have a torch. The moon was wrapped in cloud, offering zero illumination. Which meant a detour of about a mile to buy a torch from a twenty-four-hour garage on the outskirts of town. Which served to intensify his gloom. He had no choice. Rather that than a twisted ankle or a broken leg.

Carrying his sports bag, he made his way to the garage. He was in no particular hurry. He had no pressing engagements. The pubs were still open. He passed the Commercial Hotel, reputed to have the oldest bar in Caithness. An unremarkable, box-shaped building of pale-cream cladding, lacking any noticeable frills or ornamentation. Which suited Black fine. He went in. He hadn't showered for a while, but he couldn't have cared less. The bar was small, compact. Cushions fashioned in tartan; dark panelled walls. In one corner, a group of four men in earnest conversation.

The bartender appraised him –

"Yes, sir?"

"Glenfiddich. Double. Straight. Please."

The bartender acknowledged the request, poured a glass, set it on the bar. Black paid him, sat at the other side of the room, savouring that special moment – the two-second prelude before lifting the glass and pouring the contents into his mouth. The liquid soaked the tastebuds as only Glenfiddich could. Black sat back, relaxed.

The conversation from the table opposite continued. Black, within close proximity, had no choice but to listen. His interest was instantly piqued. The dialogue bounced back and forth, each individual contributing a snippet which initially was confusing. But within twenty seconds Black understood the substance of the conversation.

The newsagent had burnt down.

He finished his whisky, left the pub, made his way directly to the shop belonging to the man he knew as Richard Hornbuckle. It no longer existed. Instead, a shell, blackened and burnt.

Black experienced a twinge of sadness.

"Bad luck," he muttered. He hardly knew the guy. He'd visited his shop every week for over a year. The guy had made an effort to strike up a conversation. Black, being his usual taciturn self, had not engaged. The men in the pub said no one had died. It could have been worse. Plus, from a purely selfish perspective, Black would never need the shop again, because he would never need to buy the *London Times*. *Shit happens.*

He pushed the matter from his mind, made his way to the garage, bought a cheap LED plastic torch, and sauntered home.

SIXTY-FOUR

THE WAY WAS EASIER than Black imagined. He had walked it so many times, he knew every rock, every twist, every contour. He was there in less than forty minutes.

To the place where his lodge once stood.

He remained motionless, experiencing a gamut of contrasting emotions – shock, disbelief. Outrage. He flicked the torch left, right, up, down. The image before him bore a striking similarity to the image of Richard Hornbuckle's shop. The carcass of a building, rather than the building itself. All black and burnt, reduced to a crispy shell. Someone had made it their business to set it on fire during his absence, and had performed the task with zeal.

He peered closer through the darkness. The surge of anger dissipated. Now, a sudden twinge of foreboding. He approached the front door, which, remarkably, was still standing. He focused the torchlight.

There, something nailed into the wood.

Black looked closer.

A fifty-pound note.

SIXTY-FIVE

A SOUND. Something. Perhaps nothing. But Hornbuckle woke. He woke because he never really slept. Not since the letter they'd received. Not since he'd borrowed money from a gangster. Not since he could remember.

He pulled the covers over, eased out of bed. He opened the bedroom door, went into the hall, closed the door gently behind him. He switched the light on, stood at the top landing.

Again. A sound. *Jesus. Was he imagining this?* It was like – the kettle had just clicked? Then a chair being pulled back, the grate of metal against tile.

"Hello?" he shouted.

Silence. He went downstairs, one careful step at a time. The kitchen door was closed. He opened it.

And stood.

And stared.

And heard a voice say, "I thought you'd never join us. And my sincere apologies. We're a day late."

SIXTY-SIX

BLACK HALF RAN, half stumbled back the way he'd come. He was reckless, but suddenly he didn't care. He'd discarded the sports bag. The torchlight twitched and jerked with his movements, images flashed as he lurched and staggered along the rocky route back to Thurso. He got to the flat surface of road, his rhythm more fluid. He increased his pace almost to a sprint.

He got to town, immediately went to the police station. The waiting lobby was empty. He approached the duty sergeant behind the front desk.

"Can I help you, sir?"

Black dispensed with pleasantries.

"I believe someone's life may be in danger."

The policeman raised an eyebrow. Otherwise, he maintained a professional neutrality, his face expressionless.

"Can you provide me with some details please?"

"Certainly. My name is Adam Black. I've just returned from holiday. I live in a house at the foot of Ben Dorrery. My house has been burned down. It's remote, so no one would have noticed. I think the same person set Richard Hornbuckle's shop on fire. You know the one, I'm sure. It's the only burnt building in Thurso. I need you to check Hornbuckle is safe."

The policeman gazed at him.

"Now that is interesting, Mr... Black?"

Black waited.

"What's your address, sir?"

Black bit back his exasperation. "There's no official address. Write down *shithole cabin in the middle of the fucking mountains.* It's irrelevant. What's relevant is that you check on Hornbuckle."

The policeman paused, as if arriving at some inward decision.

"I can assure you, Mr and Mrs Hornbuckle are fine."

Black cocked his head – "And how would you know that?"

"They've had an alarm installed. They have my direct number. You don't need to be concerned about their welfare, Mr Black. But I am interested in any information you have about Mr Hornbuckle's shop."

Black considered. "They have your number?" He took three seconds to reflect. "They're being intimidated, yes?"

The policeman gave a dismissive shake of his head. "I can't divulge any details. I'm more interested..."

Black cut in – "Where do they live?"

The policeman's face now changed to annoyance. "I can't possibly tell you."

"That's fine. No problem. I'll go to every pub in Thurso. I'll knock on every damned door until someone gives me their address."

"And what would be the point of that?"

"So I can see Hornbuckle with my own eyes. So I know that he's not harmed. So I can sort this thing out."

The policeman frowned – "And why do you feel the need to sort this out?"

Black's voice cracked with passion – "Because this was all my fucking fault!"

The policeman spread his hands in a calming gesture.

"Slow down, Mr Black. I'm not following this one bit."

"This is getting nowhere," muttered Black. He turned and made for the door.

The policeman opened the counter, followed Black, raised his voice.

"Please. I can't let you leave."

Black stopped, and still facing the exit, said softly, "Do you plan on preventing me?"

The policeman, perhaps sensing the quiet threat in Black's voice, hesitated, said, "No. But I can take you to their home. Provided you promise one thing."

"What?"

"You tell me what this is about."

"Naturally. Now let's go."

SIXTY-SEVEN

THE MOMENT WAS DELICIOUS. A moment he would not forget, to be locked away in his memories, like a rare treasure.

It had come to this. All his plans. His campaign. The man he knew to be Richard Hornbuckle stood before him, face expressing a range of emotions. But foremost, fear. Which Rom had created. Which Rom owned. Which Rom savoured. Rom Callaghan. The Gypsy King.

He sat at Hornbuckle's kitchen table. Sitting next to him, Arlene. Gorman was at the fridge, pulling out a carton of milk. Behind him stood the two cousins, silent, watchful. Also, a man at the back door. As extra precaution, he'd stationed another in the front living room, at the window, in case of unexpected visitors, which was unlikely.

He'd insisted they each wear identical clothing, purchased specifically for the occasion. Soft dark trousers, dark tops, dark gloves, black boots. To add drama to the occasion. Like they were a team of assassins. To escalate the fear. To drive it home. To squeeze out every drop of terror.

"You're just in time for a cuppa," he said. "Or perhaps a coffee? Which would you prefer, Richard?"

Hornbuckle stared, said nothing. He wasn't how Rom

remembered him. Looked like maybe he'd lost a little weight. His hair looked greyer. His pyjamas hung off his shoulders, his arms and legs skinny and sharp. Like a scarecrow clothed in rags, ready to scare the crows.

Face sunken and white as death.

Because that's what I am, thought Rom. *Death.* And Hornbuckle knew it.

"You remember me?" he said.

Hornbuckle didn't speak.

"Cat got your tongue? I understand that. You'll be in shock. You know what? I get it. Is it to be tea or coffee, Richard? You haven't answered the question. And given Mr Gorman here is going out of his way to make it for you, it would be rude not to answer." His lips twitched into a small secretive smile. "And talking of cats – that was Arlene's idea. Wasn't it wonderful? And daring? She was watching the whole time. She took pictures. Care to see? No? I understand. It's sad when a pet dies. Breaks the heart."

Arlene giggled.

Rom watched with amusement as Hornbuckle's scrawny neck jerked in and out with every swallow. And he was swallowing damned hard. Eventually his voice box worked.

"It's you," he said. "The guy."

Rom's face split into a broad grin. "Ta-da! The guy! I am that man." He gestured politely to Arlene. "And this is Arlene, my girlfriend, who, if you recall, was standing outside your shop at that particular moment, and who will never forget what you did. Isn't that right, darling?"

Arlene never took her eyes off Hornbuckle.

"Not until the day I die."

"Are you listening, Richard? Not until the day she dies."

Hornbuckle's voice lowered to a dry crackle. "You're the guy with the fifty-pound note."

"The guy you embarrassed," replied Rom. He took a long slow breath, spoke in a soft voice. "The guy you crossed."

Hornbuckle blinked. His mouth wobbled. "But I didn't mean..."

Rom cut him off – "Did you really think I'd let it go? I don't let anything go. Sit down, Richard. Take a load off. We can skip the coffee. I can tell you're not in the mood. Where's your wife? Still upstairs, all tucked up and in the land of Nod."

"I'm right here."

Elspeth Hornbuckle stood at the kitchen doorway. Rom clapped his hands, essayed another broad grin.

"We meet at last, Elspeth. You can't imagine how excited I am. Please, both of you, sit."

They complied with his request, approaching the kitchen table, bodies rigid, faces pale and haggard, terror framing every movement.

They sat opposite.

"It was you," whispered Elspeth. "You sent the letter. You did those horrible things."

Rom displayed a theatrical innocence. "Not just me. This was a team effort. I don't possess the imagination. Mr Gorman did all the nasty burning. And as for all the planning, that accolade should be given to Arlene. She's been studying you both very closely."

Arlene pressed two fingers to her lips, suppressing another giggle. "I love to plan things," she said.

Elspeth spoke, voice quiet as a breath. "Why?"

Rom's smile faded.

"Your husband caused me distress. He *humiliated* me. He and another. In his shop. Therefore, some payback. The other man used the word 'restitution'. That's what I want. *Restitution*."

He leaned across the table. The table creaked under his weight.

"We're still looking for the other one. But we'll find him, make no mistake. And when we do, do you know what I'm going to do? Do you want me to tell you?"

Neither Hornbuckle nor his wife spoke.

"I'm going to cut his fucking heart out. Cut it right out with a fucking steak knife. And I'm going to feed it to the fucking sparrows."

He sat back, resumed his smile. "But I digress. This is not about him. Not tonight. This is about you. This is your special night. The crescendo. Aren't you excited?"

"What are you going to do?" said Hornbuckle.

Rom laughed loudly.

"Don't be so fucking obtuse. The second you went out your way to embarrass me, you entered my world. And my world is not a nice place when someone does something to upset me. It can get ugly." His voice dipped low. "We're taking you both on a little trip. Somewhere quiet. Remote. We don't want interruptions." He kept his voice solemn and quiet, as if expressing bad news. "I have to be honest. You're both going to suffer tonight. Suffer badly. Like nothing you have ever experienced. Mr Gorman is an expert when it comes to pain. A real artist. And when he's finished, then I'll give you closure. Both of you. This is your great finale, Richard! Your *coup de grâce*!"

Silence. Then Hornbuckle found his voice.

"I didn't mean to humiliate you," he mumbled.

"Well you fucking did!" roared Rom. He slammed his fist on the table. Hornbuckle jumped. But Elspeth didn't move. She kept her gaze steady, not flinching, and Rom was impressed by that.

The man watching from the front living room entered.

"A police car's pulled up. Two men approaching. One's a cop."

SIXTY-EIGHT

"IT STARTED WITH A FIFTY-POUND NOTE," said Black.

"I don't understand."

"No one would. Goes to show. Every action has consequences. What's your name?"

They were in a police car, heading out of Thurso.

"Sergeant Starling. Harry Starling. And you're right. The Hornbuckles have experienced a systematic campaign of intimidation, the latest incident being the burning down of their shop."

"It won't stop there," muttered Black.

"How do you know? Arson is as bad as it gets. I don't think the people behind this will take it any further."

"That's very comforting, Sergeant Starling. As bad as it gets? I don't think so. People who take things to this level over a relatively trivial matter are – in my humble opinion – psychotic. And psychotics don't have boundaries. They are incapable of understanding when to stop. I want to meet the Hornbuckles. Proof of life. I want to tell them I'm sorry, and I want to make damned sure they're safe."

"I still don't understand."

"Nor me." Black said no more. They arrived at the

Hornbuckles' house five minutes later. Parked outside was a Range Rover and a BMW X5.

"They appear to have guests," said Black.

Starling pulled up, sat still, surveying the scene before them. He took a deep breath. He removed his seat belt.

"Stay here," he said.

"Sure," said Black, who immediately unbuckled, opened the door, and got out the car.

Starling did likewise, glared at Black across the car roof.

"I told you to wait in the car!"

"Yes. You did."

"Shit."

"Aren't you going to call for backup?" said Black.

"What backup?"

"Fair enough." Black made his way to the front gate. There was nothing Starling could do to stop him. They got to the door. Black noted a glass panel had been removed in its entirety, cleanly cut, leaving a long rectangular space, indicating skill. Thereafter, a relatively easy process of stretching an arm round, and unlocking from the inside. Provided the perpetrator knew the types and positioning of the locks.

The door opened.

SIXTY-NINE

I have no words; My voice is in my sword...
Macbeth, William Shakespeare.

A MAN MET THEM, dressed in soft dark clothing. He was holding a semi-automatic handgun, its make unmistakable. A Desert Eagle. If he chose to fire, the impact would split Black in two. An instant kill weapon, where the order of the day was certainty. The guy was no novice. A two-handed grip, arms straight, a slight bend of the knee, one foot forward for better balance.

The man spoke.

"Inside. Easy."

Black and Starling did as instructed, the man backing away carefully as they entered.

"Close the door behind you."

"I'm a police officer," said Starling, his voice strained. "Think what you're doing."

The man continued, edging backwards, manoeuvred into a room off the hall, twitched the pistol, beckoning them to keep moving onwards, to the kitchen at the far end. There, another man waited, similarly dressed, holding an identical weapon.

"Towards me," he said. "Slowly." He too backed off as they approached.

They entered the kitchen.

There were four men standing, each bearing semi-automatics. At the kitchen table, seated, was a man whose profile Black recognised. Richard Hornbuckle. Sitting next to him, in her dressing gown, frail and terrified, a woman. Presumably Hornbuckle's wife. Opposite, sitting, a couple. Maybe late twenties, maybe older. The same couple Black had encountered in Hornbuckle's shop. The bodybuilder and his girlfriend.

"Luck!" declared the bodybuilder in a voice of hushed pleasure. "Luck indeed!"

The gunman who had greeted them at the front door entered the room. Six men. Black had to assume the bodybuilder was armed. Six men with pistols, each pistol a veritable cannon. All in a relatively confined space. The odds weren't great. But they could be worse. Barely.

"Good to catch up," said Black. "Still hitting women? Or have you graduated to kids?"

"My God, but you're a cool one," replied the bodybuilder. "Do you have any idea who I am?"

"Judging by the steroid abuse, I suspect a guy with a seriously small dick." Black diverted his attention to the girl at his side. "Is that right? Does he have a small dick?"

She didn't respond. A silence fell. Tension was wire tight.

The bodybuilder spoke, his voice hard and flat. "We'll let that pass for now. A rather feeble attempt at bravado. You've got nerve, I'll grant you that. But that's all I'll grant you. Listen well, Adam Black. My name is Rom Callaghan. I'm the Gypsy King." He paused, presumably for dramatic effect. "A lot of people have heard of me. A lot of people fear me. Before this night ends, you too will learn to fear me. Before this night ends, you will plead for death, so that the pain ends. For pain is where you're headed. A whole world of it. Such pain as you could not believe. And you will welcome death when it comes, my friend."

Black fixed his stare on the man sitting at the kitchen table, the man called Rom Callaghan, and said in a soft even voice –

"I'm not your friend. I'm afraid you've misjudged this situation, Rom. I already welcome death. And pain? That can be a two-way thing. When it's dished out, it can be dished back."

Rom sat back on the kitchen chair, scrutinising Black with a glittering gaze.

"I'm sure. But my friend, Stu Gorman… and he nodded his head at a man leaning nonchalantly against the kitchen worktop, "… has some skill in such matters, as I have already explained to Richard and his charming wife. It might prove to be a long night for you, Adam."

Black regarded the man introduced as Stu Gorman –

"You don't have to worry about causing all that pain," he said.

Gorman laughed, a subtle, muffled sound.

"Why is that?"

"Because you'll be dead before you can start."

Gorman tilted his head in polite acknowledgement.

"Let's see how that works out."

"Let's."

Harry Starling suddenly spoke up.

"Everybody needs to calm down. Please. There's no need for anyone to get hurt…"

"Cut the fucking theatrics!" said Rom. "You've been paid already. And for bringing me Black, I'll wire you an extra ten. So quit the bullshit, Harry."

Hornbuckle's wife turned to Starling. She spoke, a quiver in her voice: "What have you done?"

Rom chose to speak on Starling's behalf. "How do you think we got your address? And how do you think we got in without tripping your alarm. Your husband's date of birth, yes? Sergeant Starling has all the details. He told us your movements during the day. Why do you think he was phoning you so often? Because he cared? Hardly. To establish your location. To allow us to play our games. I'm afraid your friend, local reliable Sergeant Harry Starling is also our friend, local reliable Sergeant Harry Starling. And for a not inconsiderable fee, he supplied us with all the information we needed."

Starling shrugged, dispensing with any show of fear or concern.

"I need to get back to the station," he said, addressing Rom. "Already I've been away too long. You should do the same. Want my advice? Bury them deep. And do it quick. No traces. Missing persons sounds a whole lot better than murdered persons."

Black turned, cast him a smouldering gaze.

"You should have thought this through," he said.

Starling responded with a disdainful laugh: "I did. I get rich, you get dead. It's nothing personal. It's just bad luck..."

He never finished his sentence. Black struck a quick savage blow to the neck, using his shoulders as momentum, destroying larynx and windpipe. Starling emitted a short, strangled gasp, dropped to the floor. Black stamped down, again the neck. Starling convulsed briefly, fell still.

A momentary stunned silence – then an eruption of frantic life. Rom jumped to his feet, face contorted in a wild look of shock and rage. Black half turned. Too late. Gorman's arm descended, pistol making heavy contact with Black's skull. Lightning exploded in his head. He tottered, collapsed to his knees.

"Don't kill him!" shrieked Rom.

Gorman backed off, dark eyes watching.

Black's world spun. He leant forward on his hands to find balance, but the world kept moving. He shut his eyes, swallowed back the pain. He was aware his head was bleeding. He took three deep breaths. The world slowed, righted itself. He opened his eyes. He was surrounded by men, handguns aimed and ready. He kept his focus on the ground, made every effort not to puke.

"He's killed the cop," he heard Gorman say.

"I fucking know it," hissed Rom.

The girl spoke. "Kill them now, Rom. Do it! Put a bullet through their fucking heads!"

He heard Hornbuckle's wife gasp. He looked up, attempted a weak smile. She and her husband sat at their kitchen table, as they would have done countless times before, never once conceiving of a situation like tonight. They sat, faces stricken, terror blazing in their eyes. All because of him – his pointless display of machoism one stupid Saturday morning in their newsagent shop. All over a slap and a fifty-pound note.

They were holding hands. They foresaw their deaths, and in even in this last moment, all they had was love.

Black took a long slow breath, felt the rage burn. If they were going to kill him, by Christ, he would make them earn it.

"Can I shoot one of them?" he heard the girl say. "Let me do it. Let me shoot Adam Black."

"Shut up!" said Rom. He was in a state of agitation. A dead cop was not on the agenda, surmised Black.

"We need to go," he said. "We'll take Starling too. Put the body in the boot."

"We should kill them now," argued the girlfriend, her voice shrill.

"I said shut the fuck up!" He slapped her hard. She jerked back, fell silent, shoulders trembling.

Rom looked at Black, swept his gaze round his men. "Here's how we do this. We leave the house in procession, you understand? Two men carry the cop to the car. They go at the head. I want Black behind, with three men on him. One on either side, one following." He pointed at Gorman. "You follow. You watch Black. He's a slippery bastard. Then the Hornbuckles. I'll come out last, with Arlene."

He gestured to the Hornbuckles. "Stand up."

Mrs Hornbuckle stared back up at him, her look defiant. Her voice quivered when she spoke, the tone so quiet Black could barely hear her.

"I'm not moving," she said. "I'm not going anywhere."

"Really?" said Rom. He pulled his jacket to one side. Attached to his trouser belt was a white leather sheath, from which he slid out a six-inch knife. He strode round to the opposite side of the table, grabbed her husband's hair, yanked his head back, exposing his throat, placing the tip of the knife on his Adam's apple.

"If you don't come with us, I swear I will slit his throat. Slit it so wide and so fucking deep, his fucking head will slide off backwards, and we'll play football with it in your fucking back garden."

The girlfriend's eyes shone. "I want to see you do it, Rom."

"Shut up." Rom glared at Mrs Hornbuckle. "If you don't move, and I kill your husband, then that's down to you. Your fault. You want that?"

Black, still on his knees, and watching the situation unfold, said – "Do as he says. He means it."

Rom turned. "Who gave you permission to speak? Hold your fucking tongue!" He kicked Black hard in the ribs. Black twisted his torso, absorbing the impact, the pain sudden and sharp.

Mrs Hornbuckle seemed to sag, her defiance evaporated. She stood, fragile and broken. More a wraith than a human being. Rom drew his knife away. Hornbuckle, slowly, stood up by his wife. And still, through everything, they held each other's hand.

Black watched. The anger burned like acid.

Rom focused his attention back on Black.

"Now your turn."

Black clenched his teeth, bit back the pain. His ribs ached, his head throbbed, and he was losing blood. He got to his feet. Including Rom, there were six armed assailants in the room. At this precise moment, five of them had pistols aimed in his direction. Rom was still brandishing his knife. He stepped close.

"You scared, Black?"

Black said nothing, held his stare.

"I could pop your eyeball out right now, should I choose. Or maybe widen your smile. Maybe peel your skin off. I can do anything I want. You've got a long night ahead of you. How does that make you feel?"

Black reacted with a cold smile.

"Think I'll need a face mask."

Rom frowned. "What?"

"If your knife doesn't kill me, your breath will."

Rom remained motionless for five seconds. He raised the knife, tapped the blade on Black's cheek. Black didn't flinch.

"A long night," Rom whispered. He placed the knife back in its sheath, tugged out his wallet from his back pocket, pulled out a fifty-pound note.

"If I recall, you took my money that morning. And then you slapped me on the face. Like this?" He flashed his hand out, caught Black across the right cheek. Black staggered back, shook his head, willing away the pain, righted himself. But the guy was powerful. Like being hit with a sledgehammer.

Rom dangled the note two inches from Black's face. "I want you to put this in your mouth, and I want you to chew it, and I want you to swallow it all down."

Black swallowed, focused. The world spun. He spoke, but his voice sounded far away. "Wow. You love giving me your money."

Rom smiled, revealing all his splendid white teeth.

"We'll see how long your bravado lasts, my friend."

"Looking forward to it," said Black.

The man called Gorman leant forward, spoke in Rom's ear, voice low and urgent – "We've been here long enough. We should go!"

Rom nodded, put the note back in his wallet. He addressed two of the men, began to bark out orders – "Pick the cop up." He turned to Gorman. "You and two others – take Black." He focused on the Hornbuckle's. "Arlene and I will escort you out. As I said, we go in line, so there's no trouble."

As ordered, two guys hoisted up the corpse of Sergeant Starling, one grasping the ankles, the other hooking his hands under the dead man's arms. They manoeuvred round, to enable exiting through the kitchen doorway, the going awkward. They shuffled through.

Now three men encircled Black, ushered him to follow. The doorway was too narrow for a man to walk either side. Instead, they filed through, single formation, one man in front, facing Black and backing out, two men behind. Whichever way Black looked, he had Desert Eagles aimed at his body.

Behind them, the Hornbuckle's, and then, at the rear of the column, Rom and his girlfriend. A grim procession, thought Black. Dancing to the tune of a madman, heading to oblivion.

Black braced himself. Initially, he reckoned a firefight at close quarters was to his advantage, the bad guys more likely to kill each other. But he had revised his thinking. A stray bullet might hit the Hornbuckles.

Outside then. In the dark. In the open space. The prospects of success were slim. His head pounded, he felt nauseous, his ribs ached. Death, it would seem, might now capture him. About time, he thought.

But not yet.

They emerged into the front garden. The three men guarding him changed format, on the orders of Rom, two of them gripping Black by his waist and shoulders – which meant tucking their handguns back into their side holsters – Gorman keeping a step behind. The pace was slow, checked by the speed of those lumbering with Starling's dead weight.

They got to the Range Rover. The boot opened, by remote control. The two with the dead cop were poised to sling the body in.

"Hold!" shouted Rom. Now they were all congregated round the rear of the car. "Put Black in the boot first. He can enjoy the ride with a corpse. We want him acquainted with death. Put the Hornbuckles in the back seat."

The format changed again. Gorman opened the back door, gestured the Hornbuckles in. The men carrying the cop had to shuffle back four steps to allow the two holding Black to come forward. Meanwhile, Rom and his girlfriend watched the process, like two sick hyenas.

The men tightened their grip on Black's shoulders, grabbed him by the seat of the trousers. Black hung supine and limp.

"Here we go."

"Here we go," said Black.

And then Hell came to supper.

SEVENTY

BLACK SWIVELLED, broke holds, struck the man on his left across the temple, felt the instant crush of bone. He spun, targeted the man on his right, kept his centre of gravity low, thrust upwards using the heel of his hand, striking the area between nose and upper lip, ramming a spike of bone into the brain. Turning at a crouch, he flung himself against the knees of the man holding the ankles of Starling's body. The man staggered, released his grip, lurched backwards, clawing at his sidearm. Black kicked out in a scything motion, sweeping through the man's legs. The man fell heavily on his back. Black leapt on him, using his full weight, jamming elbow into throat, snapping the neck. Black rolled away, and with agility, regained his feet. The entire process took less than eight seconds.

Starling's body was on the ground. The other carrier had unholstered his weapon, but it was dark, the sudden commotion causing distraction and confusion, which in turn caused hesitation. Black bounded forward, swept aside the man's arm. The weapon discharged. Rom's girlfriend jerked into the air, the back of her head a sudden spume of blood. Death by stray bullet. Too bad. Black continued, focused, drove his fist into the man's face. The man grunted, dropped the pistol, attempted a head lock, but the effort was ineffectual. Black shrugged it off, hacked back-hand at the exposed larynx. The man fell back, distressed. Black caught the back of his head, yanked his face down against his knee. Cartilage crushed; teeth broke. The man toppled to the side. Black kept moving, his motion fluid, darted to the fallen weapon, retrieved it, swivelled in a crouching spin, shot the man in the head.

Rom was positioned behind the BMW. His voice boomed. "Kill the fucker!"

Black sprinted from the cars, darkness his ally. Bullets ricochetted off the road. Gorman was hunkered behind the bonnet of the Range Rover, firing in Black's general direction. Black had no such shield, other than the gloom and the shadows. He sank down, minimising himself as a target, assumed a semi-lunge position, balanced himself, shot twice at Gorman. Missed. Gorman returned fire. Black felt a sudden searing pain, raised his hand in reflex. Half his ear was shorn away.

Now movement. Rom was easing into the driver's seat of the BMW, ready to exit. Black shot the wheels, shot the chassis. He heard Rom curse loudly, the car now useless, saw him sprint off into the darkness. Black aimed his weapon, but now Gorman was firing. Black returned fire, flung caution to the wind, ran straight for his enemy, shooting with every stride. Gorman ducked back behind the Range Rover, sheltered from the spray of bullets. Black reached the car, ammunition finished. Gorman raised his head. Black dived across the bonnet, slammed his fists into Gorman's face. They tumbled to the ground. Black rolled away, and in almost acrobatic fashion, regained his feet. Gorman stood, dazed, swaying. He had lost his handgun in the collision. Gorman produced a knife. Black launched towards him. Gorman thrust forward. Black dodged sideways to his left, hacked with his hand at the side of the neck, punched Gorman's right eye. Gorman slashed at Black's ribs; the blade sliced through his clothing, and laid open eight inches of skin, the cut deep and raw.

In a rage, Black caught Gorman's arm, applied a lock, tripped him, and using Gorman's momentum, broke Gorman's elbow joint. Gorman shrieked, face contorted, the blade suddenly falling from lifeless fingers. He lurched back, hunched in pain. Black scooped the knife up, threw it. It plunged almost to the hilt into Gorman's neck. He stood, transfixed, eyes wide. He tried to speak. Instead of words, a glut of blood. He sagged, fell to the ground, the weight of his body driving the blade entirely through his throat.

Black kept moving. He pulled the knife free, and gave chase after Rom. He was losing blood from both his head wound and the gash in his ribs. Soon, he would lose strength. But not yet. Rom had run in the opposite direction of the town, into the hills. Black guessed he would keep to the road, easier than stumbling across rocks and gorse. Plus, he was muscle-bound, ungainly, incapable of swift movement.

The night was clear, the glimmer of the moon providing a faint silver illumination, showing the road – a slender pale ribbon, dark wilderness either side. His body, despite his injuries, felt alive; his soul expanded. He was running in a dream.

There! A flicker of movement ahead. The figure of a man. Black increased his speed. The figure was struggling, the pace slow and lumbering. It stopped, bending over, struggling for breath. Black reduced his pace to a walk. The world wavered; he focused, blinked away sweat, kept his gait steady, concentrated on each step. But the earth swayed; the shadows whispered. Loss of blood. Time was limited. Black halted. Before him, Rom Callaghan, Gypsy King. Rom straightened, breathing heavily, great shoulders rising and falling in the effort. He regarded Black, right hand clutching his blade.

"We can work this out," he gasped. "It was all supposed to be a bluff. A joke." His voice grew shrill. "I can give you money. Don't you want money, Black? I'm a rich man. I can make you wealthy. We can sort this. Anything you want. Any fucking thing."

"How about a little justice," said Black softly.

Rom turned away, gazed into the darkness beyond. Black could read the man's thoughts, his mind doubtless in turmoil as he debated his next move – whether he could keep running. But he wouldn't get far. He was tired and clumsy and scared. The road ahead held no sanctuary for the Gypsy King.

Rom turned back to Black.

"Please," he said. "We can sort this…" With a wild scream, he lunged forward, knife held high for a downward strike. Black attempted to block. But he was weak. It felt like catching the impact of a boulder. He managed only to deflect, the knife penetrating Black's shoulder, an inch from the neck. Black staggered back. Rom released a triumphant roar, strode forward, manoeuvred a vicious undercut, tried to stab Black in the abdomen. Black swept the outstretched arm to one side, countered, plunged his own dagger into Rom's belly – once, twice – thrust upwards, slicing through skin and organ to the centre of the ribcage, then three quick stabs in the chest. He stepped back. Rom was motionless, gazed at Black, tottered on his heels. He bent his head, examined his torso, used his fingers to keep the innards spilling. He took a gurgling breath, stared wide-eyed at Black, aghast.

"All over a slap," said Black. "Hope it was worth it." His voice was slurred. Words were difficult to formulate. The wound on his shoulder was deep. The world was darkening.

Rom remained standing, rocking on his feet. "This shouldn't be happening," he mumbled. "I'm the Gypsy King."

"Sure you are," said Black. "But even kings die." With his last remaining strength, he leaned in close, made further work with the knife, striking heart, cutting throat. Finalising matters.

He turned, made his way back to the house. His footing was unsteady. Adrenaline had kept him going, but the tank was dry, his credit was done, and the night was ending.

SEVENTY-ONE

HORNBUCKLE HAD HELD his wife close as the chaos ensued. When the shooting stopped, and the silence fell, they ventured out of the car. Around them lay the dead. Hornbuckle had no words.

"Is it over?" whispered his wife.

He took a tremulous breath. "I don't know."

A shadow emerged from the dark, limping, clutching his shoulder.

Adam Black.

He saw them, waved a feeble hand, stumbled and collapsed to the ground. They rushed to him. His top was wet and slick with blood. He was losing consciousness. Hornbuckle gripped his hand, leaned closer. Black was trying to speak, but the words were too soft to understand. Hornbuckle pressed his ear close to Black's mouth.

"I'm sorry," Black whispered. "Please forgive me."

SEVENTY-TWO

AFTERMATH - SIX MONTHS LATER

FACT, undeniably, was stranger than fiction, decided Richard Hornbuckle. The police were satisfied with Hornbuckle's account, which, after all, was the truth. On that fateful night, a gang of organised and dangerous criminals had been obliterated. The police were loathe to ask too many questions. Plus, one of their own – Harry Starling – was involved, which was an embarrassment. And Hornbuckle's story made sense – Starling's bank balance showed several large deposits from an account controlled, ultimately, by Rom Callaghan. The cop was corrupt. End of.

Initially, there was a media frenzy. Suddenly, Thurso was the centre of the world. Time wore on, the frenzy quietened, eventually consigned to old news.

The Hornbuckles got their lives back. The insurance paid out, the little shop reopened, and Richard Hornbuckle went back to selling sweets and newspapers. And in a rather strange act of remembrance, he continued to stock the *London Times*, which no one ever bought.

But Hornbuckle would never forget the man who did.

SEVENTY-THREE

ELIZABETH TAPPED THE NUMBER. The phone on the other side of the world rang for twenty seconds, and then it was answered.

"You're quite the hero," she said.

"It doesn't feel like it."

"There's been a development. I need your help."

"Your friend, Gibson?"

"Not quite," she said. "I found something else. Connected to him."

A short pause. "What?"

"Something terrible."

"What?"

"A group of individuals. They call themselves the Companions. They are...she struggled to find an adequate word, "... monsters. Can you help?"

"Yes," said Adam Black. "I can help."

"My Dark Knight."

She heard him give a soft laugh.

"When can you get here?" she asked.

"I'm already leaving."

SEVENTY-FOUR

WILSON SMITH RECEIVED the initial intimation by a simple text message. The message was sparse, as it always was. A figure – one million pounds.

The highest yet.

He responded.

> Yes.

He went immediately to his study, opened his laptop, entered the password, and went to his emails. It appeared, its presence registered by a soft chime. He opened the attachment. A man's face. Rugged, somewhat flat cheekbones, dark hair cropped short, dark eyes. He closed it. The email contained a name, and last-known address.

The name interested him. It was a name he knew.

Adam Black.

Adam Black will return...

A NOTE FROM THE PUBLISHER

Thank you for reading this book. If you enjoyed it please do consider leaving a review on Amazon to help others find it too.

We hate typos. All of our books have been rigorously edited and proofread, but sometimes mistakes do slip through. If you have spotted a typo, please do let us know and we can get it amended within hours.

info@bloodhoundbooks.com

www.ingramcontent.com/pod-product-compliance
Ingram Content Group UK Ltd.
Pitfield, Milton Keynes, MK11 3LW, UK
UKHW041341280325
456815UK00002B/88